YEZAD

A Romance of the Unknown

By
GEORGE BABCOCK

PUBLISHED BY
CO-OPERATIVE PUBLISHING CO., INC.
BRIDGEPORT, CONN.   :   :   NEW YORK, N. Y.

To My Sister,
EVA STANTON (BABCOCK) BROWNING,
this story is affectionately inscribed.

GEORGE BABCOCK.

Brooklyn, N. Y.
November, 1922.

CHARACTERS

1   JOHN BACON, Aviator.

2   JULIA BACON, His Wife.

3   PAUL BACON, Son.

4   ELLEN BACON, Daughter.

5   ADOLPH VON POSEN, Inventor, in love.

6   SALLY TIMPOLE, the Cook, also in love.

7   JASPER PERKINS
8   SILAS CUMMINGS } The old quaint cronies.
9   NANCY PRINDLE

10 DOCTOR PETER KLOUSE.

11 HESTER DOUGLASS } Grandchildren of the Doctor.
12 FINLEY DOUGLASS

13 SAM WILLIS, the dreadful liar.

14 WILLIAM THADDEUS TITUS, Champion of several trades.

15 WILLIAM GRENNELL, the Village Blacksmith.

16 MINNA BACON } Children of Paul and Hester.
17 BRENDA BACON

18 ROBERT DOUGLASS, Son of Finley and Ellen.

19 CHARLOTTE DUDLEY, a Maiden of Mars.

20 CHRISTOPHER SPENCER, Astronomer of Mars.

21 FELIX CLAUDIO, the Devil's Son.

22 DOCTOR NATHAN ELIZABRAT of Mars.

23 MARCOMET, a Guard of the Great White Way.

24 JOHN BACON'S DUALITY.

Note:—A Glossary of coined and unusual words and their meaning, used by the author in Yezad, will be found on pages 449 to 463.

CONTENTS

CONTENTS

YEZAD, A ROMANCE

CHAPTER I

THE PRICE OF PROGRESS

CALM prevailed. It was a day of glorious sunshine. Fleece-like clouds lazily floated across the sky—banking 'way to the South. The drowsy music of a near-by stream lulled all nature into a midday peace. Even the birds had hushed their singing of the earlier hours.

"You are right, little wife. It is dangerous, but the time is at hand when aviation will have become perfectly safe. The reason he fell? Well, who knows? He was at so great a height, that none could see what happened. But, he might have been careless. Fortunately, I've never had a serious accident, as you know."

"No, John, you have never had, otherwise, we might not be conversing now, and——"

"Oh, shucks, Julia. People are killed on railroads, steamboats, and in a thousand ways, yet that doesn't eliminate business. Killing is sometimes necessary to progress. No accident occurs without some additional safeguard arising to prevent its repetition."

"But, you just said, he was so high in the air that no one knew what caused the accident."

"Oh, of course, the majority of us die without adding knowledge to the world. What I want you to understand

1

is, that all progress is at the expense of some sacrifice, or self abnegation."

"But you have discovered many new points, John, and——"

"Yes, but others try them out too. Not all have proved successes, if they had, two fine fellows would be here to-day. But why harp upon this matter? You knew Paul and I were going out to the field to-day. I promise you, I'm not going to touch my 'plane. It's going to remain in the hangar until I make certain repairs and more or less important improvements."

"Look here, Dad, if you don't hurry, we'll be late. Say, Mother, why don't you and sister Ellen make ready and come along with us? You've got just about time enough," said Paul, glancing at his watch.

"No, Paul. You and your Father can hurry along. Don't miss your train. You know it's nearly a mile to the depot. Ellen and I are both sick at heart. The tragedy of that poor aviator falling a mile through the air was too appalling. Though more than a week past, I seem not to rid myself of the shock. That's why I want you to give aviation up, John";—and my wife tenderly laying her head upon my shoulder, gave me an affectionate embrace.

"Please don't worry, Julia. I'm not going up to-day. I promise you that, although my name appears in all the papers.—'John Bacon will attempt to beat his own record for high flying to-day.' But for once, I'm going to fool them. I hold the record, as you know, of having ascended to a greater height than any living pilot, so I'm well advertised. I've made money at it, yet I'm not going to throw myself away without care or calculation. The

National Scientific Society has made me a liberal offer,
if I obtain certain facts at high altitudes. Still, I've
got till next June before I make the try. I'm going to
rest through the coming Fall and Winter. And now,
I'll give you my solemn word, Julia, 'twill be my last
trip."

"Oh, I am so glad, John, to hear you say that," returned my wife; then starting up, I observed a slight
pallor overcast her face. For a moment her eyes closed
and, bowing her head, she was silent.

Paul and I left her standing on the old front porch,
her eyes wistfully following our retreat as we hurried
down the dusty path toward the old New England village.
The afternoon train, soon due, would take us to the
aviation field.

As I turned to wave her a parting adieu, I suddenly
became conscious of my abrupt remarks. As if she cared
for or thought of money! Poor little wife, it was I of
whom she was thinking. There she stood, silently and sad,
watching us as we hurried down the old familiar road—
the road over which we had journeyed together for more
than a generation to and from our old-time comfortable
country home.

It was a quaint old town—far away from the "madding
crowd." For many years past, as the young people grew
old enough, away to the city they went to seek their
fortunes, leaving for the greater part behind, the old
and worn out. Good fortune smiled upon us quite early
in life, for my wife and I had been back for years from the
city's strife and swirl. The glamor of its lonesome crowds
and artificial life had no further attractions. After we
had gathered up no small portion of the gold that the

hurrying and thoughtless had thrown away, we harked
back to the still life of the country where things are real
and interests are human.

A few years later, there sprang up an aviation field
but a few miles away. Naturally I took a deep interest
in the project, as not a few of my former city acquaintances were among the promoters. My interest deepened
and soon I owned a couple of aeroplanes, together with
a national reputation as a "high flyer." Success supplied
an added confidence, almost to the point of recklessness.
My fellow aviators called it "luck." Most of those who
started with me are dead. Each one sacrificed his life,
consciously or unconsciously, for the sake of progress.
When thoroughly investigated, each accident was found
to arise, in part, from unscientific construction. Hence,
the sacrifice of life seemed a necessary factor to each
solution. Always some trivial improvement resulted.

So, it remains a question of how many lives must yet
be sacrificed, ere aviation becomes moderately safe—the
old rule of Progress, applying to the new.

It goes without saying that the perilous element in
flying has deterred me from inviting my family and friends
on these aerial ventures.

The numerous tragedies of the field, witnessed at times
by my wife and children, cured the family of any lingering
ambition to fly.

For my own part, the tense excitement, and exalted
sensation of soaring in the air, high above clouds, passing
over country, villages and cities, over lakes and rivers,
tracing each sparkling stream below, running in its thread-
like course through great patches of green, like brilliant
emerald and silver mixed—all this gave flying its zest.

Far below, everywhere the people seemed to move like tiny ants. At times, I tried to hear their cries and shouts above the mingled burr of engine and propeller, but generally failed until near alighting. Then, the approving cries imparted new inspiration to the flyer.

Once, my son and I sat in the quiet seclusion of our hangar, looking out upon the great crowds who had come from far and near, to witness flights of these wonderful bird-men. I could not help noticing that as the time came for the crowd to leave, and their cheers of encouragement grew less, the aviators were correspondingly affected by the change, in their seeming loss of enthusiasm. Indeed, I mused, this is truly *"Nosmnbdsgrsutt*—the land of flying men and women." High above me, so far up that it was next to impossible to trace their movements, were a dozen or more men and women aviators. The awe inspiring sight seemed to electrify the spectators, and produce alternately, periods of absolute silence and noisy demonstrations of approval. These great human birds, maneuvering and soaring like eagles, transfixed the beholders until released from the strain by some apparently false movement. Had there been no peril to these air men, few of the crowd would have paid for entrance to the grounds. They did so on purpose to patiently stand and crane their necks, and with bated breath, strain their eyes in fear of some horrible accident. Eliminate the danger, I thought, and the interest largely lags.

As Paul and I sat there, frequent outbursts came, of "Where's Bacon? We want John Bacon."

"Paul," said I, "you hear them calling for me?"

"Yes, Dad. You seem to be the most famous aviator alive."

"I have become so notorious, Paul, that we shall have to wait the last train out of here, or be absolutely mobbed. If people knew I was here, they'd break through the lines, and overwhelm me with flattery and noise. Of this I feel sure."

"But, you were very anxious to get your name before the public in the beginning, were you not?"—Paul quickly asked.

"Yes, I was. People began to talk about me after I had made one of my higher ascents. The advertising grew until I became notorious, not famous. Unless I can discover some scientific truth, I may never be really noted. Success and failure are but a step apart. That is the reason I intend working so hard to accomplish something on my next ascent. If I dare fly the highest, I may learn some important truth for the National Scientific Society. I intend making a determined effort, and accordingly, shall take plenty of time to prepare."

"But suppose you fail, Dad, what then?" asked Paul, anxiously.

"Most anybody will go to a hanging—the more notorious the victim—the larger the crowd. I'm sure to draw well, Paul, and I shall be cheered as long as I last. If I fall, it will bury me and my notoriety together."

"Cheer up, Dad, you're taking yourself too seriously," said Paul.

Indeed, accidents on the field had now become so frequent, that my sense of pity, in no way lessened, became more and more blunted. Accidents were necessary to progress, and seemed to pave the way to greater achievements, and carry us nearer to perfection. "Surely," I thought, "out of evil cometh good."

Paul and I waited until the crowd had departed, before attempting our homeward trip. On reaching home, a half dozen men and one woman were waiting in the parlor to see me. They were each there on the same errand. Some one had found out that I had been employed to make a fresh attempt to break my highest record, and that I had been engaged at tremendous expense, to obtain certain data for the National Scientific Society. Each of my visitors begged to accompany me in the flight.

"Just so that I can tell my friends, and my name will be in the papers. You know, Mr. Bacon—you understand."

"My name and yours, side by side," said one with enthusiasm.

"But, my dear Madam, the venture is decidedly dangerous. You might be killed."

"I am perfectly willing to take the risk. Oh, I should love to go. If you deny me, then I shall have to remain just as I am, all my life. This is my great chance, Mr. Bacon. I know where I can get a position in vaudeville, almost as soon as I touch the ground."

"'That is, if we should be fortunate enough to come down and live," said I.

"Oh, Mr. Bacon, that would make no difference—absolutely. I am willing to die for art," said she as the tears streamed down her face.

I explained to them all, that my 'plane would carry several pounds of scientific apparatus on the trip, and that with this, the load would reach its limit. I knew, that a refusal upon any other grounds would be taken as an inconsiderate denial or personal insult.

"I'm so glad you've decided to give up that dangerous

sport," quietly remarked my wife, that same evening.

"Dad's going to make one more trip, next Spring, Mother."

"I know that, Paul—and I hope no accident will occur," nervously replied my wife with a deep sigh.

"I'll end it then for your sake and the children's," said I.

"You'll certainly end it, if you happen to take a tumble," remarked Ellen.

"Oh, I'll come back, even if I do drop," I said with a show of confidence.

"Come back with your machine, or we'll never know where to look for you," replied Ellen.

"Where did you get that idea? You often say, 'I'll come back again.' What do you mean, John?" asked my wife.

"Just what I say, of course. Did I ever tell you about my old friend Doctor Klouse?"

"I have often heard you mention him. Who was he, and where did he live?" asked Ellen.

"Just a moment—Ellen. I'll tell you in few words, about one of the greatest men I ever met. He was a noted physician, and lived here in our village. He has been dead many years, having lived to be over ninety. He married very late in life. Though becoming acquainted only a few years before he passed away, I learned to love and respect him. Dr. Peter Klouse, you must know, took an intense interest in experimentation and the investigation of more or less popular ideas,—especially those relating to our presumed 'future existence.'

"Apart from his profession, his character was unknown to the populace. He studiously avoided making himself conspicuous; indeed, he made the acquaintance of few people, and had no confidants. Even I, who knew him perhaps better than any one outside of his own family, had little knowledge concerning his past.

"I enjoyed his society—any one would—for he was the most lovable man I ever knew. I miss him, even now. Often, I have sat by the hour without speaking, just to catch his beautiful words and original thoughts. He told me that his early life was spent in much research. He established a 'Home' he called it, in the far West. I would have named it an Institution for Experimental Research. He never informed me in just what part of the West it was located, but I gathered, somehow, that it was in the vicinity of the Yosemite Valley. There he built a great structure devoted to experiment and investigation. After twenty years of research, he returned here, only to find, however, that conditions were not ripe to give the world the results of his discoveries, so he reluctantly withheld all explanation.

"I believe he made a record of a few experiments. Doubtless his only child, a daughter formerly living in Washington, has preserved them, for she must have realized their value. Once I told him, that I thought him too timid in not publishing the results of these costly and interesting data.

" 'The people are not ready yet,' he answered. 'If I should publish these things, they'd mob me, call me a fool, or both. I have no money to waste. When the time comes, some one else will take my place and publish the results.' "

"Did he suggest the thought of sacrifice being necessary to progress?" interrupted my wife.

"Yes, he first suggested the idea to me, but, of course, that was not original with him. He frequently declared that lives were often sacrificed in the interest of very small or insignificant ideas. He believed that the human race was progressing rapidly toward perfection. That so soon as the individual wears out one body, he returns in a new one,—never changing personality. The better we live one life, the more advanced we become in the next, and so on, until perfection is reached. He believed that life was continuous and everlasting, and as we increase in knowledge and goodness, we lengthen the span of each separate existence. Also, memory of previous existences, constantly and progressively increases as we reach out toward perfection. Hence, as we approach that condition, our knowledge of our own bodies and Nature's laws will have so advanced, that we shall be enabled to prolong the life of the body indefinitely. Death will be almost unknown, and never feared. Indeed, he thought many would seek it, if they desired a new body."

"Then, in accordance with Doctor Klouse's theory, he's back here now, in a new body?" suggested Paul.

"Certainly. According to his researches, he claims to have proved that we come back, repeatedly,—or, until we are perfect," I replied.

"Into the same family?" asked my wife.

"Not necessarily in the same family, and perhaps, not even on the same planet," I answered.

"In what manner or way might we know a person?" asked Paul.

"By a study of the personality. The last generation really knows very little regarding the personalities of those preceding it."

"Then an old man might find some of the companions of his youth back again?" suggested Ellen.

"Yes, but the Doctor's theory was that each personality, or body, was dual, and contained two souls; the *Bonality*, representing the good in us, and a second, *Malality*, representing the evil. That they came here but once together. The *Bonality*,* or good, is presumed to dominate, and not to be influenced by the evil one within us, but rather to teach the latter self-control, that both might return, each with still more improved companions. Since the dual inhabits the same body, *Malality* is constantly seeking the opportunity to dominate, and should this evil succeed, then *Bonality*, or good, will become again *Malality* in the next life; if, on the other hand, the evil be mastered, both shall be advanced towards perfection.

"Declared the Doctor—'There is sunshine somewhere from within, beaming forth from the blackest life.'"

"Then life is continually evolving into longer spans, in proportion as human intelligence increases?" suggested Paul.

"Certainly," I replied, "and our planet is evolving and ripening, as we live with it. Our Earth represents life. It begins as do our lives, and continues in all the same successive stages, just as we are born, live and die, to be re-born again, so the planet upon which we live,— the process is the same.

"Disintegration is the last step before a new and glorious birth. Time, through its short duration, deters us from seeing this change in one life's span. Civilizations and peoples rise and fall, in the same way. The future

* The Doctor had chosen the terms *Bonality* as portraying the good, and *Malality* as indicative of evil in the dual nature of man.

is constantly being built upon the ashes of the past. An empire lives only as long as it perceives the truth, and practices justice."

"Did Doctor Klouse believe that those ideas would not be accepted in his day?" asked my wife.

"Yes, even now, his ideas will be considered revolutionary. People's minds mature too quickly, by which I mean, too early in life. He often said,—'the less there was to anything, even to a man's mind, the quicker it matured.'"

"Great minds grow slowly, and so with thought. Small thought, or the commonplace grows quickly, and as readily dies out. Therefore, he deemed himself too old to advance ideas which would take so long to be understood. Again, he would have had to suffer the sneers of the critical, and to stand abuse.

"Advanced in age before he had prepared his more mature thought, he elected to remain quiet and unknown.

"To combat even the broadest theory, nowadays, as to the origin of man, the view that man has evolved step by step from the lowest forms of life, would have meant an advance that his age would not have permitted.

"He contended that man had a soul, and was created with one. Nothing else living, he contended, had soul. If all life was mainly animal, how could we justify the killing and eating of our brothers and sisters, the beasts? It was to these questions, that early in life, the Doctor demanded of some one an answer. Later, it resulted in his determination to investigate, and though the task should part him from civilization and from friends, and require the relinquishment of many comforts, yet, the best of his life was to be given to the solution, if possible, of these problems.

"Is man and the animal related? That mystery has baffled the brightest minds of all ages. The human mind repels the idea of first starting from the lowest form of known life,—the protoplasm,—and then forward to the fish, through ages and ages of evolution. From the flying fish to the bird, by countless changes, into countless differing species, finally evolving the four-legged brute. Then, through unknown stretches of time, to the highest form of chimpanzee, and through the ages, slowly and painfully, up to the wonderful being—man.

"You should have heard the Doctor press home his thought upon that subject. 'If this theory be correct,' he would say, 'at what step in his upward evolution did man receive his soul?' 'What will his next form be?' 'The truth is, we, doubtless, came here from some other planet,' he declared. 'If I were a fish,' said he, 'I am sorry that I did not stay one. Why was I not permitted to remain fish? What was the reason for making a monkey out of me later on?' "

"Then he believed that our *Bon*ality might not immediately return, unless we lived up to our highest ideals?" inquired Paul, showing an increased interest.

"Yes. Good was the dominant spirit in every life. No matter to what degree the evil spirit, or *Mal*ality, had overcome, held possession of and dominated the will of good, an appeal to kindness might put the evil one to flight."

"Then, if a man has mastered and improved himself, over the secondary or evil self, he would certainly return a better man?" Paul persisted.

"Yes, or woman, either," I replied.

"There goes the front door bell," suddenly exclaimed Ellen, as she made haste to answer it.

"I wonder who it can be, at this late hour," mused my wife with a suppressed tone. "It's a quarter to ten now. Hope nobody's died suddenly 'round here. What would I do if there was a funeral of one of my friends,—and my best black silk ripped up. I ought to have waited a week or two later, before parting it." Then she nervously awaited Ellen's return.

Ellen soon appeared and bluntly announced: "Man in the parlor, Dad, Dutchman I think. Oh, he's so fat,— no room left in his clothes."

"What's he want? Why didn't you tell him I had retired? Confound these night owls! What name did he give, Ellen?"

"I didn't understand. I thought he said 'Poison.' "

" 'Poison,' hey. Well, I will if he bothers me," I replied, making my way into the parlor.

In the dimly lighted room, I could only outline the figure of a man. He was of immense proportions, and sat leaning back in a large morris chair. As I entered the room, I saw him make two futile efforts to gain his feet, before he succeeded. I excused the dimly lighted room, and proceeded to turn up the light.

"Mr. Pacon, I pelieve?" said the stranger, speaking with a strong German accent.

"Yes, sir, I am John Bacon. Who have I the pleasure of greeting?"—As I stepped forward with outstretched hand.

As we both shook hands, he replied,—"Adolph Von

Posen." After a slight pause, he continued, "An aviator, you are, I hear, und——"

"Kindly be seated," said I, pointing toward the chair from which he had just risen.

"I vill keep you, Mister Pacon, von minute. Chust till I exblane my new, like air, you call it vot—inventions. Chust now I send it, last Friday, to Vashington."

"What did you send to Washington?" said I somewhat impetuously.

"My new inventions. A wery vine vlying machine of my own gonstrugtion. I am a great study of air currents. Ull my life vas to berfect the air current idea. Sume air is dedt. To moving podies, air sdicks. In an open drolley, a pug is zafe to vly vithoudt peing plown avay, is it not so? Nicht wahr? To the gar the air sticks like clue. Dedt is dot air, nicht wahr? Now, to you I vill exblane my prinzibles new, aboud my inventions.

"Der to-day aeroblane can lift up twenty-seven bounds each voot square of zurface, ven one blane is used only. Add anoder blane, over directly der udder. It lifts it not, but a liddle more, nicht wahr? If gapable is one blane to lift each voot square of zurface, twenty-seven bound, vhy not iss two blanes, vone rright over head of oder, gapable in bounds to lift as much as twice,—yah, or no?"

"Yes, Mister Von Posen, I have often wondered if a single plane has a lifting capacity of twenty-seven pounds to the square foot of surface, why it does not increase or nearly double the lifting capacity when another plane is added. If we could discover the reason, we might im-

prove the aeroplane so that by increasing the plane's surface, we could lift unlimited weights, and——"

"Vait a minute. I tell you, in a hurry. I study the
pirds,—the air. Why zoar the pirds I exblain, quick, if
you but vait a liddle," replied Adolph Von Posen excitedly,
and with great energy. "A segret I vill geif you. Alreaty
I exblain dot bodies moving make dedt de air. Der air on
one blane single, brushes off, but two blanes the air holds
between, dedt, yes?"

"You mean to say, that the reason the biplane has only
a very little more lifting power than the monoplane, is,
because the air between the two planes is what one might
term dead air?"

"Dot is it, mein vriend," said Von Posen, smiling.

"The dead air then, is carried along between the two
planes; therefore, both the upper and lower planes lose
a large percentage of their lifting capacity. Well, that
looks reasonable enough, but, how do we get rid of the
dead air?" I inquired with increasing interest.

"I exblain, I exblain, Mister Pacon, to you. Now,
der air dot is dedt, is not made. You do not rid yourself
of dedt air, dot is not made alreaty."

"How's that?" said I bewilderedly. "Do you mean to
say, by your method there is no dead air? Then the
planes are not opposite one another," I suggested.

"Dot is right. You are wery smart, Mister Pacon, a
wery smart man. I talk mit you, mit delight," said he.

"How do you arrange the planes, Mister Von Posen?"

"I vill you tell. I blace der blanes in steps of stairs
like—each blane a pird fedder represents. Did you efer
a pird notice? Its vings it spreads, mit each fedder abart
und efery fedder back a leedle from der udder von, so

it makes bossible for him to soar. Nefer could he do, oder-vise,—nicht wahr?"

"I see. You would place the planes over and a little back of one another, like steps of stairs. How wide would you make each plane, and how long?" I asked.

"Not ofer eighteen inches wide each. Der blane fordy feed long could pe, yes, und downvard curved each side," he explained.

"The whole thing would certainly resemble, then, great successive steps. How many people might that sized plane carry?"

"Vell, it all debends how many der blanes. Dree blanes, fordy feed long, each side, makes surface aboud dree hundret feed sqvare. Dot vould susdain nine dou-sand sefen hundret und dwenty bounds, und carry easy —yes? Bud of steel I should buildt it, mit engines nefer less den two or more, for zafety—yes?"

It was approaching one A. M. before my enthusiastic friend broached the added reason for his visit.

"Mister Pacon," said he confidentially, "a loan must I get. You will loan me fife hundret? A model must I make, you know. Lost vill it pe foreffer, uddervise," and he hung his head in apparent dejection, and was silent for the first time in hours.

The man's incessant bombardment of broken English, backed by tremendous energy and a strong, deep voice, had worn upon my nerves. Yet, his ideas were new to me, and had taken possession of my imagination. Therefore, when he spoke of constructing a model, and requested a loan, I seized the opportunity to learn more about my visitor. Assuring me that he had been a student of air currents all his life, and was without friends, he aroused my sympathy and I readily promised him assistance.

"My machine vill tousands of lifes safe—und maype, some day,—yours," he said.

"Build a model for me, Adolph," said I, familiarly, "and have it ready by next Spring. Then, I shall be glad to try it out. If it works——"

"Vork it vill—lofely," he broke in, "mag-mag-ficent!" he shouted with enthusiasm.

"If it works well, Adolph, I will make my trip in your 'plane, in the interest of science. That would afford us both fame and fortune! It would put you on your feet so that you would never have to work again, except you desired," said I reflectively.

"Och," he replied, leaning back and closing his eyes— "Vould der day pe velcome. Rested I am not. Now, Mister Pacon, I vill promise to hire der empdy vactory mit der large douple doors, to-morrow. Dot vill pe large enough in vich to gonstrugt a mottel."

"All right," I replied. "Only yourself shall be permitted to enter, even I will not disturb you. I will see to the expense. When you have finished, and feel sure of the machine's working, let me know. I will meet cost of material, and all other expenses. You shall board in the village."

These arrangements being assented to readily with all but tears of gratitude, he thanked me again and again, and agreed to begin work on the model immediately. All the details of construction, we agreed to hold secret.

Explaining that he should need no help in the construction, it was past two o'clock that morning, before Adolph departed, leaving me to surmise the result of our venture.

As I ascended the stairs leading to my room, I was startled, not a little, to hear some one speak; stopping, I listened.

"It's I, Dad," said Paul, as he stepped from his room into the dimly lighted hall. "I've been watching a light moving from room to room, in the old Klouse Mansion across the road. Though it has disappeared now, it seems to me, some one may have broken into the house."

"You are mistaken, Paul. While out on the field to-day, your mother informed me that a young couple had moved into the Doctor's house. I wonder who they can be, to fancy the old, damp mansion, for years vacant."

"Gee, I'm glad we've secured some kind of new neighbors. By the way, I'll ask Jasper, in the morning,—he's almost sure to know who they are."

"Possibly," I replied, though a new thought possessed me.

CHAPTER II

THE GHOST

It was the twilight of an Autumn evening. Swallows flitted overhead, swiftly dove and arose again. The voice of the village gossip, Perkins, was in the wind, and suddenly one heard—

"Well, Ellen, guess yer father ain't a-comin' out yet. Nearly seven neow. Perhaps I'd better come over ag'in. Don't like t' go hum when it's tue dark."

"Oh, don't go yet, Mister Perkins,—it's somewhat romantic, you know, to sit here and talk with you. This old piazza gives one an exceptional view of Nature in its near virgin state. At Vassar, our young ladies longed for the country, and they would have been pleased to have joined us here. If you remain, Mister Perkins, father will be here soon. I see, that while you are old in years, you don't seem to have lost the intrepidity of youth."

"Oh, I ain't afraid of no dark—if yer mean thet, Ellen. I don't believe in ghosts, no, sir-ee. But b' gosh, thet colledge eddication at Vassarlene gives yer some purty smart idees. It's kinder interestin' t' hear an eddicated critter speak—even if ye don't know sartin what she's talkin' of. But I kinder side in with simple things meself. Anything simple—simple folks, an' simple—interest even. None of yer compound kinds fer me. No, sir-ee"—and

20

Jasper brought his cane down with a thud, to emphasize his words.

"Your metaphors are really good, Mister Perkins," said Ellen, "they remind me so much——"

"Well," broke in Perkins, "I've heerd of them mentofers, but have never seen wan of 'em."

"But, who's thet a-comin' in the gate, Ellen?" queried Jasper—interrupting himself.

"Why, it's Mister Cummings."

"Do yer mean Silas? It don't look like him. Either me eyes are dim, or he's shaved his whiskers off."

"You're mistaken, Mister Perkins. His beard is still in place."

"Yes, Miss Ellen, yit, to me he looks like a cross-eyed moth. I believe, too, he's comin' in here."

"Good evening, Mister Cummings! Will you join us in our little conference?"

"No, no. Much obleeged—jest had supper. Everybody well, I s'pose? Nobody sick, hey? What's yer father a-doin'—is he in? Who's thet, sittin' there with yer?—Got a beau, Ellen?"

"Why, only your old friend, Mister Perkins."

"Then, b' gosh, yer must be sittin' alone! Ha, ha, ha, thet's a gud un. Yit, when I come t' look—who's thet old bald head, dressed like a dude, sittin' ther' like a hen on a roost? Ellen, I'm surprised yer should be keepin' compney with so old a rooster as thet." These remarks were uttered with a quizzical shake of the head as Silas joined them on the porch.

"What cher 'bout, ther', Silas Cummings! Mud slingin' ag'in, air yer? Tryin' t' immitat thet dum poly-tish-shun, Jim Landis, air yer? Better yer shet up. Can't yer be-have fer once?"—shouted Jasper with a decided show of feeling.

"Let not thy angry passions rise," said Ellen, citing the rhyme, reprovingly. "You should not slander, you know," she added.

"Why don't yer take a cheer, Silas? Plenty of 'em."

"Hain't abeen invited yit," he replied peevishly.

"Then, I invite you now, Mister Cummings," said Ellen, moving a chair in his direction.

"If thet's ther case, I'll jine yer," returned the visitor. "Hain't seen yer in some time, Si, where yer bin?"

"Hain't bin nowhere, but I was agoin' deown to th' po-lit-ti-cal mee-tin',—begins 'bout eight, they say. Started airly, so t' git ther', an' git a gud seat. Then I turned in here, as I seen a jack-rabbit cross th' road rite in front of me—a sure sign of tic-douloureux. Nancy's got th' tic' neow."

"Yer don't tell me? Well, she's goin' t' prayer meetin' every nite—thet accounts fer't," dryly remarked Jasper.

"Don't yer scandalize, Jasper," bawled Silas threateningly, though Jasper paid no attention to his remark.

"Si, yer th' fust Cummings, I ever knowed, to take enny intrest in poly-ticks. Yit yer only awastin' yer time! What be yer thinkin' on? Of all th' critters on airth, a polytishun is th' most useless. Like a weather vane, he points, with his mouth wide open, toward the strongest wind. If he don't blow over, give him time, an' he'll be on every side of every question. I was deown teown last nite, an' heer'd one of 'em talk—all hot wind, an' no kind of growin' weather!"

"You ware?"

"Yes, I ware. An' I'm ashamed t' say't. I heered thet

Jim Landis talk. He sounds like a hot gale, Si. I sot deown front, but by ginger, I bet a chew of 'backey, thet I could a heerd him 'way hum."

"Then, he's quite loquacious, rather vain-glorious and spread-eagle in his style?" suggested Ellen.

"He's nothin' of th' kind, Ellen. He is a flippant, flamboodled, up-to-date, vain and flatfooted liar. Thet's what I knows," replied Jasper, thumping his cane on the floor.

"Then, he is very voluble, is he not?" persisted Ellen.

"Nothin' very valu'ble about him, 'cept to an undertaker. I listened to him till he got wind-broke. Then he came over where I set. Says he, 'How did yer like it, Jasp?' Says I, 'Jim, yer sounded like th' ting, tang, tong of a critter drummin' on a pan, an' tryin' t' induce a swam of bees t' settle. Thet ting, tang of yours orter settle some of ther bills thet yer owe. How about the bill of Widder Durmot, for ther cord of chestnut she let yer hev? An' hev yer paid Hank Smith fer yer last winter overcut yit?' says I. 'Jim,' says I, 'yer can't stampede me by yer bellerin'. Yer ain't no newspaper huxter. They're th' only human critters thet's got th' divine rite ev kings t' beller.' My friends a-listenin' said, 'Good! Good! Jasp.' "

"What did Landis say?" asked Silas eagerly.

"He said, 'Gud evenin',' an' skipped—thet's all."

"Jest look at them swallows," said Silas, pointing his stick in front of him. "See how low they're flyin'. Never saw 'em dip and fly lower. Thet's a sure sign of bad weather."

"Why, here comes 'Paw-paw,' as our English cousins say," suddenly exclaimed Ellen.

Neither of the old men moved, my daughter's allusion being lost on both. Suddenly seeing me step out on the piazza, they both arose.

"Gud evenin', John!" broke in Jasper. "We're tucken possession, yer see."

"Good evening, boys. Keep your seats and make yourselves comfortable. I'm glad to see you both looking so well. I call you 'boys' because we've known each other so long. A life-time indeed. You're as familiar, and as much a part of our town, as the great elms across the road. Let's see, you're both about the same age."

"I'm a gud deal older then Jasper," said Silas, with a touch of pride in his tone.

"Yes, I remember now; you are about three months older than Jasper. You're eighty-seven. Let's see, how old is Nancy?"

"She's jest past eighty-six, an' sprintin' on t' eighty-seven," replied Jasper.

"Thet's rite, but thet's a race where we all sprint alike," said Silas with a slight sigh.

"Where is Nancy, to-night, boys?" I asked.

"T' prayer meetin'," they answered in unison.

"Yer see, she bot a new bonnet last Spring. The durn thing sits on her head so high, she got cold in her cheeks, an' it turned inter th' tic. Neow she goes t' prayer meetin' every nite t' git rid of it," drawled Jasper.

"An' th' feather on her bonnet come out of th' tail of a bird as big as a hoss, they say," added Silas.

"They call the thing a bloom, an' say it come from Eurip. It hangs down so low from her bonnet thet it tickles her cheeks an' agitates her tic'. But, she's bound to wear it thet way, 'cause it's the style,' " explained Jasper.

"Eurip must be quite a teown. They can git more differin' kinds of critters out en it, than flees on a goat. We'll never git ther', Jasper. It takes several generations of hard workers to produce a crop of Eurip-pean tu-rists."

"Well, *you* never worked very hard, Si, 'cept t' keep compney with Nancy," remarked Jasper tauntingly.

"Neow, don't yer say thet ag'in, Jasper Perkins! You've been tryin' t' cut me out fur sixty odd years. Yer ain't succeeded yit, hev yer? No, ner yer won't nether. By gosh, I'm a good mind t'——"

"There, there, boys, that will do. Sit down, Silas! Put down your cane. The idea! You wouldn't strike Jasper, would you? You're both too old to quarrel. Just imagine it, you old bachelors, without a 'chick or child' in the world, to be fighting over Nancy since you were boys together. Yes, just think of it, Nancy's been waiting nearly seventy years for one of you to propose. Neither of you seem to possess the first spark of courage."

"We had spunk enough, John, but we never had th' heart to cut t'other out. 'Bout a year ago, I told Silas he was free to purpose an' if Nancy would hev him, I'd take my chance in marryin' his widdy. 'Twas th' fust time in sixty odd years, thet I consented to thet. I never believed in second-hand goods, but, I'd take her if she'd hed nine husbands—thet is if she'd hev me," said Jasper, his voice slightly falling with emotion.

"You can hev her, Jasper," murmured Silas, as if he had lost hope.

"No, you take her, Silas," said Jasper with evident

emotion, and then brightening up, he turned to Ellen and asked, "What do you advise, Miss Ellen? You're younger then we, an' orter know?"

"Oh, Mister Cummings, how very interesting, yet, I'm not sure if I can easily answer you. I admit that one must exercise one's sympathies occasionally"—and Ellen looked as if her reply might give relief.

"I exercise my symp's every day, rain or shine," remarked Silas solemnly, while Jasper looked puzzled.

"You know, of course, what old Doctor Klouse would have told you both?" said I.

"Doctor Klouse, did you say? Doctor Klouse!" said Silas, rising quickly. "Yes, yes, that was him! That was him! I must be goin', however, I must be goin'. Yes, yes, I must! Good-by, all. Good-by, I must go— for it's late."

As I looked up, in astonishment, at the speaker, I noticed that his face had suddenly paled. I felt sorry for him immediately, and arose to steady his tottering frame. My first impression, that some sudden illness had seized him, impelled me to request Ellen to bring a little brandy. Returning, she handed the old man a liberal portion which he swallowed eagerly. His cheeks slowly resumed their color, and his manner became calm.

"What's the matter, Silas?" I inquired in a rather agitated tone, as the occurrence had somewhat unnerved me. "You are trembling. Don't you feel well? If you will, I'll have you driven home. The horse is ready."

He made no reply, but when I offered him another portion of brandy, he said, "Thet's fine brandy."

"Be seated, Silas, and tell us what the matter is, won't you?" and again I urged him toward the chair.

"Yis, do sit down and behave yourself," was Jasper's rather bluff comment.

"You knew Doctor Peter Klouse, didn't yer, Jasper?" broke out Silas, holding out his hands as if pleading a case of some necessary import.

"Course I did—as well as you. Maybe not so well as John, though, yet, we both knowed him longer'n John," returned Jasper with a knowing nod.

"Well, I never did believe in ghosts, but I believe in 'em neow!" said Silas, and he emphasized his remark with a vigorous thrust of his cane, which struck uncomfortably near Jasper's outstretched feet. After a pause, he continued: "I'll tell yer all about it, if yer hev th' re-spect t' listen. I say this because, yer know, some folks ain't got no sympathy," he added, as he glanced in Jasper's direction. "Well, I hed a very peculiar experiance. As I said, I never did believe in ghosts, but I believe in 'em neow. Why, if ye'd tol' me thet I'd seen ghosts—an' jest as natral as life tue—I'd a said yer needed a guardeen, 'fore I'd tucken yer word fur it."

"What time a day were it, Silas?" asked Jasper with interest.

"It were jest 'bout betwixt an' between, long on th' verge of th' evenin'—sumthin' like neow."

"What color were it—white?"

"They tell us at Vassar that white is not a color," corrected Ellen.

"He were a nat-ral critter," and Silas impressed his opinion by striking the floor with his cane. "But I know he's bin dead, nigh on t' thirty years. My eyes air a little dim, but yer can't fool 'em all th' time. I seen him, as plain as daylight."

"Who be yer talkin' about? Why don't yer tell us what cher gettin' at, Si? By gum, yer gittin' old an' forgitful. What cher wait-tin fur?"

"Give me chance ter get me wind, won't cher? Don't you git ubstroppolus, Jasper."

"My, that would be a strange word at Vas——"

"Vassar be darned—Miss Ellen—let me tell yer, won't cher? It were jest a week ago las' nite. Says I to myself, after supper, I think I'll tuck a little con-sti-tu-shional. So, I made up my mind to walk out toward th' cemetary. It was putty near dark 'fore I got out thar. My pesky rhu-ma-tiz ached so bad I could hardly step out. I heerd th' dogs a-barkin', unusually common, an' it made me a leetle nervous like, an' when they bark like thet, I all's know thet suthin's a happinin' or goin' t' happen. But I didn't spect it so soon. I was walkin' slow like, kinder careless, mindin' my own consarn, an' thinkin' of nothin' in partic'lar, when all of a sudden I heerd suthin or some un creepin' like, comin' rite up from behind me. Well, I kinder thought it over a bit, 'fore I tuck action. I jest kinder careless like gradually come ter a stan' still. Thin, got a good grip on ma cane, with one hand, an' with t'other I jest grabbed th' iron fence in front th' cemetary. Then, as cool as a cucumber, I peer 'round a bit. But gol durn m' eyes, I couldn't see a thing. Nothin' in partic'lar was in site. As I was partly turned and facing toward hum, I thought 'twould be handier to go in thet direction—besides, I never did approve of walkin' by cemetaries, in th' dark."

"Why didn't yer run then, yer darn fool?" interrupted Jasper excitedly.

"Who yer callin' a fool—an how could I run with th' rhu-ma-tiz?

"So I started to hike it hum," continued Silas. "I hadn't gone a dozen steps a'fore I seen a shadder, rite in front of me. It wa'n't makin' a bit o' noise. It was jest a-creepin'—creepin's along rite towards me. It were comin' kinder slow, so says I, I'll give ye a wide berth, an' I jest hobbled rite up near th' fence,—behind some brush. Then, says I t' myself, if ye come near me neow, I'll disturb yer peace of mind with this old hickory o' mine, by ginger! An' I got a good holt on it, ye can bet yer boots. The shadder kep' a comin' nearer, an' I kep' my eyes on it every min-nit. Yit, I wasn't prepared t' git quite sich a shock—didn't expect to see a ghost, so puffectly natral. S'posed they were allus white! But there it were, rite in front o' me. I'd know th' fellow in a crowd anywhere! I knowed he was dead, for I was one o' the bearers at his funeral, but now, his face was young—as I knowed him when a boy. I'd a known him anywhere. What did he mean, says I to meself, by gittin' up out o' his grave in th' cemetary, an' go snookin' around, scarin' respectible people? I never owed him a cent thet I hadn't paid him. Thin, I give him one gud look, but I never had th' strength tue lift me cane, arter I seen his face, an' even I forgot 'bout my rhu-ma-tiz. Sakes alive, didn't I put it up th' road for dear life! Thought I heerd him say suthin, but I didn't stop t' hear what 'twas. I jest kep' agoin', faster'n old Dobbin ever trotted. Th' only thing I could hear was th' creakin' of my old j'ints, an' I was a-feared they'd git adoubled up 'fore I'd git hum. As I shuffled along, th' dogs barked more'n ever—they fairly howled—an' th' wind began t' whistle through th'

trees—mournful like. So I jest put on more steam, an'
for a while I felt as if I'd speeded up to a mile a minute.
Jist as if I were a kid ag'in and the trees lookin' like a
fine-tooth comb, a-passin' by. When I reached hum, I
didn't even bother t' lift th' door latch—I busted rite in
an' made sich a racket, thet the whole barnyard was set
in motion an' nobody slept fer the rest of th' nite.

"Gosh, I hain't had rhu-ma-tiz sense," again his cane
came down on the porch, as if to emphasize the unexpected cure.

For a few moments no one spoke. Expectancy awaited
some further narrative. Jasper, the while, shifted uneasily in his chair before venturing to speak, but finally
asked, with all the dignity he could muster, "Where did
this ere—ghost meet yer, Si?"

"He didn't git a chance tue meet me—he came up behind. I evaded him by certain tac-tics—as Miss Ellen
would say, at Vassar."

Here Ellen laughed outright.

"Did I know this 'ere critter, while a-livin'?"

"Shure, you knew him! Everybody knew Doctor Peter
Klouse. What d'yer ask that tommyrot fur?"

"What, Doctor Klouse!" exclaimed all in unison.

"I don't believe yer, Si. 'Twas a dream yer had, not
any re-al-ity!—not even er house without er lot."

"I'm not mis-tooken, I tell ye. I guess I knows real
from imitation. Besides, I lost a button off my breeches
jest as I started t' try an' trot,—an' I didn't stop t' pick
it up, nuther. Never lost a button 'fore in my life."

"Well, accordin' t' my mind, tue lose a button ain't no
evidence—it's on'y talk," said Jasper solemnly.

"But I've got th' evidince in my pocket. I got up

yisterday, 'bout sunrise, an' arter lookin', found it 'bout
noon. Thin I hiked over t' the Doctor's grave in th'
cemetary, but nothin' looked disturbed. I can't understan' how he got out an' back ag'in, an' not move a blade
o' grass," said Silas—his head bowed in thought.

"What made you think it was Doctor Peter Klouse's
spirit, Silas?" I finally asked.

"I knowed him! Didn't I? An' you knowed him, too—
didn't cher? We both knowed him fer years, 'bout here.
'Cause, everybody knowed him—an' liked him tue. Didn't
he used t' walk with his head a-hangin' an' his hands behind
his back? Didn't he walk with his back stooped, always
a-thinkin'—suthin like this?" And Silas, rising from his
chair, walked in front of us, stooping over in mimicry of
the Doctor.

"Didn't he used to stop every few feet, an' stoop over
t' examine——"

"Did he do it las' nite?" interrupted Jasper.

"I didn't turn aroun' ter see arter I got started. Didn't
he used to stoop——"

"Not all th' time," retorted Jasper.

"Wal, I tol' more'n tew dozen critters 'bout et, down
towne, yisterday."

"What did they say?"

"Said! Why, that I been a-drinkin' hard cider, th' un-
believers. Never believed in ghosts before, but I believe
in 'em neow. Listen a minute! There's two dogs with a
barkin' howl neow. Thet means a death in somebody's
family."

"Oh, shet up, Si! Ye've got ghosts an' signs on th'
brain, t'nite,"—and turning to me, he remarked: "I see
yer nue neighbors jest strike a light—they must be

wealthy, fer they burn ile lamps. Hev yer met em yit, John?"

"No. I have not had the pleasure of meeting Mr. Douglass, or his sister," I replied.

"Well, it's 'bout time yer did, John. I heerd 'bout yer son Paul a-keepin' compney with th' young gal—pretty quick work, but none of my business. How much money hev they got, do you s'pose? Of course, it's none of my business. It's considerable, ain't it?" cautiously inquired Jasper.

"If you'll write out your questions, Jasper, I'll hand them to Mr. Douglass, just as soon as I get acquainted with him. He'll doubtless answer you promptly, as he appears to be a very bright young man," I replied.

"What's thet, an owl a-screechin'? Guess I'll go hum," said Silas, rising to leave.

"Don't git skeered, Si. Nobody wants yer—yit."

"I never heerd an owl screech like thet, unless there be a calamity on its way. Suthin' is goin' t' be hit hard," said he, with a knowing nod, and throwing a parting glance in Jasper's direction. "An' it won't be me," he added with emphasis, hobbling towards home at a gait that threatened to become a trot. Off he went down the path and out into the road, digging his cane, at each step, into the soft mud.

He had proceeded several hundred feet along the road, when he suddenly stopped, and turned towards us. In the deepening twilight, I saw him raise his cane in the air, and in a high keyed voice he shouted: "Be gosh, I forgot t' say good nite."

"Strange doings," I thought, as his figure vanished in the gloom.

CHAPTER III

WHATEVER might befall as to the lives or destinies of our new neighbors, neither the provincial opinions of Silas nor Jasper could in the least affect the result. Both were now old men—past eighty—yet, they had seen little of the world. Outside of our small New England community, in which both men were born and had spent their lives, their horizon had long been bounded by the woods and streams. Knowledge of the world surrounding them, though narrowed, was, however, none the less intimate and complete. Each had vied for years, with the other, in their narrow research, trying the while to spring new surprises of what each deemed discoveries in the world's progress. The result was, that while they had read and digested many facts and figures of greater cities and distant countries with curious and interesting histories, somehow, they each felt that there was no place found in their researches quite so enlightened and comfortable as their own quiet village. To them, no people could compare in honesty and character with most of the families found in their own lives and the immediate village community.

So, while Silas and Jasper had read of the world's happenings, its crimes, and horrors, of wealth and poverty, of positions of prominence, somehow, they felt that

33

Providence had been particularly kind to them, having marked them out for comparative peace and plenty, and far removed from the terrors of poverty and crime found in other lives. From their far away viewpoint, they observed the struggles between poverty, wealth and prominence go on and on. To them, like great masses of worms, the people appeared embraced in a life and death struggle for but two things—both as transitory as the meteor's flight across an unclouded sky.

Men came and went, to be followed by others—each forgotten, so soon as the newer brilliancy appeared. To these men life was like the "brief candle," lighted and extinguished without warning.

Quaint and circumscribed, yet with a germ of truth, Silas would often remark——"After all is sed an' done, Jasper, there's nothin' like Nancy, a good character, an' old apple cider."

The families of Prindles, Perkins, Cummings, and Bacon were among the old Simon Pure New England stock, who for many generations had been prominent and most respected of the community. While many of the old Puritanical ideas still obtained, no more generous, hospitable and charitable people existed. As in all small communities, however, the people's time was much taken in the discussion of each other's faults and failings.

To these men, the larger communities furnished much of the continuous crime so incessantly talked about. They failed to see the smaller human failings in their neighbors. Hence, they secured credit of having more charity for the multitude of human weaknesses. Herein lay their mistake, for great charity being a quality of the imagination, fewer seem to possess it. City people and the government may learn of your crimes, but everybody living in the country knows of the other's faults or lesser shortcomings.

Both men were well-to-do, and in addition, they were honest. Their time was mainly occupied in slowly gathering village news, and circulating gossip. As everybody pursued the same course, nobody objected to the two busy old newsgatherers. Unless it was a case of real poverty, which was of rare occurrence, town news was dutifully disseminated with additions to its kind and quality. Unlike the newspaper that prints and circulates the same news for all, the village newsgatherers of a small community never fail to discriminate in the circulation. Happening to have the reputation of being serious minded, or of taking an active part at prayer meeting, certain town news would surely be denied you. If, perchance, you were attractive to a crowd of fellow citizens, and enjoyed a hearty laugh, your appearance among them might produce a lightning-like change in every face. One of them might suddenly ask the time of day, or when is the next prayer meeting. It took the town crone to discriminate.

Si, Jasper, and Nancy Prindle were about the same age, and ranked among the untaxed valuable assets of the old Town. Hardly a day passed but one or all three might be seen strolling down the old familiar road leading to the village. Seldom they passed my home without staying for a cup of tea and a cheery word, or to eagerly exchange some important bit of so-called news. Notwithstanding objections, there was earnestness in all they said, and when one of them did not appear for a day, I seemed to miss them. They were welcome everywhere, but I feel sure that if frequency in calling at my house was an indication of their preference, then my home must have been next in popularity to their own.

In the summer season, my wife, Julie, and I enjoyed sitting on the piazza through the long twilight. In good weather we had numerous visitors, and, occasionally, so many of our neighbors that it taxed the capacity of our rather spacious porch.

Jasper was the first to "show up" on this particular evening.

"Got great news t' tell yer, John," began Jasper.

"Let 'er go, Jasper," said I, imitating his method of address.

"Well, first I understan' that Widder Dudley's got a new silk dress. Nobody seems t' know where she got it. Sartin is, she can't afford to buy one. Looks kinder suspicious. They say she ain't got a cent in th' bank. She had it on t' the pic-nic yesterday. I know more'n seven people who'll never speak t' her ag'in, 'less she explains where she got it."

"Why, Jasper, that's anything but charitable. She has a right to buy and wear what she pleases."

"Ther's only five widders in this town, John, an' only one of 'em can afford t' buy silk. Ther' is likely t' be a big scandal. Where did she git the money, thet's what I'd like t' know? 'Tain't nat'ral for widders t' buy silk 'less they hev money or a beau, an' I know she hain't got nuther."

"Here comes Silas, perhaps he can tell us something more about it," said Jasper with a wink.

Soon Jasper had repeated this newest piece of town scandal to Silas, with the usual relish for embellishments and innuendoes. To the great surprise of Jasper, his old chum did not indicate the least surprise. He maintained an apparently stolid indifference, which finally evolved the suspicion, that the news to him was not entirely new.

"I'd like t' know where she got it. It looks kinder bad fur her," repeated Jasper.

"Do it?" suddenly exclaimed Silas, in a voice of suppressed rage. "It do! Do it? What do you mean, Jasper Perkins, by cir-cu-latin' scan-de-las an' de-form-a-tory—er—scandal? Did yer know thet ye cud git locked up fer thet? Th' idee of a member of th' Fust Baptis' Church tellin' sich wicked an', I may say, devil-lish lies. I know where she got th' dress—an' 'tain't silk nuther! It's jist an uncommon good barg'in in Farmer's Satin at eight cents a yard—ten yards which were bought by a sartin in-di-vidu-al who ain't more'n a thousand miles away. Of course, there ain't many wimmin got sich fine dresses as thet, I allow. It was a-given t' her 'cause th' overseer of th' poor sed she was needin' on 't. Neow thet explination sh'u'd shet up all this talk about th' widder. Thet's all I hev t' say."

"Think we'll git thunder 'fore mornin'," said Jasper, looking up into the sky and sharply sniffing in the air.

Silas reigned for a moment. Jasper's story of the suspicious circumstance surrounding the widow's dress, had fallen flat. He looked much crestfallen and dejected.

The stillness was soon broken by Silas suddenly jumping to his feet. He amazed me by his rapid movements, as he made from the piazza down the path toward the gate.

"What's the matter, Silas?" I asked. "Where are you goin?"

"Goin' hum, fast as my legs kin git me ther," he shouted in reply.

"Don't be in a hurry. I'll be goin'——," began Jasper, but he failed to finish the sentence.

I glanced at him in surprise—wondering why he stopped short. He was looking in the direction of the road. Then, his eyes appeared fixed upon some object. He was straining through the fast disappearing twilight, with his mouth wonderingly wide open. Of a sudden, he seized the arms of the chair, and, half rising, tried to articulate, but words refused to form. Then, the terse silence being broken by the sharp fall of his cane to the floor, it seemed to bring back his voice.

"Look!" he whispered hoarsely, pointing his long, bony finger and trembling with emotion. His eye followed the direction of a figure moving down the road. "Wh-wh-what do I see?" and then, raising his other hand slowly, as if shading his eyes, he almost shouted, "Look! John! Look! Who is thet?"

At this moment my wife stepped out on the piazza. I had risen from my chair, and all stood with eyes following in the direction indicated.

I had paid no attention to passing pedestrians, but I now distinctly saw the figure of a young man walking on the opposite side of the road. "What was there about the figure to excite unusual interest," I thought,—yet, upon more careful observation, there was revealed to my mind certain familiar characteristics and unmistakable points of resemblance. There was some one I had known. Still, my thought confused, permitted no recollection. "Yes," again I thought, "that is an old, familiar gait—I would know it among a million. Let me see, who is it?"

Still puzzled, my wife at my side closely observing me.

"Can't you recollect who it is?" she asked.

"Yes, I recall now, who it is," I answered without a particle of hesitation. Yet, a strange chill, not unmixed with surprise, seemed to suddenly possess me.

No wonder Silas made so hasty a retreat. It was not strange that Jasper sat trembling and haggard looking —his eyes closed, to shut out the figure on the road.

Now, the man we had just seen, had been dead a quarter of a century. I had helped to bury him—years long past. Still there he was, moving down the same old dusty road, so familiar to him in life. It's his form and figure, it's he—I could swear it!

"There goes a man who's been dead for twenty-five years," I said—touching my wife's sleeve. Jasper groaned audibly.

"Then he couldn't walk, could he?"—innocently ejaculated my wife, who failed to take in my view of the situation.

"But it DOES walk," I insisted. "See! See it walk!"

Jasper groaned again, which did not tend to reinsure me.

"What do you want it to do?" she asked, as if she could reach out and push it from my sight.

Jasper again groaned and murmured—"I never believed in ghosts before. Silas was right."

"Yes, Silas WAS right, Jasper, for that is truly Doctor Klouse!"

"Oh! Oh! Oh!" moaned Jasper as if deeply afflicted.

Not for a moment did I release my eyes from the apparition as it slowly moved down the road toward the village. Presently, it only appeared as a faint and indistinct shadow, until at last, wholly lost from sight, it dissolved into the fast deepening twilight. For awhile we all stood silent, our eyes strained to pierce the darkness that evidently had swallowed up this ghost of our old friend and neighbor, Dr. Klouse.

For myself, I felt a great and sudden change of view. A new truth had been thrust before my eyes. As it were, a new revelation impressed me. I felt convinced that for the first time in my life I had witnessed a real ghost, and to me, further argument or investigation would have simply been wasted. It occurred to me that Silas had seen this same ghost but a few evenings before. At that time I was inclined to laugh, so skeptical was I of his story. Not that I thought he would exaggerate, as I knew him to be perfectly reliable, but, he might have been mistaken. Now I KNEW, for the first time, that the old man was right, and I determined that the next time I met Silas I would confess as to the doubt I entertained regarding his story.

Three witnesses had recognized the figure of the Doctor. Yes, and one more, my wife had seen the retreating specter, though I knew she had never known him in life.

The testimony, however, must at least convince our friends. That of one person alone would not suffice to prove that the Doctor had revealed himself to his friends, after a period of more than twenty-five years.

But for what reason? What did it mean? There was no mistake. I was willing to wager my life on the appearance. Then I sought to arouse Jasper from his half-dazed condition, and send him on his way before a reoccurrence of this nerve straining incident. If IT should attempt to walk back again—well, it might carry the old man into the great beyond, in spite of all effort to revive him. My wife, still holding my arm, said in a sweet and calm voice—

"What are you staring at, John? Your neighbor is out of sight now. Why do you tremble so, are you cold?"

"Neighbor! Neighbor! Well, you certainly are cool. Why, it's Doctor Klouse——"

"Oh, John, tell me about Doctor Klouse. Who is he?"

"Who IS he? Who WAS he, you mean, Julie. Well, he lived in that big house across the road, yes, and he died there, over twenty-five years ago. I knew him well,—everybody in the village knew him by name, but excepting myself, he had no intimate friends that I knew or know of. He'd been married. Had one daughter, and she had married and, as I remember, lived in Washington. This only daughter had two children—a boy and girl. I've forgotten this daughter's or even her husband's name. I knew the Doctor more intimately than any one in the village. We were close neighbors and had many pleasant talks and walks together."

Here Jasper gave another groan.

"Why, we often sat on this very piazza all through the long evenings, and——"

"Oh, don't, don't, John," exclaimed Jasper, putting his wrinkled hands to his eyes,—as if to shut out some unpleasant vision of the past.

"What's the matter, Jasper, are you ill?" asked my wife.

"No, Jasper's not ill," said I, answering for him. "He'll be better soon.

"As I was telling you, the Doctor and I often sat here

together. He was a man of rare ability and held many
strange ideas—that is, they were strange to me, but I
loved and longed to hear him talk. After awhile, he absolutely converted me to his way of thinking. I recollect
distinctly the last conversation we had together. It took
place on this very porch, and——"

"Oh, let me hear about it," interrupted my wife.

"Well, he was a very old man—eighty-nine, I think;
but he was quite spry, I tell you, for a man of his age. I
happened to make some remark about his age, and hoped
he'd reach the century mark. 'Thank you,' said he. 'I
know you mean it, John. You are sincere, as I try to be,
but the sooner I go, the earlier I shall return. I am
anxious to meet my wife again.' He talked on for some
time, and finally said, 'If it's possible, John, to recall
when I come again, I intend to re-marry her.' I knew
his wife had been dead a few years. He really believed
he would return to life again. Said he, 'I believe she's
already back on Earth. I believe I have found her. She's
a little tot now, but I knew her face and form as quickly
as I saw her. I was almost tempted to steal her, and
bring her home with me! That's the reason I would
rather go now. This very night if I could! I'm anxious
to get back. She'll be a little older than I, but I care
nothing and she'll care as little. Yes, John, I've seen
her! I've talked to her, but she didn't know me, poor
little soul.'

"These were about the last words he spoke to me.
Then he crossed the road to his home——. A few days
later I helped to take his body to the little cemetery."

"What a queer man he must have been," pondered my
wife,

"Yes, that is what the great mass of people thought—— 'He's queer,' they said. The Doctor, of course, was anything but popular with the masses. He was much too reserved. Yet, first of all, honest. Plain in dress, simple in taste, and always strictly attentive to his own business. Entirely too retiring to attract attention.

"He never sought a public office, and it is doubtful if he could have been elected, handicapped as he was with advanced ideas. An opponent might easily have demolished him, as he could never be induced to vilify or abuse.

"A man of high ideals, none could say a word against his character. Honest, truthful, kindly and just, I thought him the most intelligent man I had ever known."

"I can't stand this any longer," suddenly exclaimed Jasper. "Most afraid t' go hum alone. Thet ghost has given me a frightful shock."

After wishing us both "good night," Jasper hobbled off at an unusually fast gait. We observed him closely as he tottered along, turning at every few quick steps to put his hand up, as if shading his eyes in expectancy of seeing the ghost following. This he repeated at every few steps, until disappearing around a bend in the road.

"What did he mean, about the ghost giving him a shock, John?" asked my wife, after he had gone.

"You don't mean to say, Julie, YOU didn't see Doctor Klouse's ghost?"—raising my voice in surprise.

"Where? When?" she said in evident amazement.

"Why didn't you see Jasper and I watch the ghost of Doctor Klouse pass down the road a few minutes ago? You were here! You asked questions. You must have seen it, too! You saw it move with its hands behind its back, didn't you?"

"Why, John! I'm surprised. Haven't you met your neighbors across the road yet? That was the young man that has taken a fancy to our Ellen, and even Paul has started to go with his sister—that was Finley Douglass!"

"Douglass! Douglass! Why, that's the name! The Doctor's daughter married a Douglass! Gee—is it possible! The ghost must have been the Doctor's grandson! So they're living across the way, in the old Doctor's residence—Well, I'll be darned!"

CHAPTER IV

DOCTOR KLOUSE

THE Summer had almost passed. Already the chill of early Fall nipped the evening air and forced us to frequently seek the warmth of the great log kitchen fire. Here we would adjourn from the piazza with our company, to the spacious old-fashioned open fireplace, with its large and knotty hickory logs. Before the warm glow, our company would draw their chairs in semi-circle fashion to enjoy the long evening that followed. Then was heard the cracking of nuts, the popping corn, flowing cider, and forth came the rosy cheeked apples. All differences in religion and politics were threshed out and settled once and for all. Somebody was sure to "start the ball a-rolling."

Nancy, Jasper and Silas were all "hard shells," and could never quite understand how our Ellen could believe in "Sprinkling."

"You can't convince me," Silas would declare—"Ye can't wash a sheet by jest wettin' a corner on it, nuther kin y' wash away yer sins, 'cept t' git in all over."

It was, in every sense, an animated scene. Often would the arguments wax long and positive, each picturing in fanciful—if not strange terms—the same final torrid home in which each would find himself installed forever, if persisting in heterodox beliefs. The argument generally started by an innocent remark upon some one's part, but, like the proverbial snowball, it grew in size and importance, until, by its own weight and certain applied heat, it finally dissolved. Everybody laughed and joked and made merry for the while, inevitably closing with weird and ghostly tales, or legends of early New England. Under the influence of these stories, the company finally tip-toed for their wraps and soon sought the protecting shelter of their own homes. None but the bravest went home alone, and, after all had departed, my wife and I would secure the doors and windows on the lower floor—assured that nothing remained unfastened. Truly, as one may regard it, there is something spooky and weird about an old country kitchen, on a Winter's evening, notwithstanding the great glowing fire in the open fireplace. Now and again the reflection of dancing shadows on walls and ceiling stimulated the imagination, and helped the company to trace in them departed as well as the living forms. They seemed to reflect all our suspicions, superstitions, and troubles, and suggested hundreds of new ones. When ambition was dormant, we built within the flickering shadows, our cherished air castles.

Only on evenings when the violinist arrived with the young people, wearing happy faces and their noise-loving propensities, were solemn thoughts entirely driven from that old kitchen.

One other exception may be noted. Since my engagement with Adolph Von Posen, who had reported progress from time to time in construction of his bird-like aeroplane —revolutionizing the flying worlds—he often found excuses to call when company had gathered for the evening discussion. Then was I put at my wit's ends, to keep our people from making a hasty exit. Their departure was ever stimulated by Adolph managing to sit nearest to me, while whispering his new discoveries in air flight throughout the evening. Unfortunately for the rest of us, he never took kindly to our hot ginger bread, cider, apples, popcorn and nuts.

After a few such evening calls, of uncomfortable sequence, I secured in the village some pickled pigs' feet and bologna sausage, as an agreeable surprise. It greatly pleased him, yet his surprise for us was fourfold, as Adolph, doubtless realizing his lonesomeness, had already provided himself with several large pickles and a liberal portion of cheese—and such cheese!

Notwithstanding, much pleasure and interest was afforded to these neighborly evening gatherings by the advent of the two young people, Finley Douglass and his sister Hester, grandchildren of my old friend, Doctor Klouse. They were our opposite neighbors now, and my surprise knew no bounds when I first obtained a near view of Finley. If his gait, manner and general personality had caused Silas, Jasper and myself to honestly mistake him for his grandfather's ghost then, indeed, at close view the striking resemblance he bore to him convinced me for all time that it was not the Doctor's ghost that I now beheld, but Peter Klouse himself, arrayed in a new body, but repossessing the same soul. He looked, acted and spoke as of old. I could not be in his presence a moment without feeling that his name was Klouse—not Douglass.

In view of the great affection and esteem in which I held the Doctor, it was but natural that I should seek the society of young Finley. This intimate knowledge of

Finley's personality—almost a duplication in conversation, thought, and ideals of my old friend, caused me to almost forget that he had once died. I noted that Finley's eyes were not the same color as his grandfather's, neither was his hair, but these characteristics seemed to have no apparent relation to the man himself.

It took some time before I could convince either Silas or Jasper that the ghost of their old acquaintance was none other than our young, new neighbor. Yet, little by little, they became reconciled to my view of the incident, and, after much persuasion upon my part, they were induced to meet him. Not, however, before warning both not to create a scene, and admonishing them never to mention the subject to him or to any one else. None else but my wife, Silas and Jasper shared the secret of my firm conviction. I warned them decidedly, that to relate the circumstances to others, or to express any positive knowledge of our belief, that this was the old Doctor —returned in new form—would excite derision, and might invite violence from fanatics. I felt that the very least that might happen to us would bring discord into our lives; and we might become the laughing stock of the whole community. To keep our own council, we all finally agreed.

Finley, upon being introduced to Silas, could not help indulging in mirthful reference to their first meeting, at twilight, in front of the old cemetery. How much less mirthful he would have been had he known the truth.

To my mind, the Doctor had made good his promise— he had returned! Another fact added further weight to my conviction—Finley was born on the very day his grandfäther died! His anxiety for a speedy return had been unconsciously satisfied.

Early in our acquaintance, we saw much of both Finley and his sister. Their frequent calls at our home added to the happiness of our family; but as these calls increased, my wife and I saw less and less of them. There was a delightful reason for the episode. Neither of us was willing to admit to the other that anything unusual was going forward, while seriously hoping there was, and patiently waiting lest we disturb the desirable result.

One day we incidentally observed Finley's marked attentions to our Ellen. We entertained only one hope—that Ellen's Vassar manners and methods would not finally drive him away.

Suddenly it dawned upon us as a case of love all around, for Paul and Hester were even further advanced in their love-making than Ellen and Finley. They were engaged! They agreed, however, to wait for Ellen and Finley to "catch up," if possible, before setting the happy day for a double wedding.

For my wife and I it was a merry time at home, though a little inconvenient for all couples. Yet there was more to come, for Von Posen had fallen desperately in love with Sally Timpole, our spinster cook. It was a case of extremes, Sally having reached her fiftieth year—tall, slender and weighing less than one hundred pounds. Her profusion of curls, and large brown eyes had captured Adolph, who, only twenty-eight, short and broad, tipped the scales at three hundred pounds. His broad face—almost flat—with abbreviated, retroussé nose, imparted a strange appearance, while his eyes gave the impression of being half asleep all the time. It was a case of love at first sight. The course of their love was tinctured by an absolute indifference as to what others might think. The fact that they monopolized the kitchen every night, with Finley and Ellen in the parlor, while Paul and Hester occupied the sitting-room nearly day and night, demanded some drastic action.

"We must have the kitchen, or be forced to bed and stay there," said my wife to Sally. This compelled a compromise and additional headquarters near the wash house were arranged and a bright fire constantly kept burning. To this cosy place we transferred the pigs' feet, pickles, Sally and Adolph.

Who ever heard of a triple wedding in one household? Yet, the approaching fact seemed obvious enough.

So, for many anxious weeks, my wife and I chose between kitchen and bedroom. Of course, we pretended not to notice things, but to save my life I couldn't help occasionally peeking first into the sitting-room, and then into the parlor. It increased our hope.

My wife and I must have been similarly affected, as I observed the intense interest the love scenes excited in us both. It took us all our time to study complete indifference but to no avail.

When we first learned of Paul's engagement to Hester we celebrated the event, to our relief, by dancing on the bed together one morning in our stockings, and hugging one another in sheer delight.

We secretly continued to elaborate our preparations for the double wedding, with a few extra touches thrown in. This, in case Von Posen's mind remained unchanged, as we had learned from Sally that she'd "been engaged from the first night's spooning in the wash house." Naturally, we never discussed Ellen's prospects. We both intuitively concluded the event was foregone and without unnecessary words. Neither of us could have accused the other of interference—in case all our calculations happened to go amiss. Except for our mutual impatience to hurry matters, no happiness in our lives ever quite equaled this period. It was bliss, from parlor to wash house. Even the chickens and the cows, and all the little late Fall flowers, seemed in love with one another. The world did seem so happy to me then.

"Suppose it don't happen, Julie?" said I anxiously one day.

"You know what Tennyson says," she sweetly answered.

" ' 'Tis better to have loved and lost, than never to have loved at all.' "

"Yes, Julie," said I, "but you don't seem to recall Thomas Moore's view of the case. He takes the opposing side and says, 'Better far to be in endless darkness lying, than be in light, and see that light for-e'er flying. All that's Bright must Fade.' Yet, we need not borrow trouble, Julie," I consolingly added—kissing her.

Ellen was extremely happy. Finley was a God to her, and the lovers had already begun to live their earthly heaven. She seemed, with his words of love, "like the Chatookee that never drinks at a stream, but captures the rain drops in falling."

One day Finley came to us, in the kitchen, and asked for Ellen's hand in marriage. We solemnly consented; then quickly retired to our bedroom for another dance.

CHAPTER V

HEREDITY VS. KLOUSE PHILOSOPHY

As matters had settled down to a complete understanding, and the causes that had led to genuine love affinities were about to produce their much desired results, it will not be amiss to indite Mr. Finley's account of certain facts linked with his Grandfather's speculations.

"My mother told me many interesting facts about Grandfather," began Finley one evening as we sat together discussing not a few of the theories held by the Doctor.

"It was about a week after Grandmother died that he began to act queerly, as my mother thought and expressed it. 'He began,' she said, 'a systematic search for every new born baby, for at least fifty miles from where we lived.' He advertised in our local paper, and others published in towns nearby. The advertisement ran something like this—'Send me the name and address of any girl baby born since'—here giving a certain date, which was the day of his wife's death. He then signed himself 'Doctor Klouse.'

"My Grandfather received several hundred replies. The folk who knew him, thought he had suddenly been afflicted with some mental aberration. They shook their heads and winked at each other whenever he was present —or the subject broached. Those living at a distance and who did not know him, wondered not a little as to what the subject-matter of the advertisement meant. Some refer to it to this very day, so great was the mystery mingled with their curiosity. When he had obtained the names of all new-borns, he devoted most of his time, and every day in all manner of weathers, to calling on both parents or the mother of each little one. Under one pretext or another, he managed to see every one of the children. More than a year was devoted to steady riding and driving in making all these calls. Never once did he tell any one why he wished to see each baby. I think I am the only person who knows this reason—though now, you may guess it."

"I can only guess," I replied—with the intention of hearing all.

"He was looking for his wife!" Here Finley stopped short, expecting me to betray some indication of surprise; but I said nothing, and after a moment's hesitation he continued:

"He had promised his wife it seems, many years before, that if she 'passed away' first, he would devote all the time possible in trying to discover her identity re-born in some new arrival upon Earth. Both the Doctor and his wife thoroughly believed that they would return immediately, and that neither would lose their identity. Indeed, they were convinced that they never could, in any number of successive lives. Yes, he devoted more than a year in investigating the possible reincarnation in every infant for miles around this village. It was a task of intenseness which kept him in an eager half-feverish state of mind nearly all the time. It cost him considerable sums of money, as he had to almost buy his way into some homes.

In others, they treated him with kindly consideration and he lavished benefits in appreciation. He never thought of the cost. Yet, to him, it proved but a deep disappointment, for nowhere did he find an infant that resembled in the slightest a duplicate of his wife's identity. Most people meeting him concluded that no living physician could discover any particular identity in a baby, though the child might develop a duplicate of some one living or dead,—but the Doctor concluded otherwise. If disappointed in his quest, he betrayed no outward sign, nor did he speak of it.

"Three or four years later, he learned incidentally, that to his wife's sister, living in the far West, was born a baby girl, on the day following his wife's death. This news he joyfully received, and immediately made preparations to visit the happy mother. While strictly holding the secret of his mission, an unconscious remark betrayed to my mother informed her as clearly as if he had amply explained. Half in jest, she asked him one day, 'Looking for a Western girl, Dad?' He answered simply, 'No, for your Mother.'

"Arriving at his destination and cordially received, he beheld the little four year old—a happy, healthy girl. Though a man of education and splendid will-power, he absolutely felt sure that he had discovered the return of his departed wife. His surprise and pleasure was so great that for several days he remained wrapped in a kind of revery. Having absolute faith in his painstaking investigations and observations, covering almost a life's period, he felt assured that no false theory had possessed him, though he scarcely expected to have recognized his wife's return so easily.

"A few days after seeing the child he began a series of observations, taking in every word the child uttered. He remained in her company constantly, hovered around her, listening, watching for every word and sign of recognition. Nothing came. Convinced, however, beyond reasonable doubt that this sweet little girl was none other than his reincarnated former wife, his affection for the child grew day by day.

" 'She has returned,' he said to himself, 'but not for me.'

"After weeks of observation and thoughtful study, he finally concluded—'She has a spirit with her. Yet, a stranger to me—I cannot recognize it.' Now, Grandfather believed that every human body was the abiding place of two separate and distinct spirits. These he named, for convenience, the dual identity—the *Bon*ality and *Mal*ality in every human being. 'I, the *moral*, represent the better of me. I am in charge, and am responsible. By will, I must keep the evil or lower self, *Mal*ality, from mastering the "I" or *moral*, and placing the *lower* in control.'

"So sure did he now feel his wife's return, that the sudden desire seized him to 'shuffle off this mortal coil,' return again, and later claim her. There was some doubt in his mind, however, as to his mental vision being sufficiently advanced to recall a former existence. This would be necessary if he were to recognize the wife of some former state. He felt convinced that the human mind, in its highest imaginative or intuitive type, had nearly reached the point where previous existences would be recalled in detail more and more. Scarcely one highly intuitive mind exists. Indeed, it might easily recollect

certain vivid things of a former life, but to recognize
identity of the *morals* changed by *Duality*, in each separate life, would probably be next to the impossible. 'She
has returned, but she knows me not!' he would repeat
again, and over again to himself.

"His love for the little child grew most pathetic. The
anguish of the old man's heart was seen as the child's
small white hand rested gently in his. He longed that
none might discover his secret, until his weakened body
had dissolved in death. Then, he would be happy as of
yore. He would be near her, and touch the hem of her
garment, and hold her hand again, and every day.

"When alone, he talked aloud to the image of his intuition. To him, the childish affection of this little girl
seemed to hallow ground on which he walked.

"Yes, Doctor Klouse was a man, as intimated, with a
mighty will. He had now realized that though this world
was no place for him, he was still bound to sojourn his
allotted time.

"Returning from the West, he told my mother the circumstances of the visit, confiding the pathetic tale to no
one else. Then, two years later, he passed into the
great beyond."

*   *   *   *   *   *

From Finley I learned later that the light and love
recognized by his Grandfather in this little child, flickered
and went out in less than a year after the old man's
demise.

To aid my own future observation, I held from Finley
the remarkable coincidence of Ellen's birth occurring on
the very day of his Grandmother's death.

CHAPTER VI

A DREADFUL LIAR

THE double wedding had taken place. The happy event had become a matter of family history. So had the village gossips ceased their tattle and sly whisperings concerning the antecedents of Finley and his sister. One thing, however, had been settled in their minds, that the young people belonged to the class known as "well-to-do," and for the future would have to be referred to as the son and daughter-in-law of John Bacon—the famous aviator.

Again normal conditions reigned in our domicile. The house was large and roomy enough for all to dwell together as one happy family. There was no friction—nothing had thus far developed to mar each pleasant relation. Why then anticipate the future? Our minds and tastes blended perfectly. Each had his and her part to perform in the multitude of duties, and each one worked to lighten the several tasks of the other by trying to do more than his part of the whole. As a result everything was in order, well done and promptly. Everybody seemed happy, and Finley not infrequently remarked that we must obtain our pleasure from our work. We all believed it. All were convinced that it was the nearest to true happiness that had been achieved. So, we were a busy and happy lot of people. I found no time for the aviation field.

"In order to secure data for the Scientific Society, I promise to make just one more flight," I said to Julie.

"When will you make that one?" she anxiously inquired, as of old.

"Not until the Spring," I replied.

"Oh, I'm so glad," was all she said, reflectively.

I had now promised them all that this would constitute my last trip in the air. I was in no particular hurry regarding the start. I began to recognize the danger as I had never before. There were intervals when I had been on the point of retiring—then some added feature to aeroplane construction would suddenly appear. "This new feature insures perfect safety. We are now 'fool proof,'" would be the announcement of the promoters. So each time I decided to sustain the interest I had taken, and to try every innovation that seemed to solve the problem. Many of my intimate friends called me, "plainly reckless," and predicted that some day I'd "break my neck." All this they uttered impetuously, knowing I would take their remarks in the spirit of friendly warning—which I did. I made it known that I was making a preliminary study of air currents, with the idea of perfecting a machine which would finally revolutionize the whole theory of flying. I informed them of my mental plans and expected to submit a model in the Spring.

As agreed with my family, I had put everything in shape for the winter at the hangar, on the aviation field. This did not by any means terminate my duties to my fellow aviators, regarding numerous matters that held me a more or less conspicuous figure on the field. Time was now pretty evenly divided between the field and farm.

When not busied with these matters, a host of callers held my attention up to midnight each day, monopolizing my time with submission of all sorts of schemes and requests. While I was away, or busy on the farm, the house folk entertained them until I returned. I generally settled matters by saying—the "ladies first." Sometimes I had to hustle the callers slightly along, they pushed and pleaded so persistently. So far as the men were concerned, I would sort them into groups, saying, "All who want to borrow money, come in first." This usually had the effect of clearing out about half the number at one swoop. "Those who want to sell Life Insurance, Real Estate, Bonds, Stocks or Books—come in," I commanded. Not a few of the more knowing callers waited until the rest had gone, and then sprang upon me, figuratively speaking. These stickers were of the nerviest nerve wearers. Some wanted nothing but sympathy for woe, but most of them would ask nothing less than cold cash. Why did they call, you ask. Heaven knows, except it was because of my name being so frequently in the press. Some announcements ran—"Mr. Bacon, the wealthy aviator, will give an exhibition in his new 'monoplane.'" I was a mark—advertised like a new brand of soap. At first my visitors called at the house in single file. Soon they came in pairs, and finally in flocks. I have failed to preserve a record of the schemes presented, and all the strange inventions tending to turn things topsy-turvy. Many of these people wandered over the farm, picking most of our choice flowers and sometimes pulling them up by the roots. They pocketed vegetables, fruits and berries, and broke the limbs from the smaller trees. They would then excuse themselves—"Oh, Mr. Bacon, I just took it for a souvenir, I knew you wouldn't care." I really did not care—if that simply would have kept them away.

Not a few sought my photograph, or my autograph. That was easy, as I had several thousands of both printed, to serve out when called for. It was anything but a wise scheme, as it only increased the crowds, who called for more. In one sense, it served as a further advertisement which brought quick returns.

On Sundays, each member of our family had a small group of callers in almost every room of the house. They were entertained until I was ready. Each one, however, seemed perfectly at home—thank heaven for that.

Though I was fairly well to do, my callers suggested a thousand new ways of becoming richer. "Was there any reason," I thought, "why I should stand this army of solicitors?"

Finley suggested, and truly, that I suffered the natural penalty of being conspicuous, with the added reputation of having ready money.

Jasper informed me that I was a fool to stand it any longer. He suggested my turning an "ugly bull" loose in the front yard.

But it's a long road that has no turning, I thought. Things that have a beginning, have some ending, too.

Worn out, one late evening, I retired to my room. Sleep seemed soon to possess me. It was all very real. I began to arrange all the Town's people up in one long row. My numerous callers had broken my nerves. I told them of my determination to go away—to leave them. I looked to see if any of 'em would shed a tear or two. No, indeed. It only made them laugh at me. That was the last straw. Hold on a minute—yes, there is one poor fellow over there seemed to feel deeply. Who is he? He's the only man in the whole row that appeared to look responsive. Let me see—I said aloud to myself. Why, that's Sam Willis! What in—Why, it's that ever-smiling Sam, the most famous first premium liar in the country. Poor Sam. There he stood, bawling as if his heart would break. Calling for me to stay. So I walked up to him and explained why I was going—to the far West.

"Say," said he, drying his eyes, "take it from me, you're too serious." Whereupon this good natured blue-ribbon liar laughed right in my face. "Why, Mr. Bacon, I'm surprised, you don't know the trick. Lie to 'em, and they'll love you, oh, so much. After awhile they'll let yer alone." Then he continued, "The Lord loveth a cheerful liar—so do others. Didn't yer know yer friends are sometimes yer enemies?"

I was certain that I had seen and heard all this,—that I had been awake all the time,—that I must have been seeing things. Yet, here I found myself in bed.

Everything was quiet, my wife soundly asleep.

"I'll go hire Sam in the morning," I found myself saying aloud. "I'll make him my butler. I'll put him on the door." I was so pleased with the sudden inspiration that I reached over and gave my wife a nudge. I couldn't keep my plans to myself—even till morning.

"What are you doing now, John?" she said, raising herself. "Thank goodness, I'm so glad you stopped that snoring."

I didn't want to tell her that I believed I hadn't slept a wink. So I swallowed my resentment and told of my plans.

She didn't seem to have much confidence in what I said, for she offered scant encouragement. Still she said, "we might try it," even if it did "expose us a little."

" 'Twill be better than living in some other people's hereafter, as we've been doing," she remarked with a sigh.

Accordingly, the next morning, long before people were astir, I quietly slipped out of my bed, and made off to call on the biggest liar known since the epoch of the famous Jack Wilding.

I found him—just where all sensible people should be at that hour of the morning—abed and asleep.

It didn't take long to state my errand. Sam immediately informed me that he had held hundreds of just such positions as I offered. He told of being in one position nearly twenty-seven years. He said he could sleep standing up as well as *lieing*, but that he suffered "from tender nerves." I wanted his nerves tender, so I hired him. Sam was not a bad fellow—nor bad looking, as a matter of fact. As for dressing and vanity, he was the personification of an Asmodeus.

A host of girls in the village were in love with him. He could say such pretty, small nothings—all so harmless. He insinuated that the hair of the reddest head in town was like the glory of the sunset West. That the poor girls' freckles were beauty spots set to the time of "dainty and sweet." He was never lonesome among the girls. They followed and admired him. He could talk their way —just as they wanted him. Of course, he never told them the truth by way of hurt. The more homely they were, the handsomer he would portray them. Sam never lost his temper. He had, apparently, none to lose. So the girls just loved him. They worshiped Sam. Each one

looked flushed and happy after a talk with Sam. He never
pretended too much knowledge. On politics and religion
he was "mum." But Sam was a wise fellow—cute and
observant. He knew, he said, where people "put their
foot into it," and go "a-blundering through the world."
Unprejudiced in mind, he saw others' mistakes and prof-
ited by the knowledge gained. Having no "axe to grind,"
he never advocated reforms, nor posed as a reformer.
If he had ideals, he never mentioned the fact. He simply
said and did the things that pleased and appealed to the
vanity of those with whom he came in contact. Then, he
would make a dozen smiles grow where there was but .a
grouch before. Few knew him, because he never made
himself conspicuous, yet, he knew everybody in town—
their first as well as their last names. In this respect he
held all the advantages of the successful politician. Sam's
voice was always modulated to the soft and pleasant. If
he lacked initiative, he avoided the company of the fellows who had it. He stood aside, and saw them fret,
fume and worry themselves into prematurely "old age,"
as he styled it. He dubbed them as unhealthy cranks
in their mad rush for place and wealth. He knew just
enough to obtain a good easy living, and to cling to all
the cash he picked up. No pangs of hunger disturbed
his composure or worried him in his dreams. He was
perfectly docile, obliging, for he would go or come, just
as you preferred. Either way suited Sam. He was
married, and his wife was evidently happy, for she never
sought acquaintances apart from Sam. Such abiding
faith did she have in his perfection, that when forlorn
ladies called upon Sam at his home, to ask his advice regarding any matter, Mrs. Willis was never jealous. She

would sit as if immovable, with a never-fading smile on her sweet, round face. But for an occasional deep, half-suppressed chuckle, and her immense size, her presence would have been unnoticed.

So, we installed Sam as a sort of court jester, a Chicot, Patch, or Wetzweiler, and while not so famous and wise as these notables, he was, notwithstanding, more modern and up-to-date. We didn't dare, however, to call him butler—as that would have given him free access to the pantry.

Sam's duties were simple. He was to answer the front door bell, and admit only those who appeared as friends on the list compiled for his use. All others—well, we left it to him. He boarded and lodged with us, on the understanding that he might return home every two or three months. Though his home was less than a mile dis-tant, Sam preferred to write his wife a daily letter, rather than make the call in person, which he deemed undue familiarity. He called his wife, his dear "Semper Idem," which he said meant "always the same," in Latin. In the Summertime, he closed his letters to her with the words, "this is tempus fugit," which he declared meant "this is fly time."

Sam had been with us but a few minutes before I heard the dreaded jingle of the front door bell. I marked his measured step down the hall in answer to the bell. I was immediately interested as to who the caller was, and if not to be admitted, to learn the nature of the conversation between Sam and the caller. So, from my position in the upper hall, I quietly watched and listened.

"Is Bacon—John Bacon in?" came the voice, as Sam opened the door.

"Have you a card—your name, please, and——"

"I knew Bacon before you were born, John don't need no card from me. My name's Titus—Bill Titus—I want to see John. Is he in?"

"Why, how do you do, Mister Titus. This is indeed a surprise. I have often heard John—Mister Bacon I should have said—speak of you, William,—Bill, he generally says. Only last night, before he went away, on rather a long journey, he said to me—'now, Sam,' said he, very affectionately, 'if my old friend Bill calls, treat him kindly. Give him anything I've got.'"

"You don't mean to say, Mister—Sam, I mean, that John has gone away, do you?" said the man eagerly, as he suddenly glanced into the hall—noticing my old brown soft hat and coat hanging on the rack—and fairly screamed out, "Whose hat and coat be they?"

For an instant Sam was startled, so completely had he been taken off his guard, but he managed hesitatingly to ejaculate, "What?"

"Hain't those John's things?" Titus fiercely bawled.

"Don't, don't," said Sam, deprecatingly throwing up one hand, while reaching for his handkerchief with the other, which he quickly put before his eyes with a tremulous groan. Titus respectfully allowed Sam a full minute to repress his apparent sorrow—then, he said:

"I'm sorry if I was the cause of this sudden sorrow."

Not a word did Sam say. I felt that he was shamming sorrow, in order to think out his next plan of action.

"Forgive me, if I've been abrupt to you," added Titus.

"Surely, I forgive you," said Sam, replacing his handkerchief in his pocket. "I forgot to put 'em away," said

Sam, "they always remind me so much of him," he added.

"I hope he isn't dead. I wanted to ask a favor of him," said Titus rather dejectedly.

"Oh, no, he is not dead, or rather was not, when he left here. How much of a loan did you want?"

"Only six hundred."

"Is that all? Now let me see. He had just about that amount upstairs last night, before he went. He was then asking how it might be invested—he asked me. He always leaves it to me. I told him, so he handed me the money to care for. As I never like to have money around, early this morning I carried it over home, and said to my dear wife, 'Semper Idem,' 'take it to the city this very day and invest it.'"

"When is she going to the city?" eagerly asked Titus.

"Why, er, let me see. It's now ten forty-five, the train leaves at ten forty-seven. You've got plenty of time. Just tell my wife that I sent you after the money. Now hurry, Mister Titus. You can sign a note for it a little later, I'll trust you till then. Now be quick," said Sam, waving his arms as he got Titus under way.

"Yes, yes, I'll make it all right. So-long! Give John my regards. Good-by, thank you!" and without another word he started on a run to the front gate. Just as he reached the gate his hat blew off. Grabbing it up savagely, he made a fresh start down the old road towards the village. With a swift gait, he was soon lost to view in the dust and distance.

"Sam," said I, doing my best to suppress my anger, and as I came out of hiding, "now, you placed me in a bad light. He'll be back here, when he finds you've lied to him."

"I'm waiting outside for him now," he serenely replied. "I know he'll be back, for he forgot to ask where my wife lives."

Sure enough, within ten minutes, Titus had returned, hat in hand, out of breath and vigorously mopping his large, flabby face, while fumbling to open the garden gate. Sam politely went down the path to meet him.

"Did you get the money?" asked Sam, as he smilingly opened the gate for Titus.

"Hell, no! Like an idiot, I forgot to ask you where you lived. Such blasted luck," he said with great disgust. Then suddenly brightening up, he confidently whispered, "Ain't John got more money in the house handy?"

"You poor Mister Titus. How I pity you. You should have had that money, it as good as belonged to you. How disappointed Mister Bacon will be when he comes back—a year from now. He borrowed from me, the last ten I had—for his ticket."

"Hang the luck. Gol darn it. Say, it makes me sweat to think of what I missed, and the opportunity Bacon missed too—yer understand?" he said, significantly nodding his head, and then added, "I'm the boy that can pay interest, and good interest, you know. He's the loser. He's missed it. You tell him, won't-cher. Tell him, he just missed it by a hair-breadth. Gee-whittica, ain't that too bad."

"Very, very unfortunate," replied Sam solemnly.

"Say, Sam, what's your last name?"

"Willis."

"Well, Sam Willis, you're my friend. You're true blue, you are, and I'll be your friend. You can count on me every time. Now, I tell you what to do. When

Bacon gives you any more money to invest, bring it to this address. I'll be waiting, and I'll be good to you, understand? I'll be generous, yer know. He'll get good interest, but you'll get,—well, yer know—maybe ten per cent or so, accordin' to circumstances. Well, good-by, Sam. You're all right. I like yer, and I'll do the right thing by yer. Good-by again now. So-long."

Sam took the proffered card, and without reading it, placed it in his pocket, then quickly replied, "Good-by— er William,—I mean Bill. You'll get another chance, just like the last one. I'll save it for you, or bust," said Sam, raising his hand and voice at the same moment.

"Good! Good for you! So long," shouted Titus as he left, his face wreathed in smiles, and looking as happy as if he had the actual six hundred in his pocket.

"I don't remember that fellow, Sam," said I.

"I have his card in my pocket, he just gave it to me, let me read it. Here it is,—'W. Thaddeus Titus, champion wood sawer and corn husker. Hogs killed in the Fall.' "

"I remember him, Sam. He came to slaughter our hogs last Fall. He became drunk and lay under our woodshed for three days."

Recollecting how dreadfully Sam had lied to Titus, I determined to take him to task, which I immediately did, whereupon he replied:

"Mister Bacon," said he, "you're a big man in this small community. You've got to have peace. You cannot afford to be pestered, though it's a natural law for the weak to be attracted to the strong. Philosophers say, that two bodies attract each other inversely, as the square of the distance. The square of the distance of a host of these 'er fellows from you, makes them gravitate towards you very persistently. Yes, you're a very important man around here, you attract 'em, sir, you pull 'em as it were. Poverty is attracted by riches, liars are attracted by people who tell the truth. That's why I'm here, Mister Bacon. I believe a good liar is a great protection to the big man who tells the truth. It's necessary in this community, sir! I flatter myself, I can do it so that they love me better'n the one who sticks to the plain unvarnished truth."

I found no way to answer his argument; besides, I knew when I hired him, that his dreadful lying had made him a most popular and much beloved character to all who did not know him. After that I let him alone.

With some little initiative, I believe he would have made a name as a seller of mining stock. Like the famous Bessie Millie of Pomona, in the Orkney Islands, who made an excellent living by vending favorable winds to mariners, so, I believe, Sam could "pass out the salve," with a little effort he might sell wind to wind-mill owners.

We could always hear the front door bell. Then the echo of his good natured laugh, as he softly closed the door when the caller turned to go. Not infrequently did they drop a "tip" into his soft, upturned hand. Whenever he received one he would remark to me,—"A prince from the City," otherwise, he would simply announce—"hayseeds."

But Sam had brought more or less of joy into our household. The change was wonderful. I never saw callers leave so happily convinced. The ladies who called all fell in love with Sam. I have often seen them turn and wave to him, or girls who knew him intimately, throw

him a kiss as they went down the path. Then the men
would go 'way, sometimes bowing and politely returning,
"Thank you. Oh, thank you."

He had told so many callers that I had gone to Pekin,
or London, that frequently, when I went to the village
people would accost me with—"Glad to see you look so
well after your journey. Made a quick trip?" To which
I invariably answered, "Yes, just a flying trip—as my
mind flew there and back."

They really thought I was joking, and they laughed
whether or not they saw the point. "Why should I care,"
I thought. I know that not one of them were concerned
unless it was Silas. He, indeed, has insisted upon going
to prayer meeting twice a week since Sam's engagement
with us. It was only yesterday that he told me he was
interested in an effort "to save Sam's lost soul."

"Whatever he may have lost," I replied, "he has certainly saved the happiness of our whole family,—the door
bell's merry jingle is now only as music to the ear."

CHAPTER VII

As the long, quiet Winter evenings closed in and our company gathered around the old-fashioned open fire, and the warm glow of the great hickory logs gave zest to the meeting, we discussed the knotty problems of the day, or dreamed away our time. The grotesque shadows cast upon floor and ceiling in dancing waves of light, suggested a miniature war of flame and artillery fire, attacking and destroying the strong and powerful fort of logs.

At times I caught myself dozing off as Finley read from the dry and parched leaves of his grandfather's ancient manuscript. Many of its ideas I had long before digested from his own lips. The heat from the fire becoming too intense, more than half the company slept—sometimes an odd snore breaking in—until awakened by the sharp, penetrating voice of Sam.

"Nobody's snoring, but I'm afraid you're agoing to, so I'll wake yer up." This was Sam's method of sparing our feelings. Still, we were forced to be resigned.

The company invariably arrived by four o'clock in the afternoon. Adolph's presence seemed eternal, and very frequently it appeared as if he had remained in the wash-house from one afternoon to the next. Sally usually propped him up in a comfortable position, which she knew he would never move from between eight and ten hours at a stretch. Meanwhile, she employed herself

71

with a thousand and one things in the house. Sally, though slender and peaked, could do more work in one day than most people can accomplish in three. It was always safe to beat a hasty retreat when we saw her coming, as she insisted on her own way with firm possession of room and air. Never before had one of us attempted to stand before her shrill voice and caustic tongue; but Adolph seemed to admire it as an element incorporated in his love, so he would smilingly go to sleep under the incessant lash and smarting. The harder Sally talked, the quicker would he succumb to the lulling effect.

Each night Sally prepared the supper, cleared the table and polished up the plates. All before the old hall clock had struck six. An hour later, the light in the wash-house was turned low, an indication that Adolph had been fed to the satisfaction of his ever-increasing weight.

Always in anticipation of company, my wife had prepared a pan of rosy-cheeked apples, and a large pitcher of sweet cider was set upon the table.

While Jasper and Silas were able to consume an amazing quantity of food—considering their great age—Nancy could not be outdone as a close second. While a plentiful supply of popcorn was hanging in the corner, ready for the popping, fat chestnuts and shagbarks were to be found by the bushel in the store-room. It was pure joy for Jasper to crack the shagbarks, roast the chestnuts, and "chuck" the shells in the open fire. There they burst, emitting flame as brilliant as a flash light.

Then, all but every evening, Ellen would persuade Finley to make us some good "old-fashioned Jamaica Molasses Candy." All declared him "the dandy candy maker." Everybody ate molasses candy, and by common consent, all conventionalities were discarded. None are supposed to eat molasses candy with dignity. Even the cat and dog loved it, though mastication amounted to a tragedy. But the most to be deplored incident "touching" Ellen's candy exploit was Nancy's false teeth. Sally seemed the only one to elude the charms of molasses—its sweetness being entirely out of place with her temper.

Finley had now become the center of attraction. His resemblance to his grandfather seemed to impress all who had known the Doctor—especially the three old crones. To them, he was old Doctor Klouse returned. Therefore, they accorded him the same respectful attention when he spoke, as had characterized their demeanor towards the old physician in bygone days.

As Finley related the many familiar characteristics of his grandfather, one or both the old crones were sure to forget with the familiar "Jes so, Doctor"—so close did Finley's resemblance recall the past.

One evening he surprised us all by relating how he had found one of his grandfather's manuscripts. It gave an account of that Western trip, and years spent with experiments in the wilderness. The prospect of our learning much from this interesting document produced a delightful sensation of expectancy and so far arrested our attention that, for several minutes, neither cider, apples nor molasses appealed to the company.

"I'm durned anxious to hear that yarn," said Silas with rising enthusiasm.

"Be ye? Well, I'm as poor as Job's off ox in a knowledge o't; jist start 'er agoin', Finley," said Jasper.

"Thank you, gentlemen, if you're ready, I'll begin:

"After returning from the West, many years ago, my

grandfather roughly wrote down some of his quaint philosophical ideas. Also, the results of many experiments for his own use and benefit. While they are by no means complete, I will venture to read from the manuscript," began Finley.

"Hold on, Finley," interrupted Silas, with a warning cry. "I got some 'lasses candy stuck t' my teeth. Here, Nancy, you got gud eyes, take my jack knife an' git at this 'lasses."

"He hain't got no teeth," said Jasper in a tone of voice anything but complimentary, as Silas handed Nancy the open knife.

After the interruption, Finley resumed:

"First of all, let me relate some facts touching the Doctor's earlier life," he continued. "It was soon after his graduation from the Medical College that he began to doubt the commonly accepted theories regarding the origin of man. Mankind is apart and separate from all other forms of life, he thought. Man could not successfully reproduce himself in combination with other animals. In the language of the layman, it was then generally admitted by the medical profession, that the blood of animals and human beings did not mix. Any attempt to do so, would produce fatal results. If this is true, thought he, why should any one accept the growing belief that mankind is the result of millions of years of evolution up through the lower animals, the result of accident? Starting from the lowest form of life, some would have us believe, that through accident and environment, the animal life branched off into different families, one from the other, into millions of shapes and forms. From this one lowest form of life, to-day, have been pro-

duced all insects, fish, birds, reptiles and ferocious beasts
—the elephant, the mastodon, and the ant; the snake with
poisonous fangs, and the human mother. To accept the
idea that man was ever a beast, he thought, was an absolute denial of God. If we were beasts, we NOW are beasts,
for there is no intermediate condition. The one great
dividing line between the human and animal kingdom that
proves man's divinity, is the volunteer progression by selection, of mankind. No other kind of life in the world,
voluntarily progresses, if at all. My grandfather was
anxious to discover the reason for this human endowment,
which stands in contradiction to all other known life.
Was it something added to the human blood, or was it
something that had disappeared from the blood of animal
creation? This was his great question! How may I find
a solution of this one query? There is only one way,
thought my grandfather, and that is by the transfusion
of blood of one or several animals with human beings. If
their bloods do not 'mix,' then we may never obtain answers to our question.

"Again, suppose he could find, by experiment, that the
human blood might circulate in the body of wild beasts
and the blood of beasts in turn might circulate without
danger in a human body; and, it should be found, that
this human being still voluntarily progressed, while the
beast remained in unprogressive state, would not this tend
to prove that the human being was divine?

"Upon this problem he studied long and faithfully, until
after several years of painstaking scientific research,
coupled with experiment, his efforts were rewarded by
the discovery of serum* or 'culture' which could suc-

* See Transfusion in Glossary.

cessfully injected into the body of either man or beast—
and through this inoculation of the blood of both—permitted, without danger, the perfect intermingling and
transfusion of their bloods.

"He further discovered, that when once a human being
and any warm blooded animal had been inoculated with
the serum, their blood might intermingle by means of
rubber tubes, inserted into the arteries of each without
harm to either. The Doctor kept the formula of this
serum a secret. He never wrote it down, to my knowledge.
I have hunted among all his records, manuscripts, and
papers, but I have been unable to find any reference to
the formula except the bare mention of its discovery.

"He was successful in one or two experiments, where
he was able to transfuse and circulate through tubes, his
own blood with that of a dog. This was without any ill
effect. But, he found that if he was to gather unques-
tioned results, he must seek the quiet of the wilderness
where prying eyes would not misjudge the object of these
experiments.

"From that time on, and for more than a quarter of a
century, he experimented and worked with the one absorbing purpose, to discover, if possible, if man and animal were the same. In a measure, a thankless task to be
sure—one in which no person could be induced to take an
interest, or share a part of the necessary expense. Not a
dollar could be obtained for research work. It's easy to
raise millions for the dead he thought, but difficult to
raise a dollar for the living. Fortunately, my grandfather
was a man of means, otherwise he never could have expended so much time and money in research work. He
cared nothing for the discouraging opinions of friends,

nor the denunciatory remarks of those who viewed him in the light of a crank. Indeed, he set his ideal above all, and went straight for the mark. Knowledge, he declared, carried him out of the beaten path of the ignorant masses. It kept him happy, well and strong. It kept him smiling, but never laughing—for 'only fools laugh.' He found a world of chaos, of quarreling and fighting. Men were engaged in establishing each one, his particular religious brand. The crowds, as ever, were following the faker. Politicians and criminals occupied most of the world's stage, and front pages. The great men were generally unknown. It was, therefore, to him, like passing into the Garden of Eden to go far out into the wilderness —among the Aborigines. Away from the influence of gods and money and the social elevation of the unworthy, he could think.

"The world was beginning to accept as final, that the human race were monkeys—slightly improved. The Doctor believed that while life might be created, flesh manufactured, and environment molded and shaped, none could endow life with a soul, except through the divine and beautiful motherhood of mankind."

"Why do yer say 'mankind?' Ain't 'womankind' more perlite?" broke in Silas.

"Yes, it be—but you ain't! Shet up yer head when yer superiors air talkin'," indignantly shouted Jasper. But Silas was so accustomed to Jasper's criticisms that he had learned to pay no attention for the time being.

"So, they say we're monkeys—improved on. Darned if I can swallow thet," said Silas, shaking his head.

"But th' improvement didn't come till after you did, Si. Thet's th' reason yer don't see th' pint," chuckled Jasper.

"Why, Jasper," said Ellen—with a superior air— "When I was at dear old Vassar, gentlemen of intelligence informed our set, that a Doctor living—er—somewhere, a *Doctor Williams, I believe, had in his possession skulls of men more than 500,000 years old."

"Did he live to be as old as that? Well, I never did believe in early marriages," said Nancy, looking directly at Silas.

"He must have been wise, for he never lost his head," ventured Paul.

"But, he had a tough nut, to last that long," said Sam.

"Hold on. Listen a minute, will yer?" drove in Silas again. "Listen! Thet cricket thet's been singin' in yer hearth has stopped! Thet's a sign of death, by gum!" said Silas solemnly shaking his head.

"Will you kindly defer that dispute," said I impatiently. "Let all quietly listen to what Finley has to say about his grandfather," I added.

"Ellen informs us," he continued, "that Doctor Williams has human skulls half a million years old. We also know that the gorilla and monkey existed at that far removed period. Now, why has not the gorilla advanced in knowledge in a half million years? If both man and gorilla were mentally about the same, 500,000 years ago, man has voluntarily advanced in knowledge and learning during that time, but not so with any other living creature! History or science cannot show the voluntary advancement of any form of animal life, except as affected by environment. On the other hand, man—no matter how widely separated by countries, or seas—has voluntarily

* Dr. J. Leon Williams—Anthropology and Geology (*Brooklyn Eagle,* November 14, 1913, News Item.)

advanced, has sought knowledge, and continues to seek.
Nothing else, having life, that we know of, ever moved
forward a particle, except when environment has forced
nature to make a change.

"Man, doubtless, originally immigrated here. He may
have landed here before the Earth was quite ready. Or
maybe through the cunning of some Judas, a whole world
was thrown back millions of years. Who can say? A
conservative has ever retarded man's progress! To Doctor Klouse there seemed to be little doubt that several
classes of people immigrated here, each from a different
planet, and at varying times. The characteristics of
these people varied. Time, climate, environment, and
even intermarriage, have entirely removed the differences
which prove their distinct origin.

"The location of my grandfather's experimental laboratory is not known for certain. He erected many buildings far out in the West. He gathered his men and
women assistants engaged to accompany him. This he
did with great secrecy and care, and from widely scattered
points. The Doctor took pains to enjoin upon each
absolute secrecy, and as these people lived in widely different parts of the country, he purposely kept them apart
as much as possible. He was frank in informing them all
that he should not divulge his real name, nor did he care
to know the real name of any of his assistants. 'You may
talk,' said he, 'as much as you like, but never, not one of
you, speak of yourself, your affairs, nor of me or mine.' A
short acquaintance with the Doctor inspired them all with
confidence and esteem. They soon learned of his earnest,
sincere nature, and his high character. No one of that
little company would ever dream of betraying so good or

great a man. Whatever he commanded of them, they willingly and most happily performed. Each had been separately informed of the duties expected of him, before his engagement. They had been told that they were to accompany him to the far West—into the wilderness, then unknown to the white man. Where he was to settle he knew not until he reached what he believed to be an ideal location for experimentation. He told them there might be danger, and hardships he believed there must be. He accorded each person, or couple engaged, sufficient time to consider the matter before deciding.

"My mother believed that her father located somewhere in the mild climate of the Yosemite Valley, California. He often referred to the great pines of the valley—many of them over two hundred feet high, and of the flowers blooming the whole year 'round. In this wonderful valley he may have settled among the lofty peaks of the Sierra Nevadas. Or, it may have been in the beautiful Hetch Hetchy Valley, a delightful counterpart of the Yosemite, or, the Tuolumne Canyon, where, surrounded by lofty peaks, he might experiment or think or dream. It was his only home for more than twenty-five years.

"Here, I may read from his manuscript," continued Finley. " 'I first gathered around me a company of seventy-five people—young married couples only. Ten of these couples were colored, and employed as cooks, waiters and to serve in other capacities.

" 'In order to secure the best physical, mental, and moral examples of young men and women, I was forced to secure the services of other physicians. I engaged only those who stood high in their profession. They were chosen from widely scattered settlements, hence I secured assistants of the finest physical type. After I had located them and received their reports, I then visited each couple to make final arrangements. It was no indifferent task, and required much patience and care to select my company, and the necessary paraphernalia for the journey.

" 'More than two years were consumed in the preliminary work. As every one engaged was enjoined to absolute secrecy, it increased the difficulties I had foreshadowed. I found it would not do to publish or advertise my intentions. It might prejudice the public mind. The public mind is the intelligence of the average mind. It has ever been, that the average is very ignorant, hence uncertain, and subject to fits of hysteria. It's dangerous, in a measure, to tell the public everything. They don't comprehend. They cannot understand. Therefore, a new idea must not be sprung too quickly. There might have been objections to taking a company of young people into a wild, unexplored country—although all concerned had given their consent. A false story might have been started. The far West, then, was a trackless wilderness, infested by the Red Man, who, through his prejudice, might seek to stop our march. But, shall progress be destroyed, thought I? The man with the plow must supersede the man who sits all day consuming his energy by sharpening the arrowhead.

" 'Many meetings I held in secret with those who were to accompany me, so as to instruct them in not so much how to avoid trouble and danger, as how best to meet and overcome both. I explained to them how we should travel and divide the work, the things necessary, before beginning the journey. Our way was by wagon, overland, by mountain and plain, through forest, fording treacherous streams, with dangers incessant. All building material was transported by wagons, and carried in our train were numbers of live domestic, with many wild animals and reptiles. Each attendant was to perform a certain work every day during the journey. Each was instructed until proficient in the work before the trip was undertaken. One stipulation, and perhaps the most important one to observe, was never to become afraid—never to fear anybody or anything. Fright, invariably, begets panic. No Indian would disturb us, if we betrayed no fear—once he was convinced we meant no harm. Therefore, firearms I forbid. There being no railroads or telegraph when the start began, the wilderness faced us almost immediately.

" 'Everything arranged, the word was given—"ready." It was agreed that each couple should meet the caravan at a designated point, so that no more than passing attention would be given by those who might otherwise have their curiosity aroused. At last the villages were left behind, my concern most being to quit so-called civilization, unmolested.

" 'I had found that absolute kindness is the best defense in the wilderness, as opposed to the savagery of civilization. No harm can come to any one holding a reciprocal asset.

" 'I found the Indians, through whose country we passed, everywhere, very friendly. Many joined the caravan at intervals, displaying an intense interest as to our destination.

" 'When, finally, preparations for a permanent settlement began, I found several thousand Indians encamped around us. It would have been easy for these warriors to have exterminated our little band; but, instead, they stood watching our every movement. Once understanding that we had not come to interfere with them in any way, they appeared pleased, and by signs volunteered to help me. I was not slow to take advantage of their aid. Though each seemed in the other's way in trying to perform the simplest duties, I instructed my company to exercise the greatest forbearance. The result was most satisfactory, as it was not long before several hundreds were lending assistance in erecting stockades for the necessary buildings.

" 'Supplies of fresh game and fish were abundant. The Indians liked our methods of cooking, so superior to primitive methods, that I was compelled to establish a commissary department regulating the cooking for several hundreds twice a day. They enjoyed the continuous feast at regular intervals so much that I requested the chiefs of tribes to add others of their number to the ten of my men already overworked. This, they understood, and when new bands arrived they were told by the chiefs that the caravan, being private, they might stay as long as they wished, provided they prepared their own meals.

" 'The Indians were children to us, and we treated them as such. We avoided carping, never threatened them, nor acted in an untoward way, with the result that they fairly worshiped every one in our little band. It was at times necessary, however, for us to keep them at a civil distance, when not employed. They readily understood this, and I believe they preferred in many ways to live their own, rather than our lives.

" 'Danger seemed never to threaten us, but if presented, they were willing to stand as a great bodyguard, willing to sacrifice life in our defense.

" 'All extra game and fish was salted, smoked and dried, so that when Winter came the stock accumulated served for the first time regular meals daily during the colder season.

" 'Following, through the summers of the entire twenty-five years, located among these Indians, many of them learned to cultivate the soil—raising corn, wheat, barley, oats, potatoes and other vegetables in immense quantities.

" 'The demands of the Indians so increased that supplies for over ten thousand were soon in view. Each year the area of cultivation increased, until all needs were satisfied.

" 'A few began to cultivate on their own account, though, generally speaking, like children, they lacked initiative. Ambition, as we understand it, they knew not. The Indians around us were not confined to any particular tribe or stock, but were distributed mostly among the Kawias and Panamints of the Shoshonians. Some were of the Konkons and Maidres of the Pujunan stock, while others hailed from the Pomo and Gumas of the Kulanapan and Yreman tribes.

" 'Occasionally quarrels arose among our Indian friends, but by terms of kindly persuasion, we succeeded in restoring comparative harmony—a condition that had never before been obtained.' "

Here Finley ceased to read from the Doctor's Notes, but, looking up, continued to address our company.

CHAPTER VIII

"The exact place where the Doctor performed his investigations is unknown, but from his records much may be gathered.

"The main, or experimental building, was constructed upon plans drawn by the Doctor before leaving for the West. Though erected by the Doctor's assistants under his direct supervision, the Indians were invaluable in the heavier building work, and did much to assist in the transportation of material. Constructed entirely of lumber from the surrounding forests, horses could not always be employed to haul the heavier logs down the abrupt and rocky mountain sides.

"The main building occupied a position upon the apex of low lying hill within a broad valley, that sloped gradually to the South. It commanded a magnificent view up and down this beautiful valley, hemmed in, as it was, on the North and South by the lofty peaks of the Sierras. These great mountains, with their snow-capped peaks, filled the beholder with awe, and inspired one with the grandeur of Nature's mighty work. How small, how insignificant was man. How feeble his efforts, when compared with the mighty phenomena of those lofty heights piercing the highest clouds and parting them asunder. Words fail to describe this beauty, or picture the awfulness in earthquake of their menacing bodies. Below them, the peaceful valley of the Yosemite, rich in soil, prolific and luxuriant in vegetation. Every environment seemed to court the perfumed air and tempered the sun's rays. All inspired to thoughts of youth and love. Lilies and golden-rod, violets, ceanothus, manzanita, nodded in turn to the wild roses and azaleas, which spread out in broad beds and banks of bloom, to welcome each approaching Spring.

"On the hilltop, about fifty acres invited the construction of a high, roughly hewn wooden stockade, built chiefly, so the Doctor designed, to keep out wandering animals, and to indicate that callers were expected only at the great front gate. An all but similar gate adorned the extreme North side. Aside from the main building, there were a number of out-buildings which served as store-houses, as well as several smaller dwellings for the different families. These latter were erected, mostly, South of the Main building. To the North, lay the barns for horses, cattle and other animals.

"The cottages for colored laborers, who cared for the animals, were nearby. These folk never entered the grounds at the South half of the main building. The Doctor succeeded in making this so positive a rule, that the colored help on the North side seldom knew of the presence of the white assistants. The main building oc-cupied the center of the group. Oblong in shape, it extended East and West six hundred feet, fifty-two feet wide, and two stories high.

"The lower floor of the main building being divided at the center, ran East and West its entire length. It in-cluded solid, sound-proof partitions extending from floor to ceiling, rendering communication between the North and South halves practically impossible. The South half of this lower floor was divided by partitions into separate rooms, each room being twenty-five feet in width. These partitions extended North and South from floor to ceiling, and were likewise sound-proof, so that all communication between them was impossible. Nor could these rooms be reached, except by a door leading from a long, narrow piazza on the outside of the main building—extending the whole length in front. In each room a large window on either side of the door faced South, and admitted a flood of light. An abundance of air poured through ventilators beneath and over these windows. 'Way up the valley might be heard the deep roar of a waterfall, as its ribbon-like stream fell over the great rocky precipice, some six hundred feet, into the valley below, creating great clouds of mist which ever rose above the great trees at its base. The sunbeams, on clear days, playing upon the mist, produced those delicate and radiant rainbows which hung above, like halos of so many benedictions.

"The rear, or North half of the main building, was partitioned off in like manner to the South. Both sides had, therefore, the same number of rooms and of equal size. The North windows were smaller than those on the South half of the building, and in addition, were covered with fine gauze screens. Double doors opened outwardly, from each room into a large court-yard, a thousand feet deep. The courts were separated from one another by plank fences, ten feet high, and the North rooms were built alike both in size and finish. The interior walls and ceilings of apartments were covered by an immaculate coat of whitewash—frequently applied—adding to the sanitation and guarding the health of the occupants. The floors were of stone and kept scrupulously clean by frequent scrubbing. Communication between the yards was afforded by means of a small door cut through the side of each fence close to the building. These doors were never opened, except by the attendants to the occupants of the rooms, so that no intercourse between apartments was possible.

"The entire floor of the second story was occupied exclusively by Doctor Klouse. My grandfather avers, that no person ever crossed the threshold of that one door —the room's only entrance—after his having taken possession. This door was located at the East end of the building, and reached only by two distinct flights of stairs, wholly enclosed. Both led from a private yard, one on the North and the other on the South side, where the Doctor took his daily exercise, changing alternately, one yard for the other—as fancy or the temperature inclined him. Both the stairways were protected by strong doors, always locked. No one but the Doctor held the key. Communication with the second story of the main building was, therefore, effectively cut off. A thick fence, fifteen feet high, extended across the width of the property from East to West, constructed on a straight line with the center partition of the lower main building. Thus, a complete division of both the main building and the whole estate had been consummated.

"The inhabitants of the South and North halves of the building were as completely isolated from one another as though they had been separated by hundreds of miles. No individual, civilized or savage, no animals, foods or supplies went through either side, except by its central gate. The same rule held good for the South gate. Food for the dwellers on the North side came only through the North gate, and the employees and their families were divided about equally between the two colonies.

"All labor was divided and separately attended to by employees of the North and South. A close examination of the premises would disclose that all rooms on the South side of the main building were intended for persons of higher intelligence, and, in all essential respects, constructed and appointed with superior intent to those on the North side.

"It was equally easy to discover that the rooms to the North, while clean and comfortable, were intended for animals. Strong steel bars and bolts suggested to the beholder that many of these rooms had been designed for the habitation of wild animals.

"The South rooms were fitted in up-to-date fashion. Nothing that was known then, by way of home comfort and convenience was lacking. Each room was furnished with book-cases, lounging chairs, couch, bed, and all the bathing conveniences of the time.

"Ventilation was perfect, and the temperature did not vary more than five degrees throughout the whole year.

"The summers in that part of the valley were seldom warm, nor the winters ever extremely cold.

"The rooms on the North side were as scrupulously clean and convenient, but, as they were occupied by many species of animals, both domesticated and wild, the interior of each room was arranged to accommodate the occupant with every necessary requirement.

"The Doctor began experimentation by selecting, from his white male employees, twenty of those who were men-

tally and physically nearest perfection. A prime condition of this service was, that each would volunteer the use
of his body in the interest of science and in just such manner as the Doctor deemed best, it being understood, however, that no permanent harm could befall the subject
knowingly. In other words, each was guaranteed against
any fatal result. So sincere was their confidence in my
grandfather, that no visible hesitation appeared among
them to accord his every wish. Everything in readiness,
each man was assigned one of the South rooms, where he
would be confined for several years.

" 'Probably, you may not pass outside your room
during the required period of time, frequently to include
from one to two years.'

"As a matter of record, the experiments rarely took
less than two, and not infrequently, three years. During
the interval, none were permitted to go beyond the walls
of their rooms. Indeed, owing to the nature of the experiments, it would have been physically impossible to
do so, without inviting death.

"In the North apartments, directly opposite those occupied by the young men, were placed the females of
twenty wild and domesticated animals. One species to
each room. Among the domestic animals were the horse,
cow, dog, pig, sheep and goat, and among the wild were
the lion, tiger, buffalo, monkey (chimpanzee), elephant
and rhinoceros.

"The Doctor had gladly submitted to the trouble and
expense of these arrangements for the contemplated experiments, with the one single purpose in view—to seek an
answer to his question:—

" 'Did the human race evolve from lower animals?'

"Thinking men, down through the ages had asked this question, but none had ever found a concrete answer that satisfied mankind. The human race, if divine, opposes the idea, insist some of the theologians. The Animal theory is alleged by Science. So, back and forth, have the adherents holding one or the other view, disputed and fought, while the great veil which separates the knowable from surmise, has never for a moment lifted to admit the light regarding the mystery. Yes, it had been raised. So, my grandfather believed. Can it be penetrated? Can this mystery be solved by any human method? The Doctor was convinced it could. Had not man always drifted away from his inspired ideals in proportion to his acceptance of the theory that he had slowly evolved from the lowest animal life?

"The Doctor was aware of the oneness of nature, and that all life existed under the same natural immutable laws. To transmit the blood of one of the lower animals into a human being, with the idea of restoring vigor, was an admitted failure, and seemed to prove, that it could not be successfully accomplished, without the introduction, as he termed it, of his saline solution or Elixir. In order to discover whether humans differed in any undiscovered essentials, from the lower animals, he believed it essential to, in some measure, equalize their natures. There was only one way to obtain this result. There could be only one equalizer, the blood. Everything in nature, so far as we know, depends for its life upon the circulation of its particular kind of sap, or blood. When that ceases to circulate, life ceases to exist.

"Transient transfusion of the blood from the human being to a lower animal, and from that animal to the same human, would produce only temporary results. To equalize their natures, if possible, it would be necessary to have their bloods circulate together, from one to the other, continuously, and for a considerable period of time. It might require several years before he could prove absolutely whether man was an educated animal, or a human being divine.

"By a continuous transfusion of blood between his human subjects on the one hand, and the lower animals on the other—so arranged that their bloods would circulate continuously—he hoped to prove through several years of trial, that neither they nor their offspring would change mentally. It was possible that human thoughts and passions might be transfused, through blood intermixture. But would one cell—so to speak—of knowledge be added to the human or animal mind, though blood should be caused to circulate and intermix for years? To him, that was the question which would decide the issue. Again, would the human mind lose, or the mind of the offspring deteriorate by reason of such an attachment? Physically, there might come changes to both, the Doctor thought; but, human identity or personality, could not be destroyed or changed, he believed. If the human being and the lower animal, with their offspring fail to become equalized physically and mentally during this process of blood union, then, is not the human divine?

"The Doctor's human subjects had no knowledge of the animals arranged in opposite rooms on the North side of the building. Neither did the attendants of the animals know, who or what occupied the South part of the building. None but the Doctor knew the animal located opposite each human subject. The employees of the South side attended only to the needs of human subjects, while those on the North provided the necessary needs of animals, each, however, under the direct supervision of the Doctor. Speaking tubes were arranged throughout for his convenience. These connected all apartments with the Doctor's private second floor, from which he was enabled to communicate with each employee—whether subject or attendant.

"The circulation of blood between a human subject in a South apartment, and a lower animal occupying a room opposite, was made by means of two small flexible hollow tubes, bound together in pairs, and extending between each North and South room. They were covered to the thickness of about one-half inch with material impervious to moisture, and a non-conductor of heat or cold. They were attached to the side walls of every room, while several yards at the ends remained perfectly free. A pair extended from each room of the human subject, through the ceiling to the second story, reaching to the Doctor's laboratory. Here, they crossed to the center of the apartment, where they again extended upward and across a small glass table, retaining a temperature of blood heat. The tubes descended from this table across and down through the floor to the animal room opposite. Here again, an extra length, provided several yards, so that the ends might be carried to any part of the room with perfect freedom.

"At the point where the tubes crossed the table in the Doctor's laboratory, they were made wholly of glass, and provided with a small thermometer.

"At both ends of each pair of tubes were attached two large hollow needles—one needle for each tube. These needles were inserted by the Doctor, in the arteries of the arms, being secured by linen bands in such a way that while the human subject had perfect freedom of action in movement to any part of his room, still using, without disturbing the needles, the arm to which they were attached. Once the needles were inserted and bound, they suffered no removal while the patient remained well. In like manner, two needles were inserted into the arteries of the animal occupying the room opposite, and while moving with a freedom equal to the human, still limitation was enjoined by the length of the tubes.

"Before inserting the needles, the Doctor inoculated each subject with his secret serum. Once the needles had been inserted the blood of each subject circulated freely through the tubes, and across the table in the laboratory above. Here the Doctor could watch and note the intermingling blood, and, by aid of the thermometer, observe the varying changes of temperature. Walking down through the center of the room, at a glance he noted the interchanges in each of the twenty pairs of human beings and animals.

"For the first time in history—so far as human records stand, this wonderful union had been accomplished. This achievement of my grandfather—without knowledge or assistance from without—stamps the Doctor, I submit, as a most unusual man." Finley pronounced this opinion with much emotion. We all tacitly agreed that he was right.

Finley, after a libation of cider, in which we all heartily joined, resumed his narrative:

"At first, all the subjects treated appeared somewhat dull and listless. Yet, as the days went by, all resumed their normal condition, developing no ill effects from the union. The Doctor kept constant watch of the laboratory thermometers, and frequently made blood tests for signs of trouble. It was not long before he made the discovery that the main thing to note with greatest care was the quantity and nature of food taken and required by both subjects. He found a frequent cause of trouble to be overeating. This he proceeded to regulate, by serving the proper quantities best suited to the pairs. If examination in the laboratory disclosed the beginning of the slightest physical disturbance, he would immediately withdraw the needles, and both subjects brought back to the normal condition before continuing the experiment. 'Eternal vigilance' was his watch-word.

"So careful were his observations and the facts deduced minutely recorded, that he could tell at the instant, any approach of trouble in the condition of a subject pair.

"The first, or preliminary test, lasted for a period of eight months. It was a painstaking and cautious trial, and intended only to demonstrate the safety of the undertaking. It was, however, of sufficient time, to prove physical changes in both subjects. For example, the young man whose blood mingled and circulated with that of the elephant, began to show changes in the color and texture of his skin. Strange as it might seem, it had become several shades darker and was unusually thick, tough, and wrinkled—resembling, slightly, the elephant's hide. On the other hand, the elephant's skin had grown softer, and was perceptibly lighter than before.

"The appetites of each had also gradually changed, until both seemed to relish each other's food. Many things now eaten by the elephant, as uncooked potatoes and other raw vegetables, the man had also attained a relish for. The human subject frequently expressed wonderment to the attendant, at his markedly changed appetite.

"It was not surprising, therefore, that the appetites of all human subjects and animals were somewhat similarly affected, though more or less dependent upon the class of pairs attached.

"Then, the subjects were accorded a few months' rest, before again being joined each to a new and different animal. The experiments continued through several long years, pending which time it was found unnecessary to remove the needles from either subject treated. So intense was the Doctor's vigilance, that neither sickness nor death paid a single visitation. This was mainly due to the fact that the human subjects were continually occupied, and the animals were given due exercise. The periods of work, study, and recreation had their time and order each day. To demonstrate their natural inclination and voluntary desire toward a higher progress, during this experimental period, each subject was permitted to follow natural inclinations. The Doctor was agreeably surprised to see his human subjects select their own studies and class of work, and the easy ability with which they voluntarily acted. He had proved one thing, the union with the animal had not affected in any way their initiative. It was at this point that he began to give them lessons in science, medicine, history and the languages, in each of which, their remarkable progress surprised him. The human subjects grew constantly in intelligence from day to day, this, in spite of the fact that each continued to somewhat resemble physically the animal to which he had been joined. No degree of physical change seemed to destroy the personality or impair the mind. In like manner, the animals suffered physical change in the loss of hair, and all gradually assumed a human color, but——

"All the teaching of years, combined with exercise and training, and the co-mingling of human blood in their veins, added nothing to the animal intelligence. Not the slightest difference was noted between the animals taught certain tricks while receiving the benefit of human blood, and those of the same species not united with the human. Yes, the Doctor and his assistants undoubtedly worked, and diligently for many years, with a view to add some human degree of mental uplift to their intelligence, but the attempt only proved a failure.

"Dogs, pigs, goats, and indeed, scores of domestic animals with many wild ones, were taught certain tricks, until they had learned to perform well the things so taught. The offspring of each was taught similarly during twenty successive generations. The teaching was repeated, yet, the taught of the last generation, knew no more than the untaught at the Doctor's initial trial.

"More than twenty generations of one particular dog, each generation coupled with the same human subject, were taught similar tricks under exactly the same conditions. Not a single animal of any generation showed the slightest advance in human mental initiative. The latest generation of the dog, so trained, showed no greater proficiency in the beginning than did the first. He was equally as hard to teach as had been his early ancestor, so, finally, the last generation was purposely denied a final training. What was true in the dog's case, was true of all the animals.

"After years of patient teaching, with human blood flowing continually in his veins, the dog remained the same dog, the pig remained pig. The last generation could do nothing new voluntarily, nor could it be taught more easily nor understand better than at first. The Doctor had proved, he believed, that man is not an animal, but a divine being wherein is planted an identity that nothing can hide, nor even death destroy. It took years of patience to prove that, while many things may assume or occupy similar physical bodies, only in the human exists the divine spark."

"Well, Nancy, Jasper an' I will see you hum. Mr. Finley, 'bout time we went," said Silas, rising to go. At his signal the company all arose to see the old cronies take their departure.

" 'Tis 'bout time we went," injected Jasper, hurrying to seize his hat and coat, so that he could be in ahead of Silas on Nancy's right arm.

"Before I go, I'd like to ask Finley a question," he said with a grin.

"Go ahead, Jasper," replied Finley encouragingly— "What's on your mind?"

"Did the man who was attached to the dog, bark?" asked Jasper, with a chuckle.

"No, Jasper, but both knew how to growl, both before and after," Finley solemnly answered.

"Come along," said Silas to Jasper. Then he added as he took Nancy by the arm, "You git on the outside of me, Jasper, and I'll 'tend to Nancy."

"Not by a gol-darn sight," answered Jasper, hurrying

over to take Nancy's free arm. "Yer can't play no tricks on me."

" 'Tain't no trick. Nancy al'a's leans to th' rite, an' I kin hold her up better'n you kin. I'm stronger," answered Silas, stiffening up proudly.

"Jasper's strong, too. I'll lean his way to-night," said Nancy gayly—and all three departed with a merry chuckle and a longing look behind.

CHAPTER IX

THE HOUSE OF SILENCE

"THERE goes the bell, Sam. Wonder who 'tis. Hope it's the old people come to spend the evening. Oh, I do hope 'tis," cried Hester as she came running down the front stairs.

"That's who 'tis. It's the 'divine three.' I see the shadow of Nancy's bonnet through the glass," replied Sam cheerily. "Listen!—Si is singing,

'As I went out, by the light of the Moon,
I spied, I spied a big raccoon,
A-sitting on a rail, a-sitting on a rail.
I sneaked him by the tail, and pulled him off that rail.
Ting a ring, a ring, ring, hiro dinkum donkey.' "

"Shet up, Si. Yer played thet song out fifty years ago," said Jasper.

"Oh, here they come! Oh, goody, my goody! Finley will read us more of that story now," cried Hester as she ran out to tell the news to the family, gathered in the great kitchen.

"Well," said Jasper, after all had removed their wrappings, and as he stood rubbing his hands—"Well, Samuel, it's kinder cold to-nite."

"Yes, 'tis, Mr. Perkins," said Sam in reply. "It's 'bout as cold as we've had it 'round these parts. Why, do you know," said he, addressing Silas, "I read in the papers, 'tis forty-two degrees below zero—in the shade"—he added.

"Due tell. Yer don't say so. By ginger—thet's why thet's colder'n Sam Hill."

"Oh, Silas," said Nancy, putting her finger to his lips reprovingly, "you swore then."

" 'Tain't swearing, Nancy, never swore'n my life."

"Must git rite hum agin," said Silas, starting to put on his great coat. "Hold my cut, Jasper, will ye? Forgot t' let the wa-ter out ter pump, an' then th' hog an' little uns must be made more comfortable."

Just at this moment, Paul stepped into the hall, and seeing Silas preparing to go, said, "Good evening, all. Why, Silas, where you off to?"

"Going hum, fast as I can git there," said Silas, busily putting on his great fur gloves, which he always commenced wearing in September and then continuously until the return of warm weather in the Spring. "If I don't freeze t' death," he added.

"Freeze to death? Why, it's not cold enough to freeze," explained Paul.

"Why, Sam says it's more'n forty degrees below," said Silas, becoming excited—and all began to laugh at Sam's little joke.

"Don't cher titter in my face," said Silas, moving warningly towards Sam. "I prayed for yer, last nite, in prayer meetin'. Yer de-sarve a gud trouncin', yer do. Whet du yer mean by 'et, yer pesky thing? Hev yer been lyin' t' me ag'in?"

"My dear Mister Cummings, calm yourself. I did read it in the paper, but, 'twas last winter's paper—here's the

paper now," turning over the page—"and let's see, there's
the time. 'Forty-two degrees below zero, in Alaska,' "
said Sam, pointing his finger in triumph to the para-
graph. "You wouldn't wait to let me tell you where I
saw it, Uncle Si," added Sam.

"Don't yer call me 'Uncle,' yer pesky critter. I hain't
related to no one thet tells sich whoppers, but I'll pray
ag'in fer yer, jest th' same," warningly retorted Silas,
and then, noticing that all were on the point of laughing,
he caught up the spirit of the joke, and broke into a
squeaky, "Hi, hi. By gol—thet's a putty gud joke, arter
all."

Laughter may be said to warm the atmosphere. It
undermines the pompous mein. It sends dignity from the
room, and permits the participant to settle down to com-
mendable reflection. It's a real tonic to the self-con-
scious. Without it, many among us would die of "stiff-
neck." Yet, laughter, so productive of good results may
be easily abused. If not genuine, there is danger in an
overdose. I have observed stiffness at the banquet where
no one talked. A laugh started, brought all down to one
beautiful human level. The tonic being taken, became
catching and invigorating.

As our village friends gathered in the great kitchen,
every one wore a smile. Sam had restamped his merriment on every face. As for Si, he insisted on repeating
the process.

"Thet Sam's a great—feller. Gol-darn his funny
ways. I'm agoin' ter laff fer a week, by ginger."

Under the inspiring influence of a liberal helping to
hot ginger-bread, provided by my wife, accompanied by

a supply of good sweet cider, with the assurance of plenty more in the over-sized pitcher, a merry laughing company was assured for the evening.

"Fine ginger-bread," remarked Jasper.

"Yea-s," answered Silas, "putty gud. Las' nite I drempt I saw th' table spread with thumping loaves of ginger-bread—so one dream is out."

It was not a little difficult to keep the merriment long enough, from bubbling over, to afford time for announcing that Finley was ready. After a goodly second helping of cider, matters became sufficiently quiet, and all settled down to listen with marked interest.

"The company of the wilderness, as we shall now call it," remarked Finley, "prospered physically, mentally, and financially. My grandfather cared for and watched over all, as a tender father over his child. By reason of his skill, he protected them from disease by preventive methods. Under his direction, all partook of food that he knew would insure strong and robust bodies. They became immune to any lurking disease germs that might possibly attack. All were happy and contented. His method of education was to teach them what they most needed to know. Twice every week, all under test, were visited by the Doctor or his assistants, for the purpose of discussing general educational subjects. All were paid generously for their time, and since they could spend but little except through occasional messengers sent to the nearest market point, their savings rapidly accumulated. When later, the company emerged from the wilderness, each had funds sufficient, with frugality, to support a family, without further labor. While no deaths occurred during the sojourn, more than sixty births evidenced my grandfather's pronounced skill and efficiency in experimentation.

"Deaths among babies and small children he declared to be a crime. Overfeeding, improper or impure food, foul air, and over-clothing kills off most of the little ones. This he frequently insisted upon, as well as inculcating the principle that there was no danger in eating too little.

"The offspring as well as the wives of the subjects whose blood had been experimented upon, were, strangely enough, neither mentally nor physically affected by reason of the union. It was further noted, that neither the mother nor offspring of animals united by blood with man, betrayed any human trace or ill effect. Nor were successive generations of the same animal perceptibly affected, though each underwent a precisely similar experiment.

"I have already said, that the Doctor had succeeded in demonstrating how mental characteristics of man and animal could not be transmitted. In other words, while man and animal may combine physically, they cannot mix mentally.

"Indeed, during and subsequent to these experiments, the human mind continued to go forward voluntarily, ever improving, while the so-called animal mind remained at a standstill—adding or taking nothing.

"The results obtained were highly gratifying to the Doctor. It encouraged him to try new processes. The knowledge gained so far, he considered, would be of vast value to the world—some day.

"Perhaps it might save the faith of thousands who

stood wavering between absolute infidelity, and faith in a divine being. Of course, infidelity only means, that a man is unfaithful to that which he cannot believe. So far, he believed he had shown that we were not simply the highest type of educated animals; in fact, that we were not animals. All previous investigation along scientific lines had led many to believe that we were. Many had gone down to their end, accepting it as truth, cursing the day they were born, and blaming an unknown deity for the evolution of the human conscious mind. Think of the lost happiness in one poor human life, with that belief as the final! By the knowledge and thought of our divinity alone, cannot our personality go forward in love to perfection? The Doctor was so overjoyed with his discovery, that he went around shouting to his subjects, 'We are divine!' 'We are men!' 'You're not animal— never were—it's a lie!' 'Think of your mother, boys, was she not divine?' 'I never saw a mother who was not divine.'

"At this juncture, the men thought he had gone suddenly mad. None understood what had happened by transfusion of blood. For the first time, they felt not a little uneasy. His spasm of glee did not last long—indeed, he was too busy to become insane."

"My progenitors on father's side were named Fish, which seems to prove, as we think at Vassar, that they were originally fish or fishermen," interrupted Ellen.

"But your name's Bacon now; what was that originally?" asked Sam.

Everybody laughed but Ellen—she apparently did not see the joke.

"Why, I don't exactly know what it was originally, but I imagine it was Lord."

"Oh, Lord Bacon you mean?"—interposed Sam.

"You look out fer your'n, goldurn yer! Ther ain't no pint to yer jokes," broke in Si.

Finley held up his hand in reproval and quietly resumed his narrative:

"I want to acquaint you with one particular observation of my grandfather, which I think is worth repeating: 'The more knowledge human subjects acquired, the more the knowledge increased of those who came in contact with them. Even the Indians appeared to smooth the rougher elements of character in proportion as they visited the Doctor's camp. So, their wives and children showed a marked progress, the more frequently they came together.' This gradual improvement was due entirely to the Doctor's efforts to encourage frequent conversations. 'MOST WONDERFUL OF ALL TEACHERS,' declared the Doctor with emphasis. 'Some people are stingy with knowledge, as others are with their money.'

"I believe most firmly in the principle, myself," remarked Finley. "Give it freely and all mankind will steadily advance. So you see, my friends, these evening conversations of our own, beget reflection in us all.

"Permit me to relate another most interesting experiment: There had been born in the camp, two beautiful, healthy babies—a boy and a girl—children whose fathers had been subjects. To secure for scientific test these new born children, with the possible danger of sacrificing life, when no beneficent result might obtain, made the Doctor hesitate, but only for a while. 'No life shall be sacrificed,'—he promised the parents. No permanent harm would be permitted under any circumstances. 'I need the babies,' he said, and so their parents with heavy hearts, agreed to the proposal. The mothers of both children would see them daily, but the subjects, their fathers, would be denied until the time for permanently leaving their rooms came. 'We believe, we have faith in you,' the parents declared, but the parting was none the less hard. He told them of his plan, so that they also might take an interest in the outcome. They had learned that progress came through sacrifice. To make it, was to assist in humanity's cause.

"The Doctor planned that the mothers with the children and several assistants, should thereafter be given a cottage, South of the main building. The house was convenient and beautifully situated. He had prepared their reception, by dividing off a convenient court on the South side of the cottage, and entirely enclosed by a high, solid plank-board fence. Through this, narrow horizontal apertures were made, about five feet from the ground. Through these, an adult might look from the outside, without danger of being detected by any one in the courtyard.

"The yard was reached from only one room. It was so arranged, that no one in the room could see anything outside, but an observer in the yard could readily see every part within the room. This cottage was called 'The House of Silence,' and the Doctor's positive command was, that none should be permitted to speak or make a sound that the children might overhear. The Doctor's careful watching through many weary years, proved the progress a human being left alone might possibly make, of its own initiative.

"No human being, so far as known records show, has left any testimony regarding this mystery.

"Let us now see what discoveries the Doctor further made to prove that the human being could never have evolved from lower animals.

"The two babies were allowed to be constantly with their mothers in the 'House of Silence,' until after they had reached the age of two years. While the mothers were near, neither one uttered a word during the Doctor's experiment. After reaching their second year, the children became accustomed to the change, until they finally toddled about entirely nude. If they felt cold, they instinctively sought the soft blankets always lying temptingly about, and they cuddled together in quite apparent comfort.

"While playing together in the court-yard, during the colder weather, they rarely appeared uncomfortable or affected by the cooler air."

"There's a draught somewhere 'round here," interrupted Jasper, shifting uneasily in his chair.

"Present it at the bank," observed Sam, good naturedly.

"Th' kind thet I mean 'ill give yer th' sniffles—called 'cold in th' head.' Understan' neow, don't cher?" replied Jasper.

"The kind I mean gives yer—cold in the feet," laughed Sam.

"This foolishness must stop," I protested. Every one being silent, I added, "Go on with your story, Mr. Finley."

"Speaking of draughts and colds," continued Finley,

"I must tell you that the Doctor had a most decided opinion upon that subject.

"He believed that the people who suffer most frequently from colds, are those who overfeed, or become debilitated through lack of sleep. Also, the overburdening the body with clothes, has in it, an additional menace.

"As I was relating, the children grew with nature. Outside the songs and sounds produced by birds, wild animals lurking near, or the distant cries of the camping Indians, all was still. The gentle South winds, creeping up the valley, doubtless inspired visions to their dull and slowly developing imaginations. The picturesque surroundings set off by snow-capped mountains, whose precipitous sides were covered with forests of giant trees, and visible from all points, helped to impart suggestions.

"Care was taken in cool weather to keep the room where the children slept at the proper temperature. Most of the year they chose, of themselves, to sleep outside on the bare ground. No amount of silent suggestion upon the Doctor's part changed their natural selection of surroundings. Since no ill effects from constant exposure to chilling nights, or even rain, were noted, no alarm was felt.

"After the children had become strong enough to run alone, extra room was added for exercise and a larger activity. Little by little, love of freedom in the open seemed to possess them. Even when the cold and storm drove them to shelter, they appeared to enter their rooms reluctantly.

"As they grew older, they began to utter certain low cries. Peculiar gurgling sounds of differing degrees of intensity, the meanings of which were apparently under-stood between themselves. After awhile, the attendants and watchers were, in some measure, able to interpret the meaning of the sounds. They found that each had a sep-arate meaning, indicating moods of surprise, anger, joy, or fear. It appeared, indeed, the foundation of a new language, and as their minds slowly developed, seemed to take on additions as new surprises were unfolded from day to day. After awhile the sounds became so varied in tone, the Doctor made notes, and was himself enabled to interpret the meaning. And so the record grew.

"Every act and sound recorded, was discussed by the employees and the Doctor, evolving a continued progress from day to day.

"Strange sounds would naturally startle such chil-dren. In like manner, we note, that the passage of an aeroplane over a farm, will drive the fowls to cover. Fear seems instinctive, and only decreases as a knowledge of our surroundings helps to its elimination.

"The children were carefully fed, food being arranged always in one certain place. They knew exactly where to find it, and it was always furnished in abundance. When they had eaten enough to satisfy hunger, no amount of tempting food would induce them to partake of more.

"They never failed instantly to observe any new object placed in the court-yard.

"In the beginning, they regarded an object with sus-picion, and shyed around it until they found it immov-able. Then slowly approaching, they found it harmless and were reassured. Bats, balls, marbles, and dolls of many sizes and kinds, were placed in the yard from time to time. After becoming accustomed to the toys, they played with or fondled each, as fancy seemed to dictate. They delighted to gather them near when they slept. Either one of the children would have fought hard to protect these small objects. As the evenings closed in, they chose usually the last toy handled, and went to bed with it.

"The Doctor noted, however, a natural preference for small rag dolls, displaying for these objects an almost human affection.

"By the time the children had reached their sixth year, the Doctor began to observe a greater progress in mind development. To note their treatment of common things, he had placed certain small articles within reach. He desired to see what they would do, or to what use they would put them. All were careful to withdraw each article unobserved, after they retired for the night.

"Pen and paper, and different colored crayons were placed within their reach. At first, they played with these, but after months of observation, they discovered that the crayons would mark. The markings evidently excited their curiosity because the process was continued for days at a time. Then, they discovered that the ink would also mark, and began to make scratches with the pen upon the paper supplied. It was an experiment extending over two years, before they thought of dipping the pen in the ink. Thousands of times, they failed, or jabbed the pen into some object, but slowly they had learned through their failures to destroy neither pen nor ink. They seemed to enjoy dipping their fingers into the ink, wherewith to make weird marks on the fence, or on their bodies.

"Now, the Doctor placed other objects within the children's reach, such as bicycles, kites and everything that a young, so-called civilized boy or girl could desire. These were all carefully removed each evening by the silent and adroit attendants.

"It was not long before they found a use for everything given them. They rarely applied, correctly, the use intended for the object, nor did they succeed in mastering more than the simplest things; but, it was easy to see that their minds were gradually expanding day by day.

"Small pieces of colored cloth and string were put within their reach. In the beginning, they would play with them, in all sorts of ways, but before long they commenced to decorate their bodies with the string and cloth in strange combinations. More and different colored cloths were added, resulting in their using them in varying and novel ways.

"When they reached their seventh year, the Doctor considered it safe to put a baby dog in the court-yard, to live with them, being careful to keep it tied at first, so that the children might not become frightened or alarmed. At first seeing it, they scampered back to shelter in the house. Fear had possessed them. Only hunger and thirst finally forced them from their seclusion. Their maneuvers during this experience were both pathetic and laughable at times.

"Two weeks elapsed before the children went into the yard where the dog was tied. The dog on seeing the children would jump and wag his tail as indicating his delight, but the children evidently mistook the meaning, as a hasty retreat followed.

"When finally they observed the dog not following, they gradually grew bolder, and became sufficiently familiar to approach him almost within reach. Within three to four months they learned to play with him. Then slowly he became their inseparable companion, sharing all their games, and part of their bed.

"The children were much happier after the dog had entered into their daily life. Fed separately, and in a distinct part of the room from that of the children, he never failed to find his place. It would have been difficult, however, for the dog to have disturbed their food, as it was always placed well out of his reach.

"It took more than four years' familiarity with a ball before they learned to throw it. Neither one tried to catch when it came close. They would roll, but they made no attempt to strike at it. Everything that was done, ended at a point indicating the slightest amount of thought. They readily ran, jumped and would climb like monkeys the highest trees in the court-yard. Out on the slenderest branches they climbed most cautiously, carefully. This to the great distress of the mothers who kept constant vigil over their acts, and to the growing uneasiness of the Doctor and his attendants. Their antics in the trees appeared so hazardous, and accidents so certain, that means were provided to prevent them climbing above the lower branches. Wide wooden platforms were constructed, after the children had retired for the night—wide and high enough above the lower branches —so that they could not reach the higher ones. These platforms afforded protection in stormy summer weather, and the children invariably sat on the limbs beneath them, with seeming intense delight.

"The dog, given the same opportunities to learn, made no progress. All he knew, he had learned from the antics of the children. Dogs had been dogs for more than five hundred thousand years, notwithstanding the examples and teaching of mankind through the ages. Though a close associate of man, he had made no permanent advancement. To the Doctor, the query frequently occurred—'What advancement has been made voluntarily by any living thing, in the world's history, except through man's influence and teaching?' "

CHAPTER X

"WHILE the children remained very small," continued Finley, "the attendants observed many surprising manifestations as the known expression of human worship for a deity. You cannot realize the joy this discovery imparted to the mothers of the children. 'If no other proof were needed to establish their divine origin, this discovery alone, should serve to teach the most skeptical'— thought the Doctor. No people of Earth, no matter how widely separated by lands or seas, have failed to establish to their own satisfaction a divine origin. Every nation or tribe, and of every age, the Doctor averred, has endeavored to express a love for and adoration of the Divine. This through some direct or indirect means. Opinions have always differed as to what the means may have been, but all recognized a higher power. Individuals seeking a reason for this divine heart yearning, and failing to find it, either denied or became skeptical of deity. No person, to the Doctor, could entirely smother his divinity. The stubborn might deny it, but there is no human being so low in the scale of intelligence, that does not possess the attribute.

"Timidly, those children often stood looking up at the great warm Sun—closing their eyes to guard against his brilliant rays. With upturned faces, impassioned, yet rigid, they often stood in silence, for almost an hour at a time. At first the attendants believed that they were only warming their bodies, but later developments proved that this was a silent devotion to a great something of which they had no knowledge. Oftentimes, in apparent exhaustion, after standing with their upturned faces, they would suddenly prostrate themselves on the ground, face downward, for many minutes. Occasionally they made little mumbling sounds, as if to express their inadequate thought in words.

"Day by day, these expressions of devotion grew, until finally, every morning when they came out to play, if the Sun was shining, they would repeat the seeming devotion. If the weather happened to be bad, or the light of the Sun was obscured by the clouds, nothing unusual in their action was noted. The morning Sun appeared to be the only reminder.

"The observers felt impressed, that it was not the warm rays they sought, for the reason, that they often stood so near the stockade, that its shadow cut off the light.

"Many of the watchers were so impressed by this beautiful expression of devotion, that they themselves, unseen by the children, would devoutly join them. Though only a few feet from each other, no matter how wide the span that might separate their intelligence, in both alike, seemed to exist that same spirit of worship—inborn in the human breast.

" 'Now I know,' concluded my grandfather. 'Never shall I be swayed again by doubts as to our divinity. The people of the earth, civilized or uncivilized, whether divided by lands, seas, languages or customs—all manifest devotion to some deity. This is no accident! Ever has mankind struggled to show, by some kind of devotion, that divine love was implanted in the human race!'

"As time elapsed, the children grew more beautiful in mind and stature.

"Carefully watched over by the attendants, they seemed contented and always happy. During the first ten years, their lives had been spent in absolute isolation from the rest of the world. To them, the world was as unpopulated as it might have been to the minds of Adam and Eve.

"Through the quiet teaching by impersonal means, of the Doctor and his attendants, these children made greater advance during that ten short years than had Adam's presumed posterity in a thousand. On the other hand, the children's companion, the dog, though given equal opportunity for advancement, had nothing added to his intelligence; nor had he, during this time, shown by the slightest act or indication, that he was any more than animal. In this way, the Doctor had demonstrated to his own and entire satisfaction, the Divinity of Man, through the children's natural worship of the Deity. He, therefore, felt that since the experiment had accomplished its purpose by demonstrating all he had hoped to prove, to continue further would be unjust to both children and their parents.

"The delicate mission of training the children from their then wild state was left entirely to the Doctor.

"He began at first by talking to them, without appearing in their presence. Gradually they became accustomed to his voice. None could picture their surprise, their bewilderment, when they first discovered him in person. Yet, when they had mastered sufficient confidence to approach him, their advance was surprisingly rapid. In a short while, he found them answering to their names. Then their mothers revealed themselves, and finally, new people ceased to be a surprise to them. In less than a month, they became accustomed to these changes, so that no fright was noticeable. Within twelve months, they were enabled to converse, and by the close of the fifth year, their advancement in education was equivalent to that of children of similar age. No mental setback or impairment seemed to have been produced by their years of semi-wild life, though the task to divorce them from nature was, to say the least, onerous. Their superior form, however, great strength, agility, and beauty, were Nature's endowments resulting from the freedom of their wilder state. The parents, as a result, betrayed great happiness.

"Indeed, every one concerned learned to love these children." Then, by way of indicating to the company that his story had ended for the evening, Finley, lowering his voice, concluded—"I'm sure I should have loved them myself."

"Adolph wishes to tell you, Mister Bacon, that the model is 'most ready," said Sally, in a shrill voice, suddenly showing her face at the door.

" 'Most ready!" I murmured in amazement. "Ask him where he found his material. I was to supply him, but so far, he has requested nothing. I had thought that you and he were so busy, he'd forgotten all about his promise. Tell him I'll go down to the hangar and look at it."

"He won't let you see it—he told me so. He keeps it in his trunk," said Sally with decided positiveness.

"In his trunk!—You mean the plans are in his trunk. The machine is doubtless in some hangar, or the old factory loft.   Tell Adolph I'll wait until he has it ready on the aviation field before I go to see it.   That is, when I come to make my last trip.   You can give him that message, Sally——"

"I'll tell him, sure enough.   But, have you got a little gasoline, Mr. Bacon?   Adolph has spilled his soup all over himself.   He needs to have a scrubbin'.   But I forgive him—he is so handsome!   Oh, I like those fat men—they're so warm and comfortable looking."   And Sally cast her eyes upward as she collected material for Adolph's cleansing and made for the laundry in the utmost haste.

"Poor Sally," I thought.   "Her love affair has so bound her to Adolph that her dreams have centered only on fat men, while Adolph's imagination has been confined to models only.   I wondered if Sally had become the model, while the larger aeroplane had been neglected."

CHAPTER XI

NANCY'S BEAUX

"Gud mornin', John! Little airly t' call—but suthin' hes happened. I'd like t' git yer advice, if you'll give it t' me," saluted Silas, one cold winter's morning, as he slowly stalked into the kitchen and wearily assumed his accustomed place in front of the fire. It was some minutes before he continued to speak.

There had been a heavy snow fall the day before, and I felt that his long tramp had exhausted him. My wife immediately prepared a hot drink which he swallowed with apparent relish. He then removed his outer garment and long boots, and arranged himself in a comfortable position before the great log fire.

"Well," said he, with a long sigh and some little touch of sadness in his voice, "I guess yer won't see Silas much more."

I guessed what he meant, but felt unwilling to encourage his moody frame of mind, so I quickly asked—"Why? You're not going to move, are you? Going West, Silas?"

"No, I ain't goin' West—I'm agoin' up—or down, don't know zacly which. I got m' ticket—but don't know which station they'll put me off at."

"Got your ticket?" said I, with some show of surprise. "What do you mean, Silas?"

"Just what I'm talkin' on! What y' s'pose? Fact is,

120

I dropped in t' hev yer make me a Will. I've got my ticket t' go, in th' shape of a warnin'. You know, old Doctor Klouse used t' say, everybody on airth got a warnin' before they died, an' thet warnin' was a 'through-ticket' t'—well, it depends which of th' two depoes their tickets reads tue. I've got th' ticket—but—but, my eyes are tue dim, an' my mind is tue dull t' read th' address. Will yer draw up th' Will, John?"

"Why, of course, I will, Silas. Perhaps when I have finished you'll feel better," I said sympathetically.

"Maybe, but a warnin' is allas a ticket—t' trouble to come. Sometimes yer can sell the durn ticket, but then, nobody wants one without the return privilege"—mournfully drawled Silas.

I thought it best for the moment not to dwell upon the subject. If he wished later to tell me voluntarily the nature of this warning, I would use every effort to drive the subject from his mind—if possible, by ridicule. Both Silas and Jasper very often consulted me concerning their private affairs. I therefore felt little surprise that he should seek me out in the matter of writing his last Will and Testament.

"I want all my property to go to Nancy an' Jasper—equally divided betwix' 'em. Thet's all ther is t' my Will," and Silas hung his head for the moment.

Without further comment, I drew up the Will as directed. When duly signed and witnessed, he insisted that I listen to the story as to why he had selected Jasper and Nancy as his heirs. So with all attention, I listened to his well-meant and pathetic narrative.

It developed that he had loved but one girl in all his life—Nancy. By way of true appreciation, it was

both fitting and proper, that he recognize the life-long
friendship of both Nancy and Jasper, by making them
his equal heirs. He had no living relatives. Then, in an
undertone tinged with deep kindness he said, that money
would give Nancy many added comforts. She had, for
many years, been dependent upon the never-failing support of both himself and his friend Jasper. But for their
combined assistance Nancy would have suffered the extremes of poverty. True, her parents had bequeathed her
the old homestead and a little cash—these, and a few
poor relatives. That was past fifty years ago. The only
non-assets now remaining were the poor relations.

Silas and Jasper, as the former expressed it, had managed to "keep tabs" on Nancy's financial status, and
when her cash ran low in the village bank, they, between
them, deposited a sufficiency to her credit. For over fifty
years they had contributed equally, while Nancy never
realized where the money came from. None but the aged
banker was in the secret and he knew both men to be well
to do. They were quaint old fellows, to be sure, but they
knew no policy save rugged honesty, backed by loyalty
and a character above reproach. I had no desire to be
further inquisitive, but he insisted that I should know
his reason for the bequest to Nancy and Jasper.

To me they were three inseparable friends, while most
of the villagers regarded them only as three old cronies.
Village gossip had long intimated that Jasper and Silas
were rivals for the hand of Nancy, and that the rivalry had
begun some sixty years before. Neither man ever mentioned the subject to me, though the two frequently sput-
tered and quarreled together in my presence. This afforded an opportunity sometimes to chide them a little

for not having had the courage to propose to Nancy. Their silence on these occasions convinced me that I had probably hit the truth.

"You keep th' Will, an' when yer hear thet I've been tucken, then tell 'em,"—was his only instruction. Of course, I promised. Then he proceeded to relate:

" 'Bout three 'clock las' nite, I heered a awful crash, an' breakin' of glass in th' sittin' room. It woke me up right out of a sound sleep. At fust I thought th' storm had broken th' glass, but, on second thought, knew ther wa'n't much wind, so thet couldn't be. Then sed I, must be some hungry critter thet wants t' git in, so says I, 'Hey, there, don't break the windy. I'll open th' door fur yer.' I got rite out of bed an' opened th' kitchen door an' says, 'Come in an' git warm.' But do yer know, I was but talkin' t' th' air—for nobody was there. Well, by gosh, thet made me a leetle narvous, but what do yer s'pose hed happened. Well, there layin' right on th' floor was my gol-darn Sunday lookin' glass—all a-smashed t' pieces. Then says I, thet's a sure sign of death. Well, as 'twas 'bout 'nower fore I ginerally git up, I dressed myself an' sit down afore th' fireplace. Well, I got a leetle sleepy like, an' was kinder dozin' off, when I heered some one speak, jest as plain as day. I didn't hear what they sed at fust, so I kept kinder quiet an' listened. Suddenly th' voice spoke up an' sed, several times, 'fore I listened in pertic'lar, 'Yer time is up—yer time is up. Yer heart will stop—yer heart will stop. The glass is broke, perpare t' go.' Well, I jest jumped rite up out of my cheer. 'Twas nuff ter make any one melancorly. I thought th' voice was Jasper's. But nobody was ther. Th' only thing I cud hear was th' old clock agoin',

jumpity jump—jumpity jump—an' my ole heart keepin'
time with it, jumpity jump—jumpity jump. I've thought
it all over, John, an' I know it were my warnin'," said
Silas solemnly, and his cane came down on the old oak
floor with a vigorous thud. Then he sat for some moments, with his head bowed forward, before he spoke.
When he continued: "So I came over, John, jist as quick
as I'd done th' choores. I'll hurry, says I, fast as I can,
an' git ready. Th' warnin' didn't say how long I'd got,
but I rather thought they'd give me a couple of days.
Then th' gud Lord kin jest hev what's left of me, an'
Nancy an' Jasper kin hev what he don't care for."

I tried for the moment to cheer him up, but my efforts
were in vain, as he seemed thoroughly convinced that he
had received a last warning of approaching death. For
awhile he sat as if thinking over something that he wanted
to further tell me. For some time, with his head bowed
forward in his hands, he sat silently. Suddenly looking
up, with tears in his old and fading eyes, he earnestly
said—"It's not fer myself I'm thinkin', John. It's Nancy,
yes, an' Jasper. More'n sixty year ago we all went t' th'
same old distric' school. Th' old red school house rite
up this old friendly road—'bout a mile. We were in th'
same class togither. We boys was as strong as oxen.
Folks used t' say, thet we was about as fine lookin' tue
bucks as ye'd meet in a day's travel. 'Course, I don't
want t' flatter myself, but I was a bit handsomest of the
tue. I used t' git my choores done airly, so I cud stop fer
Nancy on my way t' school. Wall, she were th' puttiest
little lamb yer ever laid yer eyes on—by ginger. I was
mad clean through when I learnt thet Jasper Perkins was
tryin' t' shine up t' her tue. When we three came hum

from school nites, I'd try t' cut Jasper out;—sometimes
I did, an' sometimes I didn't. When I got a chance, I
spoke kinder careless like 'bout th' color of Jasper's hair
—as 'twas red, an' called her 'tention t' th' freckles on
his face. She allas shy'd me off by a-sayin'—'*Yur* gud
lookin', too, Mister Cummings.' Somehow, ruther, she
tuck it, thet I was praisin' him up. I couldn't tell which
she tuck to the most—me or Jasper. But thin, John,
thet's the woman of it. I never asked her, an' she never
said.

"We all lived putty close t'gither, an' in those days
our three families stood fust. We allas hed best pews in
th' meetin' house, by heck. We hed th' most land, an'
every one of us hed a bedroom rite off th' parlor.

"W'll, Nancy's father, gran'father, an' great-gran'-
father, with th' wives, cousins, an' aunts, was about tickled
t' death t' think she had got th' two best young bucks
in th' country t' wait on her. They said they didn't
care shucks whether it were Jasper or me that won. I
kinder think, though, they sided somehow toward me—at
least, her great-gran'mother told me so,—'fore she lost
her mind.

"Well, I've lived t' see th' day when every one of 'em
is gone. Fate or suthin' seemed t' say, we three should
jest stay around. Some of th' other young fellers tried
t' spruce up t' Nancy, but I tell ye, we made up our
minds thet there'd only be tue real rivals in th' country
fer her, an' so we skeered them all off as easy as smokin'
out a woodchuck. We knew, fer all thet, 'twas nip an'
tuck twixt us tue. When Nancy went out fer a stroll
in th' meadow, with us two, she allas dressed up in her
new linsey-woolsey, an' Jasper an' I in our new Kentucky

jeans. Yes, yer bet yer bottom dollar, we was a putty big sight fer them parts. Of course, we went barefooted in th' summer, but we looked nice at thet. Some Sundays when we wore boots, there was more'n a dozen lookin' out at us, as we come up through th' chicken yard t' th' house. When we got t' th' house they'd tell us what a grand site we made t'gether—yer might build on it, John.

"I think Nancy liked both of us, but yer couldn't git out of her which she prefer'd for she said she didn't want t' hurt th' feelin's of neither, so, yer see, thet's the woman of it ag'in. She sed, if one of us started t' spark another gal, she'd decide rite away on the one left. Or, if one of us were atucken off, why then she'd have no chice. I kinder suspect that she liked Jasper a little the better 'twixt us, fer I often seen her eyes kinder twinkle-like in his derectshun.

"I tell ye, John, how 'twas: There were a spellin' bee up t' th' old red school house one nite—rite up th' old road here at th' four corners. We two rivals hed asked Nancy t' 'low us see her hum thet nite. We was kinder keepin' our eyes on one t'other, an' so, when Jasper asked her, I ast at th' same time, an' bein' a woman an' a lady, as she was, why she give her consent t' both of us at onct. So, yer see, John, Nancy was a corker at diplomatics.

"Well, when we got started t'ord hum, we each tuck an arm. Naturally, I did th' most talkin', an' was so busy thet it were only by accident I saw Jasper squeeze her hand. Thet riled me up rite away, so to hold my rite-a-way, I jest squeezed her t'other hand, an' wa'n't partic'lar whether he seen me or not. Then I made up my mind thet I'd have a little better understandin' with him, afore goin'

further. We both hed t' come back over th' road from her
house. He must hev suspected somethin' fer he were very
quiet. Th' ground was all covered by ice an' snow, worn
down hard in th' middle of th' road. It were slippery
walkin'. Suddenly th' ginger rose up in me—like fire.
Said I, 'Look a here, Jasper—it's you or me. Understand? If I lick yer, you keep way from Nancy hereafter.
If you lick me, I'll do th' same. D' yer hear?' Well,
John, he didn't answer a word, but flung off his cut, an'
I did th' same. Then without a word, we grappl'd one
another. He tried t' throw me, an' I him. It were nip an'
tuck, all over th' road with nuther of us gittin' th' best
on it. Back an' forth we fought, fust on this side, then
that—sometimes gittin' out in the deeper snow side the
road. I didn't know he were so strong. The harder I
worked t' throw him, th' stronger he seemed t' git. We
must have been at it ten minutes, an' we were both a
blowin' like steam engines, when suddenly I seemed t' git
so mad thet I cud have bitten a horse-nail in tue. It
seemed t' have given me extra strength, fer I got my boot
wedged 'twixt his legs, when he slipped, an' back he fell.
His head struck th' ice with a thud, thet made me sick in a
jiffy. There he lay, as still as a settin' hen. I didn't
say nothin', I couldn't—couldn't git my breath. Finally
I sed, 'Yer got enough?' He didn't answer, so I kinder
collected my courage, though I knowed suthin' dreadful
had happened, an' I sed as brave as I cud make out—'Git
up, Jasper!' an' then I saw he didn't move. 'Twas awful
cold, too, thet. nite. Then I thought, s'pose I keep rite
on hum—in th' mornin' they'll find him froze to death.
My conscience was clear. Who'd know 'bout it anyway?
If he got up an' walked hum himself, then he couldn't

accuse me, cud he? Well, I started fer hum, an' left him stretched out in th' road. I tried t' think how I'd next get Nancy, but somehow his face would git rite in front of hers, an' it looked so solemn-like I couldn't think of her. I must have got nearly hum—a mile away—afore I began t' realize what a skunk I was. Jest as soon as I thought on't, I know'd thet I ought t' be one, an' out amongst them critters. I then turned 'round, an' I shot a bee line down th' road 'tord where I'd left Jasper. When I got to ther spot, there he lay, jist th' same as I'd left him.

"I holler'd, 'Jasper! Jasper!'—loud's I cud holler—but ther were no use. I got down on my knees, fust t' see if he was livin', an' second t' pray in case he weren't. I wasn't sure whether he were livin' or not, an' instead of prayin' I jest lifted him on my shoulder an' carried him back t' Nancy's house—th' nearest place. He were a sick man, I tell yer. When he fell, he nearly cracked his head open.

"I went t' see him next day, an' says he t' me,—'I'm here, Silas, livin' in Nancy's hum—thet's nearer'n you'll ever git t' her—but I won't take advantage of yer.' An' he never did. So we've courted her t'gether fur nigh on t' sixty year. Everybody aroun' then has gone 'cept us.

"Now I got this warnin', John, so there'll be only tue left.

"Jasper kin hev her—an' my money in th' bargain."

Here Silas slowly arose to return home. After bidding me good-by, I watched him disappear. It was the last time I saw him alive. A few days later the "warning" had come true.

CHAPTER XII

TELEPATHY

It was late in March before Jasper and Nancy—both dressed in deep black—came over to spend the evening. It was their first appearance since the death of Silas. They were unusually quiet and took little or no interest at first in transpiring commonplaces. But under the influence of Sam's diplomatic and happy disposition their spirits revived.

The evening conversation usually began and ended by a heated discussion of the weather. This was a favorite subject with the old people, until worn thread-bare. Then, Jasper led by waxing eloquent between liberal helpings to hard cider, upon subjects of sin and the wickedness of the world, and the breeding of evil habits.

None but the weary listener to these rantings could conceive the patience needed to hear stories and comments repeated over and again, sometimes four to five times during a single sitting. There he goes on "Sin," I said to myself. Then it would be on "Temperance." If Jasper happened to imbibe more than the two quart pitcher during an evening, we were certain to hear about temperance to the limit of snakes or figures on the wall.

As we lived in the atmosphere of patience and kindness, we had learned, however, the hard lesson of becoming good

listeners. Then, some deference was due to old age. We
had time, while Jasper was passing out.

As the conversation waned, I generally nodded to Finley, as a signal to begin. He was so afraid of offending
some one by commencing his story too quickly, that my
aid was acceptable.

The absence of Silas seemed to prompt Finley to refer
to the subject of warnings, and the foretelling of events.
Also, thought transference, or the communication between
one mind and another; *Relaesthesa*, or the power of per-
ceiving distant events, without the intervention of other
known phenomena.

"The questions," began Finley, "to be considered to-
night are, first, is there such a thing as Mental Telepathy?
Are our likes and dislikes of our fellows the result of it?
Second, do we have warnings?"

Finley frankly admitted that his Grandfather had made
many records, too voluminous to read in one evening.
He would, accordingly, only read certain extracts from
these records—adding but few comments of his own.

"Natural likes and dislikes, or, more properly speaking,
affinities and antipathies, are apparent among animals
as well as men. It is probable, as in the case of man, that
animals instantly form likes or dislikes of everything they
meet for the first time. Human beings, through their
higher intelligence, may reverse their opinion later, but
in most cases the original impression returns. The human mind through the eye or touch, frequently conceives
a feeling of like or dislike of another. It is, at times,
necessary only to obtain a glance at some person we have
never met or known, in order to beget this feeling of affin-
ity or antipathy. This discriminating quality of the

mind is so acute in some, that a single glance will disclose the whole moral character of a stranger, and instantly inspire the beholder with an impression of love or hate.

"Animals unmistakably display the same qualities. People are frequently thrown together, who from the first moment secretly dislike or hold an antipathy for each other, which each may succeed in concealing for years. Yet, these impressions of love or hate, are apt to reveal themselves sooner or later. There is no apparent reason for these known phenomena, unless they be accounted for through some invisible part of our physical make-up, intuitively obeyed. It is not obvious enough to believe it as the result of any reason, because no tangible premise is found.

"Mental telepathy, or that sense by which the mind is capable of transmitting thought at distance, to one or more people, is, as far as we know, confined exclusively to man and therefore must be of divine quality. The proof of this fact was the crowning point of Dr. Klouse's investigations and proved to him beyond a doubt man's divine origin. No animal, as far as we know, is capable of transmitting thought any distance through the air.

"Telepathy was unknown to the Doctor. It had not been discovered then, and so he chose to call it, in his day, the 'Invisible Transmission' of thought.

"He gathered from widely separated communities the testimony of many thousand people whose experience proved that they had received mental messages from others. These communications covered almost every known subject of human interest, and many had been received through thousands of miles. The testimony of so

many people seemed to prove the existence of this wonderful human quality. They had little or no object in
stating anything but fact. The sender of the mental
message as well as those who received it, frequently testi-
fied, without the knowledge of the other. Of course, the
majority of those testifying to the facts, viewed the incidents with awe or superstition. People whose minds
harmonize and who speak the same tongue, may transmit
and receive human thought without regard to sex or re-
lationship. To attune our minds so that we may catch
the mental messages of others requires that we shall live
the best possible life, morally and spiritually. The mind
must be attuned to its very highest physical condition.
Imagination is, without question, the highest quality of
the mind, and imaginative minds are those receiving mental
phenomena more freely. People possessing this high mental quality generally inherit it. Other minds, while fed
by perfect physical bodies, might not be able, except
under most favorable conditions, to receive human mental
communications. We largely inherit our ability to hear
these messages. The air is filled with passing communications all the time. Not all understand or receive benefits, but each of us recognize some of them, part of the
time. A person may concentrate his mind upon a given
subject, desiring another hundreds of miles away to hear
it. If the mind of the other is attuned he or she will
receive the message. If not, some one, or scores of others
speaking the same language, may catch the message,
though to them quite meaningless. All philosophers,
writers, thinkers, receive much of their thought from this
source. 'The thought suddenly came to me,' they will

aver. 'It came as an inspiration,' one will say. Really, their minds caught it up from space, or out of the air. Indeed, the Doctor was convinced that every mind 'picked up' ideas and thoughts from the air.

"I believe," said Finley, "every new thought expressed is the result of our ability to mentally seize messages flying in the air, understood by us, and set in motion by millions of other minds. As boats at sea pick up the wireless messages so soon as flashed, so the human mind, when rightly attuned, picks up the human thought flashed forth by others. Inspired thoughts are intentional or non-intentional communications, sent forth by others, which we may capture. It is impossible for any person to hold a secret thought. As soon as the thought forms, it is immediately wholly or in part, taken possession of by others. An imaginative mind readily receives mental impressions. It is a type harmonizing with a large number of other minds. The greater,—the more sensitive, the more healthy and strong,—the more it may gather out of space.

"When one language dominates the earth, being understood by all people, then will our progress be more rapid. All thought is immediately transmitted to the air, and through air into space through the ether, even to the planets around us, if we will but let it. Therefore, thoughts are literally transmitted to the Almighty when we lift our voices in song and praise. As they penetrate and permeate everything, they are directed to the Creator and are heard and understood. To whom, therefore, they are willed, the messages go. Our inability to receive the mental impress is due to our physical or mental imperfec-

tion, or, it may be, to our lack of spiritual harmony. We lose, by our faults, which, if corrected, joy
and comfort by these silent messages can assuredly be
ours.

"Hundreds of different languages exist; how impossible
it is, therefore, to convey by mental Telepathy, thoughts
to others differing in language. How important, then,
to encourage a universal language.

"There is, however, a universal language that everything understands. It is the language of the Universe.
Not expressed in words, but in phenomena reflecting itself to the mind, when attuned to the laws of Nature. It
speaks unceasingly, and if we will but listen, we shall finally understand. When we take time to listen, we can dis-
tinguish thought impressions. It is forever trying to get
in touch with us. Attune thy mind!"

Finley also indicated that he knew of the warning given
to Silas. He declared to me that this message doubtless
came "direct from his Maker." We thought best, however, not to mention the subject to our guests. We had
a reason.

"Down through all the ages," continued Finley, "at
certain epochs, great men and women claim to have received inspirations direct from the Deity. Also, that
they were the appointed instruments or Servants through
whom these messages were to be delivered to the people.
Some, who made the claim were, doubtless, impostors, but
not all. When certain people brought the message of
love to mankind, these were direct communications. Thousands are receiving to-day divine messages, and refuse
to believe it. Others, no matter how humble or exalted
their sphere in life, know it. Their minds are attuned.

If you want to catch a divine message you must, therefore, attune your mind."

"You act uneasily, Sam," interrupted Paul. "You don't seem to like the Doctor's conclusions."

"No, I can't swallow that," said Sam, "but I agree in all he says about affinities," he added.

"*You* never had anything but affinities, and they all wear skirts," continued Paul.

"If they only wear smiles, they have the full dress of happiness for me. I never did admire the rags and tatters of a bilious disposition," dryly replied Sam.

"The Divine," continued Finley, "communicates constantly with those whose minds are properly attuned. He also warns or notifies every human being in advance of every human event. Listen, and you may know when you receive your death warning. Sometimes we are notified months before the occurrence. Every thoughtful person can recollect some circumstance in his life, when he knows he has received a warning of some kind. Attune your mind if you desire to hear the messages."

Here Finley continued to relate incidents where people had received previous information of occurrences transpiring at a much later date. All occurrences are probably predicted by some one. Almost every great calamity has been predicted—sometimes months ahead. Doubtless, most of these are of Divine origin, and the individual through whom the prediction is made, is very often an obscure and lowly person, whose mind happens to be in accord with the Supreme.

"Who knows," continued Finley, "but that some person warned the people of Martinique, in the Lesser Antilles, of the great eruption of Mont Pelé in May, 1902, when

the Town of St. Pierre was destroyed, involving the loss of
40,000 inhabitants?   Without a doubt, some message or
warning of the calamity was received weeks before it took
place.   Most of us are so engrossed with our small, selfish
affairs, that we heed not the warnings always sent in
advance.   The Doctor continues," said Finley:—"We
should be guided and advised by the 'Still Small' voice.
When the Supreme communicates with us we cannot mistake it.   It is through these warnings that men are inspired to sacrifice, that others may take note, learn, and
progress."

"The next time we meet," interrupted Jasper, "I'll
bring th' village blacksmith. He knows as much as any
man in teown. I've been tellin' him 'bout th' Doctor's
opinions. He knowed him! He's a leetle lonesome neow."
Then Jasper and Nancy arose and were about to leave.

We all thanked Jasper for his thoughtfulness, and felt
equally impressed that the blacksmith's opinions, garbed
in any particular form, were quite as valid as our own.

CHAPTER XIII

THE VILLAGE BLACKSMITH

WILLIAM GRENNELL conducted his blacksmith shop on the main street of the village. It was one of the old landmarks of the place. No one living seemed to know just when it was built. The older inhabitants assured their friends that it had been there since they remembered anything, and, added, that their "grandpas" had often spoken about the old Grennell shop, while they were yet small children.

There it stood, with its low, sloping roof, sagged in the center by age. A large, squatty stone chimney poked its way out defiantly. Its sides planked with rough hand-hewn oak were now dark and discolored from smoke that constantly poured forth from the forge, and hung like a pall over the small black building. During week days a passerby might have seen the smithy stripped to his red flannel shirt, his great erect frame wielding with steady arm the heavy iron hammer with the ease of a Hercules. The rhythmic rings on the anvil repeatedly turned steel at white heat into shape. The music of his ever busy anvil was a familiar sound. It made up part of the village life. It helped to put the spirit of ambition in many. It quickened the pace of both man and beast. Acting like a tonic on the feelings of those whose energy waned, the tuneful ding-dong, ding-dong of the anvil's

measured song beat better time than the village band. As
the sounds shot forth from door and window, through
crack and crevice of the old shop, they were carried as on
wings far down the village street—over the meadows,
dales and hills, and re-echoed again and again.

Generations of Grennells had occupied the old building.
Men tall in statue, large and strong of body, and with
wills like iron. Strong of character, simple in tastes and
with hearts that beat and hands that worked for truth
and honesty. In learning, the Grennells' reputation was
only excelled by that of the "infallible" village parson.

William Grennell lived a short walk from his shop.
The old house had been the former home of both his father
and grandfather. Here William was born, reared and
later married. A few happy years together—then
came rapid changes. Death's toll began with the grandfather, then his father. Finally came the severest blow;
death took his beautiful girl wife, like a tender flower
quickly passing—fading from the view.

As nature's recompense, she left behind her a little
child—a girl, Daisy Y. Grennell. None understood what
the middle initial stood for, and so the village folk called
her simply Daisy Grennell. A few great sobs of pathos
and suffering shook and swayed the blacksmith's oak-
like frame. Returning resolution, and the will of the
strong man dominated. With that intelligence and ex-
cellence of character so well becoming, he had determined
that his little daughter should know only of sunshine—
should feed and live upon it. There should be no vacilla-
tion or wanting on his part. He would steel himself to the
endeavor. The little girl grew, knowing but the love of
only one great parent—one so full and satisfying, so

strong and all protecting, that more could not have filled her tender years with greater happiness, nor blissful peace of mind. She was his idol, his hope. All his interest, his present and future plans, were for her. Her welfare was also his. Patiently nursing, patiently watching her day by day without faltering, through a long illness, he had tenderly held her in his great arms. Pressing her to his bosom again and again, singing lullabys as softly as he could to his "Daisy Y," "Daisy Y," the while controlling his great strong voice, in modulating tones to her sensitive ear, until the song, hushed to a whisper, only indicated with greater force his unsuppressed happiness. Convinced that she had passed into a deep sleep, or some beautiful dream, he saw to it that she was gently and carefully tucked away in her ever-ready cot.

As she grew to young and beautiful girlhood, attending first the little red school, and later the Grammar School of a nearby town, his interest, love and adoration only increased.

Human love could not change the divine law. The silent message came one still day direct to the heart of William Grennell. The darling of his hope, stricken with a fatal malady, was fast passing away. Pray—beseech as he might, no response came beyond the law.

* * * * * * * *

A few weeks after I met Grennell. Though he looked broken, he greeted me pleasantly, and said that he had learned through Jasper of the meetings at my home. He had promised Jasper he would attend the next one. He then informed me that he had taken a peculiar interest in the writings of Doctor Klouse, whom he had known as a young man. The Doctor was also well acquainted with his father, and so it befell that the village smithy was added to the company, meeting to discuss the writings of Finley's grandfather. The chair left empty by Silas was now filled. For Grennell's benefit, many subjects previously discussed were gone over, this, to the evident delight of Sam Willis, who kept the now familiar, though somewhat dry subjects, more enlivened and the whole company in better humor by his good natured exaggerations.

The improvement in the smithy's appearance was by this time manifest. Dejected and solemn during his early visits, he now went away happier, and, at times, laughing at Sam's senseless talk.

"I wonder if we ever return to life again, Mister Grennell. I understand you agree with the Doctor's theory?" inquired my wife one evening.

"I suppose I agree with most of the Doctor's ideas," he answered.

"Some day we shall know positively," ventured my wife with a sigh.

"We know now. There are many men and women, now scattered over the world, whose characters are unimpeachable, and who recall certain incidents of a former existence. We cannot ignore the testimony of so many honest people," said Grennell earnestly.

"Hope is strong in most of us," remarked Hester.

"What did she say?" hoarsely whispered Jasper, and turning toward Nancy inquiringly, with one hand to his ear, more readily to catch the reply.

"I thought she said 'dope,'" giggled Nancy.

"What about it?"

"I think she said, 'Dope is strong in most of us,'" whispered Nancy confidentially.

"Ye don't think there's any in the cider, does yer, Nancy?" he anxiously asked.

"Not 'dope,' Nancy," said Sam in a loud voice, "but 'elope!'"

"I refuse t' talk scandal with yer, Sur," shouted Jasper, rising and shaking his cane at Sam.

"What's scandal?" asked two or three of the company simultaneously.

"Oh, nothin', nothin', 'cept certain in-di-vid-u-als had better be keerful, or somethin' sartin will trans-pire,"—replied Jasper, shaking his head and eyeing Sam menacingly.

"Hope for a future is ever strong in the human heart, but we need more evidence to convince the majority," said the blacksmith.

"I know I was a mosquito when I was here before," interjected Sam.

"The idea!" said Ellen reproachfully, "how do you know you were, Sam?"

"'Cause I remember biting Jasper on the nose, when he was a kid."

"Yaas, I rec-lect it tue," quickly broke in Jasper. "I tried t' swat cher then, but yer sneaked a-way in th' dark, but by gosh, I got cher now all rite,"—and Jasper raised his cane in the air as if to bring it down on Sam's head.

"I'm a good mine ter," he said, in mock severity, the while chuckling to himself and making a vain effort to conceal his merriment.

"By ginger, Sam, yer a gud un—yes, yer be," he said at last, resuming his seat and taking a fresh helping of cider.

"What further evidence do we need, when we know in

our own hearts, intuitively, that there is a future state? Nothing in nature really dies. It merely changes from one thing to another," said my wife.

"The house changes, the occupant changes," remarked Paul.

"Yes, the house changes, but the occupant may change houses," suggested Finley.

"We may settle the matter between ourselves by devising a plan whereby the first after death to return to this life shall make himself known to those of us still living. What do you think of that plan?" asked the blacksmith.

No one answered at first. Each one assumed a thoughtful air. Naturally, we all turned toward Finley for his opinion in all unfamiliar subjects.

"Shall I answer?" he said hesitatingly, addressing the company. For reply, there was a general nodding of assent.

"If we," he began, "could uninterruptedly concentrate our minds upon a certain word, keeping it daily before us during the rest of our lives, I believe, some one of us would be almost certain to recall it on their next return to Earth. The word would have to be an unusual one, containing few letters. Let us try the experiment."

We all eagerly joined in the spirit of the undertaking.

"It will be necessary, if we are to achieve the best result, for all to write the chosen word in ink," continued Finley. "Set it down, so that each shall retain the copy so long as life lasts. Each one is to inspect it daily, being sure never to divulge a word or hint about this secret compact. We should make every effort to keep the word in our dying thoughts. As each of us take our departure, we should, as early as possible in the next existence, make ourselves known to those still living, by writing the word. The act of writing the word in a future life, may be entirely subconscious and without reason for doing so, but I feel that the tremendous impression made by the word during this present existence will manifest itself in the next.

"We are aware, that we may impress our minds with a fact, that we may transmit it to posterity; and succeeding generations will call the fact 'instinct.' Now, if we concentrate our thought, I believe, a few of us have sufficiently well developed brains to carry the fact into succeeding existence."

Finley's suggestions were admitted by all to be good. After some discussion, we enthusiastically agreed to try the experiment. Certainly there could be no harm in trying. What was this word to be? That was the problem. After an endless number had been suggested, to be finally rejected for one reason or another, my wife said, "Why not use the word 'Weissnichtwo,' meaning 'I know not where?' "

"Too long, Mother," objected Ellen. "None of us could learn to write it in this life, to say nothing of the next."

" 'I know not where' would make a pretty word for a collar button," said Sam.

"Or a key hole, in the dark," suggested Ellen.

" 'Zobara' might be a good word," broke in Hester.

"Who was he?" asked Paul.

"It's not a 'he,' it's a 'she.' She was the 'Mother of Love,' " explained Hester.

"A very 'good' word indeed," laconically remarked Finley. "But she was also the 'Mother of Mischief.'

'Harut' and 'Marut,' selected by Heaven to be judges on earth, fell in love with her."

"They must have been human judges who had forgotten their place of departure," dryly remarked Sam.

"I'll give you a word that signifies the most important thing on earth. More of it is used than of anything else. You can feel it but you can't see it. Without it, everything of life would immediately die. When it's hot, it's very disagreeable. Some people insist in using it that way. When it's too hot, or too cold, it kills. It spreads disease, famine, and destruction everywhere on the earth's surface. Yet it works and plays and plans for us. It transmits and creates beautiful music. It brings and carries. It reaps and plants. It's the first and the last thing we take. We all need it, and must have it every minute of our lives, and——"

"I don't be-lieve yer, Sam. The first thing I tuck was milk, an' th' last thing I shall take will be a little cider, there now"—exclaimed Jasper excitedly.

"Wait a minute, Uncle Jasper. As I was saying, we bring it with us when we are born, but we can't take it with us when we depart."

"Well, that sounds impossible, Sam. What is it?" asked Paul.

"Air," he replied.

"Sam, yer a smart chap," said Jasper, thumping his cane upon the floor.

"What word would you suggest, Mister Grennell?" finally inquired my wife.

"Well, I recall a term very precious to me, though I don't know its meaning—still, I've hunted high and low. On the evening my little girl was born, my dying wife beckoned me to the bedside, and in a faint whisper said, 'Will, name her Daisy Yezad.' My heart was breaking. She didn't seem to have the strength to say good-by. That was all she said, and I cannot rid myself of the strange word. So I called her Daisy Y. Does any one here know what Yezad means?"

Not one of us had ever seen or heard the term before, but we all regarded it as an excellent selection. Each of us wrote down the word, "Yezad." In order to record the term in a permanently safe way, Finley took down the old family Bible, and, opening to a blank page, he wrote the word, and each one present signed underneath, his and her own name. We all agreed to study, memorize, and concentrate our minds on the word daily, for the rest of our lives.

"I'm afraid I shall get it mixed up with Zebra, Jasper," remarked Sam.

"Stripes is nat'ral fur yer, Sam," replied the old man, "an' sum day, if yer don't look out, ye'll have 'em an' plenty."

CHAPTER XIV

FURTHER PHILOSOPHY OF DOCTOR KLOUSE

"LET us all draw chairs around the fire. I scarcely expected you and Nancy this cold night," said Finley, addressing Jasper.

"Yer don't call this cold, do yer? Why, it was so warm thet I thought I would hev to shed my cut 'fore I got here. Wa'n't it, Nancy?"

"Ye-e-s, Jasper; I wasn't cold," she pleasantly answered.

"Wasn't cold! Why, do you know it's two degrees below zero, outside?" exclaimed Paul.

"But you know, Jasper and Nancy dress very warmly when they go out—winter or summer. Jasper dons thick woolen wristers and stockings, all the summer long," explained my wife in an undertone which could not be heard.

"Yes, and Jasper often wears a heavy overcoat on evenings in the hottest summer weather," said Ellen in a confidential whisper. "He says he's afraid of draughts. Thinks there are as many kinds of drafts in the air, as we find on banks," she laughingly continued.

"When I was a boy——," began Jasper.

"When I was in Georgia," interrupted Sam, "I've seen the thermometer go more than sixty degrees below zero, yet people could bathe in perfect comfort; fruit and vegetables of all kinds were not even frost-bitten."

146

"Yer don't say so!" exclaimed Jasper in surprise. "People in bath-in'. They must a wore furs."

"No furs South of the Mason-Dixon Line, Jasper, 'cept what's on top of a black man's head."

"Thet gives yer away, Sam. I don't believe yer. Any critter who don't know th' difference twix' fur and wool, couldn't tell whether 'twas fourth o' July or Christmas."

"Hope to die, Jasper, they do bathe when it's sixty below."

"Where, in a cake of ice?"

"No, Jasper, in their bath tubs."

"You git out o' here," shouted Jasper, raising his cane threateningly. "In a bath tub, hey? Fruit not frost-bitten, hey? S'pose that's in the bath tub, tue? Say, you, you scallywag——," but he went no further, for Nancy, who had been pulling at his sleeve, finally succeeded in subduing him.

"Sam, is there plenty of hickory in the wood box?" quietly inquired Finley.

"Yes, there's hickory knots in the wood box, and hickory nuts on the table. Twice blessed be the name of hickory," he replied cheerily.

"Make it three times, and include yer head," retorted Jasper.

"If you don't mind," said the blacksmith, "I should like to hear a few pages of the Doctor's observations read to-night."

"Since Jasper has suggested that Sam's head is hickory, just read us something to prove it," remarked Paul.

"Everybody comfortable? Pass the apples to Hester, and move that pitcher of cider so Jasper can fill his glass," I suggested.

"Mr. Bacon, if 'twant for this cider, me and Nancy wouldn't hev much t' live fer, would we, Nancy?"

"No, Jasper," she shyly replied, "except to get married—some day."

"By gosh, I forgot about thet."

"I will now read a few pages from the Doctor's observations," pursued Finley. "The following are the results of an honest search for facts. I realize that many of them will be considered foolish. Before condemning them, however, let critics analyze their full meaning. This done, they shall doubtless arrive at the same conclusion."

Finley proceeded to read:—

"Mind is born, it cannot be acquired. Personality is the soul, it cannot change. Education polishes, but does not perceptibly add cells to the brain. A narrow unreasoning mind is not changed a particle by education. No kind of a mind can perceptibly change. Education and environment simply develop what is there, but careful living and a healthy body will do more than both. Humanity is in love with a person whose life is healthy, rather than large intellect that suffers from indigestion. The most refreshing thing in all the world is a happy, pleasant disposition. Good health is the first step toward charity to all men.

"Blood is the life of the mind's existence. The average person's brain lacks either in quality or quantity, or both, hence their thought must always be limited.

"The larger the brain, the greater the amount of blood required for nourishment. Hence, if the body be weak physically, or the blood thin or poor of quality, the large brain lacking nourishment, causes the person to appear dull, dazed, or uninteresting. We are apt, if they are children, to believe they lack intelligence.

"Many teachers unconsciously disregard the slow, dull child, and are enthusiastic over the phenomenal pupil. The one too strikingly in advance will invariably, later in life, be a mental disappointment, while the dull child may develop a wonderful intelligence and individuality. On the other hand, the larger brain, though nourished thoroughly by a goodly supply of blood, may suffer from apepsia—by over-eating, over-drinking, or other physical abuse.

"People of larger brain-power are apt to suffer most from indigestion, stomach troubles and headaches; therefore, they should exercise greater care in eating and drinking than those whose brains are smaller, or less active. The reason for this is, that while two persons equal physically, but unequal mentally, require the same quality and quantity of blood to digest their food, the one having the greater mentality must eat less, or suffer from indigestion, or other serious consequences. The greater brain saps the blood of its vitalizing force, and leaves the digestive organs weak, requiring a smaller amount and more careful selection of food.

"Unusually large mentalities require nearly all the blood nutriment that their bodies are capable of producing, hence, little vitality remains for proper physical nourishment. For this person, the greatest care must be exercised in eating, as well as conserving energy in every possible way, so that proper balance may be maintained; otherwise, serious consequences would immediately follow. Over-eating for the mentally active would mean indigestion, headache, and, if persisted in, severe complications. Over physical labor would bring about similar results, for no man of great brain capacity can labor and think at the same time. Small and inactive brains and great physical labor are apt to go together. Again, the great cause of human ills, overindulgence in eating and drinking is not so apt to interfere with the mental processes of the laborer of limited mentality.

"A strong mentality should possess a strong physique. Sometimes, the mind is strong, while the body is apt to be weak. A weak physique with a large mentality produced a Channing, who remarked that he was all his life 'dying.'

"Many inherit large, active brains, with weak bodies; hence, we are not apt to hear much of them. Mostly, they pass out unknown. While many are called lazy, they are really not. They simply have large and sturdy looking bodies, with no real energy for labor. Among them may be found, upon intimate acquaintance, philosophers, thinkers, and reasoners. Thousands of them exist everywhere. They are generally broad minded and charitable. No class of people on earth are better informed. Individually, their circle of influence is small, while collectively, their influence is great. Many of them are without the energy to make themselves known. Their influence is felt only in a subtle way. Should ever the day arrive when labor becomes little or no more, the world will seriously then recognize them for what they are. The hour will arrive when man will all but cease to labor, by utilizing the unlimited energy that surrounds us. We may then devote our bodies and minds to the higher purposes of human progress. Thus, we may develop in divine wisdom and human devotion to love and peace. With increased knowledge, we shall yet be enabled to employ a greater energy by making it eternally serve us, and entirely eliminating labor with its present disgraceful tearing-down physical process, mainly due to our present ignorance.

"It is quite certain that a person having great mental capacity, ought to have a strong, healthy body to sustain the same.

"Without such support, the person must suffer from inaction or dullness, this, in proportion to inherited bodily weakness. Thus, we often find persons of surprising intelligence, in menial positions, simply through the lack of energy. Their energy is absorbed by the mental requirements. Numerous philosophers, unknown—except to a few friends—are eking out a bare subsistence because the needed energy is lacking. Their dynamic force is not sufficient for body and brain. Philosophers are apt to be slow and inactive. Those whose heads bulge a little or none toward the back, may be happy in the thought that, while they enjoy greater capacity for imagination, their lack of bodily strength is sure to wane in energy and activity.

"A small brain with a large physical dynamo has produced many world-famed specialists, proving that mental activity when backed by a concentrative will and great energy, attains higher results than the individual gifted with larger brain but lacking in physical force and perseverance. The latter is apt to spread activities over a much wider area. The physical must counterbalance the mental in order to secure the adjusted life balance.

"Half the race might acquire fame and fortune did they only possess larger dynamos of energy. We are not, of course, losing sight of those who over-eat, drink, or waste their energy by bad habits. Or such whose physical condition is weak and broken by excessive labor.

"How important, therefore, is vital energy to our success in life. Yet, should we look down on the inactive, or so-called lazy? Are they always to blame? Is not their condition due to lack of energy? Something altogether outside their control? Are not many weak mentally and physically? Would not hard labor be a punishment to all such? So-called bright and active persons often lack mental capacity. Some minds do not grow beyond the age of twelve years. Others may be fully developed at twenty, thirty, or later. Therefore, great minds are such as develop and grow so long as they live. At that point, where a person stubbornly refuses to change his opinion, or to accept a new idea on sound, logical deduction, may it not be said that this mind has ceased to further develop?

"Let us now consider those persons of great energy, but of small mental capacity. Though the mind has ceased to develop, we find their physical energy is increased rather than impaired thereby. Hence, if their energy be concentrated, a certain great success is sure to result. Every walk of life exhibits men of this type— eminently renowned. These men are lost, their words sound empty, and ofttimes their ideas are positively silly, when they attempt to reach beyond the profession in which they excel. One profession is enough for any one mind to cover. No person can be a successful theologian and mechanic at the same time. In all matters, except their chosen profession, such men are absolutely helpless. The evil day arrives when they are finally undone, when they have either forgotten themselves, or the ego has led them to altogether unsuited paths. In this domain, we discover successful butchers giving positive opinions on opera; beer and whiskey manufacturers laying down the laws of health; ministers telling ladies how to dress; judges giving advice to mothers, and politicians telling the dear public how to become honest citizens. A judge should be a man of imagination. He must continually place himself in the position of others, if he would deliver wise and just decisions.

CHAPTER XV.

"ALL matter contains force," read Finley. "Life expresses intelligent force. Intelligent force expresses itself in so-called vegetable and animal life. Both forms are made up of chemical elements, which are controlled, or kept together, by intelligent life. When this intelligent life departs, the elements disintegrate. None of the elements is lost, they simply scatter, and await the time when they are again called into action by intelligent life. The amount of intelligent life varies from the lowest form of weed to the highest type of human being.

"It is a well-known fact that among the higher types of what are termed vegetable life, we find all the senses of hearing, seeing, feeling, and probably taste. There is no adequate reason for doubting that every leaf contains several eyes, and that it gathers from the great storehouse of all the elements of food—the air—its life and strength. It is possible that each separate leaf may send to and receive messages from others of its kind. Therefore, vegetable life may be conscious life, for aught with eyes that can see, must possess a brain. Degrees in size and shape represent proportionate degrees of consciousness. To claim that vegetable life has a certain amount of consciousness may be a new thought, which may undoubtedly and will eventually be found to be a

154

fact.   Animal life, so-called, begins by common consent with the lowest form of intelligence, the protoplasm.

"Popular theories start, even mankind, from a beginning—as well as all animated life.   The evolution from this embryo beginning is believed by many to have produced every kind of fish, bird, reptile, insect and the varying species of animals existing or ever having existed upon or in this globe we call Earth.

"Think a moment of the tremendously large animals that existed, as we are told, from nine to fifteen million years ago, and those existing to-day—all having evolved from a common source.   The wasp and the butterfly, the elephant or the ant, the horse and the toad, the snake or beautiful lady, all, coming down through the ages, from one common ancestor.   The thought is repelling, unthinkable.   Insofar, as human life is concerned, it is impossible, and no one has or can supply 'The Missing Link' between the Animal and the Human.   I shall give my reasons for this most positive statement later.

"For centuries people have asked each other the question, 'Is mankind a higher form of animal?'   Did he, like the monkey, wear a tail, and for uncounted centuries roam the earth on four legs?

"If there be a supreme intelligence directing all things, why did he start the human mind millions upon millions of years ago, from the lowest form of life—the protoplasm, slowly evolving it through the unknown ages, step by step, through the fish, the bird, the mammal, and finally into man—made in the image of God?   Why did the Maker go to so much trouble?   If an intelligent being made the protoplasm, could He not have made a man in the beginning, and saved all that extra work and ages of time? To admit that we began from the lowest form of life, is to deny the existence of supreme intelligence. If life slowly and painfully evolved through the long ages, from Nature's lowest forms, up to the wonderful, reasoning human being, civilized man, why does he not continue to evolve still further to some higher man form? According to present theories, he was once a bird. He did not remain one. Later on, according to this theory, he was a monkey, he did not remain one, though some of us may act like one. Can man retrograde? We have now represented on distinct parts of the earth, the very lowest, and, at the same moment, the highest type of man. But we have no type so low, in intelligence, that he is not easily distinguished from the highest type of animal. No one dares to claim that the human race can sink so low as to retrograde, to take reverse steps in its evolution. It might become idiotic, diminutive, out of shape and animal like, but can never take a step backward and first become, again, the missing link, then the monkey, and thus continue in its backward march. Mankind's progress has ever been forward and upward. There is no return to the protoplasm by reversing steps through degeneracy, neither can the mammal return to the bird, in any reversed order of retrogression. Everything in nature proves progress to higher and better forms. This, under the intelligent direction of mankind, but nothing of itself voluntarily. Human history and research have proved, that no matter how far separated may have been the tribes of mankind, each, by itself, has voluntarily moved onward and upward. On the other hand, no living thing apart from man has evolved a single forward step or increased its knowledge one particle.

"A few writers have suggested that the monkey represents a form of degenerate man. This questions the principle of evolution, by accounting for the higher form of monkey through man's degeneracy. The question of the soul is also involved, if we must accept either evolution or revolution.

"Before considering this subject, let us, if we can, first arrive at some acceptable definition of soul. Soul is something separate and apart from life. Soul expresses itself through the mind of mankind alone. Soul is the personality. It is the real person who lives in and directs the body, and is entirely separate and apart from the physical being. Its existence is forever. It operates through the mind, yet, it is not the mind. If as a great many reason, the soul is the mind, and mankind evolved from the lower forms of life, then, everything living has more or less soul—in proportion to its intelligence. If we must accept the popular and scientific proposition, that the mind of man has, through uncountable ages, laboriously and slowly evolved from the lowest form of life to its present exalted condition, then the mind, or soul, must have been of little consequence in the lowest form. Man, in that case, was an unreasoning fish for many ages. Then a flying fish, a flying bird, of little 'instinct,' i. e., of small and limited intelligence. Really, a dull cow or horse for ages upon ages, then monkey, and finally the unknown 'missing link.' What inspiration had the coming man THEN, to take each succeeding step forward, that no animal NOW takes?

"How can the lower forms of life improve, or evolve into higher forms, without example or man's intelligent and guiding hand? You reply by saying, man never had example set him. No, nor has he NOW. Yet he is progressing and perfecting himself and everything around him—voluntarily. It matters not, whether mountains or seas separate him from his brother, or whether tribes live in close communication with one another, voluntarily man goes forward.

"Man is a reasoning being. No animal reasons. They may be taught to imitate, but never to reason.

"Tales are told to prove that animals do reason, but, outside the domesticated and taught by man, the animal mind has not materially changed in ages. Climate and environment alter in a measure, and necessity drives him to differing foods, which may change his color, or his form, but time has not evolved a greater or a more reasoning mind. Should the mind of any animal through example, or by lengthened process of teaching, develop, will not the next generation return to exactly the same original state? If the domestic animal, dog, can be improved some little by generations of training, would he voluntarily improve, if left to himself? If man was once lower in the scale of intelligence than the dog now is, why did he voluntarily advance? The dog, now, has the assistance and example set by man, but he cannot even be forced to advance permanently one particle; therefore, are we to believe that we are but highly developed animals, whose minds have evolved by the process intimated, or, we are divine, have we not always been divine—a divine being with a personality—a soul given by God? Which position, fairly taken, seems the more reasonable? To say that I WAS an animal proves that I am one NOW. Must I, therefore, recognize every form of animal life on the earth as being a relative? Must I impose continually upon these relations for my living? By killing a bird, am I destroying a future and possible new race of man, or, a former relative?

CHAPTER XVI

THE DREAM

WHILE comfortably seated alone in my kitchen arm-chair late one evening, in the early part of July, a loud rap, a-tap, tap, sounded at the door leading out to the laundry house. "Who can it be, at this late hour?" I said aloud to myself. "It cannot be Sally—she would not rap," I thought.

It was an unusually cold and disagreeable evening for July. It had been raining all day, and it was now beating still harder against the west windows. I could hear the creaking branches of the large maple tree, standing near the house, as the wind blew against them, causing a rapid creak, crack, tat, at increasing and irregular intervals.

Sam, with customary thoughtfulness, had built a wood fire. The night grown chilly, I had drawn my chair up nearer to the fire's dying embers.

To watch better the occasional flashes of lightning, I had turned down the flame of the oil lamp. From my easy chair, and with a feeling of increasing security, I enjoyed the drumming sound of the rain, as it beat against the windows, accompanying the roar of the wind through the great giant trees outside. It seemed to lull, yet raise a feeling of half comfort and half fear. The moaning wind, the tat, a-tat, tat, and the low rumbling distant thunder, with occasional brilliant flashes of lightning, caused me at moments to feel uneasy. The vibration of the thunder shook the windows, rattled the kettles and dishes in the pantry, and caused the old stair leading to the chambers above to quake, as if some spirit bent on mischief was trying to noisily descend and do the house and me harm. Several times, I imagined I heard some one softly breathing on the stairs, and then, an easy tread. In a little while, another quake. Each moment, I would turn my face in the direction of some darkly outlined winding form, vainly straining in expectancy, to see a shadowy, creeping figure. As I looked, cold chills ran up and down my back, and I felt as if my hair was standing upright.

Several times I had timidly asked, "Is that you, Julie?" and no reply coming, my lonesomeness only increased. Therefore, when the rap, a-tap, tap, again sounded, my nerves were so unstrung that the knock startled me, and for half a minute I did not have courage enough to utter a word. But when the third rap, a-tap, tap, suddenly struck my ear, accompanied by a low mumbling as if some one were swearing in a subdued foreign tongue, it impressed me with a feeling of bravery and a welcome return of nerve.

"Who is it?" said I, as gruffly as I could speak.

"Von Posen, I am. In let me go," answered the unmistakable voice of Adolph.

I hastened to open the door, and after arranging him comfortably before the fire, he began by saying that his marvelous hydro-aeroplane was complete. I had already informed him, that within a few days, I expected to make a trip for the National Scientific Society. I had also promised the family, that this would be my last trip in

aviation, and I desired to use the machine Adolph was
building, as it would be larger, more powerful and safer
if the principles of construction worked.   Adolph replied that the machine/would be complete and ready by
the time specified.

Now, here I had Adolph, on this stormy night,—
Adolph the enthusiastic inventor.   He had come to tell
me the machine was "done"!

On making this announcement, I felt as though I might
fall upon his neck and name him, "my great and noble
friend."   As it was, my joy knew no bounds.   So far
was he concerned, that he did not appear in the least
affected.   It was several minutes after this occurrence,
before I suffered myself to speak—fearing to betray
any agitation.

"Why, my dear Adolph, you have not asked for more
than two dollars' worth of material since I agreed with
you last Fall.   Are you in debt for everything?"   I
anxiously inquired.

"No-o-o.   I buy myself und cash pay," he proudly replied.

"Well, well," I said to myself.   "So he deceived me.
He DID have money when he came here, or he has pro-
cured it, somehow, since.   Ah, I have it!   He has borrowed it, perhaps, from Sally.   She's been with our family for years.   She has always earned good wages, and
I know her to be frugal—saving.   Indeed, I never knew
her to spend a cent of her own money.   Now, Adolph
has been keeping company with her—yes, he must have
borrowed Sally's money.   I'll ask him."

"Adolph," I slowly began, "have you—been—er—getting or borrowing money from Sally?"

"No-o-o," he answered.

"Then, how could you have bought material—a couple of gasoline engines? And everything!—without money?"

"I buy, I pay. Noddings you pay!" is all he would say.

I thanked him for calling, and requested that he have the machine on the field the following day. If the weather favored, I resolved to try it out, and then attempt my last trip. I also told him, I would repay his kindness in advancing the money for further construction.

Adolph, rising, promised to have everything in readiness to show us. Then, in haste, he rejoined his adorable Sally who patiently awaited his return to the wash house.

After he had gone, I again settled back in the old easy-chair, trying to picture what this wonderful machine would look like.

The news of its construction was ripe, it had already leaked out. I rather blamed Sam for selling this choice piece of information to the papers, but, of course, he denied the fact, declaring that he would never dream of selling news bearing so much import for less than a thousand dollars. I subsequently believed that Sam had purposely let the news leak out to some city reporter for little more than fifty cents. It must have been Sam, I thought, for there wasn't a word of truth in the published items.

As I sat thinking, occasional flashes of lightning lit up the path leading from the east kitchen door to the front gate.

"Hark! Who's that?" I said, half aloud, as the sound of a voice pitched at high key, sounded above the roar of the storm without. "Somebody talking! They're on the road, outside," and I as quickly ran to the door, and swinging it wide open, peered into the blackness of the night—but alas, I could discern nothing. Soon, however, a flash from the sky plainly revealed the road in front. To my amazement, as plain as though it were midday, I recognized Jasper, slowly passing on his way home. What could have brought him out at that hour, and on such a night? It must be now past one o'clock!

"Jasper, Jasper!" I yelled at the top of my voice. Not hearing him reply, I again called out, "Hey, there,—Jasper! This is John!" Now he must hear me, I thought, and I breathlessly waited, straining my eyes to penetrate the darkness,—but no answer came. What could it mean, I thought. "If I don't hear him call back, I'll don the heaviest coat and go out after him"—I mumbled to myself. Just then, there came another distinct flash of lightning and again I saw him. He was standing erect now—out there in the storm. His hair and beard were blowing with the gale. The flash was only for an instant, but it revealed him standing there, apparently fighting off some one. Just then, I heard him call with vehemence—"I tell you, keep out of my way! You're always lurking around with your old white horse."

"Can I help you home, Jasper?" I heard the voice ask.

"No, you can't help me home. Don't touch me! I always hated the sight of you. Git out!"

Here, the conversation deeply interested me. Who in the world could be bothering him at this hour? I walked out on the kitchen piazza. Though it was very dark, Jasper seemed to notice me immediately.

"Good morning, John," he shouted.

"What are you doing out there in the storm at this hour?" I called back, without answering his salutation.

"Won't you come in and get warmed?" I added, beckoning hastily to him.

"No, I'm all right, John. Old age is always exposed and gets accustomed to storms."

"To whom were you talking?" I asked.

"Why, that was old man Azreal. He had his old white horse right across the path, and as I came along without warning, nearly run into it. He's a reg'lar old night hawk. He's always around late botherin' people. He's lookin' fer feed now along th' roadside, fer his old horse. He's th' hungriest critter I ever seen. Gosh, 'twas a cloase shave fer me all rite. An' he's got his old scythe an' is cuttin' what he can find fer that bony animal."

Without bidding me a further good-night, Jasper disappeared in the darkness. Though I watched and waited for a considerable time, the frequent flashes revealed no one in sight.

Slowly I returned to my chair. The noise had evidently awakened one of the family, for I heard my wife, Julie, moving about in her room.

The chill seemed suddenly to have left the air. It had also ceased to rain, so I left the door open to admit the invigorating air. Ah, now I took a deep breath. I filled my lungs with its sweet and pure, health-giving life. How my blood tingled as I drew in the deep draughts, laden as with the sweetness of new-mown hay, and the pungent smell of garden flowers. It imparted a strong and gratifying sensation, and made me feel as though I were suddenly transformed into a modern Samson.

The wind had now died down to a gentle summer breeze. The fire in the grate felt no longer comfortable, so I withdrew my chair some distance. Under the influ-

ence of pleasant feelings, my mind naturally reverted to
the subject of aviation. In this position, I had been quite
a time sitting, when I heard the front gate, as if some
one opened, and was again softly closing it. I listened
awhile, but hearing nothing more, adjudged the whole
thing an hallucination. But, again the noises were repeated. I arose now from my chair; tiptoed to the open
door, and peered out and down the path leading to the
gate. I could discern no one, though I stood watching
for several minutes. Then I heard a movement around upstairs. The creaking of the stairs announced that some
one was coming.

"Who is it?" I inquired.

"It's only me," softly answered Paul.

I did not ask him why he had joined me, and without
further words, I again sat down. Paul drew a chair close
to mine. For some time neither of us uttered a word, and
the lateness of the hour had made me somewhat drowsy.

"I came down to keep you company," he said finally.
"It's past two o'clock. Why is the door wide open?
Darkness invites danger, Dad. Evil ever surrounds us.
Those who invite danger, soonest suffer from it."

"I have no fear, Paul. Many believe that, what happens, could not have been avoided."

"Did not the old Doctor say, Dad, there is an unchanging law in nature, affecting every act we do? And so life
is made up of acts dependent upon our own judgment of
right and wrong. One minute our doings agree with that
unchanging law, the next minute our acts oppose it. And
so our lives are made up of agreement first, and then dis-
agreement with nature's laws—right—then wrong,—
good and evil. If we study ourselves, we may learn to so

guide our acts, that they will be more often right than wrong. They will build us up instead of destroying. By opening the door, you are inviting danger. Self-preservation is the first law of nature."

"But, what have I to fear, Paul?"

"First, only ourselves—our judgments. We sometimes destroy ourselves. I overheard you calling to Jasper, and I heard him tell you that old Azreal was again stalking around. He may yet see the door open. If he does, Dad——," here Paul sobbed aloud—"he will give you a warning,—you'll never forget."

"I've always been pretty healthy, Paul. If he ever tackles me, I win out," I rejoined.

"That's the trouble with us all, we're fools, and glory in our own strength."

"The mere mention of Azreal's name always gave me an uncomfortable feeling. He is so unpopular in town that only the old and disappointed ever seek his acquaintance," continued Paul. "As for me, I have never thought him half as bad as he's pictured. He is related to Doctor Birth. They are friends, not enemies, as most people believe! They do fine team work. The doctor does nothing but sow, Azreal does all the reaping.

"Yes, both are very successful," Paul remarked. "But what of Doctor Science and Lawyer Fact? Are they not more important in the community,—in teaching us the way to live?"

"No, Paul. Old man Reason is our greatest helper. Next in importance to the sowing and reaping farmers, he stands ahead of everybody hereabouts. Some people deem him insane, and foolish, and generally avoid him. Alas, what a calamity in our lives, when we refuse to lis-

ten to Reason. How they close their ears to his sig-
nificant voice. He alone preserves the good. Indeed, the
affairs of this town will never be conducted properly,
nor the people come into their own, until they listen to his
voice. Old Crimes never yet listened to him, nor never
will. He hates Reason!"

"Will some always suffer through poverty and dirt,
due to their lack of respect for Reason?" asked Paul.

"No. Old Father Time will some day correct these and
other evils. He's methodical, slow but sure. He'll accomplish his work in due course and set things aright."

"Yes, but he's so dreadfully slow," said Paul, impatiently.

"To some people, he may appear so, for those who love
Pleasure seeking he's too fast. Time passes here every
day, and I often use him to advantage. Frequent use
entitles me to the right to pronounce him a most valuable
business man. Of all the business men in this section, I
think he leads. If you use him aright, he'll help you. He
hates these lazy fellows who are ever trying to impose
upon him. You, perhaps, think him slow, because you
can't hurry him."

"I know he's a great friend of Azreal," persisted Paul.

"Yes, he's a friend of all, if they understand," I answered.

For a few minutes, neither of us said anything more.
Finally, Paul laid his head over on my shoulder, and as
I sat quietly thinking, I became conscious he had gone
to sleep. His head was so close to mine that his heavy
rhythmic breathing prevented my hearing the approach
of a figure, whose dimly outlined shadow suddenly appeared in the open doorway. Before I could utter a word,

unannounced, it silently strode into the kitchen to within a few paces of where we sat.

"Sh-e-e-e-!" it said, holding up a warning finger to its lips, as I drew back with a movement as if to arise, and defend myself; for I instinctively knew it meant harm. The very atmosphere surrounding it seemed to have turned cold, and instantly affected me with a faint or sickly feeling, that caused a cold perspiration to stand out on my face and body.

"Don't move, John, or you'll wake up Paul," said the apparition.

"Who are you?" said I, in a low but firm tone.

"Be very quiet," warned the form, again placing a long, bony finger to its lips, and after gazing around in silence, as if to make sure that no one was alert, it continued, in a voice almost inaudible.

"Fear not! I am Azreal! I have a message for you. I tried to deliver one to Jasper, but he fought me off, and ran from me. I took advantage of the opportunity to call—while your door was open."

"But that is no excuse for calling at this late hour," I said reproachfully.

"Do not complain, John! I deliver my messages of warning only when the minds of those for whom they are intended are most free, which is invariably through the night. I reap, however, at all hours. Why do you fear me? I am a friend to everybody, but a few welcome me as such."

"They do not understand you then," I consolingly answered.

"True. When Reason is absent, Suspicion is always present, though Suspicion sometimes begets Reason.

Everything lives on something. Some things live on many things. Many things live on one thing, but I live upon everything. That proves that I'm not particular. What I take belongs to me, but I take nothing without life, for 'tis the life and not the old body that I want,—for planting in a new body."

He now spoke so low, and in such a far away tone, that I had great difficulty in hearing above the sound made by the soft summer breeze as it blew through the piazza. For a few minutes again, neither of us spoke, when he said finally,—"You are going out on the aviation field to-day?"

"No, not to-day—why, yes—it's after midnight—to-day,—this afternoon," I stammered. Then I thought I heard him softly laugh, and recognized a little chuckle of apparent satisfaction, as he rubbed his long, bony hands together. It grated on my nerves and sounded in my ears, as though his hands were made of cracked ice, which he was quickly rubbing together.

"I now warn you, John Bacon, not to make that trip! Your imperfect machine defies the law of gravitation. That law shall prevail against you, but I shall be there to keep you company, and to administer comfort while you occupy your present body. Beware! If you go——"

"Father! Father! Wake up! Wake up!" cried Paul, "you are keeping the whole family awake with your heavy snoring. It's after two o'clock. You've been making a frightful racket, and I have come down to wake you up."

"Have I been asleep?" I stammered.—"Well, I'm glad 'twas but a dream."

CHAPTER XVII

ON THE FIELD

On retiring, and after a brief slumber I awoke early. The first thing that came to mind was my dream, touching old Azreal and his warning. After I had taken my accustomed morning walk in the garden, however, aided by that glorious July day, when every tree, shrub and plant seemed to lift its head in thankfulness for the scrubbing and bath Dame Nature had given to all during the night, I soon forgot my experience with Azreal in my dream.

Ah, how the fresh balmy air sent the blood coursing through my veins, thrilling and filling me with new energy. How I gloried in my strength! What delight it imparted, as I took one deep breath after another of that clear and perfumed air. And all nature seemed to share in my rejoicing, each living thing becoming active and busy in its work. Ants and bees, and butterflies, were each steeped in their activities. It may have been that they, too, viewed the world as I then beheld it. Through my now optimistic eyes everything, everybody, had been tinged with the beautiful. No expression in words could quite depict my feeling of thankfulness to my Maker and for every worldly blessing.

"John Bacon"—I repeated to myself—"here you are, strong and healthy, lacking nothing that your heart can reasonably desire. Amidst surroundings second to no Garden of Eden, and an environment of love and truth, that a Calvin might have envied. Why should I not feel joyous and be thankful for all these blessings?" The question was put with all sincerity to my inner self. I bowed my head, and in humility, awaited the answer. "I am thankful"—came the quiet response. I raised my head quickly, feeling refreshed in body and mind, and went into the house.

"Where is Sam?" I asked of my wife.

"He's at his station, in the front hall," she answered.

"Well, and where's Sally?" then noticing the latter coming from the pantry, I accosted her. "Oh, say, Sally —do you think Von—Mister Adolph Von Posen will be ready with my machine on the field to-day?"

"I never interfere with other people's business," she replied, as she turned with an abrupt swirl of her skirts, and vigorously slamming the door, disappeared from view.

"Don't mind her, John," soothingly suggested my wife. "She told me that she and Adolph had just experienced their first quarrel. It appears she accused him of taking onions from the stock in the laundry. He passed this quietly enough, but, when in anger she accused him of breathing on her pansies in the window box and killing them, he put his hands in his pockets, closed his eyes and struck out for bachelor apartments in the village."

"Sam," I said, turning, "will you go down to the village and help Adolph move the machine out on the field? We will all be there to meet you. You may require several horses to do this, but hire as many as needed. We shall retain our own here, as we intend to drive over instead of going by train. I have much scientific material to take up with the 'plane, that must go from here with us. Be sure to be there early, Sam, as I expect a big crowd. The meet has been advertised extensively—this beautiful day is sure to bring everybody out," I emphasized.

Just, however, as we were all about to start in the old "beach wagon"—conveying a dozen or more of our household and friends, Ellen became so ill suddenly that Finley was sent post-haste for our doctor. Thus, commenced our disappointments. We quickly realized that neither Finley nor Ellen would be on the field to witness my final flight. Both wished me an affectionate "God speed," and made the prediction that the trip would prove intensely interesting and profitable in every particular.

We reached the field long before the crowds came. The anticipation of seeing the great, powerful hydro-aeroplane that the ingenious Adolph had been over a year secretly constructing and the admiration and surprise it would certainly create, when the public, coupled with my envious fellow aviators, would for the first time behold soaring like a huge albatross in the cloudless sky, induced in me a certain excitement and nervousness.

Yes, there, standing in front of the hangar, was Sam and Adolph Von Posen, but where was the new machine? I scanned their faces for a reply, yet both only looked perfectly serene and altogether happy. Sam was smiling, while Adolph looked perfectly calm and self-satisfied. Yet the hydro-aeroplane was not there.

In order to overcome the shock of feeling and uncertainty, I began within myself to excuse the fact by thinking that perhaps the 'plane had been delayed on the road, but if that were the only cause of complaint I

was then prepared to severely take them both to task for
not staying by this priceless invention.

"How do you do, ladies and gentlemen, you all look
as happy and quite as blooming as this day is lovely,"
said Sam, politely taking off his hat and making a low
bow as we came within hearing distance. "And my dear
Mr. Bacon," he added, after a pause sufficiently long for
all to mumble a return of the salutation, "the genial
character and wonderful genius, my bosom friend, Adolph,
here, has now only to show you his ingenious contrivance, with a view to produce a wave of admiration
to pass through your intelligent faces. He has it right
here."

"Right here?" said I, giving Sam a savage look. "Do
my eyes deceive me, or is he simply lying," I thought. "I
don't see it!" I shouted with vehemence.

"It is der baber in, right here!" returned Adolph, pointing to a bundle done up with newspapers and secured by
several yards of pink-colored string.

"What do you mean?" I demanded with more force
than politeness. "Do you mean to say that the eighty-
foot aeroplane you have been constructing for over a year
is wrapped in the dinky, picayune and greasy-looking
bundle at your feet?" and doubling up my fists I shook
my right close to his face.

"I am gladt you vill like id. I show you," he replied,
quickly stooping over and breaking the strings.

"Don't! Don't show me. I don't want to see it. I
told you to make the planes eighty feet in length. How
long did you make them?" I questioned.

"I make them eight inches. A sample it is. I try it.
It like a kite flies, lofely."

"Don't undo it! I don't care to see it," I protested, and the disappointment nearly unnerved me.

All our friends had come upon the field especially to behold my try-out of the wonderful hydro-aeroplane I had so frequently described and pictured in such glowing terms. Then again, the news had gotten into the papers, and was now widely advertised. Doubtless there would be several thousands on the field who had paid and others still to pay their entrance fee to the grounds, every one would be compelled to go away dissatisfied. Public opinion is ever suspicious of those who make excuses. "Reasons for failure don't count for much," I thought. The public salaams to success, no matter how obtained, if even in the dark.

Adolph had, with undoubted ability, neatly and scientifically constructed this eight-inch model entire with engines, and in detail complete, out of cardboard and strong, coarse thread. It was a wonder to look at, a marvel of ingenuity that must have demanded unflagging patience and great persistence. Of course, it was a mere toy to behold, and signified no practical purpose—except as a model. A couple of fat mice could not with safety have flown in it.

But why should I blame him for an honest mistake? His unfamiliarity with English was the cause of the whole trouble. I said "eighty" feet, which he misinterpreted for eight inches. Here is an additional reason, I thought, why language should become universal.

Of course, on second thought, I went carefully over and examined the model when I had reasoned myself out of that angry and disagreeable mood. I also complimented him upon his achievement and shook him heartily by the hand. He was a man of truly marvelous imagination and ability.

Differences in language, I divined, also meant differences in customs, habits and tastes. We do not understand each other sufficiently so we are generally either suspicious or patronizing. With Adolph, on analysis, we differed in taste and smell alone.

I could see disappointment plainly written on the faces of my wife and son, though with me, they continued to speak lightly of the consequences. They realized that there would be some, who, with ill grace, would take the disappointment of my failure to appear in the much-heralded hydro-aeroplane, while the crowd, in the aggregate, would not discern the difference. To me it was a keen disappointment—my first failure, indeed, to do as I had promised.

There was no time to lose. So, with Paul's assistance, I brought out my old machine. After looking it well over and carefully—for it had not been used in a year— we filled the tanks with gasoline, tested the engine, and after some little adjustments everything was found to work perfectly. I then arranged all the scientific instruments, took my position out on the field and awaited a favorable opportunity to make the ascent.

I had prepared the old machine so quickly that none of the aviators had noted the fact until I was well out on the field. Only two asked me as to the whereabouts of my new machine. They were busy with their own business and had no time to investigate mine.

The two old cronies, Sam, the blacksmith, Paul and Hester, and my good little wife—all followed me out on the field and formed a circle of happy, smiling faces, with each voice of encouragement trying to out-do the other. Back of it all, I could penetrate their mixed sadness and anxiety. They were well aware that I would make a determined effort to break my own record for flying at the highest altitude of any human being. They all wanted me to accomplish the feat, but they also anticipated some danger.

Sam had not been standing with us long before I discerned scores of young ladies making their way to our party from several different directions. As soon as the vanguard had arrived, immediate interest was lost in everything but Sam. While some few of my friends still stood close beside me, forming quite a respectable company, Sam became the attractive center of a whole flock of feminine beauty. They were of all ages, young girls, old maids with curls, and a fair assortment of widows. Every one sought a private interview with Sam. With one by one, for about a minute, he talked low and earnestly. With each one he made a positive appointment, carefully recording the promise and date in a little book he carried for that apparent purpose. Strange enough, they all minded him like so many soldiers, and departed blushing and smiling in anticipation. Of course, Sam never kept a single one of the appointments. He simply deceived the ladies—each one in turn. Yet, they never seemed to mind it.

For each unkept promise, Sam either worked, or walked or amused himself, or quietly slept a few hours without being disturbed. "They like it," he was wont to declare. "Honest men are generally aggressive, and wimmin hate 'em. It's more comfortable to be a harmless liar, provided you lock yourself in."

On this particular and momentous occasion, Sam, at last, saw fit to turn from his over-flattered group of listeners.

"Excuse me, young ladies, the show is about to commence. I have the weight of this whole—juxta-position on my shoulders, and, as the poet would say, 'We need more air,' and so, my lovely companion, I bid you a most sumptuous adieu. In other words, I'll see you later. Ta, ta," said Sam, swinging gracefully out of the circle that surrounded him, and coming toward us. Indeed, he had shooed them away.

The field was now teeming with life, the excitement increasing every minute. Thousands had come out on the field to enjoy the sport. All were in their best attire— every color of the rainbow represented in dress and parasol; and as the onlookers moved over the field, the scene took on an ever-changing kaleidoscope of vivid hues.

As I scanned the field, I beheld people from every walk of life, and every shade of character. The good and bad, the liberal, the stingy, the brave. The coward, the wise man and the foolish—all were represented there. Midst it all was the jovial and the solemn, side by side, as natural as sunshine and shadow. Yet, human interest in the marvelous was there; the conscious desire to go forward, higher and higher in our mastery of the elements. This really brought them together. Then, in union there is strength—the unconscious purpose of strengthening and carrying forward the everlasting human flight toward perfection.

Perfection can be reached only through the masses. Only in the consensus of opinion we find how far the world is advanced. Individuals may lead the way far in the vanguard, but their ideas must await the army or mass, to catch up, before the advance is certain.

The crowd had now become more noisy. Their exclamations—"There he goes!" "Oh! He's going to tip over!" The "ohs" and the "ahs," the yelling and laughing, all at the same time, this, with the constant buzz and whirr of the machines as the aviators drove back and forth over the field, imparted to the whole scene a strangely modern significance.

We were all amazed when one of the aviators started off with two passengers. It was a sight never to be forgotten when the machine rose gracefully as a bird. As it circled around in spiral-like form, ascending and dipping in the air, it seemed almost human. So perfectly and steadily did it describe circle after circle in spiral arcs, yet going higher and farther, and all but fading from view, like some great guiding spirit assisting humanity to reach some infinite goal, it supplied an inspiration beyond words. When I saw the speck slowly move in an easterly direction until lost to view, I felt as though we had forever parted.

Thirty minutes elapsed before I saw it return overhead. It was then making a bee-line toward the field where we stood, and at more than railroad speed. Down it came, rushing as if it must dash to pieces against the ground; then, suddenly, as it neared the earth, the planes changed their angle, and as gracefully as a swan it alighted gently and without a jar. One mile high and ten forward into the sky, and the return, in perfect safety! "Think of it and dwell upon it," I thought.

"It's half after three, Dad," said Paul.

"I'm all ready," I replied.

As I turned to bid my wife good-by, a vision of old Azreal's white horse seemed to arise before my eyes. A sudden shock passed through me, and I must have staggered not a little, for my wife instantly inquired if I was feeling well. For the first moment in my life, I heartily wished that all might have begged me to remain right where I was. I then could have furnished an excuse to obey that whispered warning—"Remain where you are."

Instead, however, I dimly heard the crowd's insistent cheer, that prolonged yell. They were calling for me—I knew. My wife was flooding me with encouraging appeals, and all my friends, in turn, were trying their utmost to heighten the occasion with joy and promise. Yet, I felt dizzy and sick at heart—for the first time in my life, like a coward. If the earth could have opened under my feet and permitted me to descend out of sight until all excited yellings, as of demons, had ceased, I would have gladly, aye happily, rejoined my family and confessed my weakness. It seemed as if I was being driven to perform something, that an invisible spirit warned me again and over again to desist from doing. But another force—foolish pride—labeled bravery, overcame the warning and my sense of self-preservation. So, like others gone before me, and others yet to come, I disobeyed the kindly premonition.

The good-bys had been said. So, carefully donning my great fur coat and cap, and turning up the widening collar, I took my seat in the machine. Starting up the motors, I let them, for the moment, run at moderate speed with a view to limber and warm them up. Within a minute or two without further design I turned on full power. As the machine rose gracefully in the air, I turned a little and waved my hand to Julie—a parting salute. Then I shouted a last "Good-by."

The whirr of the propeller made so much noise, however, that I could not hear the return salutes, yet I saw from the happy faces, 'mid waving of hats, parasols and handkerchiefs, how the people had joined in shouting their persistent encouragement.

I had been careful to overhaul every part of my engine before starting. Had tested and examined every wire and fastening, including the gasoline tank. As I began to rise I felt conscious of the low hum of a thousand human voices. I did not dare look down. I had determined to fix my mind on the manipulation of the planes. I kept an ear, from the beginning, on any unusual sound that might ensue from the engine's rapid and even stroke. I had made hundreds of previous trips, yet, somehow, I never felt so absolutely alone before. After the lapse of a few minutes, with sounds of the field left far behind, I was tempted to return, but mastered the suggestion and continued to rise rapidly. The whirr of the propellers—making twenty-four hundred revolutions per minute—and the noise from eight pistons, seemed lost in the vastness of space around and above. There was little wind. For purposes of aviation, the atmosphere was perfect. The excitable and violent spirit "Vato"[1] slumbered, or was far away from "Nosmnbdsgrsutt."[2]

[1] "Vato," wind spirit that could excite violent storming wind.
[2] "Nosmnbdsgrsutt," the land of flying men and women.

CHAPTER XVIII

FITTINGLY, the day pointed heavenward, and the Sun's beneficence had robed the Earth in all his glory. Here and there, scattered over the zenith of a great, broad arc, were occasional small, fleecy, softly tinted clouds in gossamer of dainty thinness, which in contrast with the deep, clear blue above imparted a sense of pellucid sereneness and tinged with cheerful quiet a confidence that all the world claimed peace and good-will to man.

A feeling freshened within me was intensified by the rhythmic chug-chug of the eight fast-moving pistons which, replacing martial music, quickened the heart-beat and reflected in my face and hands the hue of perfect health.

The temperature on the field registered seventy-two F., a comfortable and ideal degree to induce an unusually large concourse of people. This, as well as the many feats the aviators were expected to perform, gave great hope and promise for the management. So far as this understanding immediately concerned me, the populace knew it was to be my last supreme and crowning effort, before permanently retiring from the aviation field. Further urging upon the part of the management was, therefore, unnecessary.

For several previous days my fellow aviators had sent

in their congratulations upon my engagement and the generous consideration to secure for the association all scientific data. In turn, I was compelled to explain at great length many of the duties incidental to this final trip. Among other things, I was expected to secure specimens of the air at the various altitudes. To take down, as well, the temperature at each two or three hundred feet—up to the highest point reached.

Prepared for this service, I came upon the field with about six dozen large, sealed glass tubes, exhausted of air. After ascending two thousand feet, I broke the seal from one of the tubes. A sharp hiss followed, caused by the air rushing into the exhausted tube. I immediately resealed the tube, and marked the record upon the tag attached. At every additional three hundred feet of altitude, I broke a seal and secured a specimen of the air. This work, together with keeping watch over my machine, intensified the labor, to say nothing of the precision exacted.

The experiment was not new, but none had succeeded in obtaining air specimens at altitudes of a mile or over. Certainly, specimens had been obtained from mountain heights, balloons and kites, but mine was to be the first effort made from the aeroplane. Indeed, I believed I would exceed, by many thousand feet, a height greater than any known balloon or kite had ascended, or could possibly ascend.

Though the pecuniary reward was comparatively small, for the scientific values attained, the honor was an incentive sufficient to repay all the effort I might make.

In addition to carrying thermometers filled with the spirit of wine, to prevent freezing at high altitudes, I took a condensing hygrometer for measuring the humidity, and many other instruments. These I arranged in convenient positions in front of the machine, that I might observe more accurately the ever-increasing rarification of the atmosphere around me.

At moments, the stillness seemed oppressive. Time and time again, I thought I heard, away down in the depths below, that far-away voice crying, "Good-by, pa-pa, good-by-y"—I listened. Yes, out of the depths below— every little while—I felt sure I heard the cry repeated. With bated breath, and ears strained to catch the slightest sound, I listened, to convince myself whether or not I heard a voice calling, or whether it was purely imagination due to my strained condition. Could it have been the voice of Paul or Ellen calling? I never knew.

The atmosphere had now become too cold for those thinner gloves, so I removed and replaced them with a pair of heavy furs, more suited. To fortify against the increasing intensity of the cold, I pulled the cap well down over my ears, turned up the collar of my great fur coat, so that it remained well poised above my nose in front. I had just completed pulling on my gloves, when —Horrors! Was I falling? Taking a hurried look downward, I estimated that I must have been three thousand feet above earth, and directly over a farming section. Glancing at the aneroid barometer, my estimate was confirmed. It read, "three thousand one hundred feet," while my Centigrade registered 0° C., or about 32° F. Yet, I was much surprised to find the air so cold. The only way I could account for this low temperature at the altitude indicated, was, that I had encountered a much colder and dryer strata of air.

Now, a cock-crow struck my ear. I imagined it sounded quite near, yet, the barometer indicated that I had attained an altitude of more than sixty-two hundred feet. The thermometer read —3° F., or about —20° C. At this height I found myself amidst dense clouds and the mist became so heavy that my furs dripped water. In this cloud I continued to rise until examination of the barometer showed that I was 12,640 feet above sea level. While still cloud bound, my thermometer rose to 28° F. Sounds on earth were perfectly audible, and the rooster's crow seemed only a short distance off.

My machine had, for some time, been taking an upward and eastward course. I estimated, at the moment, that I must at least have been some ten or twelve miles east from the starting-point upon the field. I changed my course, still climbing higher, in a westerly direction. It was not long before I could hear, at first rather indistinctly, but growing more audible as the moments elapsed, the sounds of a great volume of voices on the aviation field.

I now had been out of the cloud but for an instant when I felt my coat, gloves and cap suddenly stiffen, and looking down discovered I had all but turned into a human icicle. The accumulated moisture on the fur had become a chest of solid ice. Leaning forward to look at my instruments, I was surprised to find that the barometer indicated a height of twenty-two thousand three hundred and seventy feet, or nearly four and a half miles. Below me I could see nothing but the cloud through which I had passed; while above, about a mile higher, I discerned another cloud. Doubtless these clouds looked insignificant from the ground, though the one immediately above me must have been about a mile in length. The cold was now intense, but I suffered little, for my fur garments were heavy, and the additional protection of the ice crust tended to prevent any further loss of heat. The air had now become so rarified that much difficulty was encountered in breathing. During the passing moments, I had occasionally broken the seals of the vacuum tubes, allowing them to refill with air, then promptly resealed them. The dread that now possessed me was of aerophobia, which in great altitudes manifests itself in hysteria or extreme nervousness. I made up my mind, at all hazards, to combat this feeling. Strange additional sounds arrested my attention, other than those arising from the multitude below. One recalled the sound of a railroad train, and its apparent nearness was surprising. I manipulated the machine on its ever upward course, first east and then west, in order to always cover the aviation field. When the sounds arising from the multitude decreased it was then evident that I had gone beyond the field in one direction, so I turned again toward the sound. Hearing the voices, I was content, but so soon as my machine moved too far away, east or west of the field, then I immediately became and felt as one alone.

Other dangers, however, not to be lost sight of, threatened, at the tremendous elevation I had now attained. By a new reading of the barometer, I found myself at twenty-nine thousand two hundred and eighty feet—more than five and a half miles in air. The atmosphere had now become so rarified that it was quite painful to breathe.

The thermometer indicated —20° F., and growing colder, I dared not expose the least part of my face. I concluded to expose my eyes no longer to the cold, as I could guide the machine perfectly by sound. I had de-

termined to proceed as long as I could obtain air sufficient to breathe. Soon I discovered my limit had been
reached. Finally I decided to take one more glance at
the instruments; then quickly make a descent. With
great difficulty I gathered sufficient will to open my eyes
and look forward. The barometer gave thirty-four
thousand feet in the air, while the thermometer marked a
temperature of —54° F. Not until I had made this last
attempt, did I fully realize my utter helplessness. I no
longer distinguished sound except an ever-increasing ring
within the ears and an accompanying drowsiness which
I felt I could not overcome. Realizing the seriousness of
my plight, I exercised all the power of will left, to arouse
and shake off the condition. But in vain. All my facul-
ties refused to respond.

I was now genuinely tired—very weary. I needed
sleep. Then there came the awful realization of my condition, and soon the mind might convince itself that a
short nap would not be harmful, but if so, it could really
make no great difference after all. This alternating feeling continued for a few moments. Then an instant of consciousness would flitter through the feeling of drowsiness,
intercepting it and arousing me temporarily. But my
seemingly rigid body did not respond, and nature could
again throw her cloak of unconsciousness around me, and
mercifully shut out all feeling, until strength enough again
returned. Through one of these half-conscious spells I
became suddenly aware that I no longer heard the chug-
chug of the engine pistons. Was I asleep? Or was it all
only a horrible dream? No, it is not a dream! Yes, the
engines have stopped. Why? Why have they stopped?
With a mighty superhuman effort I aroused myself. I

felt now as if all nature, or the power of a hundred demons, could not again put me to sleep. "Why had the
engines stopped?" I cried aloud. "The gasoline has
frozen!" seemed like a returned reply. "Frozen!
Frozen!" I hoarsely whispered. "Yes, yes! The gasoline
must have become solid in this temperature. God, I
forgot that it would freeze! Look! Look! The thermometer marks —150° F. Almighty God!" I yelled as
loud as I could cry out. "I am bereft of a chance! Oh!
Oh! Horror of horrors!" I hoarsely cried, my whole body
quivering like a leaf, while the perspiration became frozen
on my brow.

Now, I'm awake!—I laughed in hysterical glee. I'm
awake! Awake! Then my great plane pitched forward
—gave a lunge. It shivered as if consciously shocked
at the prospect of a six-mile plunge.

Beginning to sink, I stood upright, and with all my
strength, whispered faintly out of a dry and parched
throat, "Help! Help! Oh, God do help me! I'm falling—I'm falling! Ju-lie! Pa-u-u-u-l!" Then everything
was dark and still.

CHAPTER XIX

DROPPING THE PILOT

How long I remained in the unconscious state there were no means of ascertaining, but it seemed not to exceed two or three seconds of time. Coming to my senses, a hurried glance at the barometer showed an altitude of thirty-three thousand feet. Doubt was at once removed, but that my plane was fast falling, which brought again the instant realization of a perilous situation.

Within the fraction of a second I knew again that not a solitary chance remained. The engines had stopped! The gasoline had frozen! Now the machine was descending at lightning-like speed. I could feel my face blanch, and my blood seemed to have frozen within my veins. The horror and suspense seemed to paralyze my very soul; and, as the plane rushed downward with increasing fury, all the important happenings of life seemed outspread before me—rushed before the mind's eye as a moving picture. Seconds seemed like ages of time. Then the vision departed, and I became transfixed with mortal terror. First, sinking back in my seat, as if to avoid the awful consequences, then, clutching wildly at the air in my madness of despair; and dying ten thousand deaths as the 'plane descended with ever-increasing speed, lurching, yet plunging in its swift descent. How my heart sank within me. Alone, above the clouds, and flying as a meteor

toward the earth, rushing half consciously toward the inevitable! Then, I prayed for unconsciousness—but alas,
prayer was for three seconds only. I involuntarily stood
up numb, lifeless—sick. I again clutched the wheel mechanically—with bare hands. My gloves becoming heavy
with frozen ice had dropped when I became unconscious,
and had released my hands from the steering wheel. I
clung on again with a death-like grip, my jaws meanwhile chattering and my whole body shaking from spasms
of fright.

Suddenly, and without warning, I felt something, even
colder than the intense chilliness of the atmosphere,
grasp my hands. A new terror seized me, for, behold,
standing and confronting me, WAS ANOTHER PER-
SON. The figure entirely robed in black, had its head so
bent forward, that I could not regard the face, thus preventing me from discerning whether it was man or woman.
With a terrible vise-like grip, it placed its hands over mine,
and seemed to force the steering wheel around,—first one
way, then the reverse. I had not the strength to resist,
neither could I utter a sound. Any attempt to cry out
seemed only the more to choke off the words.

How it was possible for any one to have hidden in the
machine, and to have accompanied me thus far unnoticed,
I failed to understand. Then again, the somber and frail
robe of the figure seemed far too thin to afford protection against the temperature of the altitude now attained,
the thermometer indicating more than fifty-five degrees
below zero. Surely, any living thing unprotected by suit-
able garments would have succumbed in less than a
minute. What could this stranger mean or be doing
here? How had this figure stalked or crawled in front of

me unobserved? Why was it turning the steering wheel so determinedly, and in so mysterious a fashion? Why did it crush my bleeding hands in its icy grasp? I might query and question, but alas for the reply!

Now my aeroplane was slowly turning! Soon it stood perpendicular in the air—the great eight-cylinder, or one hundred fifty horse-power engines having by reason of their weight, swung beneath. As the great machine swayed and oscillated in its downward course, the speed seemed to have increased tenfold. As the mighty machine rushed and plunged, the air from below seemed to lift me by its power, as if blown upward in the air by some cyclonic blast. The siren-like screeching sound caused by its rapid fall still increased, until it became a horrible, high-keyed shriek. As we rushed down, ever down, my mysterious companion seemed to increase that vise-clutch on my hands, squeezing with mightier strength. Yet, the pain of all this was, somehow, driving fear from me, increasing my strength, and inducing a calmer attitude. Ultimately, I leaned forward and addressing my companion, in a choking voice full of anguish, I cried with all the strength left me, "Will you please let go my hands?" And then, noting that the stranger paid no attention, I quickly demanded—"Take your hands away! Let go! Don't you see we are falling—to—to certain death?" Still the figure did not move, nor could I imagine who or what it was. The pain was now more intense and as the form took fresh hold of my hands, a steady, throbbing ache seemed like unto a huge club rapidly beating, and driving by its torture to the border of unconsciousness, or holding me to suffer while dying through countless deaths.

Then came relief, as my strength seemed to temporarily return. Again, I gathered myself together in another mighty effort to wrest myself from the strangling grip. Oh, for some release! I turned, I twisted, tugged and pulled; yet the stranger appeared immovable,—those long, bony tentacle-like fingers retained their hold.

Again I cried, my breath coming fast, and breathing with intense difficulty: "Let—let—go! Don't—you—see—w-we a-are—f-falling, y-y-you—f-fiend! Damn you! Damn you, let go!"

"Calm yourself, John," the voice at last returned, in clear, measured tones. "It is I, Azreal. Your friend and neighbor." Thus addressing me, he looked up. Truly, it was the same Azreal, yes, the same that appeared to me in my dream of the night before. Here he was before me. There was no time now for reflection—I knew it would all soon be over. I readily discerned the Earth beneath; it looked as if coming rapidly toward the 'plane to greet and save us on its great loving bosom.

"We will arrive there soon now, John. Be calm," I heard Azreal softly whisper. Indeed, his gentleness amazed me.

Still clutching the wheel with all remaining strength, I felt each hope, all vain desires, fast slipping from me. Should I then, throw myself with one mighty effort, into the loving arms of my companion Azreal!

Down, ever down, we flew. The 'plane plunging and turning, and shrieking with human-like agony of fear. How the wings ripped and tore to shreds and tatters as swaying from side to side, rolling and tumbling like a fast revolving wheel, they cut through the air! Now, the wires snapped, while the wings broke and threshed, their

ends beating through the upward howling wind. Strange
and darkling colors now oppressed the sight. The ear-
drums numbed, save for the thousand-and-one weird beat-
ings beyond all human ken. And withal, the ever-present,
half-conscious dread of life extinction—repellent to the
vigorous soul.

"Oh, wife! Oh, my loved ones!" I cried despairingly.
Oh, for just one more chance!—Only one more—and
then? But I knew it could not be. "Then submission,"
I thought—resignation to the inevitable. A hush seemed
now to have fallen upon all. But again the faces on the
field were revealed, ashen colored and drawn, as if some
startling calamity were at hand. Yes—they were watching—looking up. Yes, and there stood Azreal's old white
horse in the midst of all. There was Julie—my dear
wife. And Paul and Hester, and all others of my family
and friends. Did they know it was I who was falling?
Yes, and I shall plunge them into life-long grief! The
human agony of that one thought alone would have suf-
ficed to dethrone the mind. But, at that moment I heard
Azreal say again, "Come, John." "Yes, Yezad, Yezad,
Yezad"—I repeated aloud, and then, in another instant,
I knew no more.

Upon again opening my eyes, a brief second later, I
beheld the aeroplane with my own body dropping from
the machine. I saw both shoot downward with meteoric
speed. Pain and all anxiety had now entirely left me. I
felt happy, calm and supremely serene. Strange, I no
longer saw Azreal, and his old white steed had also disappeared. The concourse of people were still watching—
looking upward. Suddenly, as the machine and my body
struck the earth and seemed to rebound, there arose a

mighty cry of horror. As this, mingled with exclamations of intense grief increased, pandemonium reigned
around the field, and panic-stricken groups rapidly re-
treated from the scene.

I heard distinctly the hysterical cries, mingled with
sobs, and realized to the full, the excitement and sorrow.
But it no longer affected me as it might have a while ago.
From the group of young and old in front of whom my
body had fallen, I beheld a young man suddenly spring
forward over my quivering body, now spread upon the
sward a jellied torn mass. His companions followed him
with hands uplifted and half-averted faces, as if to shield
their hearts from some mighty blow. I saw the same
young man fall upon his knees and prostrate himself
upon my lifeless form, and one by one, his young and old
companions came and knelt beside him.

But, ah! One woman from among them has toppled
over, and I see a very old man and another woman rubbing her hands and attempting to restore—to console her.
Now, they all kneel as if in prayer, and I see their bodies
heaving as they sob and utter subdued moans. Then the
young man is looking up in my direction—he raises his
hands slowly and painfully. Then rising to his feet, he
all but staggers upon my prostrate form. His hands are
pressed to his brows. Stopping short, he again looks up.
Listen!—he is speaking as he stretches forth his hands
toward the sky above. Finally sounds are wafted to
my hearing. They are the murmurs of voices full of pain
and suffering and tear-stained faces. The young man's
anguish is too deep for words. Twice I hear him speak.
He is calling, "Father!—Father!" Then all is still. As
I move forward and upward, I see them lead him away.

CHAPTER XX

THE earth had now disappeared from view, and I found myself apparently alone in that great measureless realm known as space.

So interested had I become in watching the young man and the afflicted woman whom he appeared to treat as a Mother, and the small group of people surrounding them, who so pitifully demonstrated their intense grief, that I had not, up to the moment, entered upon any consideration of my changed condition. Far and beyond it all, as I now swiftly receded from this sorrow-stricken group—and the field was fast emptying of its wild, thoughtless and terror-stricken concourse—I became conscious of a feeling that I was impelled on and on, destined to reach some distant destination.

My body lay upon the field; that I knew. Yet, I could see and think as intensely as ever, lacking only in the longing for family or friends. I felt as if bereft of all regrets—all loving memories forever left behind. There was one exception. A deep sorrow filled me, for evil done my companions during life on earth. All sensation appealed to me as mental only. "In this realm," I thought, "my body would be superfluous and unnecessary."

An examination of my surroundings now revealed other and startling surprises. To my utter astonish-

195

ment, while I failed to rid myself of the impression that I still possessed a body with hands and feet, I could neither see nor feel either. Indeed, I was invisible to myself. I did not breathe. Neither did I walk or run. I seemed only to will myself along while borne through space—without feeling of heat or cold, or atmospheric pressure. My one desire was to reach some destination where I was about to will myself. Suddenly, my thoughts were arrested by many new and wonderful visions rapidly appearing in surrounding space.

While my desire was to go on and still on—whither I knew not—new interests retarded the consummation. Since all bodily feeling of either sickness or pain, or sense of touch, no longer retarded my mental freedom, I became immediately enthusiastic in my attitude toward the Universe and filled with deep sense of wonder and admiration. It was purely a psychic state, wherein everything is either mental pleasure or mental pain.

But very few of the many things revealed were anticipated by me. My next and greatest surprise was the sudden discovery that I was not alone! It was no slight shock, this startling revelation. I had a companion!—A man, who was moving along with me, and only a few feet away. His face was turned away, but from a quick survey I adjudged him to be about my own age and build. There he was, as if floating along with me in silence. "Where did he come from?" thought I—"and who is he?" Then, there was a something so familiar about him that when he finally turned his face in my direction I willed myself to beckon him with my invisible hands.

He must have seen the movement, for he smiled and looked straight ahead. Yet, he made no effort to come nearer. So I waited until sure he would again see me. Then, smiling in return, I beckoned. This time he came quite close. Being near enough, I imagined, to hear my voice, I attempted again to address him. But, to my dismay and great disappointment, not a sound nor word could I utter. "This is too bad," I said to myself dejectedly. "Yes, it is too bad," returned a mental message to my mind—just as plainly as though my companion had spoken aloud.

"Whose voice was it?" I asked myself. And immediately came back, "Mine." "Who art thou?" I mentally demanded, but no reply was returned. This puzzled me, for something seemed to indicate that he had heard my query. In moving over somewhat closer to him, I observed a certain familiarity of form and features, that I hitherto believed had been alone characteristic of my own body. But why was he so diffident? Why did he not reply, or let me understand the reason for his silence?

He was a solemn looking individual and gazing straight ahead. "Maybe he's the devil," I thought to myself. "I'll find out who he is, if I have to touch him with my invisible hand." I thought this, with some feeling.

Certainly, there is one thing about the human that does not change in life or death—our mental feeling. What was I to think of a fellow who ignored my presence? But I had learned to control my temper while on Earth, so I suppressed all feeling and mentally asked, "My dear companion, art thou from Earth?"

"Oh, yer make me sick! Can that 'thou' business! Cut it out! What cha mean yer lost yer nanny? Say, you mug, where did you bob from? Say, where'd yer leave yer shirt?"

His reply was far more familiar than I expected, and a little less elegant than anticipated. I had, however, the satisfaction of immediately knowing where he was from. A direct answer from the form would have been superfluous.

"I came from the Earth, too," I replied.

"Well, I came single," said he with a grin.

Then, as I observed a small wandering meteor rapidly approaching, I mentally raised my invisible arms, and telepathically cried out, "Look out! Dodge, or it will hit you!" It must have been traveling at a far greater speed than I had calculated, for as I mentally shouted my warning, I saw it strike him near the center of his body, and pass entirely through the form. It was moving so rapidly that the shock did not appear in the least to retard its speed. I expected to look up and find my companion gone, but, instead, he was still floating beside me—looking none the worse for the strange occurrence.

"Say, what da yer mean by poking yer arms in front of me face? I saw the dum thing a-coming, an' say, I saw the bloomin' thing pass right through that nut of yours. How'd it feel?"

"Why, I didn't feel anything," I replied, "but I saw it pass right through your body," I added.

"The hell yer did! I haven't a body, an' me arms an' legs are gone! You're all right! You're all there, but keep yer fins out of me vision!"

"That's strange, you seem all there, too! We both see each other, but we can't see ourselves. We are invisible here, to no one except ourselves!" I replied.

As we journeyed on, our confidence in each other increased, until I finally related my last experience on Earth.

How I had been induced to try and beat my own record, in a higher altitude of aerial flight; how the gasoline became frozen in the tank of my aeroplane; my failure to take into consideration the necessity of protection against the intense cold of an altitude of about six miles; the consequent stopping of the engines, and the fatal sleep. Of having been overcome from lack of oxygen; then, my loss of control over the machine during the few seconds of sleep, and the fatal plunge to earth. I explained to him all the details of my eventful last trip. He listened with apparent interest to the recital, not interrupting me once during the whole explanation. When I had finished, he calmly said, "Say, stranger, that's the route I came by. What's your name?"

"What's your name?" said I, giving him the Yankee answer.

"My name? Well, I hain't got none this trip. I'm just a fellow's *Malality*—his name was Bacon—John Bacon. But he was all right—a gentleman. I had a good home. He'll know me when we meet, but he don't know me now. *Bonalities* and *Malalities* are strangers after death parts 'em."

"Then, you are my *Malality*—for I am John Bacon! You are really my dual self, who has tempted me, filled my mind with evil, and with whom I have been mentally wrestling, to subdue and overcome, all my life. So YOU are my *Malality* self? Well, if it were not for old association's sake, I would say, 'Begone!' Thank heaven, I'm rid of you! But, I know you couldn't, with any prospect of success, change your disposition in one short life. I'm glad if I've been of any benefit to you, but, I hope to get a *Malality* that won't tempt me quite so much as you have done, and I trust you'll make your next *Bon*ality a better companion."

"Well, you've been a pretty good kid to me. I feel as if I'd been to Sunday School all my life, but I managed to get the best of you a few times—you bet." Here my companion grinned savagely, and then continued: "Say, old top, you made a good, healthy home for both of us, but you acted meanly in keeping me down all the time. What was the use of your studying so hard, and keeping me waiting around for you to get through? What did it all amount to? If you had let me have my way, you'd have had a good time. Maybe we'd have been up here sooner, but what's the odds, we'd have gone right back again. But, I got you drunk once, John. Remember it? Ha! Ha! You were sick as a dog. What a nice bun you had on. I did my best to break your will then— curse you. But you were such a 'goody-goody' son of a bum, you didn't have enough sense to be decent to me."

"I did the best I could for you. I tried to make you better—and I think you are."

"Well, I may be a little better, but it will take several of your kind to put me in the *Bon*ality class. I ain't particular whether I get there or not. The world owes me a good living. Let others work—your kind—I'd rather take it easy. Give me plenty to eat and drink, and an easy time, an' I'm satisfied. Next time I go back, I'll have me way."

"The next time you go back to Earth, you'll return here a better man. You were about as low as they make 'em when you started out with me, but you've improved."

"Oh, cut that josh. You make me sick. I'd like to see you drunk again."

"You said that many times," I answered.

"Yes, I know I have, and I meant it. Do you remember? Let me remind you about it. Do you remember when that bloke Dickerson invited yer to take a drink? You followed him right in, like a baby. He was a man after me own heart. He had a sleek and oily tongue all right. He could throw the cards, fight, and put up the biggest bluff of any man. Why, he was a top-notch pal. He would cut yer throat, or stick yer in the dark, and go to sleep like a kid, right after. If you'd been a good feller, he wouldn't have filled yer beer glass with whiskey, when you stooped over to pick up his half dollar, you boob. He hated yer because yer always refused to have a good time. He filled yer glass when you weren't lookin', an' yer got drunk, didn't yer? Now yer see when yer got drunk, in order to punish yer, I made you give him every dollar you had. If you'd allowed me to have my way once in a while, maybe I wouldn't have done that. See?"

"How unfortunate for you, I didn't let you try. If I had, I would have gone back to somebody's *Mal*ality. As it is, I still am *Bon*ality—the individual aiming at right. Dickerson never showed his true side to me but once, then I found he was gentle, kind, and considerate. They tell me, that when he was a young man, he was of excellent character. His *Bon*ality dominated. Then he began to drink. No one can drink without weakening his will, and once the will is weakened, his *Mal*ality begins to obtain the upper hand. Nothing but a *Bon*ality of tremendous power can break the hold of our second nature. *Bon*ality represents the good. When they are sent forth into the world, with them is placed a second, a *Mal*ality—one who is below the worst or weakest *Bon-*

ality. It is the duty of the *Bon*ality to teach and overcome the evil second self, and thus lead this hidden evil to a higher, or better life. This I tried to do for you, and I know you are better now than in the beginning."

"That's the way you've always preached," returned my companion, "but no ill will do I hold. Maybe you're on the right tack. The next bloke, however, will suffer if he lets me loose," he added.

Time is not measured, in eternity, so how long we had been together there was no way of determining. Neither is there measurable distance, for all that is necessary is to will the mind to be at any desired place, and instantly the spirit is there.

Our conversation covered many subjects, as we went forward; the principal issue, however, was our present condition. We both understood that we had left the Human, and were now in the Spiritual. While we journeyed along, side by side, we met thousands upon thousands of spirits, always in pairs, and of all ages and nationalities. With many we held conversation. Every color, kind, and creed, black and white, brown and yellow —every race from the face of the earth, now mingled together, and all in general conversation. There was no difficulty to understand each other. There is no language in the realm of infinite space. All ideas were expressed through the mind, hence no figure of speech interfered with thought as expressed in intercourse between minds.

How different was all this on earth, where a multiplicity of languages had shaded, prejudiced or oppressed the human mind. This language condition will always interfere with that great ideal state—"the brotherhood

of man." When we know one another, we are not so apt
to hate, nor war upon our fellows. In this universal
realm, all were perfectly happy in the thought that each
was understood by the other.

"If we ever return to earth again, our objective should
be to advocate one language for all nations of the earth,
many tongues being the only barrier that now separates
nation from nation, and prevents the desired oneness of
mankind. One language would doubtless lead to eternal
peace and brotherhood. What a simple solution of their
many present difficulties—a universal language," I exclaimed.

The stories and confessions of crime, murder, war and
injustice, that I heard from the minds of many *Mal*alities,
were counterbalanced ten thousand fold by the tales of
love, duty, and self-sacrifice, from the *Bon*alities, clearly
proving, that mankind is rapidly advancing by the uplift.
Happiness is on the increase! Goodness is a million times
more common now than a few centuries ago. Hundreds
upon hundreds were floating along with us, doubtless,
long before their time, because war had precipitated their
presence. But, indubitably, they will return better men,
next time, as they had sacrificed themselves for humanity.
So we all do—consciously or unconsciously. We die that
others may live—better lives. This, we shall ever do, but
in lessening degree, until mankind becomes perfect. What
a glorious thought possessed me, as we journeyed on
through ethereal space, the widening vault ever vibrating
with scintillating sounds and longings of pronounced
progress.

CHAPTER XXI

THE MOON

THERE being no measure of time in space, it was impossible to estimate how long my *Malality* and I had been in communication with others similarly situated. Soon, however, we all realized our close proximity to the Moon.

"We're about two hundred and thirty thousand miles from home on Earth, according to my reckoning," remarked my companion, as, within a few miles, we neared its rough, barren and scarred surface.

"And according to my reckoning, we shall be enabled to confirm the many estimates made by others, as to its condition," I replied.

"It's a dead one," said my *Malality* in disgust.

We were now so near, it was quite easy to study its surface at close range. The Moon was indeed dead. Not a particle of water appeared upon its entire surface, not a cloud in the sky. Indeed, there was no "sky," for its atmosphere had entirely disappeared. When all the moisture on its surface had been finally absorbed by the sphere itself, the air had disappeared.

We descended to her bare surface, in the vicinity of the great volcanic crater Secchi, at the base of which was formerly the great sea of Tranquillitatis—both of which are visible to the naked eye from the Earth on a moonlight night. Together, they present one of the darkest areas of the Moon. The whole surface of the satellite appeared as if it had been rent and torn, ages ago, by a hundred thousand volcanoes—all now entirely extinct. They presented to our vision a series of unbroken chains of volcanic mountains covering every inch of the Moon's surface. In the vicinity of the Serenitatis depression, appeared another dark section, representing what was probably a former ocean bed. Its internal fires were undoubtedly extinct, for we could trace no indication of life from within its craters. Indeed, no evidence of life was visible anywhere, as existence in the sense of life of any kind, would have been impossible, owing to the absence of air. When celestial bodies finally lose their great protecting air blanket, they are subject to the two extremes—intense heat from the rays of the Sun, and the frigid cold of surrounding space.

We were much interested in the discovery of small planets from five to fifty miles in diameter. These we termed "Small Moons," as they revolved in their orbits around the Earth. We saw several hundreds of them in the space between the Earth and Moon, all rushing along in their orbits at varying speeds. There must have been also several thousands beyond the Moon, all within a few hundred miles of its surface. Further, we had evidences that when the Moon was in her glory, her people had built great cities in which they had lived for ages, in peace and comfort.

As indicated, on our way from Earth to Moon, we passed countless numbers of small planets. Some were moving together in clusters, others in long, endless streams, while a few were alone and revolving independently. The separate ones were by far the brightest and largest in size. "How like the human family," I thought, "the weak and seeming unimportant, forever in clusters, or forming in endless streams following beaten paths. The big and bright, generally stand alone." No two planets appeared to be in the same stage of development, each representing a different degree of perfection. Many were in a gaseous state, representing the new born; others, old, wrinkled, or dried up, presenting the old age of planet life.

We passed one stream which, if visible to people on Earth, would have appeared as a comet. We estimated this procession to be more than two millions of miles long. From our view-point, it looked like a huge reptile made up of an infinite number of luminous bodies, all speeding through airless space and led by a great blazing star. This mass was traveling at a rate of three hundred and fifty miles a second, in an orbit around the Sun that would take more than a thousand years to circle. In the race some were certain to be left behind.

In addition to this vast number of gaseous bodies, we encountered countless meteorites. The most numerous among these are the aerolites, whose composition is made up almost entirely of stony matter. Strange as it may seem, the so-called siderite meteorites, which Earth's astronomers claim are composed of metallic iron alloyed with nickel, were not observed.

We were informed by strangers we encountered, that the so-called siderite meteorites observed to fall on Earth, were nothing more or less than collapsed torpedoes, or flying machines, sent forth by the inhabitants of some far-distant planet. They either miscalculated the density of our rarified atmosphere, or had lost control of their nickel and copper constructed machines, unfortunately, plunging through the atmosphere so rapidly, as to fuse, so, falling to Earth a moulten mass.

These strange travelers told us, also, that the human race voluntarily, and by this means of transportation, distributes itself throughout the universe. So, it may be possible, the people of Earth will yet find means to send emigrants to new planets in the ages yet to come.

Earth's astronomers estimate, that about forty million aerolites daily strike our outer atmosphere, and through friction are fused, consumed, and fall to the surface, in dust. Only the largest of these are seen by the people on Earth, and then only on clear nights. While, doubtless, all produce a quite distinct noise in their rapid approach through the increasing density of air, they are entirely consumed so far away that sound rarely reaches Earth.

As we reached Caucasus Mountains, at the foot of which, on the west, lies the dried up ocean bed of Serenitatis on the Moon's Northern Hemisphere, we observed, far away to the east, the great volcano Aristillus looming up several thousand feet. Near the base of the extinct crater, we discovered ruins of what once seemed to have been a magnificent city. The city's broad streets were constructed from highly polished green tile, the surface of which was corrugated and had withstood the rigors of alternating extremes of temperature for untold ages. These ages of meteoric bombardment had destroyed the greater part of the city, which we estimated to have been some twenty miles square. All the buildings were originally white tiled, with roofs of tile surfaced with gold leaf. The builders had evidently mastered the art of tile production. The buildings themselves were uniform neither in size nor height, showing clearly the builders' versatility. The city faced south, where in the distance, across the dried up ocean bed, could be seen the crater Autolycus, and beyond the Apennines Mountains.

This city, in ruins, was the last mute evidence of mankind's presence on the Moon. How wonderful it must have been when its great human throng proudly walked its streets! I could see back into the dim past, these buildings of pure white and gold, and their streets teeming with life and the shouts of the young and old. What music in the children's laughter, as they freely rode or walked about, 'midst richness and beauty, and love and song. It must have been a city of twenty millions or more and much further advanced in human intelligence than are the Earth's people. What had become of them? Had they been slowly decimated by lack of water? It is known, that as a planet's internal fires cool, the moisture on its surface and within its atmosphere is absorbed, leaving the sphere entirely dry.

Scientists of the Moon, discovering the slow disappearance of water, must have made desperate efforts to overcome disaster. Irrigation began, and, coupled with the construction of immense hydraulic pumps, provision was sought for the future safety of the race.

Did they finally migrate to some nearby planet, one in condition better calculated to sustain life? Was this feasible?

They evidently had tremendous water systems, for everywhere we discovered evidences of great hydraulic pumping stations and immense canals.

The Moon's surface was now unprotected from the direct rays of the Sun on the one hand, and intense cold on the other. Wherever her surface is subjected to the Sun's direct rays, the rocks become so heated that they soften almost to fusing point. When the Sun's rays do not directly strike, the temperature is reduced to several hundred degrees below zero.

Think of a ray of sunlight so hot as to melt stone, while in the shadow, a temperature so cold prevails, that the Mississippi River would freeze solidly in a few seconds.

Why is the Moon so bright? Is it due entirely to her reflection of the Sun's rays? There being no protecting blanket of atmosphere around the Moon to deflect Sun rays, or to act as a distributor of heat or cold, together with the perpetual striking of meteors, tends to increase spasmodic heat upon the Moon's surface.

The air blanket surrounding our Earth to a large extent fuses these falling bodies. Only in rare instances do they ever reach the Earth's surface.

Looking down upon the exhibition of meteors falling constantly upon the Moon, we become convinced, that some day, the Moon would run against one so large, that it would lessen her speed, so that she might make but one annual revolution around the Earth. "What dire consequences," I thought, "might follow this catastrophe? Would the tides of the ocean be so infrequent that their waters would become fouled? Would the Sun's influence alone on the tide be sufficient to obviate the possibility?"

Our attention finally centered upon two small spheres, less than fifty miles away. They were each about five miles in diameter, side by side, traveling at high velocity. As they sped on, we saw them repeatedly strike together, the force of the impact causing them to rebound a mile or two. At each blow, we could see, that friction was gradually heating both, until they attained a heat so great that fires belched forth, increasing in intensity, until both glowed at white heat. The area of this intense heat constantly increased at each blow, until both spheres became a moulten mass; their forms finally becoming oblong in shape, and lengthening out until the ends of each seemed to fuse together.

As they disappeared from our sight, both had merged into one gaseous ball, greater by many times than their former combined size. We had witnessed the birth of a new planet; though small and correspondingly short lived, a planet, nevertheless, that shall go through all those varying stages recognized in a human life. Hundreds of these formations were going on around us. In this process, they seemed to swallow each other in a blaze of fire, rolling, turning, and twisting in their concentric energy, while traveling in orbits at hundreds of miles a minute.

So numerous are the dead planets, wandering through space, that no approximate calculation of time could show them as paired, and regenerated. New planets appeared to dodge everything in their paths. Can this be a natural law?

Here, I indicated to my *Mal*ality, that we had seen enough, and suggested that we continue our journey. At this moment, we discovered, that we could WILL ourselves anywhere—and instantly be where we willed!

Taking a parting view of the old Moon's dry, and cracked surface, with the deeper furrows, we turned our faces in the direction of the Sun. It was at once evident to us that his smaller child, the Earth, lives a useful life.

It has been calculated that the Sun and his system, including the Earth, is rushing at the rate of twelve miles per second towards the constellations Hercules and Lyre, where Vega, one of the most beautiful and larger of the Suns, is located. This star of first magnitude appears to be rushing at the rate of forty-four miles a second towards the Sun. But, what must be said of the consequences of their meeting in the dim and distant future? The Sun is a million times greater in volume than the Earth, while Vega is a thousand times greater than the Sun. Our Sun's system is estimated as not far from that vast center of space encircled by the Milky Way. Evidently, it has traversed the intervening space from the South of that region.

Ahead, lies a cluster of stars towards which we are speeding at about three hundred sixty-five million miles each year. Vega is madly rushing towards Earth, as if to welcome us. Will the final meeting result in forming one great planet, on which may dwell the perfect?

We asked ourselves this question, but, as we journeyed on, neither of us could reply.

Being now completely overcome by a desire to end our sojourn, we willed attainment of our destination.

CHAPTER XXII

THE GREAT WHITE WAY

THERE was no conceivable lapse of time between the moment of willing our journey's end and the instant arrival at our destination.

The dazzling beauty of the scene that met the gaze of my *Mal*ality and Self is indescribable. A great vivid shaft of light, twenty thousand miles in diameter, shone forth from Beginnan, a great black planet in the system of Vega of the constellation Lyre, and extended like a great heavenly searchlight into space, for countless billions of miles. So pure were its rays that Earth's sunlight, in comparison, looked pale and dim, yet, its magnificent and dazzling beauty, instead of blinding, only increased our sense of vision. So perfect and powerful was its magnifying force, that we were enabled to see objects at will, and at any desired distance. Yet, there was an absence of glare, reflection or shadow casting. From our far outward position, however, this glorious stream of light was opaque. Our eyes could not penetrate the mysteries beyond its bounds.

As we neared its outer edge, and were about to step within the resplendent bright beam, there suddenly appeared, facing us, a long row of tall patriarchal looking men, standing erect and with solemnity, a few paces apart. They seemed to extend in a long straight line, reaching from Beginnan out into fathomless space. Expectancy was plainly marked upon every face, as they each peered into outer darkness.

As we gazed, we saw hundreds of Individuals with their *Malalities* arrive at the outer edge, to face, in turn, one of these border sentinels and hold a short, silent conversation. Then, was assigned a different *Malality* to each *Bonality*, and a new *Bonality* to the *Malality*. This done, the bearded, silent sentinel pointed in the direction of some distinct planet, whereupon each pair, or two companions, would together take their departure for the older or newer world. The change was in order to secure perfection in the struggle for man's endless existence.

Strange, but my companion at once recalled, and the reflection dawned upon myself, that we had made the journey to this same place before. That we had seen the same familiar faces of the chosen patriarchs, all clothed in garments of immaculate white, yes—hundreds of thousands of times before. We had probably seen each one of these selfsame sentinels, guarding this Great White Way.

The arrivals were coming and going * forward in a

* "Living humanity is composed of about one billion, two hundred thousand millions of human beings, the number of men and women being approximately equal at any given time."

"Of these there die annually 35,879,520 of both sexes."

"Daily there die 98,848 male and female."

"In an hour 4,020 die."

"In a minute 67 die."

"In every second just a fraction more than one human being dies."

"Now as these stream out of life there streams in at the other pole precisely the same number of human entities—no more, no less; the cosmic balance is absolute. Life, like a pendulum, swings in and out of matter, steady, unfailing in regularity, ceaseless in activity. When, in an hour, four thousand and twenty human entities pass through the gate of ebony and death, there enter, in the same hour, exactly four thousand and twenty human entities by the ivory gate of birth. It is the out-breathing and in-breathing of the cosmic life. It is balanced and it is eternal."—VANCE THOMPSON.

continuous and never-ending stream of people of all ages—arriving and departing invariably in pairs. Occasionally, a newly arrived Personality who had reached perfection of character, was allowed to enter the impenetrable light, and we beheld him no more. We distinguished no perfect Personalities as arriving from Earth, and for a while marveled at the thought. Finally, we remembered being told, that the Earth was far behind all other planets in civilization, and that the mass of people were human savages—ready to war upon and destroy each other, without knowing why. Even the most educated savages among Earth's men sought to justify murder and lesser crimes. We had been told that a mighty tide tending to the creation of a better world on Earth, had begun.

As we both stood facing the light, the voice of the nearest sentinel was heard. I knew by the expression upon his face—when he greeted us—that we were not unexpected. He was a man of remarkable personality, a figure stately in bearing, and of form divine. He revealed the most perfect type of physical perfection we had ever seen. In stature he was more than ten feet high. His massive head appeared all out of proportion, however, to his body. His face glowed with unusual intelligence, and a powerful will inspired within us immediate confidence. I had never met one on Earth, who had so quickly imparted the feeling that now possessed me.

As we took our positions directly in front of him, he held up a hand as if to warn against going further toward the shaft of light. He quickly scrutinized us both, as if to read the story of our lives from out our countenances. And that is really what he did, for I then recollected what I had been informed on previous visits there; that the whole account was plainly written on every face, each being silently judged by the patriarchs. I knew that if my life was so written, that it might be read from my countenance, it was useless for either of us to waste words by relating how good we had been, or for the patriarch to inform me how wickedly we had lived in our last existence. All was manifestly revealed for him to read and judge.

"Fine looking old gink, ain't he?" remarked my *Malality*—taking the proverbial "step" from the sublime to the ridiculous.

"You've carried your slang right up to judgment," I remarked. "Why don't you wait until you get back to Earth where it is more common," I said in disgust—fearing the white-robed figure had overheard him.

"Well, he doesn't like hypocrites any better than you do. I'm going to 'B natural,' as they say in music," he replied.

Before given an opportunity to say more, the sentinel spoke in clear, soft musical tones—"Welcome, pilgrims from planet Earth."

As with ourselves, his lips were immovable, nor was there any sound when he spoke, though we both understood perfectly.

As he greeted us, he stepped back one pace into the light, thus concealing the upper part of his body as completely as though it had been in utter darkness. It was evident that all of the guardians of the Great White Way stood upon the outer edge of the light column while holding conversations with arrivals from the various planets.

When not thus engaged, they drew back into the light which immediately enveloped and entirely concealed them within its brilliant 'bounds.

"*Mal*ality of John Bacon. Return to Earth with the *Bon*ality next to you!" commanded the same voice.

"What, that guy?" exclaimed my former companion in a tone of disgust and glancing at the sentinel with a scowl, as he pointed in the opposite direction.

I turned to see who his new *Bon*ality might be, but to my astonishment was unable to discern anything, for an invisible curtain of darkness lay between us.

"Can't see you, John, but good-by, ol' pal," I heard him say. Then all was silent, I felt and knew, almost quicker than I could think it, that he and his companion were, at that moment, reborn upon Earth.

Then the voice spoke to me, saying, "You have made favorable progress. I read through your countenance an improvement in character. All my brother guardians rejoice with me. We are delegated first, to welcome you, then read your past life, and direct your return. Every act of your life, evil and good, is plainly stamped upon your brow. The good will forever remain, while the bad shall be overcome and changed to good. In your new life, obey the Natural Laws. When in doubt, go to Nature, study her ways and be wise! Your progress upward to a better existence will ever be determined by how well you control your *Mal*ality—the perfect mastery of *Bon*ality, yourself. Know thyself. Evil acts are committed, wholly under the influence of your *Mal*ality. Become master of yourself. Remember, you create your own punishments as well as your own rewards!"

I stood there before him, in respectful silence. Then,

my mind returned to thoughts of dual self. He had gone now. How strange it all seemed! Yet, would he return further improved, or would this new companion weakly permit him to get the upper hand? I fully realized the responsibilities of every Personality. To master our *Mal-ality* is to master the world!

"Yes, and heaven, too, for when you are complete master, we want you here," broke in the sentinel. He continued then, "My name is Marcomet. I am a man from Mars who has attained perfection. Most of the people on Mars have advanced to a like state of perfection, and are here with me. You, from Earth, have so far progressed that I may accord you the privilege of stepping forward into the light." With an all but imperceptible bow, and a graceful sweep of the hand, he bade me enter.

As I passed forward into the rays of dazzling brightness, he turned slightly, and looking up toward Beginnan, with another graceful wave of his hand, he exclaimed,— "Behold!"

As this thought was communicated, I had not the complete presence of mind to reply—so great was my astonishment—and so completely had I become enraptured by the magnificent sight that met my gaze. The scene opened before me, an endless panorama of gorgeous splendor, inspiring one with an intense feeling of joyous ecstasy, yet bringing to the mind a sense of quietness and serene pleasure. The scene that met my gaze was of indescribable beauty.

Stretching out before me, in broad columns, up and down the Great White Way—as far as the eye could see —were endless lines of human beings of all ages, each by thousands, passing on toward *Beg*   ome in couples, went hand in hand, while others passed alone. Occasionally a young man and maiden, or an old couple might be seen arm in arm. No raiment concealed their bodies, nor did they carry worldly goods. Like unto my own, their bodies had been transfigured.

So absolutely was I enraptured by these scenes, that all realization of sound was, up to this moment, confused and uncertain. Presently, there dawned upon me, the swelling notes of beautiful music, vibrating and re-vibrating all along that vast White Way, filling it with highest charm of sweetness and melody. Presently I perceived that the vast multitude of voices had joined in at certain intervals, swelling the blending notes until it seemed that the very gates of heaven had opened and all therein had suddenly burst forth into music and in song. I became so enraptured by the strains that it lulled me to a feeling resembling a beautiful dream. As the delicate chords were wafted far into the distance, and mellow vibrations melted away, each murmur recalled the music of some distant singing brook, and gradually, as a dewdrop fades before the Sun, I realized that there was no greater joy than music.

Marcomet, in all his splendor, now stood without, welcoming the new arrivals and benignly directing the return of others.

CHAPTER XXIII

MARCOMET

MARCOMET soon returned from the outer sphere, his manner indicating that he was in deep meditation, as if considering some serious problem. For a long time he stood peering into space, his eyes turned toward the great Sun, Vega, and the pearly white planet, which no mental earthly eye had ever beheld—Beginnan. My own eyes, following the direction in which he looked, revealed its magnificent beauty—the seeming center of the universe and humanity's final home.

For billions of miles, in either direction, I beheld the onward and upward march of countless Pilgrims on their way. On they came 'mid laughter and song, the merry prattle of children, the tender lullabys of beautiful motherhood, and the sparkling wit of the young. All were perfect. Perfection means love, music, song, and the cultivation of supreme happiness. Knowledge is but the stepping stone to all this.

Notwithstanding countless human beings arriving from each one of the millions of planets in space, I saw no two who resembled one another. There were, however, several who appeared to be in authority, and who, completely arousing my curiosity, induced me to ask Marcomet who they were. One commanding and distinguished appearing

person, who carried a great golden trumpet, was especially prominent.

"Who is it?" I asked, indicating the person.

"I will point out a few of them to you," he replied.
"The first is Gabriel, 'Chief of the Angelic Guards.' Next
to him stands 'Uzziel, second in command.' He represents
God's strength. Behind them stands 'Zephon, the Guardian Angel of Paradise,' and the beautiful 'Zophicel, the
swift-winged cherubim.' "

"Who is that erect figure leading the pure white horse,
at the head of that mighty army?"

"That is 'Michael, Prince of Celestial Armies,' and
the horse he leads is 'Skinfaxi,' he who draws the 'Chariot
of Day.' Observe, sitting inside the chariot, 'Veronica,'
the maiden who handed her handkerchief to the Man of
Sorrows on his way to Calvary. It is recorded that he
wiped his face in it, and returned it to the Maiden. Ever
after, the cloth retained a perfect likeness of Him photographed on it. Walking near the chariot you see
'Noukhail, the Angel of Day and Night,' now preparing to
mount the Day Horse."

"Tell me, Marcomet, who are those two walking together in perfect step, and leading the way for others?"

"They are 'Zimri,' of the six wise men of the East, led
by the guiding star to the birth of the Man of Sorrows,
representing human wisdom. Then Beatrice, near him—
the wisdom that comes of faith. Following them are a
few others of Earth who were persecuted by the vain and
ignorant for daring to express their wisdom. There you
observe Anaxagoras of Clazomenae; 'Averroes,' the
Arabian Philosopher; 'Dee,' 'Bruno' who, by the order

of the Inquisition, was buried alive in Rome, A.D. 1600, for asserting that the Earth was not standing still. There," pointing, "is 'Crosse,' electrician; 'Galileo,' one of the first greatest astronomers, who was, in 1616 and 1633, imprisoned for the same cause. 'Offerus,' the bearer of Christ, is there; and walking together is 'Cleombrotus,' the Advocate of Plato's book on immortality and happiness, and Eloa, the chosen one, and friend of Gabriel."

"Who are those extremely sober-appearing three, coming forward in the distance?"

"They, also, are from Earth. Though wise beyond the average, they were wont to hire out to talk and entertain fools and hypocrites. They are the famous court jesters, Chicot, Patch, and 'Wetzweiler.' "

"I see no kings, nor soldiers, nor the men who have stimulated war and strife," I remarked; "none at all whose images stand high in stone and bronze, on pedestals, to decorate the public squares and parks of Earth!"

"Ages shall pass before one who has aided in destroying human life shall enter here," Marcomet slowly replied in measured tones. "Men engaged in the destruction of human life, advocating the killing of others, indeed, taking life under any pretext, return to the lowest order of a future Duality. The penalty for taking life depends upon its justification. There is only one Judge," he said solemnly.

"Move to the edge, and glance into the outer darkness," suddenly commanded Marcomet. "Observe those who have for many ages waited out there, preparing their minds for some more reasonable view of existence. There, many shall stand for hundreds of years in Earth's time measure, before they improve sufficiently to act as *Mal*-alities.   Others remain here thousands of centuries. These human beings present the lowest types of the human mind.   They are now fiends—sadly I say it—and mostly from Planet Earth, where each will return later as a *Mal*ality.   Over there," said Marcomet, pointing out into the blackness which my eyes could with difficulty penetrate, "sullenly stands 'Zanga,' representing revenge. For years he has sulked.   Time will make him somewhat more tolerant, and then he will be permitted to go forth in company with a strong *Bon*ality, to learn the higher lessons of life.   Near him stands Item, a vile creature, money broker, cheat, villain, bully, who cajoles and curses, who fawns, flatters and filches.   There come two more celebrities.   'Whang,' the avaricious Chinese miller; and 'Jonathan Wild,' the man of ten maxims, a cool, calculating, heartless villain.   Others are coming in the distance.   'Lumpkin,' fond of low society.   'Lucifer,' representing price; and 'Linne the Spendthrift.'   Then there is that old offender, 'Mrs. Frail,' full of affectation, wantonness, malice, and folly; and accompanying her is 'Fribble,' of weak nerves, a contemptible mollycoddle."

"What wickedness is now being plotted by those yonder, whose heads are close together in earnest conversation?   Their lips move not, and their hideousness is only equaled by that of a Frankenstein."

"Plotters though they be, no evil will result from their present state.   Apart, they are cowards, and will cease their plottings.   The one on the right is 'Asmadai,' a lustful, destroying angel; 'Asmodeus,' a demon of vanity and dress; and the one with the stooping shoulders and a long beard is 'Kartaphilos,' the Wandering Jew who struck at the Man of Sorrows, and was formerly door-keeper for Pontius Pilate."

"It is now time for you to return," said Marcomet.

"Did my efforts to overcome my *Mal*ality earn a better companion for my next experience?" I inquired.

"It will be far superior in all respects," replied Marcomet, and then, continuing, said—"Our Dual companions are far different in each separate existence. When the *Bon*ality has absolutely conquered it takes its place here among the perfect. The *Mal*ality that was mastered becomes a *Bon*ality in its next existence. Then, it tries to overcome its *Mal*ality in order to become perfect, and so, the struggle goes on, until each one has finally attained perfection."

"How many separate existences may each one have to pass, before attaining perfection?" I asked.

"Some have had but one, though all now remaining have lived through countless lives," he answered.

"Does knowledge help to attain perfection?"

"It helps, yes, for it leads us to a better understanding of the natural laws of the Universe. People who have knowledge, however, do not always follow its teachings. Ignorance often lives a better and purer life than knowledge, though it cannot lead to progress. It is often truthful and negatively good. It does not require an education to be good. Neither does an education guarantee higher morals, nor a better disposition. Faith in our own divinity, however, guarantees an improvement in both of those high qualities and many more."

"Are the people of Mars more advanced than those of Earth?" I inquired.

Marcomet did not immediately reply, but remained

as if in deep meditation. Then, turning to me almost appealingly, he said: "John Bacon, I have a message to the people of your Earth. I have looked in vain for a bearer of that message, until you appeared. Earth's people are at present the furthest removed from perfection of all the peoples occupying the billions of planets in space. Through the act of a Judas, the Human Race upon Earth at once descended to the very lowest condition. From this it is now again rapidly rising. You can be of the utmost service to your fellow men upon Earth if you will attempt to change their minds with the story that I shall now relate. There are many who will not believe when you repeat my story, but do not let this deter you from the telling. Skeptics there are, and shall be, when men allow *Mal*ality to prevail. Now, do you promise, John Bacon, to tell Earth's people my story so soon as you arrive at the age of understanding? Will you do all in your power to circulate it, that they may know their true origin?"

"I will do my best to remember your words, and will repeat it as you tell me," I returned.

"I came from Mars several million years ago, long before the surface of that planet began to dry up. Since I must frequently refer to time, let me remind you that while a day on Mars is only thirty-seven minutes longer than Earth's day, our years are nearly twice the length. The Sun rises three hundred and sixty-five times a year on Earth, but on Mars it rises six hundred and eighty-seven times a year. So you see, when a person is a year old on Mars, he is very nearly two years old on Earth.

"Both planets were born during the same century,

twenty-two million of Mars' years ago; therefore, Earth must be nearly double that age. The Sun hurled the Earth into space, a distance of nearly ninety-two millions of miles, while Mars—a sphere about half its size—was thrown into space about one hundred and forty millions of miles, consequently, they are about forty-eight millions of miles apart. Because Mars is so much smaller, the process of cooling took less than half the time of Earth, hence, millions of years before the Earth was prepared for human inhabitation, Mars had been settled by the human race, and was advanced in all branches of human knowledge. Indeed, Mars never was so deficient in human knowledge as Earth's people are to-day. As I have already indicated, this unfortunate condition exists as the result of the greatest calamity known to the history of worlds. It is a misfortune that has brought untold misery and suffering upon the innocent, and from which they may not recover until communication with their nearest neighbor, Mars, be established. The people of that planet have patiently awaited through untold centuries for Earth's scientists to devote their energies in constructing wireless electric stations for the receipt and transmission of messages between the planets. Whenever this is done, Mars will find opportunity and the means to communicate certain necessary information which, when acted upon, will aid, advance and relieve Earth's people of all laborious toil. Scientific advancement on Earth will then have reached a stage that its people need alone employ the forces around them in order to transform their planet into a veritable heaven for all.

"Briefly, I will narrate of Mars' human history. The

history of its people may be said to date back to the first day of the first year, and to continue in one unbroken record to the present time.

"Every important fact has been carefully noted in an imperishable record, consisting of certain compositions which will neither burn, break, nor deteriorate by time. Yet, these are so light and thin in substance, that a complete record covering Mars' entire history may be carried with perfect ease under the arm of a child.

"By an electro-radium process, the record is transcribed on sheets less than one ten-thousandth of an inch in thickness, and of the average book page size. Upon this records, including all the happenings from day to day, are carefully preserved. Thus the important events covering a period of a hundred years are easily transcribed upon one sheet. Ten thousand of these records reach but one inch in thickness, and contain the history of Mars for a million years. While such a record would weigh but a total of one pound on Earth, they weigh far less, or about four-tenths of a pound, on Mars. Each of these plates is capable of recording about one hundred times the amount of reading matter contained in a complete twenty-nine volume work of Earth's largest encyclopedia. Since no news is ever printed or read on Mars, all important events are recorded on these 'radio-sheets.' Every man, woman and child is supplied with a small instrument, no larger than a coin of Earth, and called a 'Readograph,' which, when placed gently against the 'radio-sheet,' adheres to it, and repeats, by talking aloud, similarly to a phonograph, all that the *Readograph* touches. It repeats the record as often as the *Readograph* is applied, with the volume and tone of the original voice.

"It is quite easy to find the record of any day, month, or year desired, by moving the *Readograph* over the face of the radio-sheets.

"There are many other and wonderful instruments employed on Mars, and of these I will inform you later."

After pausing for a moment, he continued:

"I see, in the distance, a stranger coming. I must greet her. I will return and relate the earlier history of Mars and the wonderful achievements in settling your Earth and Moon."

It was not long before Marcomet returned. I noted that he keenly glanced at me, but not until he had informed me that a woman had arrived from the same part of Earth on which I had resided. Then I ceased to question him.

He failed to inform me who the woman was, and a peculiar sensation seized me. One that I cannot well describe, though it seemed to impress me that the arrival was one whom I had known in life, and whose Personality had left more than one human imprint on my being and character.

CHAPTER XXIV

THE PLANET MARS

"Of all the stars you behold from here," said Marcomet, turning with a graceful sweep of his hand toward the outer universe, "few are so small as Earth's Sun. Suns are void of atmospheres. They exist in gaseous states until, through solidification of the gases, they reach the moulten state. Unlike planets, they each have no brother Sun to induce a surrounding atmosphere."

"If all the so-called children of the Sun were originally thrown off, why did the process cease in its persistence?" I asked.

"He began to throw off planets when much younger, or nearer the gaseous state, and ceased when the moulten state was reached,"—replied Marcomet.

"Where does its heat go?" said I.

"Energy or heat rays find lodgment in some Sun or the planets of the universe. It is transferred continually, from one body to another, some billions of miles away, through the vast expanse of space—this, without loss."

"What will become of Earth's Sun when it reaches the moulten or burned-out condition?" I asked, becoming intensely interested, "as well as the Earth, Mars, Jupiter, and all the rest?"

"Hold on," returned Marcomet, raising his hand in admonishment, "one question at a time, please. As to your first question, 'What will become of the Sun when he burns himself out?' He will become a wanderer of the skies until he meets, through mutual attraction, a planet of equal or greater size. The force of the collision becomes so terrific that both instantly change into one whirling gaseous mass. As time elapses, this reformed mass hurls into surrounding space parts of itself, representing smaller child worlds, which this mother Sun warms, cares for, and protects, until they are enabled to care for themselves."

"What becomes of the children of the Sun when he goes off and leaves them?"

"Why, they each go wandering away in search of marriage to another Sun."

"When the Sun throws off his so-called children in a gaseous form, what constitutes the formation of a planet such as ours?" I inquired.

"The mass of superheated gas gradually becomes cooler and, growing smaller and more compact in form as this process continues, it soon becomes a hot and solid mass. As the surface of this mass begins cooling, through the action of the mother Sun, the elements of an atmosphere gather, forming a tremendous and all-enwrapping blanket of moisture, thus gradually but continuously tending to cool the surface. In the beginning, all the moisture precipitated is drawn back by the Sun and thrown off as surface heat by the planet into the surrounding atmosphere. This forms into fog, clouds, and steam. In time—counted by thousands of years—the surface becomes sufficiently cooled, so that moisture condenses, gradually increasing in amount until the planet's face is covered with water. As this water begins to saturate by gravitation the hardening outside surface of the Planet it comes in contact with the moulten mass within, resulting in explosions and eruptions at the surface, puffing the mass into uneven surfaces—as hills, mountains, plains and valleys, the waters the while receding to the lowest levels. Thus, part of the surface remains high and dry. As the ages pass, the water is kept pure by saturation and alternate evaporation in the surrounding atmosphere, the Sun and gravity being the active agents. By this process the water area decreases, while increasing the land surface.

"As the internal fires of the planet cool, the waters at the surface follow and are gradually absorbed. So, you will perceive, that as the water seeps through more and more land appears. Then lakes and water in the higher altitudes become dried up and, over certain parts of the planet's surface, patches of dry area begin to appear. These are really deserts—the first warning sign of an uninhabitable planet. There are now two desert belts extending entirely around Mars as, also, nearly around Earth. They appear on both planets when in the Tropic of Capricorn. These will slowly extend until they cover the entire surface of each planet.

"As the moisture of a planet becomes absorbed, that element of the atmosphere decreases in proportion, until final absorption leaves the surface of the planet unprotected against extreme heat of the Sun on one hand and the intense cold from the outer ether on the other.

"The highly improved telescopes and other intricate instruments of Mars, which I will later describe to you, prove the heavens to contain billions upon billions of Suns and Planets. So great, indeed, are their number as to be absolutely uncountable. With this vast number of Suns existing in ether, with the heat arriving from each, it might be deemed that their rays would finally heat the entirety of space, raising the temperature to an unbearable heat. But heat rays pass through ether without loss, for there is nothing to hold them. Does it seem possible that a heat ray or beam of light will pass from your Sun, ninety-three million miles away from Earth, and through the ether without loss of heat energy? Such, however, is the case, and were it not for the protecting envelope of air and moisture which catches and dissipates the heat, nothing of animal or vegetable life could exist upon the surface of Earth.

"Earth is much larger than Mars. Both were shot into space with sufficient force to carry the former about ninety-three million miles into ethereal space, while Mars was impelled some forty-eight million miles farther on. So you see that everything in Nature, whether a Sun or a human being, goes through the same process of birth, life and death. Life is the only thing that really exists. There are no Kingdoms or divisions, for whether animal, vegetable, or mineral, it is the same life, in varying forms, each going through forever its positive living and negative or dying process. As soon as born it begins to die, and as soon as dead it begins to live. Part of everything is forever dying, or forever being born. It never ceases, under natural conditions. In the realm of ether only is there absolute suspension of chemical changes."

"Then Mars must have cooled many thousands of years before the Earth?" I suggested.

"Yes, for millions of years before the Earth was fit for human habitation, Mars was a flourishing planet," replied Marcomet. "If you heat two stones of unequal mass to the same degree, the smaller will cool off first. Mars, being the smaller of the two, naturally cooled millions of years before the Earth.

"The Sun nearest to your Earth's small Sun is known to your Astronomers as Alpha Centauri. This Sun is estimated to be twenty-five thousand billions of miles from Earth.

"It has a planet which your Astronomers have not discovered, nor will they ever, as all planets at that distance show black. I will, however, give you the name of the planet since it has to do with the settlement of Mars. Its name is Alphacent. It is a planet fifty times larger than your own. The people of this great world have, from unknown time, conquered not only their own atmosphere, but all surrounding space. The inhabitants continue to migrate to other planets as fast as conditions warrant, or as they become adapted to human existence. These people have sent forth a continuous stream of emigrants to new planets and established thousands of world settlements throughout space. The migratory instinct is natural in everything. Indeed, it is a law of the Universe to master or settle, first, the dry land, then the waters, the air, and finally the great and infinite ether, that vast space through which everything swiftly and unimpededly moves, each in its own trackless path of frigidity.

"As mankind, throughout each of the uncounted planets, masters the land, sea, and air of his own immediate world, he naturally seeks to emigrate and settle the worlds next in readiness around him. The people of Mars were animated by this spirit."

"Where did the people of Mars first come from?" I asked Marcomet.

"From Alphacent! It is the most advanced of the planets in science. The history of Mars informs us that these people had watched the slow progress of Mars' development for many thousands of centuries, before entrusting human existence onto its surface. Finally, when they realized its preparedness they impelled electric torpedoes, filled with emigrants, for the new world of Mars. One expedition was alone necessary to convey ten thousand emigrants to Mars. Thus the expansion of the human race in the great Kingdom of Worlds added another conquest to Man's glory. Yes, and it laid the foundation for the establishment of peoples upon the beautiful family of planets around your Sun. Later, the people of Mars commenced sending expeditions, the first being to the Moon. The people on Mars increased very rapidly, and finally covered his whole habitable surface with a uniformly advanced population in all respects similar to the mother people. They settled upon the shores of his beautiful oceans, lakes and rivers, in the verdant valleys, and upon the tops of low hills, as no high mountains exist on Mars. His surface has always been more or less flat, for which reason easy transportation obtains. At the time I left, the people on Mars were perhaps the most advanced in knowledge of any Universal race.

"The surface of this planet is marked out in communities of exact size. The soils, water and air are all scientifically analyzed, thereby insuring accurate information as to its adaptability for agriculture, horticulture, manufacturing, and health. There is no guess work in these things. No cities are permitted to exist, but each person must own several acres, which are cultivated for his own private use. All general cultivation is adhered to by the community, each sharing in the work for the benefit of the whole.

"The community's lands are laid out in squares, all the streets and sidewalks being of pure white artificial stone with a polished surface, preventing wear or waste through too rigorous weather. The houses are of similar artificial stone, variation in color prevailing in beauty or for decoration's sake. All the people array their bodies in silks of variegated colors, draped gracefully around their bodies, while the only footwear to be found are sandals. Their silk is much finer, lighter, and stronger than that produced on Earth, therefore, when tightly woven, is an absolute protection against the elements. Through sunshine or rain, these garments prove of absolute comfort and beauty. They are necessarily light, strong, sanitary, and so serviceable that each garment may, with care, be worn several hundred years. Nothing but self-propelling electric vehicles, the wheels covered with a soft resistant material somewhat similar to rubber, but practically everlasting, are permitted in the thoroughfares of Mars. Thus, the hard, smoothly-polished stone receives but little wear. All machines on Mars are noiseless, and Electromotive force performs all the labor. It cleans, heats, cools and lights homes, public buildings, and all the streets of Mars. Aside from the *Readograph* referred to, other instruments that may be carried in the folds of the people's loose silk raiment, and no larger than an ordinary watch, are used to converse at any distance, one mile or many. A wireless instrument, to be described later, is of boundless utility. Many of these wonderful instruments were taken to Mars by emigrants from Alphacent, but others are the product of his scientific inventors.

"Long before the emigrants arrived from Alphacent on Mars these people of the greater planet actually assisted nature in preparing the latter's surface for the future race of people. They planted his entire fertile surface, and stocked his waters with fish, much as the Martians, a few hundred thousand years later, did for your Moon."

"Tell me, Marcomet, why they did this. Would not nature have accomplished all this in due time?" I inquired.

"Yes, nature provides a way for distributing all seeds and animal creations upon every new planet. Indeed, nature is forever sowing and reaping, whether the planet is fit or unfit—nature ever sows. Nature, however, requires thousands of years to accomplish what the intelligence of man may obtain within a few short years. The people of Alphacent knew this. Consequently they devised means of planting upon and over a whole planet at one time. It is a very simple undertaking, after you know how. They assisted nature to hurry vegetation so that a new world might be established. I will explain to you later how the people of Mars successfully accomplished a similar undertaking with the assistance of torpedoes. When the emigrants arrived on Mars everything grown on Alphacent was found in readiness, awaiting the guiding hand of man to improve and cultivate, yet, assisted by the magic of nature, in the process of multiplication. Knowledge from Alphacent had fortunately passed on to Mars.

· "They began anew, where they had left off on the old. By knowledge thus accumulated, a marvelous progress set in. Mars fairly blossomed like a vast and well-kept garden. Improving upon the old in his rapid strides toward perfection, Mars became a transcendent world of great promise. His climate was so healthful and salubrious that human life was prolonged more than ,four thousand per centum. The first million years of Martian history is filled with accounts of his humid and excessively damp climate, causing everything on the planet's surface to attain an enormous size. Gradually, as the planet's water became absorbed, and more land appeared, the size of everything grew proportionately less."

"Has labor, then, been entirely abolished?" I inquired.

"Yes, almost entirely. Everything is performed by electrical power, radium and liquefied air. These three elements are of insistent utility. A sufficient force of any one of these three elements may be carried in a small tube weighing less than one ounce. It is capable of propelling an individual ten thousand miles through the air in an electro-aero-chair. The people of Mars do not employ railroads, but travel and transport everything by their electro-aero-chairs or the electro-aero-car. The first of these conveys but one person only, while the latter are utilized for the transportation of all freight. The 'cars' vary in size and power, according to each proposed purpose."

"Then no boats are necessary?" I inquired.

"No. The air is a sea void of shoals or sandbars. Earth's people shall some day master it, then they will readily discover the non-utility of both land and water."

In silence I bowed my head, and with keen expectancy awaited his next announcement.

CHAPTER XXV

THE INHABITANTS OF MARS

"In transmitting thought you will observe, in my conversation, that I employ only familiar terms of Earth, so that you may the better comprehend my meaning, and avoid confusion of ideas," remarked Marcomet.

I thanked him for the kindly consideration accorded, though he mildly protested by acknowledging that it was a duty as well as his pleasure.

"Were the emigrants from Alphacent a very highly developed race, physically and mentally?" I inquired.

"Yes, I have already informed you of this. They are far in advance, physically and mentally, of any existing race in the universe—so far as I know. In size and stature, at the epoch referred to, they were veritable giants, averaging fifteen feet in height. They were students of nature, for they each, and without authority, analyzed and investigated for themselves. Nature, you must know, answers every question put in truth by the diligent and persistent searcher. Hence, disease was absolutely mastered by these people, and death was almost unknown. Since they knew that life was a succession of separate existences, the custom of the people was not to live beyond the age of near or about three thousand years. At that period of life a complete renewal of the body seemed best, and it became customary to publish a notice so that every one might learn of the individual's intention through the *Readograph*. Such a notice usually began,—'I hereby give fifty years' notice of my intention to be re-born.' Hereupon, the properly appointed individuals would immediately make a physical examination of the person announcing the intent. Notations of certain parts of the body showing excessive wear were taken. If an examination disclosed that the Individual was at all hurrying matters, and the parts showing decay could be substituted, consent would be denied, and a denial of privilege would be published in a like manner, withholding and forbidding them to leave. A substitution of all worn parts would then be made. On the other hand, if rebirth was thought best, no denial to the person's intention would be made. Then, the person had a right to elect a time after the expiration of the published period."

"Do you mean that they were enabled to repair any worn-out parts of the physique from time to time?" I asked in astonishment.

"Yes, they could safely substitute any worn-out part of the body, as well as construct and replace diseased nerves, correct and prevent hardening of the arteries, and so regulate the chemical requirements of the system as to keep it in perfect balance. Does this seem remarkable to you?" he added.

"I must confess it does," I replied.

"Think a moment! Are you not aware of the many marvelous surgical feats now performed on Earth? They now do in part what some day shall be done in whole, but only as Earth's people grow away from war and savagery. So long as the energy of nations is dissipated in strife and the support of strife makers, and the deifying of all such, progress will be slow and difficult. By comparison, you of Earth spend a cent for science to every thousand dollars for 'glory.' Science, even now, imparts to you the art of renewing noses, ears, stomachs, livers, and teeth."

I had humbly to admit the fact.

"After one publishing a notice to depart had proven to be beyond repair," continued Marcomet, "notice was privately served on all relatives and friends, that permission had been granted for the re-borning. Each inhabitant of Mars had a name and was given a number, both of which was the same,—written and in figures—in each successive existence. It was the duty of the individual in each new existence to announce when the age of fifty years had been reached, and giving his true name and number. There was no way to deceive by a mis-statement for the individuality was invariably recognized by the people, long before the required age had been attained. Under fifty, they were considered infants with names unrecognized by any one except the parent. At the age of fifty, the name of identification in their previous existence was returned them. Their mental training was so highly developed that it became essential and was not difficult for any person to remember the three thousand years of their prior existence."

"Then, one always had the same name, but what of them before they reached the age of fifty? What name, if any, did they bear?"

"Already I have informed you that every one was considered an 'infant' prior reaching that age, and until positively recognized would be referred to as a 'male infant' or 'female infant' of such and such parentage.

It was customary for parents to give their offspring pet names by which they were known to them alone. Frequently the parents, or infants themselves, upon reaching an early age, that is, fifteen or twenty, would disclose their identity, and immediately adopt their true name and number."

"You have not yet told me, Marcomet, how the aged voluntarily terminated their lives," I suggested.

"In a carefully selected location on Mars, where perpetual warmth and sunshine continues during most of the year, a wonderful garden of magnificent beauty existed. It was adorned with lilies, forget-me-nots, roses, daisies, honeysuckle, and hollyhocks—indeed, all the flowers of delicate scent and pungency. Their fragrance unfailingly ever filled the air, and their soft and delicate colors delighted the eye of the beholder when contrasted with the deep green of the stately elm, and the graceful willow. The trees, shrubs and flowers seemed, as it were, to reproduce every human character. The weak and strong, homely or beautiful characters seemed each represented there, as a perpetual reminder to those who had passed. The garden was laid out with gorgeous magnificence, without stint of richness in color and as near perfection as man can build. Filled with dancing fountains and miniature cascades, with cool, white manufactured marble paths, winding off in varying directions, but leading where—no one could know. It was a weird, dazzling, awe-inspiring sight when beheld from without.

"This garden was entirely surrounded by a high, white marble fence, through which the eyes of the passerby might peer, in an attempt to penetrate the depth of flowers and foliage, to result only in disappointment.

"There was but one entrance, and that by a single gate. The weary traveler, who had permission, passed gladly through, as the gate was ever unguarded. None was denied the right to enter—no human or divine penalty for seeking its welcome portal. Those who passed in appeared to do so eagerly and with joy. As the pilgrim faced East and went forward through the palatial portico, he was observed to proceed until he reached a point where numerous paths led off in different directions, terminating in an endless maze. It mattered little what path was chosen as each one here and there branched off until it fairly bewildered the traveler. Exhausted and weary, he now lay down to rest 'midst all the splendor of the scene—for none might find his or her way out again. The beauty and promise to each traveler became overwhelming. We each choose our particular path to the beauties yet unseen, but the windings in the labyrinth all lead—here. Do you understand?" asked Marcomet quietly and with emphasis.

I dreamily nodded, bowing my head in assent.

Without awaiting my return from absentmindedness, he continued: "The growth in the population of Mars, you must know, was rapid, and from the very beginning their progress kept pace with and in many ways excelled the mother country. The birth rate of Mars after awhile was, however, in exact proportion to his death rate. Nature took care of that. As deaths were infrequent, so were births. Births gave occasion for much rejoicing. Indeed, the joy of the Martians was unbounded as they contemplated a personality being permitted to return, instead of being directed to a new world, as frequently happens."

"How was Mars governed?" I ventured to inquire.

"There was no centralized 'government' on Mars. The people of each separate community, having certain well-defined boundaries, governed themselves through two educational bodies, co-equal in power. The people as a whole, however, enjoyed free intercourse between communities—all enjoying absolute freedom everywhere. There were no printed laws to govern Mars, as none were deemed necessary. Each person lived by the law of custom—well understood. Intelligence, order and the high human attributes of the Martians were so general that, aside from the existence of the unwritten law of trained habits and intellectual customs, further devices would have only tended to impede progress.

"There were two distinct organizations for each community. These constituted the only authority, and were distinct and separate in function from one another. For your convenience in understanding quickly, I shall call the first organization The Senate. Any person, male or female, over one hundred years old, could become a member after passing a rigid examination in chemistry, geometry, psychology, or certain other groups of scientific knowledge wherein they excel—one or more. There was no positive rule as to the exact science, if they only merited recognition. The examination covered a tremendous field of learning, but the candidate was only expected to take the subject in which he believed he excelled. They were passed and admitted by such members as were best qualified to judge the scientific subjects in which the candidate deemed himself expert. The qualifications of a candidate in any branch were judged solely by the members specializing in that branch, though a versatile examiner might belong to several branches."

"Which branch stood first in importance?" I asked.

"The members were never graded after admittance into the Senate. No one was permitted to lead. Each group of specialists were self-governing, though all matters of general importance, as effecting the entire community, were submitted to the whole body. Perhaps among the more important branches were some of those specializing in certain branches of chemistry, for the reason that certain of these branches were in full charge of the public health. They studied, to wit, the chemical needs of the human body, and the chemical values of foods. They studied and examined each person, so that every one was able to determine for himself continuously what was necessary to eat and to do, in securing vigorous health, thereby immunizing himself of disease. They had learned that disease was an effect and not the cause. Their investigations tended to discover more appropriate chemical compounds for the human system, such as strengthening the tissues of the body and thereby substantially lengthening human life. They were aware that no disease of any kind could obtain if the body be made proof against it. Studying disease is of utility only after people become afflicted. Weak bodies are subject to more forms of disease than are liable to be mastered."

"Was there no mystery about disease on Mars?"

"There is no mystery in all Nature that can long defy the searchers after truth. They must, however, be persistently and intelligently conducted. The Martians have mastered them all," replied Marcomet proudly.

"You just mentioned, I believe, that another educational body existed in each community of Mars?"

"The other body I shall call the 'House,' as it was

composed wholly of men and women Astronomers. Naturally, you would think their work had most to do with the surrounding Suns and Planets. But this was not altogether true, as that body also attended to everything pertaining to the surrounding air and ether beyond. All transportation by air and beyond was under their immediate supervision. The members composing this body were made up of the greatest minds in the communities, hence, the recognized superior minds of the realm. The same method of examination for admission was employed, but there were always fewer candidates, as the examinations were more exacting and difficult. It required minds formed and born, rather than educated, to enter this body. Natural ability embodies imagination, patience, persistence, broad mindedness, and an extended capacity. No education supplies these. Both Senate and House were open day and night, many members being continually present.

"The buildings wherein these bodies met were usually situated upon some high eminence, being large and imposing, and constructed of a white manufactured stone, the surface of which resembled highly polished china. It was much harder than the finest steel, and absolutely weatherproof. The buildings were imperishable. Many built several hundred thousand years ago are still in a perfect state of preservation."

"What were the qualifications of citizenship on Mars?"

"Eligibility to citizenship demanded that a person be at least fifty or more years old, and the qualifications were that he shall pass a satisfactory examination held by ten Senate members before he is entitled to all the benefits of citizenship. The examinations were alike in every case, and the answers given demonstrated fitness. The benefits of citizenship accorded certain rights and a grant of land with a house thereon, also, the right to visit, petition and be heard before the Senate of the community wherein they reside. A citizen of one community was free to visit, live in, or travel at will in all other communities."

"Then, children under fifty, and people incapable of becoming citizens, did not travel as they desired?" I suggested.

"No. They might go abroad with parents, but not alone. Their parents were absolutely responsible for them until they reached the age and requirements of citizenship, even though a thousand years old before succeeding in passing the examination."

"If there were no printed laws, lawyers, courts or judges, how then are differences settled?"

"When disputes arose in the family between children, the head of the family—the mother—decided matters. Her word was final. When these differences were between citizens, both were required to immediately appear before two Senate members, some of whom were sitting day and night. They presented their own case, without any aid, and witnesses were not permitted."

"After both sides of the case were heard,—then what?" I eagerly asked.

"Then two Senators immediately decided the matter in dispute, and fixed the penalty, provided both agreed. If they failed to agree, the disputants had to appear at once before the other Senators, and continued to do so until two of the latter agreed on the case. When a decision was once rendered, neither of the disputants, during life, might mention the matter again, nor was any one allowed to ask either of them the success or failure of the issue."

"What was the penalty in case they ignored the Senators' verdict?"

"The penalty was to advertise the person's offense throughout every home in the realm. Indeed, the worst disgrace suffered by any person was to be held up to public scorn; therefore, cases of disobedience were very rare."

"Since there were no published laws, then there were no political bodies?"

"None."

"Did not some form of evil exist?"

"Yes, among people that were not absolutely perfect."

"How, then, was evil regulated or suppressed?"

"By example, moral suasion, and publicity. All knowledge of existing evil was known to certain Senate Members only, who quietly regulated or suppressed it."

"Would free intercourse among nations and the employment of one common language on Earth remedy evils?" I asked.

"These would help. One language on Mars gave all the feeling of perfect security. Several languages would have destroyed the harmony, cause suspicion, or induced one who failed to understand another, to humorously regard his language, manners or customs. On Mars, when people betrayed any disrespect, or quarreled, then to school they had to go, and there stay until they had learned to thoroughly master the weakness."

"Then, I suppose, some remained in school most of the three thousand years of their lives?" I suggested.

Here I detected a playful smile which seemed to cross Marcomet's face, as he replied solemnly: "Yes, and when they came back they began all over again."

"Were there no rich and poor on Mars?" I asked, suggesting a change in query and answer.

"There were neither rich nor poor, for the excellent reason that there was no money. They had no use for that commodity. Each individual contributed a certain amount of work for the benefit of all. Then all surplus belonged to the whole. Menial labor was practically unknown. They had learned how to harness the energies, so freely supplied by Nature, to perform all menial labor. The more delicate energies of human body were not permitted to be abused or broken by the harder toil. Their brains and hands were for working out life's higher problems, in its upward march."

"Upon what scale was labor performed on Mars?" I ventured.

"The labor was all done by machinery—upon a huge scale. Each community specialized in certain things, according to soil, climate and natural conditions. In farming, for instance, the soil best adapted to raise certain things was selected. Sufficient of everything was provided, so that each person had plenty."

"You have mentioned certain motive power used on Mars?"

"Electricity, radium and liquefied air were formerly employed. Liquefied air is not now permitted, for the atmosphere has become so rarefied that it cannot be spared. Electricity was, however, the most common power for many kinds of service. Small batteries, weighing less than two ounces, were attached to the clothing, and gave to the individual on Mars enough light, heat and power to last from ten to fifteen years, without renewal."

"How was it released by the person carrying it?"

"At will, and this concentrated energy-instrument was so constructed that there was positively no danger to the person."

"What incentive have living beings to strive for if there be no reward as a consummation?"

"There can only be one noble incentive worthy of our striving. The reward of a greater knowledge. For this, Martians have ever striven with an intense desire. Hence their exalted position in the great family of worlds."

CHAPTER XXVI

PREPARATIONS

SIMULTANEOUSLY with Marcomet's concluding remarks, I observed a great company of several hundreds, standing in pairs, and in long line immediately outside the great white way. Marcomet seemed to await their approach, for he turned from me and went toward them.

When they arrived and stood before him as if to be judged, Marcomet willed that I should not overhear his conversation. As he addressed each one, I had no means of divining what he said.

I saw others join them, re-form into different couples regardless of variation in age or size, and then, fading apparently away in pairs, they seemed as if bound for a new existence.

"Was that not a large company for so short a period?" I ventured.

"No," replied Marcomet. "Time is not an entity here, but, since it obtains on Earth, I may tell you that this large company came from there. A transatlantic steamer foundered at sea, and that accounts for the great variety of ages you observed. The accident happened, according to Earth's time, less than one thousandth of a second ago.

"When I shall have completed my narrative you will be back to Earth again with another *Mal*ality in less than a second of time. You will understand that, according to

Earth's time, you have been here only the fractional part of a second!"

Without further comment on the subject, he resumed:

"The inhabitants of Mars dress only in light, loose raiment, gorgeous in color and luster, draped to the form, manufactured from a material lighter in weight and much stronger than your finest silk. It is impervious to dampness and a non-conductor of heat and cold."

"Are there no prudish people who object to this loose, comfortable form of covering?"

"I have already said that there are no bad people on Mars!" he replied.

"But, I inquired about pru——"

"Prudish people?" he interrupted interrogatively, and then for what seemed a minute he stood gazing into the far beyond, as if to repress a show of vexation. Finally he faced about and said: "Prudishness is only another word for wickedness. A prudish mind is an evil one. As is rightly said, 'Evil to him who evil thinks.' A person is evil in proportion to the domination of his *Malality*. Wicked people see wickedness in others. Purity sees purity alone. Honesty, not innocence, is pure. The home is the foundation rock upon which honesty is built."

"As the people of Mars advance nearer perfection," I asked, "what incentive will there finally be for good—when all the bad is eradicated? If there be no bad, how can people know what good is? We would not understand light if there was no darkness," I said.

"It matters little how high the average of goodness may be, there is always something higher and better to strive for. There is the same proportional difference between the good and the very good, as there is between the bad and very bad. Perfection is an entirely relative term. Certain degrees of perfection attain definite results, as certain degrees of evil carry their own penalties."

I now became conscious of the arrival of several more people and their Dualities. Again Marcomet began to pair them, and to send them forth anew, until there was but one couple remaining. I waited for some time, in respectful silence, so that he might give them final words of instruction. When he appeared to have overlooked them, I turned and said, "Are you aware that a Personal and Dual spirit awaits without?"

"Yes, there are millions waiting whom you do not see. Behold!" Raising his hand, as if in command of an army. And suddenly I had revealed to me a great multitude of people, stretching far out into space. The vision was but for an instant. As he lowered his hand the vision, like an apparition, dissolved from view, but the lone couple I had seen were still in evidence.

"The Personality you see desires to speak with you," said Marcomet.

"He does?" I said with some surprise, turning to scrutinize the faces more closely.

"You don't appear to know me, John," said the figure. "Don't you remember Daniel Lurkin?"

He had hardly told his name before my recollection of him came back.

"You have changed, Daniel. Your face looks harder. I missed seeing you at Brighton last summer. Where were you?"

"Why, didn't you know, I died early last Spring—in—May, I think."

"What ailed you?"

"No ailment. I was hanged. Didn't hurt though, worst part was the anticipation and fear of pain, like a person's first experience in a dentist's chair having a tooth pulled. Fear is the worst part of it. You seem surprised?"

"Yes, I am, Daniel. What crime did you commit?"

"Why, I killed a man for stealing my wife away. I thought I was justified in removing him, but they tell me up here that a woman who is willing to be stolen from her husband, should not be hindered, neither should any one undertake to punish the moral thief; he punishes himself."

"Why are you detained?"

"Like a multitude of others, I'm not fit to return. After a few million years of intense thought on the subject of my crime, I shall then be fitted to return."

Then Daniel and his companion disappeared and I saw them no more.

"Where is the executioner, Marcomet? Has the State a right to kill that the individual does not possess? In justice, shall he not be punished, too?"

"Removing persons for the good of society is a duty." Continuing, he said—"To allow a few to break down or destroy the accumulated intelligence and wealth that for ages honest and industrious people have built up, without some effort to destroy them, is cowardly. Ignorance and the savage instinct is at the bottom of all wars, as well as all disease. We should not seek either, but cultivate every means to prevent both. We are best prepared when we are strongest, for strength, whether intelligently or ignorantly applied, will dominate. Ignorance sown in strength will ever overpower intelligence sown in weakness. Strength with intelligence cannot be subdued. Be prepared for any eventuality, whether in preventing crime,

or staying the occasion for war. Take this message back
to Earth! If war threatens, be prepared as no one else is!
Then arbitrate the difference. When the differences are
settled to the satisfaction of all parties involved, begin
anew to prepare, as never before. In this fashion will
all war be abolished. It will destroy you if the course
prescribed be neglected. Supreme power should be vested
in no one. Let every community be sufficient in all respects unto itself."

"Where does the greatest danger to liberty exist on
Earth?"

"Sometimes, though not always, where there is the
greatest liberty. For liberty attracts the downtrodden,
and, being accustomed to oppression, their pent-up human
passions seek in the name of Liberty to wreck the world
with license."

"Does every one work upon Mars?"

"Every person over fifty years old may be compelled
to work at least one hour a day. Since every one works,
all the daily work of Mars is done in less than twenty
minutes."

"Since there is no medium of exchange, how do people
procure their necessities?"

"Each community raises everything on a gigantic scale
—sufficient for all. This is inspected, distributed, and
its surplus retained in great store houses furnished with
preserving plants, and so perfected, that everything may
be preserved indefinitely, in a fresh and ripe condition as
when first gathered."

"In what amusements do the Martians indulge?"

"Their greatest amusement is in watching the people
of Earth."

"What are they amused at?" I said, with some show of indignation.

"By being amused, I mean they are interested in Earth's people because, indirectly, all the white races can trace their ancestry to Mars—but that is another story."

CHAPTER XXVII

THE PSYCHOLOGRAPH

"John," said Marcomet, turning to me, "your friend Jasper will soon be here."

The thought had hardly been uttered before Jasper and his *Mal*ality arrived arm in arm together. Though I was not permitted to communicate with him, nor he to see me, Marcomet permitted me listening to much of the exchanged thought between them. I overheard their interchange of thought. As I listened, I knew Marcomet was inquiring about Jasper's *Mal*ality.

"Yes, he's been a putty gud companion," I heard him say. "But I've worn out more'n one pair o' breeches jest sittin' on his pesky idees. It's a gol darn interestin' trip, I tell ye. By gum, I'm tickled t' death thet I tuck th' trip. Ain't yer glad tue?" asked Jasper as he turned to his *Mal*ality. But, receiving no response, he continued— "Well, by gosh, I never knewed my shadder was so solom afore. Yer must have got th' best of me when we went t' prayer meetin', but th' rest of th' time I kept yer where yer belonged, didn't I?" Again Jasper eyed him suspiciously. "Say, Parson, I should say Marcomet, let me have him agin fur another trip. I've learned him t' keep his tongue quiet so much, thet he can't talk, by ginger. Next time he won't see, 'less he be-haves."

Evidently Marcomet felt satisfied that both should return together again, as I heard Jasper say, "I'll take gud care of him, an' bring him back t' yer better, next time." And then, getting as close to Marcomet as he could, in a low tone, I overheard him ask, "Has Nancy arrived? No? Well, I'll wait 'til she comes, if I hev t' wait a thousand years," and the man of Mars seemed satisfied to grant his request.

But, even here, I discovered we must part from friends. Suddenly the curtain was silently drawn between Jasper and me, removing him from my vision and hearing—forever.

"One of the most noted scientists of Mars," said Marcomet, as he resumed his narrative, "invented a small electric instrument which could be fastened to any part of the body, and when so attached, would permanently record all the thoughts of *Bon*ality. It could not, however, record the thoughts of *Mal*ality. This instrument became a tremendous factor in bringing about better moral conditions, and its effect upon the daily life of Mars was fast broadening."

"What was the instrument called?" I asked with much interest.

"The *Psycholograph*. The inventor, as in all cases of new discoveries, presented it to the people of Mars, but under the jurisdiction of the Community Senates alone it was to be used for the benefit of all."

"I presume that the interest of all the people was so excited that each wanted to wear it?"

"It produced the greatest consternation among many, while in others only an eager desire to wear it," replied Marcomet. "When the excitement created by the discovery had somewhat subsided, the Senates ruled that every person throughout the whole realm of Mars should wear the *Psycholograph*, this, for the purpose of recording their true character and disposition. The instrument automatically recorded all the thoughts of the Personality. The method used was to question the person after the *Psycholograph* had been attached. The first question put by a Senate member might be 'Do you love your wife?' If the person answered 'Yes,' truthfully, it was the Personality speaking, and the instrument would record the reply. If, however, the answer given was not true, then no record would be made. A person's true character was known by the number of recorded answers made to questions put. The instrument was the means of immediately discouraging lying."

"What became of the records? To whom did they belong?"

"To the Community Senates. The *Psycholograph* recorded everything in code, therefore, being impossible to read these without a key. This latter was in charge of a Senator duly appointed.

"I have already informed you that before the age of fifty years is reached, every child is given a number, the same as possessed in a previous existence. Hence, each person's number is a positive identification everywhere. The instrument is so attached to the person that, after being fastened and sealed, it can never be removed. When records of a person are taken on the *Psycholograph*, they are filed in the Senate Archives, under that person's number. He or she may alone examine them, unless the Senate publishes the record, with a view to punishing the person for a wrong. Or unless it be the wife or husband of the person, in which case either has absolute access to the other's record. Since each person knew his own number, he was able at all times to secure his record without difficulty.

"After a record was made by the *Psycholograph*, one could then examine the same by the aid of a key, and thus learn from it all his weaknesses and how far he had allowed himself to be dominated by the evil one within. Each one knew, by reading the record, the weaknesses his character disclosed. It was not necessary for others to tell you of your faults. You knew of them yourself, and quickly learned how to guard against and master the most dangerous ones."

"Was the instrument used for sifting out all wrong-doing?"

"It was used for that purpose but a few times. It became unnecessary to seek out wrong after the Senate rule was made. Those who acknowledged their faults, were forgiven. All wrongdoers confessed their faults, thus earning immunity."

"Before whom did they confess?"

"Before any Senator, who would secure a *Psycholograph* record of the wrongdoing. After this the record was sealed and filed away, never to be opened unless later the person committed further wrong. In such case, the records were published so that the public might know the person's disgrace. No greater punishment than this was suffered by an individual. To inflict this penalty was the greatest of all punishments."

"Were records of all persons destroyed after their death?"

"Yes."

"Were the Martians required to confess to wrong-doing?"

"If they knew they had done wrong, they did so voluntarily, because it was customary and because they earned immunity. But every one acted as his own judge in all moral relations. An act was morally right or wrong according to the view of the person involved, every one deciding that matter for himself."

"Then, what an outsider might consider morally wrong, the persons involved would decide to be right?"

"Yes, that was their business. No person had any right to condemn another for things not affecting him. The public never interfered except to protect public morals. Private acts were never public matters.

"If an old man of twenty-five hundred years and a young maiden of three hundred years decided to marry, the person attempting to interfere with the union, without good reason, would be held up to public condemnation. But, any ten persons over fifty years of age, who believed that one or both of the parties to the union were acting in bad faith, could petition the Senate to use the *Psychograph*, and thus learn the truth. If the record showed bad faith upon the part of either, no union would be allowed."

"I should think then, that it would be wiser for each couple contemplating marriage to have *Psychograph* records taken, thus avoiding the danger of unnatural unions? They might, in order to show complete sincerity, exchange records?"

"You have anticipated," replied Marcomet. "They do this very thing. Every couple invariably exchange records, before marriage. Frequently the bride has cause to say, 'I could love your *Bona*lity, but I never could stand your *Mala*lity.' "

"Then many unhappy unions are avoided?"

"Certainly. No young man can say to every girl he fancies, 'I love you.' 'Furnish me with a *Psycholograph* record before I express my feeling to you,' she would reply. Or she might reply, that she loved what she believed was his Personality, but before deciding she would like to examine the record to find out whether it was the man's Duality that had been making these fanciful love protestations."

"Do they frequently part, after reading each other's records?" I asked.

"They rarely progress so far in their love making as to part disappointed. When both show a record not very flattering, they marry because they deem it the very best they can do. Others shudder at the thought of what they have avoided. Whatever they decide, each enters the marriage state knowing well the character of the mate chosen. No one is or can be taken advantage of."

I could not help remarking—"I wish they had that little instrument on Earth. What troubles they might avoid!"

Marcomet looked not a little surprised at my abrupt exclamation, but I could discover a pleased expression in his eyes when he replied: "You'll have it soon. You have succeeded in recording the voice, and you will succeed in recording thought. Your inventors must take care to record the *Bona*lity's thought alone."

I could not help speculating upon this part of his narrative. On Mars they must keep the *Bona*lity always in the foreground. How much, soever, evil the *Mala*lity might be would never be known or suspected if the *Bonality* dominated.

If the *Psycholograph* showed that *Bonality* spoke truthfully, and both parties loved the other, there was no way, of course, of knowing what *Malality* both carried, nor would they ever know, unless they later weakly allowed that side of their nature to expose itself.

" 'Love is blind' on Earth, but not on Mars," I thought, and Marcomet had made the whole matter clear to me.

"In order to effect a perfect union, the instrument must disclose that each one's Personality loves the other. If, after a couple have once married, either wife or husband has reason to believe that the other's affection is on the decrease, each has the right to subject the other to an examination by the *Psycholograph.* If the result discloses that the wife's love is unchanged, though his love has somewhat abated, both are required to continue the union, so that she be given an opportunity to win back, if possible, the husband's affection. The instrument would invariably show why his love is growing cold. One of the reasons might be that he is dissatisfied with her cooking, or that she has grown careless in her personal appearance, or perhaps she is slack in her housekeeping, or that she has fallen in love with some one else. Here, therefore, was her opportunity to make a strong and honest effort to correct the weakness, if weakness it might be. The *Psycholograph* was frequently resorted to in order to know what progress was being made along these lines. Can you imagine a woman's happiness in again winning back the lost love? If honest effort prevailed this beautiful result was certain. For, does not honest endeavor bring its own reward? What woman would not make an effort to retain the love of him whom she loved?

"Now, on the other hand, suppose the record develops that her love for him has lessened, and that he finds it is because he is lazy, indolent, shiftless, brutal, or has fallen in love with another woman, or a thousand other weaknesses that man develops through his ignoble nature. The disclosure would, without fail, have an instant effect upon him, and he would hasten to mend his ways.

"On Mars, however, man can't advertise his reformation. On Earth man alone rules, and he has ever been proud of his prerogative."

"Can a married person love more than one?"

"The *Bon*ality can love but one, and if we master our other self, so that we are not dominated by *Mal*ality we never can love but one. Men or women who love more than one, thus express the weakness of their will, and their failure to control the companion over whom they should exercise it. One who loves two, may love many. Pity the one who thus destroys the hope of many lives."

"What is love?"

"We know, first, what love is not. The common error is to mistake passion for love. The affection called passion is the only 'love' existing among animals. The young man who can say to different girls, 'I love you,' twice during the same evening, is merely telling them how he feels. Love is the adoration of our highest ideals. It does not mean the common, low, and melodramatic word so popular on Earth. It begins and ends in faith. It may be slow in growth, but its renunciation will be likewise."

"Are there divorces on Mars?"

"No. Either the husband or wife may subject one another to an examination by the *Psycholograph*. If at any time the husband desires a record of his wife's *Bonality* she must submit herself to the *Psycholograph*, and vice versa. If the husband has been unfaithful or has even been thinking wrongly, the instrument would disclose the whole matter to his wife. The husband would likewise have knowledge of his wife's secret thought."

"What happens if unfaithfulness is shown?"

"When a new affection enters either life, the moral law teaches that no one has a right to interfere. It would be manifestly a crime to compel two human beings to be joined forever in wedlock when love existed only on one or neither side. A simply published renouncement is all that is necessary, when each may go his or her own way. God desires love and happiness, but it cannot come ready-made by laws or manufactured by customs. People cannot be forced to love each other, as it becomes immoral to compel."

"You have told me what happened when the love of wife or husband diminished, and how hard each strove to regain lost affection, but you did not explain the result in case love could not be regained, and the loss continued?"

"It obtains as a puzzling condition, and ever will, when one's affection grows cold in the face of every adequate and beautiful condition. Of course, such cases are rare on Mars, but when they appear custom then wills that the persons must live apart until the *Psycholograph* shows an improvement. If, within a reasonable period, there is no return of affection upon the part of the one grown cold, then either may re-marry. Their conception of life is to seek forever happiness in its highest and most blissful form. They must, therefore, follow, morally, the true impulse of their own heart, their *Bonality*.

"The public is not permitted, under any pretense whatsoever, to invade the privacy of a Martian. Every life is sufficient unto itself, and must account instanter for transgression of the moral law. God judges! He does not permit any one to supplant him. Those who do judge, however, now stand without, not fit to return until changed," said Marcomet, pointing towards the immense groups of individuals, many of whom had been outside for many ages.

"They are so far wrong that they are deliberately held here for a quiet contemplation of their assumption. There is nothing so dangerous as the person who judges others before they have had a chance. Some people have been waiting ages to overcome this evil," continued Marcomet with emphasis.

"Then the incentive for hypocrisy has been lessened by the *Psycholograph?*" said I, wishing to change the subject.

"It very nearly wiped all out. There is no 'class,' so to speak, on Mars, therefore, there is no so-called 'society.' This small instrument drove out 'superior to thou' in honest pursuits, and cleaner thoughts. Indeed, it saved them from degradation. Money, it must be remembered, is not the only factor in creating the class idea. We have no money on Mars, yet we had, until the advent of this instrument, a well-defined upper class. It was created from unworthiness, supported by hypocrisy, and kept alive by assumption. When light was thrown onto their real life, through the *Psycholograph*, the classes all rushed to cover until the storm blew over, then they went to work. They did not intend to be dishonest or hypocritical, but overfeeding and associating exclusively with their own kind subsequently made them act queerly. They did not realize that continued intermarriage within their own social set was producing degenerates. When lapse of time exposed this poor, weak social class, the people did not ridicule, but rather pitied them.

"What a rejoicing there was when each one assumed his work in life, so that, within a few years, they were wont to look with pity on their previous condition."

CHAPTER XXVIII

THE ASTRONOMICAL SOCIETY

"One of the famous men frequently referred to throughout the ancient histories of Mars, and whose interesting life all the children of the realm delight in reading, was known as Christopher Spencer. While he lived that particular Martian life millions of years ago, people never ceased to admire his personality and achievements. Part of his life was spent upon Mars, where he was born, but he migrated from there to the Moon in early youth.

"The Spencer family had been a noted one through many thousands of years, owing to its uniform and excellent character, coupled with a high degree of intelligence. For several thousands of years they, or their ancestors, lived upon the border of the great and beautiful Lake of Lucus Lunae, fed by the 'Rivers Ganges,' 'Clitumnus' and 'Chrysorrhoas,' and connecting with the 'Caricus,' which flows towards 'Fons Juventae' and 'Messeis Fons.' These rivers are now dried up. Their great beds have been utilized to form canals. The Ganges Canal now beautiful in itself, connects with the Community, but, alas, beyond the city lies only the desert of Stagnum Pegaseum. There is, withal, but one cry from the great voice of the people—water! Water! More water!"
Here Marcomet turned from me, his head bowed upon his

breast. To me it seemed a long time before he sufficiently recovered to continue speaking.

"Most all the inhabitants have departed from Mars. But that's another story. I will not weary you with the relation," he said. "In the age, however, when Christopher Spencer was born on the shores of the beautiful Lake of Lucus, the community of Stagnum Pegaseum was the most popular on all Mars. The community entirely encircled this wonderful Lake of pure and limpid waters. One, indeed, of dazzling celestial beauty—famous throughout the realm. The Lake was fed by great rivers of wonderful purity. Along its banks grew beautiful semi-tropical vegetation in uniform environment, and of picturesque magnificence. Nature, in time, dried up the rivers and the Lake, aye, even to the last drop. But man, with indomitable will, combined with perseverance, has since restored them!"

Here again Marcomet paused, as if to emphasize his words. A feeling of pride seemed to well up within him as he uttered each thought.

"Through immense hydraulic pumping stations, the present inhabitants have brought to the surface the very water that once flowed above it. Unfortunately, Christopher Spencer's parents died while he was yet a child, less than fifty years old, and as his remaining relatives were then few, or none, he found himself friendless and alone in the world. By that, I do not mean that any one suffers from lack of companionship on Mars, but in one respect the people of the entire universe are alike, in that they have no particular interest in people or things out of sight. Few knew him, therefore of human friendship he knew little. He was educated in the public institutions of the

Community in which he lived, taking up Astronomy as the goal of his ambition. He had great natural ability for this particular branch, and, in a comparatively short time, his name became known as a young and ardent astronomer of remarkable proficiency. This soon gained for him the privilege of applying for membership in the Astronomical Society. After passing the necessarily successful examination, the Society received him into membership with honor. Before he had obtained his one hundredth year, his name on Mars had become famous. The fact that he was a man of strong character, great ability, and an inventor of renown, added to his fame and popularity. It was not many years before he was the recognized leader of the House.

"Spencer's aptitude in the solution of many perplexing problems in which Astronomers had failed, now excited profound admiration. Though very high advancement in the science of Astronomy had reached a point where great telescopes were enabled to discern, and examine with ease the surface of the farthest Planet or Sun—bringing them so close to vision that objects on their surfaces appeared as only a few feet away—the problem of penetrating clouds, mists or fogs, was as yet unsolved, and was thought among Astronomers to be impossible of solving. Therefore, all planets during the formation process, and when they had reached that stage when vapor surrounds them— to incredible depths—were impenetrable by the most powerful telescopes, so that no certain knowledge of Nature's processes could be obtained. Then, Spencer's genius proved its adequacy. To solve the problem, many had tried, but Spencer knew it could be done. His first experiment was in penetrating fogs on land and sea. After many discouragements, he succeeded in perfecting a machine which pierced fogs of any depth. This achievement encouraged him to apply the same principle to the telescope. He succeeded, and finally applied the principles of the wireless telephone to the same instrument, naming the completed machine the *Transtelephonescope*. This instrument in concreted form was manufactured in dimensions which not only brought objects billions of miles distant to within four or five feet of vision, but its receivers were so constructed that the listening operator might hear the faintest sound when coming from that section of the Planet to which the disc of the *Transtelephonescope* pointed. It was quite as easy, through this instrument, to see as well as to hear far beyond a billion miles. Of what utility and how interesting it would have been to have had a similar instrument set up on another planet! It would have been possible to carry on conversations with perfect ease though billions of miles apart. Would it not?" said Marcomet, turning suddenly and facing me.

I nodded in assent. Indeed, I was so interested in his narrative, I didn't think quickly enough to reply.

"I will tell you later how all this was accomplished by this very young man," said Marcomet. "It could penetrate vapor of any depth. To its disc, sound-receivers were attached, with extensions regulated and attuned to numerous smaller ones, each branching off to the private rooms and experimental chambers of the members of the Astronomical Society. Here its members received and recorded the news from other worlds, and re-transmitted it, so that each family could keep in touch with all that was going on through the *Readograph*. Sounds from other planets, or in the space surrounding them, could be heard. The *Transtelephonescope* was so delicately constructed that when pointed at a planet where information was desired it would only record the sounds from the exact spot on the planet pointed at. Hence, there was no confusion of sounds.

"Many of these powerful 'Scopes'—as they were popularly called—were set up in different districts of each community, each in charge of Astronomers who took turns in watching and recording matters of importance transpiring on the planet under observation. Their efforts never ceased through day or night.

"Through the 'Scope' we studied the languages and customs of the planets, noting their progress, observing their wars, catastrophes, accidents, and taking moving pictures of all in their natural colors. Combining and recording everything with the sounds accompanying, and exhibiting the results to the people of Mars for their entertainment and instruction."

"Why do you hesitate?" I asked, as Marcomet almost abruptly stopped short, peering into the distance—his eyes fastened upon Earth.

"I was thinking of the pictures that had been taken of that Planet," he replied, pointing in its direction. "Whenever our people seemed somewhat impatient or dissatisfied, the Astronomers would turn the discs of their 'Scopes' toward Earth, taking a few moving pictures, and then exhibiting them to our people. Many scenes from that unfortunate planet would invariably cure any one of a feeling of dissatisfaction. 'Thank God I live on Mars,' the discontented one would say. '*There* is indeed hell,' others would remark, after viewing the pictures of sav-

agery and war. There were scenes of cruelty and injustice, everywhere. They observed the strong oppressing
the weak; the rich and powerful taking from the masses
the fruits of their toil; the blasted lives through broken
vows, and promises unkept. In every hamlet, we saw
prosperity and disaster, sunshine and sorrow, love and
hate, laughter and tears; all at the same moment. Then
pictures were given of mankind from the very beginning
on Earth. His savage battles from the time when, in his
ignorant, hardened nature, without provocation, he would
as quickly crush the innocent, cooing baby in its mother's
arms, as he would crush out the life of an enemy with a
club. Indeed, he saw no penalty in either act. But, as our
people viewed and now view all of these scenes, they knew,
and know, that Nature holds a penalty in store for every
wrong, as well as a reward for every act of generous sacrifice, holy living, justice, and the noble desire for ultimate
perfection.

"They saw in the pictures, a few years later, the thiev-
ing wretch of a previous existence, now returned to an
ox-like existence of incessant toil; the gambler to a life of
pain and sorrow; the libertine to a life of sickness and
disease. Those who had followed lives of murder, hate and
injustice, were here again, reaping the results. For none
may escape the penalties weighed out with minutest exact-
ness, though it might take a thousand separate existences
to satisfy one individual debt. Earth's society penalizes
itself by punishing its individuals. The prisoner is no
more guilty than the judge who inflicts the penalty upon
him—unless charity and mercy, with a desire for the good
of all, prompts the sentence!"

"Did not the people of Mars, themselves, suffer, to

think that all these horrible things could be enacted before their eyes, and they still helpless to assist or advise?"

"For thousands of years, Mars' scientists have struggled to devise some method of communication, but without success. Yet you may tell the people when you return. It will some day be brought about, through your wireless telegraphy.

"So far as Earth's scenes of crime affecting our people, I assure you they did not, for the Martians understand that the actors in crime pay every particle of the debt— no discounts with Nature! 'Do wrong, if you will, but you shall pay for it to the last minute particle!' they would say, when they beheld a human brute commit a wrong.

"There is an interesting little world which has had a wonderful history," exclaimed Marcomet, suddenly pointing at Earth's beautiful Moon. "We, for ages, had watched and studied this attractive satellite, with increasing interest. Through its various stages of development we observed, until finally, impenetrable banks of mist enveloped it, making further study impossible. We realized that it would take several hundred thousand years for this mist to cool the sphere sufficiently to allow the surrounding moisture to condense upon its surface, and thus clear the atmosphere so as to enable us to regard it again, toward its planet development. We were impatient to find a means of looking through the mist.

"Not until the arrival of Christopher Spencer, a few thousand years later, and that wonderful invention, 'the Scope,' had been discovered, did the astronomers continue their observations. When they first turned the discs of their great instruments upon this 'Queen' of the skies, and gazed easily through the mist surrounding its surface, it produced a sensation among them that has not been paralleled to this day. When the news describing it was flashed through the public *Autoreadophone*, the wireless voice to every similar instrument, in every home of Mars, great was the excitement of the people. Then occurred a rush to all observatories of Mars, to behold this 'new born' of the skies—as they felt disposed to call it.

"These staid and sober-looking astronomers could not even refrain from joining in the general rejoicings, nor could they restrain their child-like antics, so great was the delight. If the Moon had been a human baby, it could not have excited greater or more profound curiosity."

"Is all the news of Mars flashed by the wireless voice?" I inquired.

"Yes," replied Marcomet. "Public news is spoken into an *Autoreadophone*, which is repeated aloud on every machine in Mars, each being attuned to receive public messages."

"What do you mean by 'attuned to receive?'" I said, perplexedly.

"All 'phones,' as they are commonly called, are adjusted so that the messages, instead of talking aloud, are transmitted to permanent records which later may be read by applying the *Readograph*. However, when you desire to receive or send a message on the 'phone, it is necessary to attune the instrument to the same degree of current status as that of the instrument to which you wish to speak, for each machine's electro-motive force is permanent. 'Phones are all set at the same tension and every person knows how to attune his 'phone to receive and send messages. In order to talk through this instrument, however, they must first know and obtain the attuning force. Of course, friends exchange these records, but no one else may call up.

"It is customary for the people, early in the day, to attune their instruments to the public wireless voice. The families gather after breakfast in their spacious houses and listen to the news. While all private houses in Mars are but one story high, and contain no more than the necessary rooms or divisions, many of these are built two hundred feet high, with several galleries usually extending entirely around the one public or principal room.

"Every convenience known to science and art is universal, the only difference being in the construction and decoration, due to the individual taste of the occupants, as everything belongs to everybody.

"Electricity, caught from the air by ingenious devices, is universally employed for heating and lighting their houses, grounds, walks, and roadways, or cooled by iced air circulated by powerful electric fans set in the walls of houses, on the walks and roadways, or wherever necessary, according to the pleasure, comfort, or desire of the individual. Cooking, in all forms, is done entirely by the same devices. Power is plentiful everywhere—more than sufficient for Man's needs. Nothing is so cheap on Earth as electro-force if the people would learn how to harness it. Instead, ten thousand men on Earth work to invent some new power that will destroy their fellows, or blast the lives of millions of innocent women and children. If they would only bend their energies toward harnessing the inexhaustible power around them, they would serve in relieving all from distasteful toil, so that each might devote his time to the more noble work of improving his body and mind in learning to live and how to die! The fair day and hour will dawn, however, in spite of the many minds that cannot see into the future!

"As an instance, I give you this:—

"One morning, as the people gathered early in their great rooms, the unseen voice was heard through the 'phone by every listening inhabitant of Mars. The first announcement created a thrill of interest—almost wonder. The voice was that of Christopher Spencer, the greatest astronomer Mars ever had. His first words were: 'I have examined the surface of the Moon, and find it has cooled sufficiently to admit of vegetation, which has already made its appearance. Not, however, in quantities of any one or more kinds sufficient to sustain the life.'

"When the people heard this, a mighty cheer went up in every home, the combined noise of which sounded like distant thunder on Christopher's 'phone. It was some moments before the sounds subsided sufficiently to allow him to proceed, but when all was quiet again he continued:

" 'Four years ago there was not a sign of vegetable life on the Moon. I knew it had to appear, but how? None could convey the various kinds of seeds; then, how was the Moon's surface to be planted? About two years ago, I noted that several weeds and flowers had sprung up. How did they get there? I watched through each day and far into the night. At last I discerned a spot about a mile in diameter. It was situated on a high plateau. There was no sign of vegetation anywhere within the boundaries of that circular mile. About six months later, as I was intently watching, I saw a beautiful meteor come out of the sky and burst thirty to forty miles over the spot I was viewing. There was nothing strange about this, except that I thought it singular why the meteor should explode over that particular spot. I was amazed one morning a few weeks after to see weeds, grass and flowers coming up in scattered patches, all within that circle! This impressed me deeply, and I soon proved to my own satisfaction that *the meteor had brought the seeds!*

" 'Then I at once realized that Nature's method of planting was the same throughout the universe. Vegetable and insect life is transplanted from one planet to another, through the direct and natural communication of meteors. The meaning of it all was, obviously, that everything from the smallest dust particles to the largest bodies coming in contact with a planet's atmosphere came through the medium of meteors. There are seeds and other forms of life in embryo, daily blown or brushed off these visitors as they begin their rapid descent through atmospheres. In addition, quantities float in space, until drawn into some atmosphere. Then, on they slowly seep and float to the welcome Earth, where later they blossom into new life, after millions of years of suspended animation!

" 'We of Mars, know that the temperature of space is about —400° F., cold enough to kill anything, one would think, but since there is *no air* in space, nothing can disintegrate, all life being held in suspense.

" 'Hundreds of insects and other forms of life never before seen by Earth, are discovered upon Mars yearly! They come into our atmosphere daily. Are you aware that space is filled with countless species of bugs and insects, held in suspense in their embryo or ovum form, all ready to spring into life as soon as they fall within the attractive force of some passing planet? Wherever this life is distributed, whether in the torrid or frigid zones, when the temperature rises sufficiently, it will spring forth on our planet Mars. There sleeps, in partially suspended life, enough embryo and seed, that if the zones suddenly became temperate or torrid we would discover every form of vegetation. The warming air sets all life free within a few weeks after the extreme cold and ice have disappeared.

" 'Meteors fall upon all planets in great number, most of them carrying some form of germination.

" 'I now hear several asking where these seeds—this life form—came from? Well, I'll tell you. You doubtless meant to ask me where the meteors came from. I believe they are smaller portions thrown off by planets breaking up through the shock of striking another or other planets. Some come through the explosions of volcanoes, when this life is thrown far into space. Volcanoes, in endless number, cast off tons of soil filled with seeds, the momentum carrying them up far beyond the attraction of gravitation into the ether of space. There it remains suspended for ages, except it comes within the attractive force of some nearer body.

" 'I am convinced that the ether of space is an absolute preservative for anything in it. Time does not change it. Nothing dies in the embryo state, in space. All processes of life may be partially suspended. It cannot perish, neither can it develop while in the waiting state. Not only new life, but, doubtless, new thoughts, come to us out of the heavens!

" 'This morning, out of the heavens, has come to me the thought to migrate to a new and beautiful world.

The Moon is being planted by Nature. It will take ages to accomplish the feat. Let us, the people of Mars, assist Nature, not only in planting, but in stocking it also! What do you say, fellow citizens, shall we begin to plant it with seed—now? Wait a moment. Don't answer as yet. I say, when the vegetation is ready on the Moon, then man and beast invite emigration. Let us first assist Nature to expedite the planting. Then we will establish a new empire! Now, what say you all? Yes, or no?'

"Like the roar of ten thousand distant cannon came back a mighty 'Yes.' "

CHAPTER XXIX

FELIX CLAUDIO

"THE excitement incident to Spencer's announcement over the phone that he desired to assist nature in the planting of the Moon continued unabated. The wisdom of an undertaking of such magnitude was freely discussed by the people, many openly advocating and commending, while a few were as positively opposing and condemning the proposition. The development of the opposition was due to a lack of faith in its feasibility, and not to a lack of confidence in Spencer—as will appear later. While the people were invariably called upon to freely express their will in all matters dominating their lives, both the Senate and the House depending on their jurisdiction regarding the subject, the final decision was made by one of the two bodies.

"In the House and Astronomical Society, nothing but enthusiasm and praise was accorded Spencer among his fellow scientists. Christopher Spencer was the recognized leader in ability and enterprise. They all knew that the people as a unit had given their consent, and that the condemnation of the enterprise carried very little weight. Not a voice was raised in opposition to him among the people, and none among the Astronomers, until the appointed meeting for the discussion of the subject was held.

"There lived in the same community as Spencer a man by the name of Felix Claudio. He was a young man of about two hundred years of age, and belonged to the same Community Society of Astronomers. As an Astronomer, he was considered exceedingly deficient, having barely succeeded in passing the necessary examinations, and then only after sixty years of continuous effort. As an orator, however, he excelled all others, being the recognized leader of the Astronomers in the Forum and foremost as a public speaker. He was young, ambitious, and popular with many who had listened to his eloquence, but who had not learned how arrogant and sarcastic he might be, or how caustic his tongue, when opposed. Among his fellow Astronomers these failings detracted somewhat from his popularity. A vacillating mind delights to agree with everybody, but the cunning character expresses no opinion until the opportunity arises to land on the winning side. Such minds let others do the preliminary work and wait until victory is in sight. Then they take positions in the foremost ranks and contrive to steal all the glory. Watch, just watch them now on Earth, steal silently into the women suffrage movement, when victory is in sight. All evil is about equally divided between both sexes—for man is the son of a woman, and woman is the daughter of man.

"Claudio was a patient listener, and waited until he felt quite sure he was on the winning side before he expressed an opinion on any subject. In case of defeat, he took it to heart. It stung his pride. He became bitter and ready to vilify all successful opponents.

"On questions of most importance he waited until the early skirmishes were over, with the parties drawn up in

battle line. Then he chose the stronger side. Then it
was he used his oratorical powers to lead those who stood
with the strong, and denounce the weaker side. With him
it was not a question of right, but one of might. There
was only one exception to this rule of Claudio's, and that
was, always to oppose anything advocated by Christopher
Spencer.

"It was but a few weeks after Spencer's announcement
through the *Autoreadophone* that one morning he further
addressed the people as a whole, and in his accustomed
way, on the subject of the Moon.

" 'I have discovered many new and interesting things,'
he told them. 'I shall demonstrate to you by facts and
figures,' he continued, 'that the temperature on the Moon
is about the same as that of Mars, zone for zone. It is
cold at the poles and torrid at its equator, but, through
the circulation of its oceans, most of its surface is semi-
tropical. Of course, we shall see the Sun there at an
average of about seven hours a day, for the whole day is
but fourteen hours in duration.

" 'On account of the fact that the planet Earth is now
in a moulten mass, and entirely enveloped by a dense
blanket of almost boiling mist, the Sun's reflection upon
its disc is not sufficient to give us Earthlight—nights of
great brilliancy. Earth is, however, more than fifty
times larger in mass than the Moon.

" 'I have been endeavoring to estimate how many million
tons of seeds, with how many insects, certain food, animals
and fowls, it will be necessary to send on our first expedition. I have not succeeded in ascertaining the exact figures, but I shall be prepared to submit them at the next
astronomical meeting. I wish to announce, also, that I

have now thought out the style and method of construction of a certain form of torpedo that will successfully accomplish the work of transportation to the Moon. Shall we proceed?' he asked, and back came the answer from several million people in one thunderous voice, 'Yes!' Truly the people had spoken as one person, yet, in the face of this mighty endorsement, Felix Claudio was openly opposed to the whole proposition, and by the wiles of his eloquence sought to completely turn the tide of public sentiment against it, but in vain—as you shall see.

"It was not generally known why Claudio so bitterly opposed Spencer in everything the latter advocated, particularly in the stupendous project of planting the Moon. The wise ones understood, however, that it was due to something more than an honest difference of opinion. It was, indeed, pure jealousy, a human weakness thought to be wholly eradicated on the planet Mars. In him, however, the passion was as unreasonable and as deadly as ever.

"Both were suitors for the hand of Charlotte Dudley, one of the realm's most noted beauties, and springing from a family of many noted Senators. She was a lovely young woman of ninety-five summers, the youngest of a family of eighty children. Her parents were now at the zenith of their influence, and in the prime of life. Both her father and mother were two thousand and fifty years old, with every physical indication of their rounding out a life of fully three thousand years or over.

"Charlotte's parents looked upon the attentions of Spencer, the famous young astronomer, with much favor, encouraging and commending their daughter's choice, though strenuously opposing the idea of marriage before she had reached the customary age of one hundred years or over. They were accorded the right to set the marriage this early in Charlotte's case, as she was the youngest daughter and the pride of the whole family.

"As to Felix Claudio, neither the family nor Charlotte regarded his attentions seriously, though his persistence in making regular calls was more than embarrassing on occasions when Christopher was present. Christopher was about Charlotte's age, while Felix was more than one hundred years her senior. She steadfastly declined his proffered affection, and ignored attentions which he sought to force upon her.

"When she learned of his open opposition to Christopher's plan of planting the Moon, the knowledge of it rankled in her heart. At the first opportunity she upbraided him for his jealous unfairness and perfidy and forbade him to call longer upon her—to which command he paid not the slightest heed.

"Words do not express, however, the secret resentment and jealous rage that now boiled in his heart. His every thought was now centered in a plan to secretly undermine the character and discredit the motives of his opponent. The affront received at the hands of Charlotte hurt his pride more than anything that happened to him before, bringing out and intensifying all the evil within him.

"As for Christopher, he regarded the activities of Felix in a friendly way, and had never by thought, word, or deed, showed the slightest concern. He openly invited criticism and welcomed any opposition based upon a fair discussion of the subject presented, but in personalities he declined to indulge. Therefore, when Claudio attacked his character, custom and his idea of manliness forbade him enter into a public controversy. He held his peace and awaited the day when the Astronomical Society should meet to finally decide the question of his project. He knew no fear, though gentle and retiring in disposition. It was an accepted rule that orators were generally of small caliber, and were actors in words rather than doers of deeds, all, however, being necessary to the general progress.

"At the appointed hour, the Astronomical Society met to discuss and decide upon Christopher's plans. It would require the favorable endorsement of every Astronomical Society on Mars before the project could be undertaken. It had become the custom for all the remaining societies to follow the leadership of the one introducing or initiating an idea. All were constantly in direct communication with each other through the medium of the *Auto-readophone*. When, therefore, questions affecting the whole realm were to be decided, they all stood as one body. Every private house on Mars not only heard the whole discussion perfectly, but could see the entire chamber and the people in it as plainly as though they stood beside them. This convenience, however, did not remove the desire to be on the ground, nor will it, for human curiosity not alone helps ambition, but cultivates desire.

"The clamor for 'gallery' seats in the Society's great auditorium was the greatest known for many centuries. When the short proceeding for the consideration of Christopher's plan was opened, every Astronomer was present and there was not an empty seat in the public galleries. I have already said, that there are no officers of the Society, not even a Secretary being necessary, for the records of all proceedings are automatically taken down and transmitted to everybody by the 'Phone.

"Christopher Spencer was the first to address the Society, repeating, in a short, simple way, the plan contemplated, without suggesting in detail how he proposed to accomplish the undertaking. Claudio immediately followed in a long address of abuse and sarcasm, questioning the sanity of the promoter, casting aspersions on his motives, dwelling upon the loss to Mars of millions of tons of seeds, together with the wasted life and energy that was sure to follow certain failure. There were no other addresses.

"As it is against custom on Mars to encore, there was no demonstration to denote the feelings of the Astronomers. The form of voting upon a question is simple. The one opposing a motion has the first right to call for a rising vote. This Claudio did. He said, standing, 'All in favor of dropping forever this proposition, will please stand up!' The manner of Claudio was dramatic, but as he cast his eyes around the chamber, and saw that no one was standing but himself, his face underwent changes in rapid succession of surprise and anger. It was evident to all that if any one had harbored any doubt as to the feasibility of Spencer's project, Claudio, by his abuse, had changed them. The question was settled. Mars would now undertake the planting and stocking of a new world!

"The project required the construction of an immense torpedo, sufficient in size to carry several million tons of seeds, various species of animals, birds, and insect life. Let me tell you how this young Martian accomplished it."

CHAPTER XXX

As I waited for Marcomet to resume, I saw the veil which separated me from those without gradually dissolve, revealing to my gaze a scene of indescribable fury, for there, standing vividly before me, as far into space as I could discern, was a vast throng of persons of all ages, male and female, whose incessant cries were terrifying and most pathetic to hear. Their intermingling voices were loud, alternating in ceaseless appeals or bitter denunciation, distressing lamentations, or sullen profanity, 'midst the continuous babble and chattering of those who ranted, argued, and swore, until one by one they became silent or impassive.

As the curtain was drawn, shutting the scene from my view, I meditated, contrasting the conditions of these unhappy and sorrowful beings on the one side, and the sublime peace and everlasting happiness manifested by those I observed on the other, from my position on the border of the great white way. Could I forever remain in this hideous predicament, while the others passed on to glory? Thus bewildered, I asked—"Are these two great contrasting scenes illusions?"

"They are both realities," calmly replied Marcomet. "You behold without, the *Mala*lities who must wait until

287

subdued, when they are fitted to return. All will return finally."

As he spoke these words, I felt as though I had been relieved of some great burden that had rested heavily upon me. It encouraged and imparted the desire to know more about human beings of other worlds, whom I shall some day meet.

"The day following the decision to plant the Moon," continued Marcomet, as he resumed his narrative, "Spencer was about to enter the beautiful Zenodochium to meet and consult with newly arriving astronomers from those distant communities. They were all strangers to him. He was greatly pleased and much surprised to find Charlotte there awaiting him.

" 'How did I know you were—I mean—how did you know I was here?' he stammered, and stepped sideways in his bewilderment. She was kind enough not to notice his confusion, but, for the moment, could not refrain from an attempt to tease him, by praising the speech, and otherwise magnifying the wonderful ability of Felix Claudio. In this, however, she signally failed, for no matter how unstinted her commendation of Claudio, Christopher was sure to agree with her view-point.

" 'You can't guess who was over to see me, last evening, Christopher,' she continued.

" 'Some one we both know?' he asked.

" 'Certainly,' she said, smiling.

" 'Well, perhaps it was Astronomer Tinker? No? Then, let me see. Was it Dr. Elizabrat?' he gravely asked.

" 'Neither of them, stupid,' replied Charlotte in feigned disgust. 'The idea! Do you think I desire to marry either of those old dry-bones?'

" 'Why, I didn't know that you were prepared even to take a fellow with wet bones,' meekly suggested Christopher.

" 'You know they are both over twenty-five hundred years old. Each of them has had half a dozen legs and arms substituted for those too old or worn out, and who knows, by this time, how otherwise physically they may be worn.'

" 'As long as their heads are healthy, they're all right, aren't they?' he argued.

" 'Oh, how exasperating you are! I don't want their heads or their feet—I want a whole man or none.'

" 'How soon do you want a whole one?' he persisted.

" 'Why?' she snapped.

" 'Well, I feel about one and a half. Thought the surplus might perhaps attract you.' Then, as she made no comment, he lowered his voice and added: 'Maybe, to you, I look less than one? What do you say?' he asked, now drawing closer to her, his eyes looking into hers.

" 'I said—I asked you—who you thought was over to see me last evening,' was her evasive reply.

" 'Now, who exasperates, Charlotte? You want your questions answered. Why don't you answer mine?' he said with some show of impatience. 'Who was over to— oh, I'll answer. I know who it was. I might have known in the beginning, it was your very fine orator.'

" 'My fine orator?' she questioned again in feigned surprise.

" 'Yes, your orator, the one you praise, the one whose surname is Claudio,' replied Christopher with a show of feeling.

" 'Why, how easily you guessed it. How did you happen to think of him? Don't you think he's nice?' she asked with a twinkle in her eye.

" 'I presume I have to be going in now,' he answered, assuming the manner of one deeply hurt, and ignoring her question.

" 'Oh, please don't, Christopher. I didn't mean it. Please don't go in yet.'

" 'I—I better go in, I guess—you don't like me,' he continued, making a slight movement as if to go.

" 'Now I do like you. You're horrid to say these things when you know I—I'm disgusted with that old thing. You knew it was all pretense on my part, didn't you, dear? Oh, I think he is awful. He's terrible! Christopher, you don't mean that, do you?' she asked, looking up into his manly face, her great, lustrous eyes now suffused with tears.

" 'Why, you poor little girl, of course I don't. You look so sweet and pretty this morning, I feel like eating you up,' he answered passionately.

" 'Why, Christopher. How ferocious you are to-day! Now, I must tell you about Claudio. You know he came to me,' she began, 'as big as life, in his beautifully upholstered electric aero-chair. He began by telling my Father that he had important business with me. "How honored your daughter should feel to have me call upon her," he said. Well, Father told him that the word honor was a term that none should use unless armed to the teeth. Then he asked where I was. Father knew I had forbidden him to call, so he informed him I was out. The while, he knew I was listening from behind the screen in the room. Do you think Father did wrong?'

" 'Yes, in not giving him a foot-push. Your Dad is a wise old owl. You didn't want to meet Claudio, did you?'

" 'Why, no. Of course not.'

" 'Then, 'twas all right to let the rogue down easy.'

" 'I heard everything that they said,' she continued.

" 'Please do not inform me, Charlotte,' he hurriedly interrupted. 'It might amount to a breach of confidence.'

" 'I'm not going to tell you, only, he said things about you that are not——'

" 'Please do not mention it,' he interrupted.

" 'Oh, well, if that's your attitude, I'll not say anything, but I'm going to *watch* him,' she replied with some show of vexation.

" 'I suppose, I should be very jealous of him—but I am not. I respect you too much to feel that way. I have faith in you. Have you some—just a little, in me?' he tenderly asked.

" 'Yes,' she softly replied, her face suffused in blushes. Then, looking up, she continued: 'I think you are the best man that ever lived. You are so noble and manly, I should think anybody might love you.'

"He stood silent for a moment. Then, looking around, he cautiously said in a low voice, 'I'm afraid if we stand here too long we shall attract attention. Let's go into the rotunda'—taking her gently by the arm—they entered and took a seat under the great dome.

" 'Is it not delightful to be here?' she whispered. 'I'd just like to hug you now'—with a roguish look in her eyes.

" 'Well, proceed, I don't mind. I'll give you permission to do that anywhere. But wait a moment,' he said suddenly, becoming very serious. 'I've learned about Claudio's visit to you last evening. I know his purpose. I received an *Autoreadophone* from your father early this morning.'

" 'You did?' said Charlotte, opening her eyes awide.

" 'Yes, Claudio's plan was to send a 'phone to every Society of Astronomers, asking them to defer ratification of our Society's action yesterday. He thought to gain a little time by so doing.'

"For some moments neither of them spoke. They were thinking of what possible move Claudio would make next.

"Finally Christopher said, 'Why, the silly fellow, they ratified our action of yesterday in every community on Mars in less than ten minutes after. Every community has already agreed to contribute its share of all that may be needed.'

" 'Tell me, Christopher,' she suddenly inquired, 'why is it necessary to dispatch, in the proposed torpedo, birds and insects with the varying kinds of seeds? How will they assist in planting of the Moon?'

" 'If they all arrive safely, the insects will be of vast assistance in distributing seeds and pollen. They labor incessantly for animate creation. We believe that they do this consciously. Without them, most things in plant life would eventually go out of existence. Nature creates for its perpetuity. Things least needed, in time become extinct. When man's intelligence supersedes the work of insects and birds, the latter become unnecessary. Nature has her way of eliminating things not needed. When Nature needs anything new to meet new conditions, they appear very soon after they're needed. By sending the animals and insects, birds and seeds to the Moon, we shall assist Nature until man arrives. By so doing, we are assisting in Nature's work.'

" 'Then why should we Martians kill and destroy life that is useful?' asked Charlotte.

" 'We should not, until it be proven that they are useless to nature. If so proved, then we should rid ourselves of them. Many centuries ago, Mars had a little insect by the name of "fly." They lived upon the filth and in a large way were scavengers, though dangerous ones, as they spread disease. After man had found a way to remove nature's filth, chemically, flies were only in the way. There was no need of killing them, for, when sanitation became perfect, the flies, having nothing to do, died gradually and soon disappeared. If there be work for them again, they'll certainly return. Careless sanitation would cause them to develop here in less than ten days. Of course, we assisted them once in a while. Their services being no longer needed, we hurried their funerals with fly flappers and traps. Just as soon as Mars had learned to keep clean, the flies had nothing to do—but die.'

" 'Is it true that you are to suggest a plan to-day for the construction of the torpedo, Christopher?'

" 'Yes, I have plans prepared. I believe the torpedo, and the barrel-formed vessel to hold it, can be constructed within a great opening in the ground. As it is built, we shall sink it by degrees lower and lower, until it is far beneath the earth, perhaps by seven or eight miles. Boring a hole the necessary size and disposing of all dirt will be the most difficult problem. I believe, however, I can get everything ready within a year. The Moon will be nearest to Mars in just 486 days from to-day. At

15½ seconds after six o'clock in the morning, at the end of 470 days, I calculate the Moon will be 43,009,777.60 miles from Mars. At 15½ seconds past 10 A. M., the torpedo will be fired. It will be shot off with sufficient force to easily penetrate Mar's atmosphere, so, that when it reaches the ether beyond, it will have attained a speed of thirty-two miles per second. I propose to have the torpedo shot from Mars in four hundred and seventy days from to-day, at 15½ seconds past ten in the morning. By this calculation, the torpedo will reach the Moon in exactly fifteen Martian days, four hours, and fifteen and one-half seconds, the very moment when the Moon is nearest to us.'

" 'But, Claudio says that landing on the Moon is impracticable at the present time, as its atmosphere is altogether too dense. Is that so, Christopher?'

" 'Felix Claudio knows very well that we have already calculated the density of the Moon's atmosphere and upon those calculations I can demonstrate that it is much easier to alight in a dense atmosphere. When the atmosphere is rarefied, even as it is now upon Mars, it is impossible to make a safe landing. Mars may send out its torpedo expeditions, but it can never receive them through its own atmosphere. Our atmosphere is fast disappearing. It is now so thin that no torpedo could safely enter in it and land upon our planet's surface.'

" 'When Mars was first settled, was his atmosphere very dense?'

" 'Yes, very dense, otherwise we would not be here now.'

" 'You calculate that when the torpedo reaches the ether it will be traveling at a speed of thirty-two miles a second. Won't the speed continuously grow less until it finally stops?'

" 'No. Ether is all but a vacuum, therefore, there can be little or no friction, hence no resistance. Unless the torpedo, in its flight, strikes something heavier, mass for mass, than its own weight, it would not vary a fractional part of a second in a billion years. Mars and many planets are flying through the same ether, yet, none vary a perceptible part of a second in a hundred years. In their course, they may accidentally, or otherwise, collide at times with a larger body.'

" 'Suppose the torpedo did hit some heavy mass while going through space—for you say space is filled with matter, from ether to dust size and up to planets?'

" 'True, but space is so vast that a collision with so small a thing as a torpedo is quite unlikely. If it should accidentally strike a very large body void of atmosphere, it would become instantly a small cloud of gas, so great would be the force of the impact. There are few large bodies between here and the Moon, so that there is little to fear. Of course, there are plenty of small meteors and meteoric dust between us and the Moon, but they will be harmless, as the torpedo will travel at such velocity that anything in its path will be brushed aside as easily as a bullet passes through light.'

" 'What,—are you going?' said Charlotte, as Christopher arose.

" 'Yes, we must hurry over to the Society's rooms. I have all my plans to lay before and explain to them. I came into the Zenodochium believing I should meet a few strangers here, but I think we are late. They must have all departed for our meeting in the Astronomical Society's

House. Will you not go over with me? You can hear and note everything.'

" 'On one condition,' she replied.

" 'What is that?' he said in surprise.

, " 'That you will come over to our house this evening,' replied Charlotte.

" 'Oh, thank you. You know very well I shall be there. Say, Charlotte,' he added, 'we will take a short ride over the country to-night. I have had my new *electro-aero-chair* repaired, and we can go abroad in that.' "

CHAPTER XXXI

THE TORPEDO

"Charlotte found a convenient seat in the People's Gallery, of the great main chamber of the House. This afforded an excellent view of the floor where she could observe all that was going on. When they arrived, the Assembly was in waiting. Without further preliminaries, Christopher began to explain his plans.

" 'The torpedo that I propose to have constructed,' opened Spencer, 'will consist of a cylinder of pure nickel steel, three thousand five hundred feet in length, pointed at the front, and of cigar shape. Its rear, against which the shock of the explosion will occur when shot forth from its great steel case, will be of solid nickel steel two hundred and fifty feet thick. The whole torpedo will weigh considerably more than six million tons when loaded.

" 'The first work to be done will be in boring the hole and sinking the barrel-like receptacle to hold it. In this the torpedo must be constructed. This barrel will have to be sunk into the surface at least seven miles deep. The hole will be bored at an angle of about $49\frac{1}{2}$ degrees, pointing in the exact direction where the Moon will be 486 days from to-day. The firing angles have already been worked out, and the required quantity of liquefied air, mixed with other high power explosives, have been arranged for and their manufacture already commenced.

Its delivery in time is therefore assured. We find that the barrel holding the torpedo will have to be made at least two hundred feet in thickness, in order to secure resistance sufficient to overcome the strain the explosion will cause. In addition, this steel barrel must be strongly reinforced by hot moulten stone. We expect to bore a hole seven miles deep, with a diameter of six hundred feet. The labor will be performed entirely by machinery.

"'I have made calculations to have the torpedo attain a speed of exactly thirty-two miles per second, when the ether is reached. To accomplish this requires patience in working out the weight, resistance of Mars' atmosphere known, and the amount of explosive force to overcome all. I believe my calculations are void of flaw.

"'The walls of the outer shell of the torpedo will be eight feet in thickness. Its diameter will be one hundred and sixteen feet. There will be an inner shell or tube, which will leave a clear space of about twenty feet between the outer and inner shells. This space will be filled with liquefied air. The inner tube will be held in place by steel standards, but the liquefied air held between the outer and inner tubes will keep them apart. The twenty feet of liquefied air surrounding the entire inner tube will afford ample protection, both in absorbing the shock of the explosion when the torpedo is shot forth, and in resisting the shock, in landing on the Moon. The inner tube will be of solid nickel steel, one foot thick. A clock mechanism will be installed inside of the torpedo to control and regulate discharge. It will be so timed that when the torpedo reaches the Moon's atmosphere volumes of liquefied air will be released from pipes into the atmosphere, causing tremendous explosions—thereby resisting gravitation and regulating its own descent. As it descends towards the Moon's surface, the released liquefied air expanding will offer tremendous resistance as opposed to gravitation, until the torpedo strikes the Moon's surface. Of course, it would strike with such force that its outer tube would crack the liquefied air within—blowing it to atoms. The inner tube would remain unharmed, landing 'midst it all, as softly as would a gas balloon. So soon as the liquefied air pressure is released from the inner tube, the hundreds of provided doors will automatically fly open, releasing every living thing within.

" 'My plans, however, contemplate a little different landing than that described. You might then call this an emergency landing, or should the plan I will later describe, fail. In considering this matter, I have provided for emergency, in case the clock mechanism fails—but complete failure there shall not nor cannot be.'

" 'Will Spencer tell his brother astronomers how long it will require to prepare for the work?' interrupted Felix Claudio.

" 'If we start with the preliminary work to-morrow, everything will be complete and ready in 469 days,' replied Spencer.

" 'I do not see how that can be,' argued Claudio, 'for we have no boring machine large enough. It will take a month or two to build one of requisite size to do this work. The hole to be bored must be made at least a thousand feet in diameter. It appears to me, therefore, that Spencer is all at sea, and is occupying the valuable time of this body by more or less idle predictions based on false calculations.'

" 'Our kind brother astronomer,' began Spencer, 'must

be referred to the *Autoreadophone* for more and better information as to what I have already said. A new boring machine will not be necessary. We have plenty of electric boring machines that will complete an excavation more than six hundred feet in diameter. This, I know, will be ample for our purpose.

" 'These electric hydraulic boring machines, as you all know, will easily bore a hole at any angle, at a rate and to a depth of three thousand feet per day, when adjusted to a diameter of six hundred feet. Electric hydraulic force pumps will carry away all débris and water—as far away as you desire. If you wish to have it carried to the sea, I am impressed with the belief that a fair-sized island may be formed by the dirt. As fast as the clay is removed we shall sink the casing forming the barrel. I have arranged to have the moulten matter needed for these casings brought from our largest steel foundry, through asbestos pipes to the hole. This will be accomplished as fast as the hole is sunk, and the casing can be cast. When once we begin, we shall not desist till everything is ready. We can have the casing, or barrel, prepared within two weeks. We shall wind the casing with nickeled steel wire, and outside the wire will be placed the liquid rock, poured into all the empty space between the wire and the ground —making the barrel absolutely rigid. No explosion will affect it. Construction of the torpedo will take much longer. The inner shell will be divided in the center by two strong steel partitions ten feet in thickness, making two immense chambers, one in front, and one in the rear of the torpedo. The rear chamber will be used entirely for the storage of seeds. It will be lined with three feet of asbestos, with a view to protecting the contents against extreme heat or cold. The front end of the inner chamber will be divided into innumerable rooms or small compartments for the storage of the lava from insects' eggs, insects, and useful animals.

" 'Drilled, a little back from the center partition through the outside shell of the torpedo, will be several rows of small holes extending entirely around it. These holes will be driven down into its steel jacket, seven and a half feet deep, and, when ready, will be filled with the most powerful explosives known, then capped over to prevent any premature explosion. Each hole will be connected by a battery connecting the clock mechanism. My plan involves timing the arrival of the torpedo into the outer atmosphere of the Moon. When the torpedo strikes this element, the gravitation of the Moon will cause the heavier or rear end of it to become the head end, or part pointing towards the Moon's surface. If the time clock does not explode the charges in these holes, the air will cause certain chemical changes which will positively do so. This explosion will sever the seed-half form of the torpedo, causing hundreds of thousands tons of seeds to be spilled out into the upper rarefied air. The heavy shell, dropping away from the seed, will go plunging through the Moon's atmosphere until the friction caused by its velocity against the ever-increasing density of the Moon's atmosphere as it descends will create fusion and complete consumption before it reaches the ground. What was once the rear half of a great torpedo, six million tons of nickel steel, will gently land on the Moon's surface— nothing but dust. The seeds, however, being very light, will scatter so completely through the air's upper strata, that the Moon's revolution will carry many of them around its entire circumference before percolating gently through the air to the soil below.

" 'Let us now consider what has become of the other half of this torpedo containing the insects, fish and animals. For a moment, we will leave them just where they are, until we dwell upon some of the problems to be met for their preservation and safe transfer. We all know that the temperature of space—so termed—is about —400 degrees F. Therefore, they must have sufficient heat for protection, otherwise, they would freeze solid instantaneously after reaching the ether. To obviate this serious obstacle to success, I have arranged to regulate the temperature of all chambers and compartments within the torpedo. This automatically and by electro-rheostatic warmth varying the temperature in each according to the natural needs of its kind. Food and water will be provided each for a year. The water will flow through open basins all the time. The problem of supplying food and drink for all on the journey, we find it simple enough to overcome. I also find the problem of supplying fresh air easy to regulate while passing through the airless track termed ether. If air only was needed, I could supply the same for an almost endless time. It will be furnished in steady, fresh streams through tubes penetrating the liquefied air chambers.'

" 'I do not understand,' interrupted Claudio at this point, 'how you will prevent things turning topsy-turvy, or standing on their heads most of the time during this trip through space.'

"A great roar of laughter went up from the Astronomers, as also from many of the people in the galleries, at this remark of Claudio.

" 'Is it possible,' shouted an unknown individual from the gallery, 'that we have a real astronomer who fails to know that there is no up nor down to space?'

"Then everybody present joined in a hearty laugh at Claudio's expense. To say that the mirthful explosion his silly question had provoked raised his bitterest feelings, would be stating the fact very mildly. Rising from his seat in a towering rage, he shouted, 'I can stand the laughter of my brother astronomers, but not from you,' he said, pointing his finger in the direction of the galleries. 'You laugh like hyenas, and wag your empty heads as pollywogs do their weak and tender tails, but not one among you knows whether you're standing on your head or feet!'

"The crowd roared again with laughter. It was some time before quiet was restored. The while, Claudio glared in silence at the galleries.

"Spencer, with rare good judgment, did not refer in any way to Claudio's question, thus avoiding another disagreeable scene.

" 'The compartments of all the larger animals,' continued Spencer, 'will be provided with a moving floor which will carry all the refuse to the rear of the front half of the inner cylinder. As it reaches the end it will automatically be precipitated into a large tank, the contents of which will be continually sprinkled with disinfectants. The moving floors will give the animals constant and gentle exercise, as they move in one direction— a few inches every minute.'

" 'In what manner does our learned brother propose to release the great tanks of fish?' asked Astronomer Nathan Elizabrat.

"A wave of suppressed excitement seemed to spread over the whole assembly. Every Astronomer present shifted uneasily in his seat, and renewed attention in various ways. The crowd in the galleries craned their necks, and turned their heads that they might the better hear any explanation that might cover the query. No one could conceive how it was possible to transfer fish from oceans on Mars to those of the Moon.

"Felix Claudio could not restrain his malicious feeling, gloating the while over the question which he believed none could answer.

" 'We would like that question intelligently answered,' he sneered.

" 'Then I'm afraid you will fail to understand it,' shouted a voice from the gallery.

" 'Thank you, Doctor Elizabrat, for reminding me. I also desire to thank our brother astronomer, Felix Claudio. I shall endeavor to simplify the whole matter, rendering it plain to all.' With these preliminary remarks, Spencer awaited absolute quiet.

" 'We will return to the torpedo again. The half we left was in flight, on the border of the Moon's atmosphere. I have calculated the time of the explosion which divided the torpedo into halves will be fifteen days, four hours, and five seconds from time of starting. Just as the two halves separate, and while the hinder half of the torpedo is still going at thirty-two miles per second speed, there is automatically released, through hundreds of pipes pointing from the torpedo's bottom, tons of liquefied air. So great is the effect of these steady streams of air against the Moon's atmosphere, that there is immediately a perceptible lessening of the torpedo's speed, and, as it descends, the speed continuously slackens. In another second or two the clock has released, automatically, hundreds of doors from every chamber and compartment of the remaining half of the torpedo, except that of the animals'. Out flies every bird and insect, the lighter ones seeping slowly through the atmosphere. The great tanks of water filled with many kinds of fish are also precipitated into the atmosphere below. Onward goes the water and the fish, passing through perhaps a half mile of atmosphere, into —what? Why, the ocean, my friends.

" 'Now, the torpedo will strike the Moon's atmosphere at an angle. The calculations are made so that after the birds, bugs, and fish are freed, the torpedo will continue to travel. The birds and insects will find their way to land, but the fish will drop straight into the water. The torpedo, by reason of the constant releasing of air from the front, will alight as gently as a kitten's paw upon the floor of this chamber. The clock will now perform one more service. It will be the opening of all doors, to release to a new world the larger animals, which find their way out and in time all will multiply in proportion to man's advent into a new world.'

" 'Suppose the torpedo does not strike the Moon?' said a voice from the gallery.

" 'Then, it would keep going right on until it collided with, or was drawn by the attraction of, some mightier body in space against which, in the dim future, it would meet annihilation. Until then, it would keep on its fixed course at the same speed, through many Martian, so-called, years.' "

CHAPTER XXXII

" 'LET me congratulate you, Christopher, on your very lucid description of the wonderful torpedo you propose to build,' exclaimed Charlotte, after pushing herself through a group of people that had surrounded and were further questioning young Spencer in the hall leading to the Auditorium, after the explanation of his plans. She had pushed herself unceremoniously into the crowd, the members politely giving way as soon as they recognized her, for every one in the community knew she had become Spencer's fiancée.

" 'Thank you, Charlotte, I am glad you have thought me lucid, for some of my friends here had doubts as to having made myself clear to everybody. I noticed you were listening intently. Doubtless this accounts for the clear ideas you possess on the subject. I could see that you were much interested.'

" 'Yes, and you were interested in the people's gallery —I noted the fixity of your glance.'

" 'Not so much in the gallery, Charlotte, as in the star that rendered its galaxy the brighter.'

" 'Don't blame Spencer, boys, astronomers have to look up, it's only natural. He was searching for the beautiful, the bright—the star of first magnitude.' This was repeated by many as they bowed low to Charlotte. With this sally, the smaller groups all joined in a good-natured laugh at Christopher's expense. In a few minutes the people had all left the hall and lobby, leaving Christopher and Charlotte standing alone.

" 'What horrid men some are,' was the first remark Charlotte made after the assembly had dispersed.

" 'Why do women always call every man in whom they have no interest "horrid"? Why, they tried their best to say something pleasant,' Christopher said, reprovingly.

" 'Oh, I don't know. I presume it is because I only like one, and that's you. Really, Christopher, I grow more proud of you every day. My love for you is so great'—and so saying she threw her arms around his neck and kissed him again and again. With his great, strong arms he drew her towards him in affectionate embrace, and returned her passionate kisses.

"Then, pointing, he said—'Let us go and sit on the marble bench in yonder corner, where we will be less conspicuous.'

"Suiting the action to the word, they walked to the corner, and, sitting close together, remained in each other's embrace.

" 'Why do you kiss me?' he whispered.

" 'Because I love you,' she replied.

" 'Will you always love me like this?' he passionately asked.

" 'Yes,' she whispered.

"Then, looking around, he suddenly exclaimed in a low tone, 'What was that noise?'—as great beads of perspiration stood out on his forehead.

" 'I didn't hear anything—did you?' she anxiously replied.

" 'I thought I did. Let us keep a sharp lookout for eavesdroppers,' he tremulously whispered.

" 'Yes, yes, I will,' she said.

" 'I know what I'm going to do now,' said he playfully, but with a determined air.

" 'What?' looking into his eyes.

" 'Can't you guess?' in mock surprise.

" 'No,' she replied.

" 'Then I'll show you,' said he, pressing his lips to her cheek.

" 'Oh, Christopher, don't do that. It isn't fair. You didn't give me time to——'

" 'Sh-u-u-u, some one's coming! Sit up quickly!' he commanded.

"It was Doctor Nathan Elizabrat. There is no question but he saw them both, though much too polite to interrupt the tête-à-tête. He was about leaving the building, and would have passed on, had not Christopher spoken first.

" 'Good afternoon, Brother Elizabrat,' began Christopher with a confused air, rising.

" 'I'm so glad to see you, Doctor,' said Charlotte in a voice which did not exactly carry sincerity.

" 'I am glad to see you both,' he said, approaching with a broad smile. 'I hope I did not interrupt your little meeting,' he added with a good-natured laugh. 'This is one of the delightful incidents of your lives, my children, and no one has a right to interfere with or interrupt the smooth course of your mutual love. I know how sensitive the most of us are in fearing detection. God didn't make the birds that way. No one should be afraid to love to his heart's content. It's the purest thing there is. You should be proud of Christopher,' said he, suddenly turning to Charlotte.

" 'I am, Doctor Elizabrat,' she replied with a blush.

" 'I have great confidence in your ability, and I am certain your plans will succeed,' said the Doctor, turning to Spencer. 'It's merely a matter of mathematics,' he added.

" 'Thank you, Doctor. If encouragement alone would accomplish the undertaking, it would now be a complete success. I feel and realize the responsibility, however,' he replied.

" 'By the way, you did not mention how many dondittos you figured on sending,' suddenly said Doctor Elizabrat.

" 'I have provided space for two hundred and fifty cows, and five hundred dondittos. By the time we are ready to send emigrants to the Moon, there should be no scarcity of either.'

" 'Which do you think is the most difficult to milk by electricity—the cow or the donditto?' asked the Doctor.

" 'I think the cow is. The donditto is larger and quieter.

" 'I have several of these animals that give from twenty to thirty pounds of meat juice daily. One of the Senate Members, a chemist, doubted whether the meat juice given by the donditto will solidify as quickly in the Moon's damp air as it does here. Why, I milked one of mine a few days ago and in half an hour the juice was as solid a piece of meat as I ever saw. From it I cut several beautiful steaks. What an improvement this is over the old method of killing in order to secure meat. Well, we don't have to kill anything now, yet, what a vast variety of good things we have,' replied Christopher.

" 'I do not see how the atmospheric conditions of the Moon will change the nature of the animal. If it does, we may note also a change in the cow's physical condition. I do not anticipate any difficulty in this regard,' remarked the Doctor.

" 'Who knows but on the Moon the cow will give purer cream and butter,' laughingly spoke up Charlotte.

" 'The best butter I know of, Charlotte, grows on the butter tree,' remarked the Doctor.

" 'Why, yes, almost every planet has a butter tree, though not always known by that name. Few people are aware of the wonders of nature,' agreed Christopher.

" 'Well, I must leave you, children. Sorry I disturbed you, but make up for lost time when I go,' laughed the Doctor, as he strode into the street.

"They both sat in silence for a few moments, when finally Charlotte said: 'How are the birds, insects, fish and all the different animals to be watered and fed, after you have once transported them to the Moon?'

" 'I have puzzled not a little about preserving their food, otherwise, there are but few serious difficulties to be met. Carrying sufficient to last through the estimated time of flight between Mars and the Moon gives me but little concern, but it will be necessary to safely land with insects and animals many thousand tons of food in order to insure sufficient for at least a three years' supply. We cannot absolutely depend upon a generous vegetation before that period of time. But how shall I preserve it fresh and nutritious?'—he absentmindedly asked, and he next thoughtfully bowed his head as in deep meditation.

" 'Why, Christopher, have you so soon forgotten that we chemically treat and preserve everything here successfully for indefinite periods? The *autoreadophone* said this morning, that the community treated more than ten thousand tons of grass yesterday. Father said that, without deteriorating, it would keep more than two hundred thousand years, if necessary. I had some ripe fruit for breakfast this morning ten thousand years old. We have preserved deliciously sweet strawberries that mother declares are more than fifty thousand years old. We have them only occasionally, but they are as sweet as though just picked.'

" 'Of course, I know all that, little one, but the air of Mars is now rather light, while that of the Moon is very humid. The question is, will our preservatives have the same chemical effect there as here?'

" 'Do the lines on the spectrum show the same elements there, as here?' she asked.

" 'Yes, they do! Say, you're a wonder. Indeed, you've solved it. I must kiss you for this idea,' he pursued, as he gently kissed her on the cheek. 'They may not be in the same proportions,' he mused, 'but chances are there are a like number of elements. Yes, I believe our preservative will be just as effective there.

" 'By the way, Charlotte,' he continued, 'did I tell you where I had decided to have the torpedo land?' Christopher suddenly asked, and without waiting for a reply— 'The safest spot for the torpedo to alight will be just North of the Tropic of Capricorn, on the Moon's Northern Hemisphere. Its surface is now almost entirely covered with water, but as this cools, through ages to come, the water will seep in and be slowly absorbed. So, as the water disappears, more land will continually appear until nothing but land obtains. Time alone is the factor that

will bring about that change. When all the water on the
Moon's surface is absorbed, and nothing remains but land,
then will begin the leveling forces of nature. When all
moisture disappears far into the soil, the drying up of
surfaces begins finally on every planet, in each hemisphere, generally in the Tropics of Capricorn and Cancer.
First, belting the sphere at those points, then extending
over the entire surface of the planet, until finally it becomes a dry planet, without atmosphere. When a dry
planet is exposed to the Sun's rays, the heat is so intense
where these rays strike, that even the rocks fuse, while
in the shade, only a short distance away, the temperature
is four hundred degrees below zero.'

" 'Are you certain the torpedo will strike the land
accurately?'

" 'That is my calculation. If it does not, it will drop
into the sea. The only dry land now is a large piece
North of the Moon's equator, in the Tropic of Capricorn,
all the rest is covered by oceans.'

" 'Will you send both fresh and salt water fish in the
expedition?'

" 'No, my dear, only one kind—salt water fish. A few
centuries will produce species that will evolve fresh water
fish. It is much the same with fish, as with man. He
accustoms himself to his environment. Doubtless, all
fish lived originally in salt water.'

" 'When you release the fish from the torpedo, miles
up in the Moon's air, where the temperature reaches a
point of frigidity, won't the fish freeze stiff when exposed
on the instant?'

" 'That very matter puzzled me for some time before
I made this discovery. The fish, when turned from the

water tanks of the torpedo, begin immediately to descend through the cold air. At first they freeze, but then their rapid flight downward would at the least create so much friction that they would first be broiled, then burn up, so by the time they had reached within a mile or two of the Moon's surface, nothing would remain but dust or calcine of lime.'

" 'Why, you surprise me,' exclaimed Charlotte in an incredulous tone. 'Then how can you land them safely in the ocean?'

" 'I have arranged the tanks so that the water and fish are precipitated together. As the water and fish touch the atmosphere, the water will freeze the latter in the ice solidly. Fish can live in solid ice a minute or more. As this mass of fish-filled ice descends, its velocity through the air will produce sufficient heat so that, on the moment of its reaching the ocean, it will have become water. If all the ice fails entirely to melt in its passage downward, it will do so on reaching the ocean, and most of the fish will be saved alive.'

" 'Are you certain that the Moon's ocean is salty?'

" 'Yes, we have observed salt in the marshes surrounding it. Every planet is, chemically, about the same. The elements are practically similar through all space, thus proving that nature is one throughout.'

" 'Why is it necessary to take the fish, instead of their spawn?'

" 'Because there would be no fish to fertilize it there.

" 'Before you go, let us take a stroll over to the Aero Station,' said Christopher, as they both prepared to leave. Just then they were surprised to hear some one try to suppress a cough. The sound appeared to arise in the direction of one of the great pillars which supported the roof of the lobby. Both turned to look toward the indicating point. Neither saw anything at first, but, finally, Charlotte said: 'There's a shadow behind that pillar, the sixth one back towards the entrance to the Auditorium,' as she pointed her finger to indicate the precise spot. For a moment both hesitated before proceeding, and closely watched to discover if the shadow moved.

" 'I'll take a walk to that pillar,' he said. 'You stay here,' suddenly commanded Christopher.

"He had hardly proceeded forward before the figure of a man stepped out from behind the pillar and moved rapidly in the direction leading to Astronomers' private chambers. Neither of them could see his face, but both knew the form.

" 'Claudio,' was all that Christopher remarked.

" 'Yes, that is sneaky Felix. So he's eavesdropping, hey? Trying to overhear what we are discussing. Oh, how I despise that man,' said Charlotte, her eyes snapping.

"Without further comment, they left the building and strolled leisurely toward the Aero Station.

"For some moments both remained silent. Finally looking up at Christopher, Charlotte said: 'I think Felix Claudio is the personification of the Evil One. I'll keep watch on him. He is——'

" 'Let us change the subject, Charlotte. No harm can come to you or me, except that which we ourselves create. You wanted to ask me further questions, did you not?'

"His admonishment was so gentle, and his manner so calm, that she instantly suppressed her feelings of resentment.

" 'You are right. I will try to avoid the disagreeable subject. I wanted to ask you if there is life now in waters on the Moon?'

" 'Why, of course, there is. Water itself is life. Then, as I have already explained, all kinds of germ life and seeds from meteors and the dust of outer space are percolating into the whole surface of the Moon. Just how large a form of life may reach the surface, and later develop, I do not know. I do know, however, that without question, life is transplanted from one planet to another by this means. That life evolves from other forms, according to its environment—there is no doubt.'

" 'Then, there may be much more life there than we now anticipate?'

" 'Exactly.'

" 'How soon after the arrival of the charged torpedo will the Moon be fit for the advent of the Martians?

"Christopher stopped here and thought profoundly a moment before making reply. Then, slowly, as if calculating each reason, he answered: 'About ten years.'

" 'Must we wait all that time before being married, for you know, Christopher, I wish to marry you? Oh, I do wish men were compelled to propose.'

" 'You must obtain your Mother's consent before marrying, Charlotte. She has already told you that she awaited the event after I had finished this work.'

" 'It is so long and hard to wait, Christopher. You'll marry me then—won't you?'

" 'If I live, I will, and if I don't, I'll come back immediately and when I attain the proper age I'll certainly do so. Why, I could eat you up, I love you so,' he replied.

" 'Oh, Charlotte,'—suddenly drawing her to his breast

—'I'll tell you what we'll do,' he continued. 'We'll get married on the way to the Moon! Ask your Mother about it! You'll be old enough then, about a hundred and ten years.'

" 'That's a capital idea, Christopher, and I'm going to hold you to the bargain. Are you sure the Moon will be ready for emigrants by that time?'

" 'I am certain of it. More, I believe we can add at least one thousand years to our lives on the Moon. In other words, I estimate that every one will live to at least from four to four thousand five hundred years old there. The air is so abundant and pure, and our knowledge of the laws of health are now so perfect that we shall succeed in lengthening the span of life at least fifteen hundred years more than on Mars.'

" 'Look,' said Charlotte, becoming suddenly agitated, as she pointed her hand towards the open park opposite the entrance to the Aero Station. 'There he is again. He's been following us.'

" 'Who's been following us?' said Christopher, looking up in surprise.

" 'Why, look and see! That scoundrel, Felix Claudio!'

" 'Now, what need you care about his movements? Let him follow if he wishes to use his time so unprofitably. Perhaps he's going on an aero-trip. Yes, see, he's crossing to the Station. There, he now goes inside. You should not concern yourself about his movements. Don't worry.'

" 'I'm not worrying about him. I'm thinking of you. He is wrought up and jealous because I love you, and because you were confirmed as Director of the Moon Expedition. It's within his nature to do you harm, if he can.

He said in my presence to-day, while in conversation with your fellow astronomers, that a man in love had no right to be in control of any important matter, that state detracting his attention too much. I knew well what he meant.'

" 'Charlotte, you are unduly alarmed.'

" 'I am not," she replied with some feeling, and continued: 'A woman always scents danger to those she loves. It's her intuition. I know you are good and kind, and it is just those qualities in you that he endeavors to take advantage of. I'm going to be on the alert. I warn you now.'

" 'Again, let us change the subject, little girl. Here we are at the Station. I will see you to your electro aerochair. There it stands—over there. Before you go,' he said, 'I want to surprise you.'

" 'Surprise me, why, how?' .

" 'Sit down,' he gently commanded. 'Now look up to me. Before you start the motor, let me tell you something.'

" 'Oh, what is it? I desire to know. Why don't you tell me?'

" 'Listen. The work on the tunnel for the torpedo is progressing swiftly. It will soon be ready, and before the estimated time. Now, I am going to christen and confirm you as the starter of the torpedo. You shall have the honor of turning on the switch, releasing the charge, and sending the expedition on its way to the Moon!'

" 'How will you christen and confirm the appointment?' she asked gleefully.

" 'In this way,' said he, bending over and kissing her adieu."

CHAPTER XXXIII

"So great was the interest taken in the first step towards establishing life and civilization on the Moon, that the people of Mars willingly—almost eagerly—took up this mighty task of preparation. Under the skillful leadership of Spencer, the work went conscientiously and merrily forward. Each day found work ahead of the estimated calculations. Already, the necessary seven miles of shaft had been sunk, and, in less than eleven days from its inception, this great hole of six hundred feet in diameter—while boring—had been temporarily lined with a strong wire gauze, to prevent the sides from caving in. It was now being prepared for the stiff, featherweight paper moulds. These paper moulds were first lowered into position and then hardened, by subjecting them to a chemical wash, which not only increased its hardness beyond that of steel, but rendered it absolutely fireproof— the process not increasing its weight. Each section of paper was stuck together with adhesive glue, but after the chemical wash was applied, all the sections became as one. When the moulds were in readiness, liquid nickel-steel, at white heat, was run through eighteen-inch asbestos pipes, from the foundry two hundred miles away. This was poured into the moulds, forming a solid steel barrel around the shaft from which the torpedo was to be shot. The moulten steel, once run into the moulds, was immediately subjected to a chemical spray, which not only tempered and hardened it, but converted the released heat units into electric currents, thereby economizing by storing all unused energy. There was nothing known to the chemists of Mars in the science of metals, harder or stronger than this nickel-steel. The manufacture of the torpedo had begun simultaneously with the steel barrel, and made to fit so close that there was but five inches' play between. This intervening space was later filled by a hard grease, similar to creosote, but so treated that the friction caused by the shooting of the torpedo would prevent it from burning.

"Charlotte and Christopher could now be almost daily seen on their way back and forth to the torpedo shaft, located on a high hill named Mount Hope, in Stagnum Pegaseum. The distance from their home at Lake Lucus Lunae is about twenty-nine hundred miles. While this beautiful lake was located about fifteen degrees South of the Equator, and sixty-eight degrees East in longitude, to reach Mount Hope, one must pass nearly twenty-eight degrees in latitude North of the Equator, longitude fifty-five degrees East.

"The delightful aero trip from their lakeside home, across the Equator to the works at Mount Hope, was made by them daily. Comfortably and safely seated in their powerful electro aero-chairs, while flying at terrific speed, an observer might have noted their happy faces, as the chairs gently alighted at their destination.

"Let me describe these wonderful chairs to you. The electro aero-chairs of Mars are constructed of that same paper referred to as chemically treated, and are so light in weight, as not to exceed that of an ordinary house chair," said Marcomet. "The small, compact, and powerful electro-storage batteries used to propel them weigh less than seven ounces, while the triple motors with which each is equipped do not total quite two pounds. Each set of motors easily develops more than one thousand horsepower, making it possible to attain a speed of SIXTY MILES A MINUTE.

"Charlotte and Christopher's morning ride of twenty-nine hundred miles, therefore, took less than one hour in time on the average. They did not care to attain an extreme speed, neither of them flying the powerful aero-chairs at full capacity. Traveling at the rate of sixty miles a minute made it quite difficult to converse—though performed alone by small wireless 'phones. When, however, the speed did not exceed forty miles a minute, conversation by 'phone means was quite audible. The small wireless 'phone was so attached to the chair arm that conversation could most conveniently be carried on. While one chair might dash several miles ahead of the other during a conversation, it did not in the least affect the clearness of tone or lessen the degree of sound. The only danger confronting the rider of an electro aero-chair, when traveling at a high speed, was the liability of striking birds unable to dodge the machine with alertness. Many serious accidents had occurred to aero flyers by carelessly running their chairs at high speed in too low an altitude, thus increasing their liability of striking birds in flight. Many were killed by accidents of this nature prior to the invention of the 'scope,' and certain other magnifying glass-protection shields, which have removed all danger to users of the electric aero-chairs. At this time, accidents were almost unknown.

"Electro aero-chairs were fashioned somewhat like an ordinary leather arm chair. They were protected in front by a strong glass wind shield, the glass employed being so tough that it was capable of withstanding a blow of several tons. It also possessed wonderful magnifying qualities. Suspended strongly from a frame about six feet above, securely fastened to the chair, and operated by its occupant, were nickel-steel rods, operating the rudder, also made of the same strong, thin glass. This performed a double service, by acting as a protection against the weather, and as a rudder to safely guide the machine through the air, in any given direction.

"To this simple arrangement, an additional flat steel rod extended down the back to the rider. In front there was placed a small steering wheel so arranged as to ingeniously regulate the speed of the aero-chair, or to direct its course up, down, or towards any point. The motors, securely attached to these chairs on the underside of the seat, were so efficient that when the electric current was turned on the twin propellers would instantly attain sufficient lifting power to raise the chair and rider straight up from the ground. The glass plane, or rudder, required only a small degree of adjustment to perfectly direct its course. In case of accident to the rudder or plane while in flight, so sensitive was the machine's steering apparatus that the occupant of the chair could direct it by holding out an arm from the back. Great care had to be exercised not to expose any part of the body beyond the line of the wind shield, while traveling at high speed, as the occupant was in danger of being jerked from the chair by the force of the wind, or killed by having the air drawn suddenly from the lungs. It was customary, when traveling fast, to wear a shield over the nose and mouth to guard against such an accident. Every one rode behind a shield so strong as to afford positive protection to all riders. The magnifying qualities of these shields were so intense that the occupant had a clear view ahead for more than fifty miles. A bird flying in range of the operator's vision, fifty miles away, was as easily seen as though it were only a few inches distant—allowing time to avoid collision.

"For night traveling, the chairs were provided with powerful headlights, which gave forth a brilliant white glow, the rays penetrating the darkness, and making all objects for thirty miles distant, as plainly visible as in daylight. The light, in connection with the magnifying shield, made night travel as safe and pleasant as in the day.

"When the operator of an electric aero-chair desired to descend, as preliminary, the motors were stopped, and the planes adjusted to the proper angle. If the machine was high in air the momentum of a downward plunge, when not arrested by the operator, was terrific, and would frequently result in fatalities, had it not been for an ingenious safety device attached to each. When the chair got within one hundred and fifty feet of the ground the device was released automatically, through large air valves pointing downward. This volume of air formed a cushion for the chair and rider so that they alighted as softly as a snowflake. If one happened to be at an altitude of two or three miles, the sensation of dropping—dead weight—at a terrific speed, increasing with every added foot, was terrifying to the timid. Not every one could endure it. It made no difference in the effect of the chair's alighting, whether the operator voluntarily opened the air valves, or whether the action was automatic. Indeed, the air tanks prevented all serious mishaps in falling. The automatic discharge of liquefied air afforded a perfect air cushion upon which the machine gently reached the ground. The air tank valves were so delicately regulated that the suddenness of the descending movement released powerful streams of air, sufficient to oppose the weight to gravitation.

"Electric aero-chairs were made in all sizes, to carry from one to a thousand passengers. All commerce was carried on through their agency and during business hours the air was fairly alive. In the evening, brilliant shafts of light from hundreds might be seen swiftly passing overhead, in all directions, like huge fireflies or ten thousand comets in possession of the air. How proud were the people of their scientific advancement in mastering the air! How weird, and yet how glorious, to sail in this trackless ocean, with nothing but the compass to guide one and the numbered communities below. Covering the whole surface of Mars, each immense white figure could be seen from a passing chair, a mile below by day and, when illuminated, much further by night. Young and old used them daily for pleasure, and all the transportation was carried on by these wonderful machines.

"For lovers, it was a favorite method to carry on their courting at night, far above and out of sight. Sometimes in the clouds or above them. If danger arose of their being discovered, they put out the lights of their chairs. When, in the silence of their surroundings, they proceeded in their love making—literally 'twixt Heaven and Mars. Snugly tucking heavy blankets around themselves, in an electric aero-chair for two, on each hot summer evening, these happy couples soon arose a mile or two into the air, amidst the cold of winter's blast. But the nipping air did not lessen their ardor, for each chair was provided with electric heaters. While the doves might bill and coo from the house tops, these lovers could be seen on the edge of a cloud. All machines without special pilots were provided with an equipment for locking the feet of the passengers to the machine. This precautionary measure was taken to guard against accident of falling out, and to prevent any one from pushing another from the machine accidentally, or otherwise. It was against custom to unlock or release another before reaching their destination. Commerce on Mars being carried on by air routes alone, the business was designated, "Commerce of the Sky." Electric "chairs" and "cars" were employed in traffic, some of them reaching one hundred thousand horsepower, and carrying hundreds of thousands of tons of freight from community to community, in all weathers, quietly, quickly, and with as little apparent effort as a bird carries a feather through the air.

"All lifting and transporting being accomplished entirely by these machines, the people knew nothing of hauling by cars, heavy loads at large waste of energy. Labor was, therefore, almost entirely unknown on Mars. There, labor was accounted menial. 'The more we labor, the less we know,' saith the prophet. All farm labor was done by electric aero-machines that pulled the surface cultivators, planters, reapers, over the soil with ease. Every one is taught to think and work, but not to labor.

The great destroyers of human lives on your Earth are labor, overfeeding the body, and worry," said Marcomet. "The elements surrounding all are ample to save our bodies from manual labor. The face of nature on Mars is not deformed and disfigured by railroads and tunnels, all commerce and travel being conducted by the more economical trackless air.

"After the appeal had been made by Spencer, for contributions of seed, animals and insects, there came a generous response from every community of Mars. But no one was prepared, nor had any one anticipated receiving such an overwhelming deluge as answered the call. Spencer was indeed pleased and gratified. This public response demonstrated to every one the genuine faith in the project, and as quickly renewed Spencer's courage. The testimony of approval spoke louder than words. One thing at least became settled, there would be no lack of supplies to mar the success of the expedition."

CHAPTER XXXIV

THE SUCCESSFUL FLIGHT

"Felix Claudio's oft-repeated prediction, that the sentiment of the Martians was against the planting of the Moon, had now proved a failure"—began Marcomet. "The generous and general consensus of opinion of all the people, proved their deep conviction that, under the personal direction of Christopher Spencer, it would become an accomplished fact. They had confidence in him. This genuine testimony on their part convinced the skeptics—if any remained—outside the limited influence of Claudio, that they deemed silence the better part. No one now had the temerity to repeat prediction of failure.

"Day by day, the appointed time of the torpedo's scheduled departure drew nearer.

"Arrangements had been made for appropriate exercises commemorating the event. Details of the vast undertaking had been daily transmitted, and were now familiar to all.

"The interest of Charlotte and Christopher in the work of construction constantly grew as the great torpedo began to take form. Study and work occupied their whole time, all other matters, deemed as trivials, being divorced from their daily life. Thoughts of self were eclipsed by the necessity of application to details. Vigilance in watching the work proceed had reached its highest, for they both realized that any one tampering with a vital part might damage or destroy the torpedo. To guard against the possibility of such a calamity, rigid orders were promulgated from sunrise to sundown at Mount Hope, forbidding visitors. Charlotte never for a moment relaxed her vigilance in watching over Christopher. Every attempt upon the part of individuals seeking irrelevant information was blocked by her guarded replies to questions. She knew that Claudio had made but one trip to Mount Hope. He came in his aero electric-chair early one morning, but, apparently, he took little interest in the proceedings, as he remained but a few minutes. While there he asked certain questions of one of the young engineers. He, however, put many questions concerning the torpedo's internal arrangement, and seemed particularly interested in the amount of liquefied air required for the firing charge. He desired to know the day the charge would be loaded into the barrel. Questions were politely answered, but this last query was something about which each person chosen for the work had been forbidden to impart information. Other precautions had been taken to guard main secrets at the works. An *autoreadophone* was attached to the coat of each person working at Mount Hope, which automatically recorded every word spoken. It was therefore impossible to hold private conversation. Charlotte had learned from these instruments of Claudio's visit and his inquiries. His visit alarmed her for, woman-like, she was suspicious of his motives. She could not believe that curiosity alone prompted this cool, calculating man to take an interest in the success of an undertaking which he had previously and so strenuously opposed. Doubtless his purpose was a sinister one.

"She did not dare to tell Christopher regarding her suspicions, for she more or less anticipated his convincing arguments in rebuttal. She pictured herself confessing fault while knowing she was right, therefore, it was better not to name the subject.

" 'My dear Charlotte,' said he, a few days later, 'Did you cause an *autoreadograph* to be sent to all the inhabitants of Mars, forbidding visitors day or night within the torpedo zone?'

" 'Yes, Christopher, I did, but——,' she faltered.

" 'But what?' commanded Christopher sternly. Receiving no answer, he continued: 'You made it appear as if it were my order.'

" 'I know it, Christopher, but I——'

" 'Don't speak to me now. I am shocked and ashamed of you. Why, Charlotte, what could have induced you to do this?' he pleaded.

" 'Ashamed of me?' said Charlotte, as the color rose to her cheeks, and her eyes flashed in resentment. 'Ashamed of me! Do you mean that? Have you lost your mind? You need not answer now, Christopher, but you shall answer me later. Ashamed of me, are you? Don't approach me!' as Christopher made a move toward her.

" 'But, Charlotte, I scarcely meant it—that word slipped before I thought. Will you forgive me——'

" 'Is this Christopher Spencer?' interrupted a young workman, excitedly rushing into the room of the office building where both were standing. 'I have just found a small battery,' he panted, as he held up before them a small, flat instrument about the size of a finger ring. 'It was lying close to the casing at the bottom of the seven-mile hole.'

" 'It is a small but powerful battery,' said Christopher, taking it from the workman and examining its make-up carefully.

" 'But it is harmless unless connected by a spider web wire,' said the workman.

" 'What?' shouted Charlotte and Christopher in unison.

" 'There was a long—er—insulated——'

" 'Yes, yes, go on,' cried Christopher, his excitement rising.

" ' 'Twas insulated spider web wire. I picked up the battery and was walking away with it, when I felt a backward pull. So, groping around, I discovered the wire—I could just see it.'

" 'Yes, yes, then what did you do?'

" 'I put it in my pocket, and——'

" 'And what? You didn't put it in your pocket and walk away with the wire attached, did you? You idiot! Didn't you cut the wire first?' cried Christopher.

" 'Why, no! What good would that have done?'

"Christopher became too pent-up with suppressed excitement to answer, but Charlotte, understanding the situation, calmly said: 'If you had cut the wire there would have been no further danger of an explosion of the high explosives that will surely rend the steel holders filled with liquefied air.'

" 'There was no explosion,' said the workman in astonishment.

" 'Of course there wasn't, otherwise you would be a grease spot on the escutcheon of space,' said Charlotte.

" 'There are no wires attached to this,' said Christopher, again examining the battery. 'Where did you cut them?'

" 'When I got to the surface I had a hard time doing it,' said the workman.

" 'Did you follow the wires up? Do you know where they lead?'

" 'Yes, I traced the wires several miles in the direction of Fons Juvental or Lucus Lunae, we can't tell exactly at which place they would strike.'

" 'Whom or what do you mean by "they?" ' asked Christopher.

" 'Why, I told several of our men, and they went along to assist.

" 'Was the wire laid along the ground?' asked Charlotte.

" 'No. Some one in an electric aero-chair must have dropped it from a high altitude, for it is strung along on the tops of trees and other high objects.'

" 'When was it first discovered?' asked Christopher.

" 'To-day—only a few hours ago.'

" 'Trace the wire without delay, and——'

" 'We can't do so, because, in order to prevent accidents, we cut all that we discovered.'

" 'Oh! So you thought of that, did you?'

" 'No, though some of the other men did'—proudly answered the workman.

" 'Well, I'm sorry they thought it necessary to do much cutting after it was once out of the hole, and therefore could cause no danger. I'm sorry, in another sense, for we have lost the opportunity of discovering the miscreant who probably sought to cause a terrible and premature explosion. If the content charge had been exploded it would have caused the total destruction of the torpedo, for there was not sufficient force to impel it beyond Mars' attraction of gravitation. It would have ascended in the air a few miles and then fallen back on Mars' surface. Just think of such a catastrophe, Charlotte!'

" 'Are you still ashamed of me?' she asked by way of reply.

" 'I am proud of you,' he quickly answered. 'You did right in sending out the *autoreadograph*,' he added, musingly. They both stood oblivious of the workman's presence, gazing with concentrated look in the direction of Mount Hope. They were thinking of the narrow escape from destruction of the torpedo and the probable abandonment of all their future plans.

"Christopher remained quiet but for a few moments. Then, turning to the workman, he thanked him kindly for his care and watchfulness, and Charlotte joined him in showing her appreciation of the service rendered.

" 'Charlotte, I have been unkind to you,' said Christopher, after the workman had gone. 'I am sorry. Forgive me,' he said with tears welling to his eyes. 'I now realize this evidence of your devotion. I see through it all. You suspected some one was tampering with the torpedo, so you acted promptly. Can you forgive me, Charlotte?' he asked.

"It was late that evening when she finally said, 'You are forgiven.'

"Christopher had done his best to show how dearly he loved her, and had promised her greater consideration in future.

"A few months had now passed quietly by, without incident. One morning, about a month before the scheduled time for launching the stupendous enterprise, Spencer gave out the news through the *autoreadophone*, to every home of Mars, that, all being in readiness, the torpedo would be shot off on scheduled time. He warned all people within seven hundred miles to immediately move from that danger zone, as none could foretell the consequences of such an explosion, nor the effect upon the atmosphere when the torpedo went rushing through it.

"For months, factories had been running at full capacity night and day, manufacturing liquefied air, often storing it in strong steel carboys, transported by electric aero-cars to the tube's entrance. Tens of thousands of tons were lowered to the bottom of the great seven-mile pit. Powerful explosives were packed among the carboys for the purpose of demolishing them when the charge was fired. The explosives, seven miles below, were connected by battery, located in a small steel building fifty miles from the mouth of the tube. This steel building was erected for the purpose of protecting the one who should press the electric button that would send a great and strange instrument to a new and strange world, and also to accommodate a few chosen Scientists and Engineers, who had made every preparation to observe the effect of the explosion. Arrangements were also made to set up several thousand *transtelephonescopes* in each community, located at widely varying places. This, for the convenience of the people, to encourage interest, to increase the number of observers of the torpedo's flight through space, and to calculate its speed and direction. There was sure to be a friendly contest among all the astronomers as to who should have the distinguished honor of first reporting its location in space.

* * * * * *

"The morning of the great event having arrived, 'Seriously now, Charlotte,' said Christopher, 'when I say "ready" be sure to place your finger upon the electric button. Look to it—not at me. When I say "fire" press instantly and hard down; then cling to your chair. If you should delay pressing hard down, the fractional part of a second, all our calculations would be ruined and no one can tell where the torpedo would alight.'

" 'Why should I cling to my chair?' asked Charlotte, showing some nervousness.

" 'You will know better than I can well describe, when you press the button,' laughed Christopher, 'but be sure to press the button when I say "fire," ' he added.

" 'Depend upon me,' she replied.

" 'It lacks now only a few seconds,' shouted Christopher, giving a last warning to a small audience of scientists and astronomers. They had gathered together within the protecting walls of the solid steel thimble-shaped house. 'Are you ready, Charlotte?'

" 'I am ready,' she calmly replied.

" 'Now every one hold fast to your chairs. Remember, while the walls are padded, you may save broken bones by hanging on tightly. Your chairs won't move, for they are screwed on steel posts set far into the ground. My judgment is, that it is better not to be tied in the chairs, for that might have caused you injury, as doubtless the

strain will be terrific. Now it's nearly time. Look out!
Cling to your chairs! Brace yourselves well!'

"Every one present stood firmly braced for the shock.

" 'Only a few seconds more! Now, Charlotte—one—
two—three—ready!' suddenly shouted Christopher,
watching each tenth part of a second upon the time-
piece held in his hand.

"Every one present held his breath.

" 'Fi——re!'

"They heard only the first part of the word, for as
Charlotte pressed the button, the remaining r-e was cut
off by a confusion of sound and sensations. The building
seemed to be lifted from its concrete foundation and hurled
back again, a thousand times in a second. The whole
planet seemed to rock and roll like mighty and angry
billows at sea. Then there came a series of dull, profound
roars, sounds as if a hundred thousand sledges had
started to batter down their small steel house. The rolling of the ground continued until accompanied with a
nauseating feeling of seasickness, by which every one
present was made violently ill. Not a person was able
to stand up. The effect of this sickness was far greater
than the pain experienced in their hands and bodies.
For more than two hours after the first shock, all lay
prostrate upon the ground, and, with the exception of a
muffled groaning, as if dead. All were in a more or less
dazed and semi-conscious state. After the first one had
partially revived and was enabled to drag himself to the
hermetically sealed door to let in fresh air upon the viti-
ated atmosphere of the house, the recovery of all was
rapid.

"Great was their amazement, however, upon opening

the door, to find that a day of warm and pleasant sunshine had suddenly changed to one of hail, rain, and snow. It had now become as black as midnight, with incessant lightning flashing and filling the sky with lurid glows, accompanied by terrifying thunder, vibrating and reverberating, as if to rend the small steel house. The storm lasted for six days, gradually lessening in severity, until, on the last day, when beautiful weather followed.

"When the occupants of the steel house had sufficiently recovered, they returned to their homes in their electric aero-chairs, not one of them having the ambition to gather data. It must be admitted that, outside of the seven-hundred-mile limit, though the shock was plainly felt, none had suffered any particular inconvenience.

"When Christopher and Charlotte arrived home, a few hours after the explosion, the first news reported was the glad tidings for the safety of the expedition. The news filled them with joy, for it meant that Christopher's calculations were correct, and now the torpedo was softly speeding on its way. Their joy knew no bounds. There was not a minute of the day or night that the flight was not watched with keen interest.

"As the days passed, and the time approached for the scheduled landing of the torpedo, the astronomers, holding vigil one after another, reported the torpedo to be 'on time.' Over the *autoreadophones* went messages hourly to the people, reiterating time and time again their absolute belief that no error in the calculations for the arrival had been discovered.

"As the torpedo neared the Moon, it was plainly seen through the *transtelephonescope* that the missile was pointing directly for its objective. The nearer it approached the Moon's surface, the more certain became the watchers' predictions that it would strike according to schedule. There now appeared but one question in their minds; would the expedition land safely? That part of the story could not be told on the *autoreadophone* until the torpedo actually reached the Moon's atmosphere.

"Great was the rejoicing on Mars when the torpedo alighted safely, as calculated. No greater event ever happened than the now confirmed confidence in their ability to master the elements.

"A few days later the cow, named donditto, and the horse were plainly visible, eating from the abundant supply of preserved hay and grain. Thus were the larger animals secure. Nothing alive had been lost or destroyed. The air and waters of a new world had become suddenly stocked for Nature's work, by the intelligence of man.

"The seed percolated through the atmosphere for several days, scattering over a wide area of the surface of the Moon, the lighter weight seed seeping much slower, but scattering over a wider territory.

"Christopher Spencer was heralded as the great benefactor of mankind. His name became a household word. It was upon the lips of all.

" 'I never doubted your ability,' said Charlotte, a few days later.

" 'You were the one important thinker in the whole affair, Charlotte,' he replied. 'You imparted to me the inspiration without which I would have failed to accomplish so vast a project. Woman has ever given to mankind the inspiration, the hope, and the love. You pressed the button, too. Had you delayed two seconds, the torpedo would not have struck the Moon, but would have continued traveling, no one knows where.'

" 'It was a lucky strike, Christopher.'

" 'You are my lucky strike,' he said as he bent affectionately and kissed her.'

CHAPTER XXXV

CLAUDIO'S DEFEAT

"During ten years, following the planting of the Moon, the astronomers of Mars kept up a continuous vigil, noting the rapid development of its vegetation and the prolificness of all life. 'One year more,' they announced, 'will develop food in abundance, guaranteeing support to man, in unlimited quantities, should he make his appearance.'

"Fog and rain were almost constant at this epoch on the Moon, but the temperature was semi-tropical over its entire surface. To account for this strange phenomena, the astronomers were utterly unable. It was Dr. Nathan Elizabrat who discovered that the temperature of the Moon was uniform, and later he submitted some excellent reasons. 'You ask me my reasons for believing that the whole atmosphere of the Moon is semi-tropical,' said he, addressing the members of the House one day. 'The atmosphere of the Moon is now extremely heavy with moisture, creating an almost impenetrable envelope around its surface. The rays of the Sun penetrating this are caught up and are so uniformly diffused that the density retains and prevents the heat from escaping and the outer cold from penetrating. Later on, when the atmosphere becomes more rarefied, then the zones of heat and cold will become more marked and rapid changes in temperature will follow.

"The *transtelephonescope* was a valuable aid in determining the progress and health of all life on the Moon. Though the birds and animals were easily discerned, their cries were the only sure proof of their health and contentment. Most of the Martians were familiar with the varying sounds made by dumb animals and birds, and quite understood their meaning. Many of the inhabitants, however, made a specialty of some certain portion of animal creation, so that there was no living thing whose cries would not be interpreted by some one. It was found that every living being possessed a language expressing all the passions, as happiness or mourning, love or hate, welcome or defiance, the cry of pain, of anger, the shout of victory, and the cry of fear. All these are as plainly read by the student of nature, as though each possessed a language expressed in human words. Then we have the language of action not expressed in sounds, and the language produced through the face and eyes. Nature provides every living thing with a sound language understood by its kind, as well as a language of silence intuitively understood by all life. It speaks through everything in nature, the winds, the clouds, the waters, the trees, and through darkness and light. It invites repose, and whispers the love song. It silently bids us to seek shelter, or prepare for the coming winter's blast, or to flee the dangerous storm. No word is spoken, nor sound made, yet everything living is spoken to in that silent language, delivered by the invisible friend of animate creation.

"The Moon to-day is a dried-up or parched sphere, and upon its surface, therefore, it is not easy to imagine the once beautiful high plateau upon which the first torpedo from Mars landed. Situate in the Tropic of Cancer in the Moon's Northern hemisphere, between the great seas of Maria Tranquilitatis and Maria Vaporum, was a high peninsula reaching off towards Maria Serenitatis. In the distance, East and West, could be seen the great abrupt volcanic mountains, and the now extinct volcanic craters of Firmicus on the one side, and Secchi on the other. The whole area was then not as large as your great State of Texas. A peninsula jutted out from a large, low and marshy continent which was often, in the Moon's early history, entirely inundated, as the people of Mars viewed its constantly increasing beauty and watched each development. Their interest grew day by day, then gradually a desire to emigrate to its surface seized them. This beautiful little satellite of an unknown planet in the early stages of formation had now enthused them. The fever of desire had set in. The wiser ones knew, however, that spontaneous movements should be permitted sufficient time to develop, as often public enthusiasm is found to wear off, to be followed as swiftly by the lack of it.

"The astronomers, by reason of their quiet, methodical training, were never influenced or forced by popular demonstrations. To them each subject had to be investigated and proven with mathematical precision. They felt it was far better to permit the natural enthusiasm of the people to subside, before announcing anything that might be feasible, in the further development of this beautiful new world which now held out such alluring temptations. A few said, that all life now established on the Moon needed human care, but the majority recognized that nothing ever created but what was provided with some form of defense, though everything in Nature must ultimately succumb to the survival of the fittest. Weakness invites disintegration, followed by reincarnation. Hence, there is no beginning to life, neither is there an ending. It is a process eternal. When human life reaches perfection, all other forms of life will be unnecessary.

"Felix Claudio was now dismayed and disappointed by this new movement, which he felt convinced would increase the popularity of his opponent, Spencer. In the effort to conceal his bitter opposition and vindictiveness, he had miscalculated the effect of his own words upon the public mind. He failed to realize, as public men frequently do, that intelligent people soon discover the true motive of each word and act. Like the ostrich, which seeks to conceal itself by thrusting its head into the sand, so, human hate, while hiding behind words, renders the motive plainly visible.

"Being conscious that he had erred, he diligently set about rectifying the mistake, if possible. Had his disposition undergone a change for the better, or had he possessed a less vindictive spirit, less of cunning, he might have succeeded, but none can finally conceal the true purpose of mind. No matter what we force ourselves to say, or to act, if not true to ourselves, the truth will sooner or later be revealed.

"Claudio gave the subject much thought, finally deciding to advocate before the House an immediate plan for colonizing the Moon. As the suggestion had never been made on a prior occasion, he believed this move would serve the double purpose of restoring and strengthening his popularity, and thus undermine the prestige of his enemy.

"Upon the next assembling of the House, he eloquently

advocated that a migratory expedition to colonize the
Moon be prepared forthwith. His advocacy of the enterprise came as a surprise to all, as it indicated a complete
reversal of judgment on his part. His fellow astronomers
showed by their silence, their lack of faith in his sincerity.
There seemed to be only one among them who appeared
pleased—Christopher Spencer. He had been patiently
waiting, in the hope that some one would suggest the undertaking, feeling that his own advocacy might be considered by many as egotistical.

"Claudio's proposition called for the immediate construction of a torpedo-shaped conveyance. It might be
about one-quarter the size of the one last used. 'I wish to
make the expedition a preliminary one,' he said. 'It shall
consist of one hundred men who shall be chosen for their
services. They shall be the advance guard, to prepare the
way for a larger colony which will emigrate after the honored one hundred have signaled back to us the glad tidings
that all is well. By this arrangement, we shall probably
save thousands of lives otherwise sacrificed, should a large
number arriving there find they cannot exist. It is an experiment, my brothers, it is an experiment only. How
honored these one hundred must feel when they find themselves chosen for this marvelous undertaking. But they
ought to be the very best men we have—for we only seek
magnificent results. There is no danger—I shall hope.
With a mingled feeling of timidity and humility, I propose
that some one be chosen from among us who shall have
the honor to give out this unusual distinction. Though I
say it with pure and holy intent, and not in the spirit of
self-laudation, I feel that I am qualified and fortified by
an unsullied character, and should be allowed the privilege

of naming these one hundred. I doubt not, many of you might be acceptable for the making of the choice referred to, yet I feel peculiarly fitted by a certain ability which I know most of you have never successfully developed, and, I might add, never will.'

"Thus far no opposition had developed, and as his request appeared natural, the privilege was readily granted.

"While seated in the garden, a few evenings after— 'Why do you not oppose the proposition of Felix Claudio?' asked Charlotte of Christopher.

" 'Why should I?' asked Christopher in surprise. 'His plan is feasible. Should I not rather do all I can to promote its success? There was neither opposition nor doubt expressed as to its feasibility. It is a matter of mathematics, and not for our dislike.'

" 'I refer to his singular request, and the endorsement of him as the sole appointee to select the persons who shall make up the expedition,' said Charlotte in a tone indicating impatience and repressed feeling.

" 'I think he deserves the honor. What is there singular about it, Charlotte?' asked Christopher, smiling.

" 'Don't laugh! Can't you see I'm serious? I said "his singular request." What is his object?' asked Charlotte, leaning towards him.

" 'Why, er—he desired the honor—he was frank in saying that was his object—I suppose,' he hesitatingly replied.

" 'You are wrong—you are wrong. Oh, it's a shame to be so good that you fail to understand the devil when you meet him. You men are so easily hoodwinked,' returned Charlotte impatiently.

" 'But, my dear Charlotte, he explained his object. He said he desired the honor,'—protested Christopher.

" 'He wouldn't know what to do with "honor" if it was offered him. Those who talk about it never have any. Those who have it, keep it locked away. When he made the request he had the undoing of some person in mind—not honor.'

" 'Do you really think so?' innocently asked Christopher.

" 'Yes, I know he did. I have a good mind to petition—to have the *Psycholograph* applied so that the people might know what a hypocrite he is. Do you know who he had in mind?' she asked excitedly, and without awaiting an answer she continued, 'He had YOU in mind!'

"A comically incredulous expression overcast the face of Christopher, inducing Charlotte to laugh aloud.

" 'What are you so mirthful over? If I knew, I would join you. It must be ridiculous, to change you so quickly,' he said.

" 'It is,' she replied.

" 'Strange, I did not hear him refer to me in the least,' said he.

" 'Oh, I see. A joke, isn't it?' he inquired.

" 'I said he had you in mind!'

" 'Yes, a very serious joke,' she said, with a far-away look in her eyes. They both sat in silence for several minutes. Finally she abruptly asked, 'Has Felix Claudio invited you to be one of his select one hundred?'

" 'Oh, no, indeed he has not so honored me, but——'

" 'But, what?' asked Charlotte, interrupting.

" 'If my country——,' he began.

" 'If your country—bosh. You mean if this schemer wants you, you respond, I suppose. Now look here, while I'm living, you've only got one country and one of every-thing else—good or bad—and that's me. If Claudio names you, and he will probably name you as the first one, do not let him come to possess you, for I want you myself. I'm going to see that no schemer gets you and a few other enemies out of his way.'

" 'It's man's duty to obey woman, and your superior judgment shall always be my guide,' said he.

" 'Thank you, Christopher, you make me very happy.'

"It was about a week later when Claudio announced to the House that he had made his selection of the men who should make up the first human expedition to the Moon.

" 'I have selected,' said he, 'one hundred of Mars' fore-most citizens—the human lights in all our realm. I hope none will decline.'

"As he resumed his seat, after this short speech, a man's voice was heard from the public gallery.

" 'Who are the men?' demanded the voice.

" 'Shall I read them?' asked Claudio, as he rose—look-ing around inquiringly among his brother astronomers.

"All the members politely nodded assent.

" 'Before reading the names, I would like to make a few——'

" 'Read off the names. We don't need a speech,' came another voice from the gallery.

" 'When I get ready, I will,' shouted Claudio angrily, looking defiantly toward the person who had interrupted him. After a moment's hesitation, he began: 'The first name on my list is that of an astronomer——'

" 'Give his name,' shouted some one.

" 'The first name on my list is Christopher Spencer,' he hissed.

" 'Cross his name off,' came the shrill command of a woman's voice.

" 'What's that?' shouted Claudio, now pale and shaking with rage. 'Who says that?' he insisted, pointing his finger in the direction from which the command came.

" 'I say it, Felix Claudio,' cried the woman, rising so that all might see who she was. It was Charlotte. 'Again I command you to erase his name from your list.'

" 'I will not do so upon your command,' he shrieked, shaking his fist in uncontrollable rage.

" 'Cross his name off, you devil. I knew his would be the first. He declines, don't you, Christopher?' she loudly appealed, looking in her lover's direction.

" 'He has not declined yet. He is not going to be a traitor to his——'

" 'That remark is out of place,' interrupted Dr. Elizabrat, rising. 'This dispute is unnecessary. Mr. Spencer is here and can answer for himself. We would like to know if he wishes to decline.'

"Every eye was now turned upon Spencer. All held their breath in expectancy. It suddenly grew so still that the slightest motion on the floor could have been easily heard. Spencer sat silent for a moment, as if trying to decide upon the nature of his reply. He sat with bowed head as if looking at the floor, then he slowly raised his eyes,—looking straight at Charlotte, who was still standing in the gallery. She indicated no outward sign as to how he should decide, but one long look seemed to be enough for Christopher. Quickly rising from his chair and turning to face Claudio he said, looking the latter in the eyes, 'I decline to be a member of this party unless two conditions are complied with. The first is, will you agree to accompany us on the expedition?'

"For a few minutes Claudio stood defiantly facing Christopher. He knew that should he consent, his plans would be foiled. If he did not consent, he felt convinced Christopher would not go; therefore, his plans were again set at naught. Why not consent to go, he thought, and back out at the very last moment? He believed he could find an eleventh hour excuse which would leave him behind, and rid him of his adversary. 'I will go,' he quietly answered. 'What is your other condition?'

" 'My other condition is, that an equal number of ladies be allowed to accompany the expedition, the wives, or intended wives of men who make up the party,' returned Christopher.

" 'I will not consent to such an arrangement,' replied Claudio viciously. 'No woman of Mars desires to accompany a colony of men on such a dangerous trip,' he added with an air of triumph.

" 'Then I decline to be a member,' quietly replied Spencer as he resumed his seat.

"The men and women of Mars were about equal in numbers and degree of intelligence. While the women were satisfied with doing the courting and raising of families, and content to supervise or dominate domestic affairs, they refrained from all labor or the taking part generally in any work which might in the least detract from their beauty or the manners of an attractive and persistent lover.

"Nothing had been as yet hinted as to the ladies accompanying the expedition, but, when all the names had been read, it was immediately realized that the majority of those selected were married men, none of whose wives would allow them to depart alone. Spencer was right. Ladies should accompany the men. People with evil motives are apt to defeat themselves in their eagerness to do others harm. There was one who had listened to the reading of the names who thought she discerned the evil motive. To her mind, Claudio's desire was simply to be rid of one hundred of his opponents, as every one named had vigorously opposed him.

"He had finished reading the list, and resumed his seat, when from the gallery again came a sharp, shrill voice: 'Who'll take care of all the babies after reaching the Moon?'

"'You misunderstand,' answered Claudio, failing to see the joke. 'The men will go alone. There will be no women on the Moon!'

"'Then change their destination and send the expedition to where you will—there are going to be women and babies there,' shouted the speaker.

"The wave of ridicule that now arose became so effective that Claudio forthwith left the House in a towering rage. He felt and was a defeated man. He could face anger, but not ridicule.

"The next day he sent in his resignation, which was very promptly accepted."

CHAPTER XXXVI

"SEVERAL months had passed since the defeat of Claudio's plan for colonizing the Moon, when Doctor Nathan Elizabrat quietly broached the subject in the House. He asked Astronomer Spencer for his candid opinion on the project. Several members were eulogizing Spencer before he had an opportunity to accept their invitation. Many were apologizing to him for what they agreed was a human fault—a lack of appreciation.

" 'We want, first, the expert opinion of our most noted astronomer, before we undertake this stupendous enterprise.' This was the consensus of opinion, heartily endorsed by the whole population almost without exception. So great was the enthusiasm in his favor, that the House was overwhelmed with demands from the people, urging Spencer's immediate selection to take full charge. After considerable urging and principally at the earnest solicitation of Charlotte, Spencer decided to accept the Herculean task of transporting ten thousand volunteers in an expedition to colonize the Moon. The boldness of the conception was astonishing and incredible. No records in the history of the universe disclosed expeditions of colonization larger than the conveyance of a few hundred people from planet to planet. Now, here was a proposition to transport thousands of human beings in one immense torpedo, to be immediately followed within a day after its departure by another of equal size, carrying everything in the way of machinery and supplies needed.

" 'I desire,' Spencer said, 'that those who volunteer shall leave no one behind who is bound by love or family ties, for while it is possible now for a torpedo from Mars to safely land on the Moon, it would be absolutely impossible to send one from the Moon to Mars. The atmosphere of Mars is now rarefied and thin, and is growing more so all the time. The Moon's atmosphere, on the other hand, is, at present, very dense, affording a cushion of great resistance against which our torpedoes strike. To attempt a descent through the thin air of Mars would result in the total destruction of the torpedo.'

"He then explained how necessary it was to have the protection of a dense blanket of air for the torpedo to cushion against, and, on the other hand, how impossible it is to concentrate sufficient power behind a torpedo to penetrate an atmosphere of certain density.

" 'So you see, my friends'—addressing the House, 'that we must stay on the Moon after our arrival there. We may go, but we cannot return. Every day, as we look upon the surface of the Moon through the *transtelephone-scope*, we see everything developing, increasing and prospering in like proportion to here, therefore, we infer that atmospheric and other conditions are like or similar. It is an old Mars saying, that wherever the sensitive donditto can live, so may man.'

"A few days later, Spencer was directing the preliminary work of boring two immense holes, each to be twelve miles deep when completed. Within these, two torpedoes, both alike in size, but more than three times larger than that employed for planting the Moon, were to be constructed. One was to accommodate the ten thousand or more volunteers, while the other would be used to carry machinery, books, supplies, plans and instruments. Indeed, a duplicate of everything of service used on Mars.

"It was arranged that the passenger should take its departure a few hours before the supply torpedo, as it was feared that if both were fired at the same moment the shock would be so intense that there would be danger of atmospheric disturbances sufficient to derange their delicate adjustment, and throw them off their course. Though this serious objection overcame the liability that each might interfere with the other while passing through the ether, or later in landing, it was too hazardous to risk, especially as there was no advantage to be gained by such a course. Moreover, the tubes would have to be fully a hundred miles apart, so that the shock resulting from the discharge of one would not disturb the charge of the other. It was agreed to have everything ready within a year.

" 'You see, Christopher, that I was correct in my estimate as regards Claudio's motives. He had prepared to make a clean sweep of all his presumed enemies, in this one grand spectacular effort. He would send them all to the Moon or to some other place where the chance of their return would be impossible,' said Charlotte, one evening, as she embraced her lover.

" 'Women are invariably right. Everybody now believes that was Claudio's purpose. But you placed a kibosh on that scheme, Charlotte. He failed to realize, when he cunningly planned this wrong, that as soon as he had himself rid of these enemies, more would immediately appear and confront him. Sometimes an enemy is but a friend in disguise.'

" 'According to your reasoning, then, our friends are our enemies. What an idea! Then your sincerest friend might be Felix Claudio,' replied Charlotte.

" 'You are remarkably practical, Charlotte. You see only one side,' interposed Christopher.

" 'We women folks have to be. It is woman's sphere to possess the initiative. She scents danger more quickly than a man, and her intuition is immeasurably stronger. The highest civilization we can attain will not remove the mother instinct of distinguishing between friends and enemies. The man who follows his wife's untrammeled judgment, will best succeed. Every man should learn to surrender his prejudice. God gave the woman judgment, and the devil gave the man prejudice. I think you are likely to make a real good husband,' said Charlotte with a sigh.

" 'Look, look up, Charlotte,' he suddenly exclaimed, pointing directly overhead, 'there goes Doctor Elizabrat in his aero-chair! He is waving to us.'

"They both rose and silently returned the salutation. Soon the Doctor speeded up his machine and passed out of sight.

" 'Will he be among the volunteers, do you think?' Charlotte asked.

" 'Yes. We need all the doctors and ministers we can obtain,' he replied.

" 'Conditions may be such that we shall not need many on the Moon,' she suggested. 'The doctors of Mars are here to prevent disease. The ministers are here presumably to prevent sin. There, no disease nor sin exists to cure, still there is always plenty of work for both. When we ignore demands, we perish.'

" 'We shall need them there quite as much as here, I am thinking. I am not going to decry the progress we now have attained. If we expect to continually lengthen our lives on the Moon, and hope to live up to our ideals, we must encourage the ministers and doctors. They, with the more profound thinkers, represent the three great foundation stones of civilization.' "

CHAPTER XXXVII

"A few days subsequent to the despatch of notice to every family on Mars, that single young men and women not less than one hundred years old, whole families without restriction, and any or all of the relatives of such families were eligible to volunteer, and thereby invited to emigrate to the Moon, Spencer found it necessary to send forth another 'phone message, announcing that the limit in carrying capacity of the torpedo had been reached.

"More than ten thousand men, women and children, selected with extraordinary care as to physical and mental fitness, were finally chosen. Among these were men and women teachers, scholars, inventors, chemists, astronomers, doctors, and ministers. The unmarried were exceedingly solicitous that a sufficiency of Doctors should accompany the expedition, as the custom of Mars made it obligatory that all marriage ceremonies shall be performed by two doctors of the opposite sex. Each candidate for marriage had to be subjected to a thorough physical examination by a doctor of his or her own sex, who vouched for the health and physical perfection of the contracting person. While the *psycholograph* exposed the true mental conditions of one to another, prior to marriage, so that each may satisfy himself as to quality

354

and quantity of the love to be expected, the physical examination often prevents unequal marriages. Marriage is not rendered more difficult, but is vastly safeguarded as to the true mental value of each to the other and, finally, as to their physical fitness. By these precautions, safeguarding health and happiness, each generation adds to the physical and moral perfection of the Martians, lengthening more and more the span of life. The adverse verdict of two consulting doctors did not prejudice a case with other doctors. If, later, examinations disclosed their restoration to health, the parties were eligible to wedlock.

"Among the Doctors to volunteer was Nathan Elizabrat.

"After the full announcement that no more applications to accompany the expedition could be entertained, Felix Claudio visited Spencer, with a pitiful appeal that he be allowed to join the expedition. His name was added, though strongly opposed by Charlotte. His next move was an application to be reinstated as member of the House, his late voluntary resignation being no bar to his reinstatement. He lost no time in again joining in its deliberations.

"For several weeks during progress of the work, members of the House listened to the daily reports of Committees serving under the direction of Christopher.

" 'The passenger torpedo,' said Christopher one day in addressing them, 'will carry scores of men and women who are capable of safely piloting the machine, therefore, may I be relieved of this lesser responsibility, and accept the more difficult task of piloting the second torpedo conveying machinery, instruments, records and supplies? So great has been the demand for room upon this, that provision is made but for one person—the pilot,' continued Christopher.

"The members of the House, particularly Claudio, were generous in the praise of what appeared to them an act of sacrifice upon the part of Christopher and Charlotte. All were aware that Charlotte and her family must go with the passenger torpedo, and that it would be the only instance of the trip where friends would be parted.

" 'I am positive that our scientific calculations for the safe flight and landing of the passenger torpedo on the Moon are absolutely correct,' said Christopher, 'and I am just as positive that calculations made for the journey of the second or machinery torpedo are true. Yet, I cannot guarantee that the jarring effect produced by the sudden release of so much liquefied air and other powerful explosives, will not cause some variation from the course as calculated. No one can just now anticipate what these changes, if any, will be, but whatever may develop, I feel equal to the task of correction, for I have already provided against every contingency.'

"Since it was definitely decided that he was to pilot the supply torpedo, the question arose, who should be pilot of the first?

"While Christopher had declared there were many capable pilots, nevertheless, no one seemed anxious to take the responsibility aside from Felix Claudio. Though the latter tried to repress any anxiety in that direction, a close observer could have easily seen that back of his studied indifference there was real anxiety upon his part. In the art of oratorical persuasion he was master. It was, therefore, but a short time before he had convinced the members, including Spencer, that he was best suited for the position. Still, there was considerable hesitancy upon the part of members in confirming Claudio for so responsible a position. His eloquence and the endorsement of Christopher and Charlotte finally convinced all that he was both capable and worthy of this new confidence.

"All calculations were based upon firing the second torpedo one day later than the first. Therefore, the first torpedo with its precious cargo would be out in space several million miles by the time the second had started.

"Public interest so increased as the work of building the torpedoes progressed, that Christopher caused to be sent over the *autoreadophone* many interesting details of how certain obstacles that appeared at first insurmountable, were being gradually overcome. While in all respects the torpedoes were externally built alike, internally they widely differed. The passenger torpedo was more interesting in this particular. It was so constructed that the chambers or living rooms occupied the entire center, being entirely encircled by immense chambers of liquefied air. These not only automatically supplied the people with fresh air in proper quantities during the flight, but served as a shield of liquefied air and protected the passengers from danger of freezing while passing through the intense cold of space. While all the rooms of the torpedo were electrically heated, no amount of warmth in which a human body could exist would have been sufficient to have overcome the frigid cold of the ether, without the guarding influence of this air blanket, which minimized all danger.

"To guard against accident, the liquefied air chambers were divided at frequent intervals by solid partitions of nickel-steel one foot in thickness. Each of the living rooms

—also separated by steel partitions—was beautifully furnished, and supplied with every convenience that would add comfort to the occupant. The entire surface of each room was upholstered by strong air cushions to guard the occupant against injury. Each room was connected with great public hallways by sliding steel doors, which, when closed, hermetically sealed each room. The opening and closing of these was controlled from a central station or switchboard, and were opened only after reaching space. Each torpedo was supplied with electric power held in storage, and sufficient not only to supply light and heat in abundance during the trip, but enough to supply heat, light and power for a hundred thousand people for more than twice the time.

"Raised above the torpedo's center, resembling the conning tower of a submarine, was a lookout or observatory made of solid nickel-steel and glass. It was so constructed that it could be raised and lowered at will, and stood about three feet above the torpedo's surface. When entirely lowered, it fitted into the main body of the torpedo so perfectly that the dividing seams were not discernible by the human eye.

"The observatory was not raised until after reaching space. Large windows filled with glass, having the strength of steel and the magnifying qualities of the most powerful telescopes, were arranged around the sides of the observatory in order that the pilot might observe the progress and direction of flight, also to avoid, if possible, the many dangers which might beset them in a speed of thirty-two miles per second. The danger of striking asteroids, meteors, and small, wandering planets, was minimized by these powerful magnifying lenses which plainly disclosed the path for thousands of miles ahead.

"While only a small gallery encircled the observatory, the pilot withal had full charge of the wonderful mechanism controlling the electric light and heating systems, as well as the liquefied air chambers and great exhausts leading therefrom.

"The course of the torpedo was so calculated that on the day of firing it would be off in a straight line from Mars to the Moon, but emergency arrangements on board, whereby the course of the torpedo might be instantly changed, were also provided. This and more was accomplished by an arrangement of many ponderous valves placed over the outside in varying directions, instantly releasing any required amount of liquefied air through any or all the valves, the direction and volume of the air being controlled by pressure on the electric buttons.

"Spencer calculated that the shock produced by the instantaneous release of graduated quantities of liquefied air into space, through these valves, would tend to move the torpedo in any desired direction, though the air was shot forth into a partial vacuum. Therefore, if any formidable obstacle should be disclosed in the torpedo's path, it would be necessary only to release sufficient air from a side valve to slightly turn the course and clear the impediment. Any slight variation in the course could be corrected in the same manner.

"The distance between Mars and Moon was then calculated to be forty-three million miles. To reach space from Mars, it was figured, that the torpedo would have about one hundred and fifty miles of gravitational and air resistance to overcome. Explosives in exact quantities to shoot the torpedo into space, overcoming gravitation and the retarding effects of the air blanket surrounding Mars, were all carefully calculated by Spencer.

" 'I can fire,' he alleged, 'either of the torpedoes into space, going around the Sun at a safe distance nearly ten million miles from it—and return to the outer edge of Mars' atmosphere. But, I would not dare to enter the latter owing to its atmosphere being now so rarefied, that a successful descent would be impossible. To attempt a descent through the atmosphere of Mars would result in being fused like a meteor in its flight towards a planet.

"'The Moon's atmosphere, however, is so dense now that, with the aid of liquefied air released against its atmosphere, I will guarantee a landing as lightly as a feather.' All this was announced by Spencer to members of the House now engaged in discussing arrangements for pointing the torpedo at will."

CHAPTER XXXVIII

"Preparations for the trip were now all but complete. The construction work on the two enormous tubular twelve-mile bores, and the huge torpedoes that rested easily at the bases of these yearning chasms, had ceased after many months of continuous activity. All was in readiness to carry out the final plans of this colossal scientific undertaking.

"The last announcement, calling on all volunteers to settle their affairs and make the final preparations to assemble at Mount Hope—at least one week before leavetaking—with a view to daily familiarize themselves with the passenger torpedo, had been made. Rooms were all selected and testing instructions duly installed. Those who desired to take a last farewell from the departing volunteers, were bidden to do so at the mouth of the great aperture leading to the passenger torpedo.

"Soon those who were to make up the emigrating company were busy bidding a last adieu to friends and acquaintances. Notwithstanding the care exercised in selecting only whole families and close friends, the leavetaking was far from a merry one, for those who were to embark or those who remained felt deeply the eventual separation. Some anticipated the journey in the spirit of glee, thus helping to lighten the feelings of those who plainly carried within a heavy heart, or the pitiful countenance of confirmed grief.

"All was hustle and bustle. Notwithstanding many warnings, there were a few late arrivals, whose swiftly moving electric aero-chairs came hurrying in from all directions.

"Then the final effort to clear the zone of all débris remaining was being pushed forward with almost feverish haste by the thousand men who had been employed on the construction plans.

"All the members of the Dudley family, with the exception of Charlotte, were among the first to descend to the torpedo.

"'I desire to become accustomed to the air aboard,' explained Charlotte's father to Christopher, just before making the twelve-mile descent in the family electric aero-car, and then, pointing, he added, 'I'm going to take that car with me. It carries eight people and weighs but twelve pounds.'

"Suddenly peering down into the great hole extending into the ground twelve miles at a slight angle, he said, 'Well, Christopher, don't let any foolhardy ones tumble down this hole. Hello! Why, you've got it illuminated! A good idea! The worst of this trip is holding this pesky air tube for breathing while descending in the car. What do you do when you reach the bottom?' he inquired. 'Is the door open; can I descend directly into the torpedo?'

"'The people will all descend in their own electric aero-chairs. The main steel door is wide open. Go into that first. Don't for a minute take the air tube from your mouth. You should descend the twelve miles in about four minutes. Put out your hand over the hole——'

" 'What for?' said Dudley, doing as he was directed.

" 'Feel anything?' asked Christopher.

" 'Yes, I feel a lot of air rushing up.'

" 'That is to safeguard the people against accidents as they descend. I have several streams of compressed air running from the compressed air tanks.'

" 'Well, I'm glad there is no danger.'

" 'There is not a particle of danger. The timid ones will be taken down by experienced aero pilots. When your machine reaches out over the center of the hole, let it go down as fast as possible. The automatic indicator will release the liquefied air, so that you will alight as softly as a kitten on its feet,' said Spencer. Then he bade the family an affectionate farewell, promising to meet them later on the Moon.

"While Felix Claudio was to be the Passenger Torpedo's pilot, he had given him no authority beyond its manipulation. Dr. Nathan Elizabrat might be termed Captain of the expedition, as the comfort and welfare of the people had been assigned to his charge. He also had general supervision of all arrangements aboard, and was held responsible for the housing of the people, the storing of foods, with the regulation of heat, light, and air in every room. He had charge of the organizing committees to teach the use and wear of the air bag into which each emigrant must go a few minutes before the torpedo was fired. Failure to do this on the part of any one meant certain death. All responsibility for the safety of lives on board was divided between the Pilot and the Captain. Already, immense stores of food and water had been taken aboard, and in a few hours all would be complete.

"The second torpedo, with Christopher as Pilot, and

loaded with machinery, implements, records, and thousands of tons of everything essential to continue the work of advancing civilization, was ready, and would follow one day later. Advancement on the Moon was designed to go forward from the highest point attained on Mars. Hence the extreme care taken to select the very latest scientific instruments.

"It had been noted that failure to reach the Moon with this precious cargo containing all the paraphernalia of an advanced civilization meant the little colony would suffer almost final extinction.

"Then would follow the slow and painful efforts of mankind to ascend again to a higher level. After weary millions of years of war and bloodshed and fighting disease, in subduing the lower animals, only a step towards final perfection would be reached, when they succeeded in attaining the present high civilization of Mars. What a catastrophe it would be, to destroy everything in literature, in art, or inventions. Those who have warred on these products of mankind in the great upward struggle through the ages are now standing without the great white way. There they may remain to mourn their deeds for ages to come," remarked Marcomet with a tone of regret.

"Charlotte and Christopher were now continually together and busied themselves in caring for the needs and comforts of all volunteers. Charlotte was in incessant demand, transmitting latest messages over the 'phone, sending out messengers in aero-chairs and cars for things forgotten or left behind. She stood hurrying up the belated, answering a thousand and one questions, and giving assurance to the more nervous. Not until every one was safely housed within the torpedo, and every one was hundreds of miles away from the zone of the explosion, did Charlotte and Christopher find time to say a few parting words:

" 'The torpedo,' he said, 'with its precious cargo will soon be speeding up and out on its mission of colonization. I have done my best to guard against all accidents. But let us change the subject,' he added. 'The time for my leave-taking draws near. You must remember, Charlotte, I have yet to betake myself back to my room in the House where I shall touch the button to release, by thousands, tons of explosives which will send you flying skyward.'

" 'I'll never fly away from you again,' she replied, laughing.

"Then it was that they both reluctantly took final leave.

"Charlotte at last bravely took her position in the electro aero-chair, and started the motor. 'Good-by, Christopher,' she said, leaning out to kiss him. 'Oh, how I shall miss you, and just think how I shall feel after we have safely landed on the Moon. Then I shall scan the sky for the sight of your coming torpedo. I don't expect to eat or sleep until after your arrival.'

" 'You'd better, Charlotte,' he said, 'for a watched pot takes long in boiling, you know.'

" 'I can see it all now,' she dreamily said. 'I can scan all the people standing on a high hill, all counting the moments as they pass, awaiting the time to arrive, when we shall behold the black form of the torpedo shoot into view, looking at first like a tiny speck away up in the clear atmosphere of the Moon. Then, I can see it rapidly draw nearer, and from a speck it has grown into a spot against the clear air; then, like a meteor, I see it plunge

towards the ground from a few miles up. Suddenly it
slackens its speed, and I hear the far-away roar of escaping air, so great in quantity that it sounds like pealing
thunder. Now it comes nearer and nearer, and the sound
increases, it is a hissing and roaring thing that looks
unnatural—uncanny. Like a meteor whose speed has been
retarded, I see it coming so swiftly towards what seems
destruction, I hold my breath. My blood almost freezes
in my veins as I watch it descend through the air. What
a huge thing! It resembles a huge, black mountain in
the sky. Now I am certain that there is no power in the
universe that can stay the fall or save it from being
smashed to atoms. It must be so. How can that ponderous thing, weighing hundreds of thousands of tons,
overcome gravitation by any power? But suddenly I remember what you have taught me in our quiet talks together. You have said that the same power that raises a
body may be used to lower it. If we have power enough
to raise this mighty steel projectile and hurl it with a
force, as a Hercules might hurl a pebble from a sling, then,
you say, the same force can be utilized to break its fall, to
make the landing as safe and harmless as a bird alighting
on earth. Yes, I can see the monster descend like a great
dirigible and move about as if looking for a good place to
land. But, oh, I can just discern you, so calm, looking
at me through the turret window, and then—well, that's
all.'

" 'That's just what you will see, if nothing happens, and
then——'

" 'And then I'll ask the Doctor—Doctor Elizabrat—
to marry us. You'll be my husband, will you not?' she

asked, placing her hand affectionately upon his shoulder.

" 'Yes, I'll be yours. That,' he replied, 'has been long understood.'

" 'Oh, Christopher! Please keep near the *transtelescope* all the time. To-night I will send you a message not later than twelve, midnight. Don't, please, retire before that time, will you?'

" 'No, I promise you I'll stay up until I receive your message.'

" 'I'll be up early to-morrow morning, too, and report to you everything as regards our experience.'

" 'As you suggest, be sure to communicate with me, by twelve to-night, Charlotte, as I must be precise, quite early in the morning. Your further message should not be before five in the morning, as I want to obtain sleep. You must be going now, otherwise all our plans will be upset.'

" 'Don't forget to push the button,' she playfully called out as her chair-car gracefully arose a short distance in the air. When over the center of the great chasm her chair began to quickly descend into the huge rifle barrel, with its torpedo, twelve miles below.

"Christopher stood near the edge, that he might the better observe, as the chair began to float down into the great dark depth, Charlotte keeping up her constant waving of good-by!

" 'Don't forget to place your air cap,' shouted Christopher, leaning over the edge—but she was now too far to hear his voice. He was relieved on looking again more carefully to observe that Charlotte had already turned on the powerful headlight, and had drawn the air bag over her head so as to breathe more freely in the fast-increasing air pressure accompanying the descent. 'I knew she would not forget my instructions,' he said to himself, as he smiled with satisfaction.

"She had now disappeared entirely from view, and for the first time in many years he suddenly felt alone. 'She's gone, for a while,' he said with a deep sigh. How happy he had felt in anticipation of their approaching marriage, for many weary years had passed before Charlotte had received her parents' consent. Patiently he had been waiting more than forty years.

"No wonder Christopher smiled again as he resumed his chair-car and drove full speed toward home—seven hundred miles away. He was happy, but, withal, felt lonesome on his way to the House.

"Great was the excitement upon his arrival. As he hurried into the chamber of the House where hundreds of astronomers were assembled, a great cheer of greeting went up from floor and gallery. 'We thought something had happened to you. You are five minutes late. What was the trouble?' they asked as they surrounded him.

" 'There was no trouble. Charlotte was bidding me good-by—and other things,' he smilingly replied. The remark induced them all to look significantly at each other. 'We have only ten minutes to wait,' finally exclaimed Christopher, showing some little excitement, and then continuing, he said: 'Those who desire to behold the coming phenomena—the effect this explosion has upon the atmosphere—should obtain positions from prominent elevations immediately,' he commanded. 'Brother Astronomers! Will you please, at once, seek your positions at the *transtelephonescopes?* I want you to observe the effect of the shock. I shall deem it a special honor if you will send all important observations to my chamber off the balcony. Who will be the first to report the discovery of the torpedo in space? Who will be first among you to catch the earliest message? You will all honor yourselves in being diligent. I anticipate that less than thirty seconds will elapse after the torpedo is fired, before one of you, my brothers, discovers its whereabouts in space. In five minutes from the time, I believe many of you will be in direct communication with your friends aboard.'

"After thus delivering himself, every one quickly left the chamber, and made haste to take up their positions at the 'scopes.' Some were appointed to observe and take moving pictures of the effect of the explosion on the atmosphere, while others were to record all sounds, or search space for the first sight of the torpedo.

"Christopher rapidly approached his chamber where he sat alone, watching the seconds as each sped by. With one hand stretched out towards the electric button connecting the thousands of tons of powerful explosives, the other arm rested upon his knee, with fingers pressed closely to his forehead. Spencer knew there was small danger to befall the torpedo when fired. But there was a danger and a serious one. He had calculated that the people inside the torpedo at the instant of explosion would be quickly jerked from a position of absolute quiet to a speed of more than thirty-two miles a second. It was early realized by Spencer that nothing human could withstand the effects of such a fearful shock unless in some way protected. How to overcome this was a problem that took him much time to determine. It had been suggested that if each voyager was tightly placed into a steel mould, exactly fitting the body, no extraordinary shock would be felt. But long experiments had proved that the best preventive against certain destruction would be compressed air. Each one volunteering had demanded a strict guarantee against danger. Later, I shall disclose how each person was protected.

"As Christopher sat waiting, through the passing seconds, his mind wandered to thoughts of Charlotte. 'If the torpedo points true,' he said aloud as if addressing her, 'you will alight safely. The danger, if any,' he repeated, 'will come in its flight. I must watch it! I must watch it! I am nervous regarding the honesty of that Pilot'— and then he repeated to himself: 'I'll watch him, too, Charlotte. I'll watch Felix Claudio.' Then for a moment he hung his head in silence. Soon he looked up suddenly, and, with eyes bulging from their sockets, he leaped to his feet and fairly screamed, 'My God! It's time!' Instantly and nervously he pressed the button at his side. The clock showed exactly fifteen minutes, eight and three-quarter seconds past four P. M."

CHAPTER XXXIX

TRACKLESS SPACE

"It was but the fractional part of a second, after Christopher had hurled his super-machine into space, when there arose a series of earth tremors, not unlike those produced by a far-reaching earthquake. For the moment everything violently shook and rocked throughout the great marble building where Christopher was seated. All this was accompanied by a nauseating feeling which lasted several minutes. The earth tremors gradually ceased, the initial shock lasting less than thirty seconds.

"To Christopher, these thirty seconds were as years in time. A profound fear and physical weakness seemed to temporarily possess him. He held his breath expecting to hear words sealing his doom for having failed. Indeed, failure of his plans, or perhaps some unforeseen accident to the ten thousand emigrants with loss of all that was dear, he seemed impressed he had already heard. Then arose vivid and terrifying pictures of the dire consequences following his failure. These moved so rapidly that a lifetime passed before his mind's eye instantaneously, exposing the consummation of his utter ruin.

"Great beads of perspiration now stood out upon his forehead, and trickled down his pallid face. As he sat alone, hundreds of years seemed to have suddenly added their weight of sorrows to all his personal efforts for advancement and good, until he looked old, broken and bent.

"As if to increase his terror and intensify the situation, there now came strange sounds, gradually increasing until the heavens seemed filled with darkling and terrific omens. At the height of all this, the unaccounted sounds aroused him from his stupor. He sat upright for a moment dully looking into space as if to satisfy himself of what had happened. Suddenly he arose and rushed to the window, throwing up the sash.

"The air seemed as if in a whirl of eddies, alternating absolute calm and violent whirlwinds, but, withal, it immediately revived him. Notwithstanding the absence of clouds in the sky, the violent vibrations still obtained.

"Though looking up and down the avenue as far as he could see, not a person was in sight. 'Is every one dead, or are they all home awaiting news?' he asked himself, and closing the window he staggered back to his chair. 'My God, did I press the key, or am I dreaming?' he whispered, as he repeatedly and mechanically pressed down the electric button.

"Then his eye caught sight of an *autoreadophone* directly in front of him—all set to receive the first message. 'Why don't somebody say something, or do something?' he finally murmured, gritting his teeth. 'This long silence will drive me mad. Oh! I can't stand it. Are they safe, or are they—Oh, God! Will some one but speak? Say something? Yell out,' he cried. 'What's that? I heard something! Yes, yes, who is it? Did some one speak?' he cried with bated breath, his eyes staring in the direction of the 'phone. He listened a moment. Then suddenly came a voice, sounding as if near his chair.

" 'Is this Christopher Spencer, Astronomer?' it quickly asked.

" 'Yes, yes—yes, yes!' he cried, leaping from his chair, but he was weak, he staggered, and fell sprawling on the floor. Painfully he drew himself up on hands and knees and crawled in the direction of the 'phone. He hoarsely whispered, 'Yes—yes—it's me—speak—I hear—who is——'

" 'I wanted to announce that the torpedo is safe and——'

" 'Oh-o-oh!' groaned Christopher—and he heavily fell forward on his face—unconscious. The suddenness of the announcement was overwhelming—too much for him. How long he lay there he knew not, but it was quite dark when he returned to consciousness. Awakened by the long and persistent repetition of his name, he recalled but dimly that through his long stupor some one had repeatedly cried, 'Spencer, Spencer,' and now every second or two some one seemed calling, 'Spencer, Spencer, oh, Spencer,' with rhythmic regularity.

" 'I am here,' he faintly answered, trying desperately to regain full self-possession.

" 'Spencer—Spencer,' continued the voice.

" 'Why, that's Charlotte's voice,' he gleefully said as he staggered to his feet. 'Hello, hello, Charlotte. Charlotte, is that you? Here I am—are you well—are you well—here I am—don't you see me——'

" 'What is the matter with you—have you lost your senses? Or——'

" 'Oh, no. I am well—very well. How are you?'

" 'Why, what is the matter with you—are you hurt?'

" 'No, no. I am well. I'm so glad—so glad.'

" 'I've been calling you more than two hours. You must have been very busy. I thought you must have fallen asleep, but every one informs me that you were engaged with observations. Didn't you have your 'phone attuned?'

" 'Yes, it's all right. I'm so glad. When did our astronomers discover the torpedo?'

" 'When? Why, what do you mean? Have you been asleep? Doctor Elizabrat announced to us more than two hours ago that a Mars Astronomer discovered our torpedo one minute and fifty-four and one-quarter seconds after the explosion. We were then 3,656 miles beyond the atmosphere. Good-by, Christopher. Doctor Elizabrat desires to use the machine. I will call later. Good-by.'

" 'Good-by—thank you,' stammered Christopher, his eyes sparkling and his voice now filled with animation. The period of weakness and fear which he had overcome was mainly due to overhard and faithful work. It had undermined his health and shaken an otherwise powerful nervous system.

"As a smile spread o'er his face, he exclaimed aloud: 'Thank God she is safe—all are safe! Now I feel better. I am glad!' he repeated over and over to himself, as he hurried up the winding stairway leading to his private observatory at the top of the House.

"The *transtelephonescope* had been already adjusted at an angle which, with little correction, pointed to the exact location of the torpedo in its outward flight. After some figuring, he set the instrument in a position that proved the torpedo's calculated speed. This showed within the vision of the lenses at the exact estimated time.

"In order to prove that the speed of thirty-two miles

a second was being maintained, hundreds of *transtele-phonescopes* were set up at given angles, so that each observer would catch a view of the fleeing monster at a specified moment.

"When Christopher first beheld the mammoth torpedo speeding through space, the beautiful sight thrilled and filled him with pride. As he adjusted the lens of the instrument he scanned its surface for signs of life. The Pilot's turret, or observatory, had already been raised, but there was no one in it. 'That is not only strange, but dangerous,' thought Christopher. 'Here it is after seven o'clock,' he remarked to himself, 'and no one in the turret!' He had hardly spoken before he saw the tall form of Doctor Elizabrat enter the observatory. Some lady was with him, but as she stood behind the Doctor, he could not make out who it was.

"An hour later, over the 'phone, came the voice of Charlotte talking from her room.

"Only ten thousand messages, each indicating a record, had been received upon the private instruments to which they were attuned. To communicate with those whose instruments happened not to be in attune, it was necessary to employ the public 'phone, all instruments being readily and instantly adjustable to this.

"Christopher had previously given Charlotte the attuning degree at which both machines should be set when they desired to converse. Here, Charlotte excused herself by saying that Doctor Elizabrat's scope had been broken. Evidently some one had tampered with it, therefore, she had temporarily loaned him the use of hers. The interruption in their previous conversation was due, she said, to the Doctor's desire to transmit important gen-

eral news. She then proceeded to give Christopher a full,
detailed account of her experiences and sensation from the
beginning of the trip. On his part, he promised to follow
her, as already arranged, with the second torpedo exactly
one day later.

" 'Everything is in readiness, and waiting,' he said.

" 'I hope the weather will be clear,' said Charlotte.

" 'What difference can that make? I shall not know
whether it is clear or stormy, once I embark. It's clear
now—not a cloud in the sky.'

" 'I know it is clear where you are, but for a radius
of over two hundred miles around Mount Hope, it must
be raining violently, for the clouds are inky black and
they seem to be extending rapidly. I noticed the clouds
forming when I first looked back at Mars about ten minutes after the explosion. I was then 19,200 miles from
you. I observed the air gradually thicken over the zone
we had just left, until it became ink-black. The storm
must have been terrible, judging from the appearance of
the clouds which I observed upside down from here. I
don't believe there can be a tree or shrub standing within
fifty miles of Mount Hope.'

"It was eleven o'clock that evening before their conversation closed.

"The torpedo was now visible to every astronomer.
Not for a moment could the vigil be relaxed, from start
to finish. So far the torpedo's progress had been steady
and accurate. Claudio, the Pilot, and many others could
be readily seen peering through the glass of the turret.
Frequently, some were observed peering through *transtelephonescopes* which in the rear pointed in the direction
of Mars. Their messages to friends on Mars were fre-

quently of praise for the skill and ability of Christopher. Thus far no one had been injured—all were well.

"The national flag of Mars—which had no meaning for the Moon or other planet—had been thrust up through one of the air tubes, on a pole, and was seen hanging limp and motionless, notwithstanding the fact that the torpedo was traveling through space at a terrific speed, thus proving that space is a partial vacuum.

"The people of Mars were wild with joy over the success of the undertaking. Even the staid and solemn looking Astronomers could not suppress their delight, but entered heartily into the general spirit of rejoicing. Bulletins were continuously sent through the *autoreadophone*, from the busy observatories.

"Perhaps the most dejected man on Mars was Christopher. He longed for the hours to pass, that he might also be on his way to the Moon.

"While the messages received from Charlotte and others were mostly reassuring, he still had an unaccountable feeling that all was not right. What it was he could not divine, but he could not shake off the feeling. Never before had he experienced a presentiment or foreboding of danger. Was it a message by telepathy? Charlotte had not hinted at danger in her conversation and, so far as Felix Claudio was concerned, neither had she spoken of him. Perhaps, after all, it was nothing but reaction arising from the terrible mental strain of a few hours previous. Weary and overcome by the day's events, he now withdrew his eyes from the observation lenses and rested his head across his arms.

"The storm, by now, had spread rapidly. The driving rain on the observatory roof, and the howling wind, sounded forbidding, yet the comfortable room gave him a sense of security which soon lulled him to drowsiness.

"Slowly the minutes passed. Twelve o'clock came, but no message from Charlotte. He heaved a sigh of relief. 'If I failed to hear from her by twelve, I was not to wait. She has retired,' he mused. 'I'll wait a little longer, before calling Anthony to take up the night's vigil,' he said sleepily. Again he dozed off, and his first realization of sound was that some one was now calling his name. The noise made by the wind and rain induced him to conclude that the sound came from without, and as he roused himself, he mechanically said—'Yes, come in!'

" 'Christopher,' now plainly issued from the 'scope' not two feet away.

" 'Yes, yes, what's the matter?—My God,' he rubbed his eyes violently. 'I must have been dreaming,' he said aloud, 'I hear nothing.'

"Then there came a hissing sound through the ear pieces. 'What is that noise? Is that you, Charlotte?' he excitedly asked, as his eyes bulged from his head in suppressed agitation. And then came a short message in a whisper. It could have been but a few words, but at the end of the report he fairly shouted, 'I will start just as soon as I can make ready. I will help you if it takes my life to do it. Have courage. Good-by.'

"He was now thoroughly aroused and filled with energy. Though he had suddenly paled, there was nothing to indicate nervousness or excitement now. He walked over and touched an electric button on the side wall, waited a few moments, walked out into the corridor and called, 'Anthony!'

" 'I am on my way,' said a voice below.

" 'Anthony, I shall not need you to-night.   I have decided to remain up myself.'

" 'And go without sleep?   The devil you are,' replied
Anthony.

"Christopher paid no heed to the remark.   Without
further explanation, he strode rapidly out of the Observatory Building, and hurried across the street leading to
the House of Astronomy.

"As he glanced at the great clock in the tower, its both
hands brilliantly illuminated, he noted carefully the time,
as ten minutes past twelve."

CHAPTER XL

STRANGE SENSATIONS

"After Charlotte had waved her last adieu to Christopher, he standing on the edge of the great chasm, the upward rush of air, as already intimated, caused by the rapid descent of her aero-chair, impelled the immediate covering of her head with the air protector. This done, she again looked up through the great polished barrel into the fast narrowing vision of its entrance where the figure of Christopher stood, resembling some small distant speck. She knew that he was unable to see far down into the great seven-mile barrel, and though she now faintly beheld him, he was unable to discern her. Previously, the barrel had been illuminated, but was now cleared, and the sides polished and heavily coated with grease, to assist in overcoming friction on firing the torpedo. As her aero-chair increased in speed downward, she turned on its powerful searchlight, and in a few moments beheld beneath her the great pointed end of the torpedo.

"Though Charlotte had been of valuable service to Christopher while the work of construction progressed, yet she had never been permitted to descend into the tubes. This was her first and only trip.

"Though she had carefully covered mouth, nose and ears with the air helmet, the pressure against the rest of her body with increasing density as she continued to descend all but entirely drove the air from her system.

"At the extreme end, or nose of the torpedo, she noticed that a great square piece of steel had been removed from its surface and hung suspended above. It was the outer door leading to the inside, and in shape and form was not unlike an immense safe door. As her chair neared the opening, she was greeted by Dr. Elizabrat who stood at the entrance.

" 'You will find,' remarked the Doctor, 'a landing place inside. You are the last to arrive, Charlotte,' and he swung the inner door open.

"As her machine landed on the platform inside she removed the air helmet. 'We will pack everything away for you,' said a young man in charge.

"Dr. Elizabrat was soon at her side to announce that he would now let down the great outer steel door. 'The door,' he said, 'is one hundred and fifty feet in thickness and fifty feet square. When it closes into place it is impossible to find where the seams meet, so perfectly do they fit. The opening and closing of this entrance and everything pertaining to the operation of the torpedo, is automatically controlled from a small compartment located in the turret.'

"As Charlotte made her way down the spacious corridor flanked on either side by thousands of entrances leading into the private chambers of emigrants, she could not help uttering frequent ejaculations of surprise and admiration for the beauty and grandeur displayed in architectural design. The huge scale upon which it had been so perfectly constructed impressed and amazed her. Beautifully decorated and illuminated, it was indeed a palace.

" 'Let me inform you of one thing,' said Doctor Eliza-brat. 'The shock of the explosion will be lessened a thousand fold by reason of this great chamber of liquid air surrounding the inner tube. It was a master idea from a master man!'

" 'Christopher is certainly to be congratulated,' Charlotte answered.

" 'Here is your room,' the Doctor politely said, pointing to the door opposite. 'Your family and relatives occupy about forty rooms on all sides of you. I know you will not feel weary or alone.'

"The sight that met Charlotte's gaze on entering the compartments especially arranged for her was unexpected and amazing. Everywhere could be seen the thoughtfulness on Christopher's part in providing an endless and bewildering variety of those small things which inspire the admiration of the fair sex. He doubtless intended that they should please and fascinate—adding much to her happiness on the journey.

"As the torpedo stood on end, pointing upward at the desired angle, moving about was somewhat a difficult task. Yet, Christopher had previously explained the new conditions the passengers would experience soon after being impelled beyond the atmosphere of Mars.

" 'Gravitation will have no perceptible influence upon our speed when once the torpedo is beyond the atmosphere. For the first time in your life you will realize that there is no up nor down to space. Everything movable, including each one of us, will be so light that, after the first few days, you will have great difficulty in moving at all. Indeed, everything will remain in the exact spot in which it is put. Should some one hand you a glass of water, it would make no difference to you whether it was upside down or on its side, the water would not spill out. In drinking the water, suckage would have to be employed. If you should suddenly let go the glass, it would remain in the air just where your hand left it.

" 'During the first few days out the influence from the gravitation of Mars will allow us all to move about with care, but no more. While it might not be convenient for us to walk on the sides of our rooms or across the ceilings during the first few days, at a certain point in the torpedo's flight, when the pull of gravitation from Mars and Moon equalize, everything and every one on board will float about. None will be able to walk. I warn you all, however, not to allow yourselves to float out of the room, beyond the reach of something you can hold to. As we near the Moon, its gravitation would gradually float you along to the side of the room in the direction of the pulling force.' Just here, Christopher could have told you, that 'for a few hours of the journey, the safest thing will be to secure yourself to rings provided.'

"Charlotte found that all portable things were securely fastened, so that the shock would in no way cause injury. All chairs, tables, beds and, in fact, everything in the way of furniture was made from a substance resembling rubber, but many times tougher, and its specific gravity happened to be one-tenth less.

"Charlotte's apartments on the torpedo consisted of a living room, a *readograph* library, a lounging and bed-room. As in all homes on Mars, beds, lounges, and all large furnishing essentials, when not in use, were folded and concealed from view in walls and closets.

"All the living rooms aboard the torpedo were veritable

palaces of beauty and art. There were 'phones and 'scopes, *readographs* and every convenience for hearing all the news from Mars and other planets in daily communication with each other. The individual might see these far-distant peoples at will, and hear their voices as clearly as though they were nearby. Stories might be read automatically by the *readograph*, but the seeing and hearing of what actually happened on a far-away planet without moving out of one's seat, excited still greater curiosity and interest.

"For some time Charlotte was absorbed in studying this veritable palace afloat. Indeed, she failed to notice that the appointed time for starting was nearly due. Suddenly, however, she was brought to a realization of the matter by a loud command over the *readograph*,—'Every one must now don the air-bag. It means death if you fail to get within its certain protection.' Instructions on board had been given many weeks prior in the use of this robe, resembling rubber air-bags. These bags were about ten feet in circumference, and were made of a material much lighter, stronger and more resisting than rubber. In one of these, Charlotte quickly concealed herself, closing the open part airtight after her. Connecting with each bag, and its air chambers on the sides, was a small rubber tube, through which passed a powerful stream of air immediately distending the balloon-shaped sphere with such pressure that Charlotte found herself in the center, and, as a further protection, a steel air mask covered her entire head and body. From the inside of the mask two small air tubes leading from the mouth to the outside of the sphere admitted plenty of air for breathing.

"At five seconds before the torpedo was due to be fired,

came a loud command through the *readophone*: 'Every one take a deep breath and relax the body as much as possible. Ready!' Charlotte heard the command, and almost immediately followed a moment of intense confusion and semi-consciousness. Something had happened, or was happening. What, she could not realize, nor did she seem to gather her thoughts sufficiently to care. All was dark, and through her dulled sensation came a vague feeling that the end of things had come. She seemed to realize a floating sensation, as if descending into the depths of the sea—slowly suffocating. Then there returned more consciousness as she intuitively raised the air tube that had been expelled from her mouth. Now she began to realize that the air-bag in which she was suspended seemed bounding around the room with frightful and rapid motion. Meanwhile, she experienced peculiar and painful sensations. At first her body felt as if moving alternately through fiery furnaces and chill blasts, the heat of the former threatening momentarily to consume her. From this it seemed as if suddenly hurled upon a floating iceberg where she stood shivering, while greater forces were driving and grinding her body by furious charges. How long these alternating hot and cold experiences really lasted, she could not recall, nor could any one of the ten thousand aboard agree as to the seeming period of time each suffered a similar experience.

"As Charlotte waited, her courage grew. Suddenly she again heard a voice coming from the *autoreadophone*. It said, 'We are safe! Get out of the air-bags!'

"Charlotte lost no time in obeying the command. As the air pressure lessened, she finally was enabled to remove the breathing mask from her face. The shock, however, was so intense that she fell to the floor and lay for several minutes unable to move. Slowly her strength returned, and after many attempts she was finally enabled to stand upon her feet. For the first time, she became conscious that the position of the torpedo had changed, for instead of standing on the end wall of the room, she found herself on the floor, in an upright position, but feeling as if her weight had reduced to within a pound.

"Her first thoughts were for Christopher. How her nature deeply longed for him! He, above all else, was dear to her,—dearer than other friends and material comforts. If he could then have been there, she pictured her happiness as supreme. As she sat quietly resting in the great arm chair, thoughts crowding through her mind, her attention was arrested by a soft rap on the door leading to the outside hall.

" 'I wonder who that can be,' she said to herself, and then aloud, 'Who is it, may I ask?' "

CHAPTER XLI

" 'Welcome to the land of—Nowhere!' exclaimed Doctor Elizabrat, as Charlotte opened the door. 'I see you are all right,' he continued.

" 'Yes, thank you, Doctor,' she replied.

" 'Good! A few of us are going around from room to room to see if all is well. So far, we find no one hurt. Some, however, are badly shaken and have retired on account of their feeling weak,' he explained. The Doctor then passed down the hall, stopping at each door long enough to speak encouragingly and to inquire the condition of the occupant.

"It was within an hour after, that the *readophone* in every room gave out the message that all passengers had been seen, and, excepting a few cases of slight nervousness or temporary exhaustion caused by the shock, all were well and happy.

"Charlotte had now sufficiently regained strength to take a lively interest in things about her. With all possible haste, she stepped across the hall separating her rooms from those of her family and friends. Here she affectionately greeted them, after which she made her way towards the turret, expecting to look, for the first time, out and over the endless realm of ether.

"The turret could be automatically raised above the

387

torpedo's outside surface, and from the circular gallery
extending around the inside, one might have an unob-
structed view in all directions through its circle of un-
breakable glass. Up the broad stairs leading to the spacious gallery, she found her way, only to discover it occupied by hundreds of others crowding each other in
eagerness to view the wonders of a new world. She found
herself at the outer edge of the assembled group, where
from her position she could occasionally obtain a glimpse
through the low glass windows, whose magnifying power
equaled that of the *transtelephonescope.*

"As she stood tiptoed, straining to glance over the
multitude of moving heads in front, she intuitively felt
that some one nearby was intently watching her. She
turned to see who it was, when Felix Claudio, Pilot of
the torpedo, approached, explaining, as he left the small
gathering of people surrounding him, that he desired to
greet the bravest lady of all—Charlotte Dudley. 'She is
the bravest,' said he with a hideous, half-hidden grin, 'because she was last to board the torpedo.' With these
words addressed partly to his friends and partly to Charlotte, he made his way with difficulty towards her. As he
approached she looked him steadily in the eye and said,
in a low, firm tone of voice, 'If you speak to me, I'll retire
to my room!' He instantly stopped short and, without
further words, turned on his heel, rejoined the small co-
terie he had just left, and immediately began to relate his
experience and sensations following the explosion. A few
leaving the gallery, Charlotte finally managed to secure a
position affording her a magnificent rear view. For some
time she had been forced to listen to exclamations of surprise and wonder. She had seen the observers turn their

faces toward each other in speechless awe. For her own part, she was entirely unprepared to behold the bewildering and magnificent spectacle that now met her gaze. One glance into this vast and mysterious realm was all she could take without shrinking back with a sense of its profound grandeur, coupled with awfulness and terror. 'The stupendousness and the mightiness of it all!' she exclaimed. Little by little she became accustomed to the sight, until finally she beheld a scene of mighty suns and planets arrayed in all their iridescent brilliancy. To accustom the eye to so bewildering a spectacle would have taken many hours, so Charlotte viewed the scene, opening and closing her eyes at short intervals, until suddenly remembering that she had forgotten to call up Christopher. Without delay, she made haste to hurriedly return to her rooms where, in her haste, she had gained so much momentum that she ran against the side wall approaching the ceiling before she could regain stability.

"At first, all her efforts to get in communication with Christopher were futile. Finally their 'phones attuned. She was now enabled to pour out a continuous stream of terms declaring her love and offering praise, mingled with vivid descriptions of her sensations and surprise.

"The hour had sped far into the evening and the great dining hall had closed, yet, as was customary on Mars, Charlotte served herself. All meals were put up in a scientific concentrated form, and served in strongly embossed paper dishes, the largest of which weighed but a few grains."

"To feed a company of ten thousand on Earth would require tons of dishes," I remarked to Marcomet.

"Yes, that is true," he replied, "but time will bring the

people a thin, beautifully colored, featherweight paper, which, when chemically treated, heat cannot destroy, and it will be much stronger than china. The material will be so cheap that, once used, it will not pay to use it again. Household articles will be so treated that fire will not burn, nor over-heat destroy them. It will then be possible to preserve all surplus foods in hermetically sealed papers, and to cook them in the original packages."

Marcomet then resumed the narrative:

"While it was morning, day and evening on Mars, aboard the torpedo, they had incessant twilight. The Sun looked no larger than the Moon towards which the torpedo pointed, nor did they notice any heat from his rays. The scene, withal, was a beautiful one.

"Picture to yourself this glorious scene aboard, the old and young gathered together in pleasant or earnest conversation, or strolling up and down the long halls in pairs, for privacy or exercise. To have looked down upon this picture of contentment would have been an inspiration to any people, and an incentive to master the universe! This can and will be done," said Marcomet. "Earth needs many more chemists and astronomers. Through their discoveries, it will leap forward in knowledge within the next century, as never before.

"Though late one evening, Charlotte could not resist the temptation of taking a final look through the glass turret, before retiring to her room. She had promised to call Christopher before midnight. Mounting the stairs leading to the gallery, she was not surprised to find people awaiting the like opportunity to reach the turret. Looking back upon Mars, she was overawed. Beholding him in his dazzling brilliancy, his disk appeared to cover more than half of the heavens. Continuing to look, Mars seemed to grow more beautiful every minute, though perceptibly smaller. She realized that in a few more hours he would be left so far behind and appear so small, that the Moon would vie with him in size and brilliancy. Millions of stars that she had never seen before were now plainly in view. The heavens in all directions seemed filled with them, the familiar ones appearing ten times larger and many times more brilliant than before.

"Looking ahead, 'she beheld, reaching away hundreds of thousands of miles, millions of small bodies of all sizes, each rushing at terrific speed in a direction differing from the rest. Space, however, is so vast that the danger of collision appeared remote. This endless display of flying planets was a fascinating sight, and as her gaze became transfixed she could not help noticing two large bodies, from opposite directions, suddenly strike with such force that they instantly formed into one great brilliant gas ball, many times the size of their combined bodies. This signified the birth of a new world.

"What seemed to her more remarkable, was, that when many of these planets in pairs came together they did not ignite, but extricated themselves and proceeded in opposite courses. Why was this, she thought? There appeared to her but one answer. Each pair was positively or negatively charged, and to ignite into one they must be of opposite poles.

"Once, as she looked forward, the torpedo cut through a large floating body of gas—no harm resulting. Later it struck a mass of substance some three or four miles in circumference, without causing the slightest shock. The torpedo had passed through the mass and was one hundred and eighty-two miles away, before Charlotte could turn to see the effect, if any, of the collision."

CHAPTER XLII

THE DEVIL'S SON

"CHARLOTTE would have gladly spent the remainder of that twilight night in the fascinating occupation of making observations of the surrounding heavens, had she not feared the presence of Felix Claudio.

"It was after the gallery had become cleared of people that she began to realize the full enjoyment of her surroundings. Now rushing to the front and watching some particularly bright meteor; then retiring to the rear to take a parting glance at the marvelous display of onrushing suns and planets, each of them, in turn, catching and absorbing that endless supply of meteors—the minions of space—with their invisible jaws; then awe-struck, standing in silent admiration of the wondrous universal phenomena. The scene was ever new and strange, and its vastness inconceivable.

"While she thus stood enraptured, her attention was attracted by loud exclamations from an old white-haired astronomer—Philip, by name.

" 'Say, Felix! Felix! Do we now point exactly towards the Moon?' he asked.

" 'Certainly, can't you see we do?' Felix gruffly answered.

" 'Well, my eyes are somewhat dim, maybe I don't see exactly straight. I'll come back later, Felix, and figure it out,"—said the old man as he slowly made his way down the gallery stairs.

" 'All right. I'll be here all night to meet you,' he replied. Then turning to Charlotte, he smilingly said, 'Do you notice any error in Christopher's calculations? Are we pointed correctly, Charlotte?'

"Charlotte glanced immediately in the direction of the Moon and curtly answered, 'I cannot tell.'

"It was but a few minutes past eleven P. M. when Charlotte returned to her apartments. She seated herself in one of the large air-cushioned chairs, and began thinking over the experiences of the day. While she felt nervous regarding the old astronomer's observation, she was aware that Christopher had figured the torpedo's direction accurately. It would, therefore, be unwise to disturb the latter before morning. Still, there was something in the behavior of Claudio which made her uneasy. Also, she reflected, how pleasantly he had greeted her. How blandly he had asked her opinion of something concerning which he must have known she would know nothing. What could have been his object? Was he trying to discredit Christopher? Had the astronomers really miscalculated their mark? If so, then what? The thought of the far-reaching consequences unnerved her for the moment. However, Charlotte was not the kind of girl to lose her head under trying circumstances.

"Without removing her garments, she lay down to rest. Her native caution prompted her action for she desired to be in readiness for any emergency. 'Forewarned is forearmed,' she repeated to herself as she tried to assume a frame of mind in which she might fall to sleep.

"She had just dozed when, suddenly, a peculiarly jarring

sensation aroused her. It seemed as if she had been rocked within a cradle. The sensation produced occasioned slight nauseating feelings—not unlike an attack of seasickness. She arose and hurriedly threw on the lights of her apartment. She instinctively felt that something unusual had happened. What, she did not know. She tiptoed towards the door leading to the public hallway, meanwhile straining her ears for any occurring sound. Everything seemed quiet. Cautiously she opened the door and passed down the brilliantly illuminated hall, but nothing stirred, no one was seen. Except for the loud beating of her own heart, for the moment she was conscious of naught else. So she closed the door. After pondering awhile, she tried to convince herself that nervousness was only the result of her first night in space. Every slight occurrence had an exaggerated effect upon her mind. She was worn out, she reasoned. Her fears being not well founded, she determined to remain up for the balance of the night. It was then past midnight, by the clock.

"About to sit down, she was startled by a sharp, sudden sound, like the escape of steam through a safety valve. The sound must have been a veritable roar to have been heard at all through the thick steel jacket of the torpedo. There was no mistaking its direction—it came from the outside. It lasted but a second, yet the result imparted a sinking feeling that produced again that nauseating sensation.

"There was a slight jar accompanying the hiss, similar to that experienced when a boat first strikes upon the sandy beach.

"She listened for further sounds before moving again—for sounds from the corridor. She felt that some one else must have felt the shock, or at least heard the noise. But no sound came to her ears. 'We must have struck something,' she murmured to herself, again rising and standing, and silently listening as if expecting other developments.

"Reaching for her loose silken over-wraps she dexterously wound them about her, stepped softly into the hall and made her way toward the turret again. Cautiously ascending the stairs leading to the gallery, and not knowing why she was following a blind impulse, she had formed a resolve. Her attention was at once attracted by the figure of Felix Claudio fumbling over the handles of the great air valves. He was alone. She felt certain that her presence had not been discovered. What could he be doing, she thought, as she slowly ascended to the gallery, meanwhile crouching as if to conceal her figure behind a post of the railing. She realized that he had a perfect right as Pilot to be where he was. While hiding behind the post, she began to chide herself for her boldness, and was on the point of stealthily returning, when suddenly Claudio wheeled about, and, after cautiously peering over the banisters, looking in all directions, and breathlessly listening, he tiptoed cautiously toward the air valves. Grasping one in each hand, he quickly turned the handle once around, and listened. Charlotte could hear a low rumble like distant surge. Then Felix Claudio turned it once again, and as rapidly turned it back. In his so doing she felt the same sensation experienced before. She felt as if the great torpedo had suddenly taken a new angle. Crouching in her uncomfortable position, and sensing the possibilities of some horror—she knew not what—into which this son of Satan was now preparing to plunge the expedition, she began to plan how best to act. Should she reveal herself to him, simulating not to have noticed anything unusual, or should she endeavor to descend from the gallery and reach her room, where she would be comparatively safe to notify her friends of what she had seen? Deciding to take the latter course, she began to cautiously move towards the stairway. But Claudio again turned, this time looking in her direction. She knew not whether he had seen her, but caution taking the part of valor, she kept perfectly still, and awaited a further opportunity to proceed. Claudio still looking in her direction, now suddenly turned and gazed out of the windows. In doing so, the reflection from the Sun seemed to overcast his pallid face with a strange light, causing it to appear green and ghastly. She could not refrain from half rising, her eyes still following the Sun, which reminded her of a great full Moon on a clear, cold and bitter winter's night. He now turned again, looking out in front of him. Again she followed his gaze. He was scanning the Moon this time, toward which the torpedo was poin—— 'My God!' she whispered to herself as she unconsciously rose to her feet and stood erect. 'The Moon is now on our right! We are lost!' she hoarsely whispered in despair as she fell to her knees. 'Oh, Christopher!' and she whispered to herself. 'I must not be seen.' A new thought had possessed her—then a quick glance in Claudio's direction.

"If he had heard anything unusual, he failed to note it, for he still stood coolly gazing in the Moon's direction. Again she crouched low, and thinking herself well screened from sight determined to withdraw quickly.

" 'I beg your pardon,' broke in Claudio in a soft, purring tone of voice, moving not a particle, and still gazing intently at the Moon. Before Charlotte could regain her feet or composure sufficiently to reply he tauntingly continued: 'Why, hello! It is Charlotte Dudley! Why, good evening, Charlotte! How do you like this view?' he said, pointing his hand in the direction of the Moon.

"At first she did not reply, but arose to her feet, somewhat abashed. She instantly made up her mind that it might be foolish and perhaps dangerous to antagonize him for the moment or pretend to have noticed any change in the Moon's location. Without perceptible delay, she quickly replied: 'Why, Felix Claudio!'—in a tone loud enough to be heard should any one in the chambers nearby be awake. 'How did you know I was here?'

" 'She-h-h,' said he, raising his hand and glancing around furtively. 'Don't make so much noise. Do you hear? Keep quiet,' he continued in a menacing way. Saying this, he stepped directly in front of her, cutting off the only avenue of retreat down the stairs leading from the gallery.

"No doubt he had been watching her some time while ostensibly occupied in gazing so interestedly at the surrounding planets. During this time of seeming preoccupation, he doubtless was studying out a plan by which he could prevent her making an outcry, for he now felt sure that her purpose in seeking the gallery at that precise hour was to secure information which she would immediately 'phone to Christopher. He knew that she was the only person present and a witness to his manipulation of the air valves that changed the torpedo's course. On the other hand, Charlotte believed that she understood his nefarious designs now. He intended to point the torpedo towards a planet further away, which one he did not know, but existent somewhere. In this act of his she read her own doom. She knew that she was dealing with a desperate man, ready with infinite zeal to grasp any extreme that might accomplish his purpose. The first thing to do was to try and notify some of those aboard of what had happened, and the increasing danger as time rapidly passed. She hoped against hope in these few short moments, with strained nerves like some half-frightened creature.

"Not a sound now of any kind was to be heard. 'It's a fight,' she finally said to herself. 'If it's a battle of wits I'll win, but if resolved by force, Felix Claudio is a physical giant. Indeed, he is the Devil's Son,' she said to herself, 'and in this twilight he appears capable of the foulest murder.'

" 'Was I talking loud? Why, I would not rob any one of sleep after so eventful an experience,' she sweetly said in a low tone of voice, smiling. And then, as if to overwhelm him with her charm, she continued: 'I am beginning to get a little tired'—yawning.

" 'Getting tired of the twilight, Charlotte?' he asked, smiling in return.

" 'Oh, no. We are fortunate in not having windows in our apartments, otherwise the light might keep one awake. It seems so strange that one never knows when to go to bed unless time is consulted. But I am so lonesome,' she said wistfully.

" 'I'm here,' said he, drawing closer to her.

"Without pretending to notice his remark, she suddenly darted to the other side of the gallery exclaiming in a voice as loud as she dared: 'Oh, look! Look! See all those meteors. Some of them must be going at a speed of two hundred miles a second. Some traveling in the direction of our torpedo pass us as if we were standing still. Many may travel ahead at this speed for a billion years or more before striking something that will end their career. How wonderful it all is.'

" 'Oh, come over here, Charlotte. Never mind the stars. Think of me, and have pity,' said Claudio in a soft, pleading voice.

" 'Do you think there is any finality to space, Felix Claudio?' she suddenly asked, starting a little towards him, and paying no heed to his remarks.

" 'I really do not know. There's an end to some things though,' he said significantly, and after a pause he continued: 'Why don't you come over here and keep me company? You know I'm lonesome.'

" 'I'm lonesome, too, but there'll be an end to that,' she answered.

" 'Don't feel too sure of it,' he growled.

"Quickly catching the meaning of his veiled threat, but determined not to notice it, she ignored the remark, continuing: 'I believe there is no beginning, nor ending to anything. Beginning and ending seem but comparative. It is a thought which shows clearly the limitations of the human mind. The end of space is an unthinkable condition. We ask, after space, comes what? Not water! Not air. Then what? That's as far as thought will take us. If for no other reason, that is why I put my trust in Him. I am, indeed, too puny and weak to say that life is chaotic. Life to my mind is made up of unalterable natural laws which I must learn to obey, or suffer the consequences of a chemical change—there is no other penalty.'

" 'Why, you surprise me, Charlotte, by your philosophy. Where did you hear all that rot? Do you know, that fellow—that fool of yours, Christopher Spencer, has turned your head. Do you know that?' he hissed in jealous rage.

" 'Is that you, Felix?' came a weak voice from below.

" 'Who is that?' he demanded, turning and peering down into the now dimly lighted room, the while keeping an eye on Charlotte as a cat regards a mouse.

" 'Oh, you are up there, Felix. I will then come up,' said the voice.

" 'You stay where you are. Who are you?' again demanded Claudio.

" 'Why, don't you know my voice? I'm the oldest astronomer aboard—over thirty-one hundred years,' replied the old man.

" 'Oh, is that Philip? Well, you'd better go back to bed awhile. I'm busy,' said Claudio in a patronizing tone.

" 'Oh, excuse me, a young lady, I see, is with you. Well, I will call on Doctor Elizabrat,' he said, turning and hobbling off towards the Doctor's apartments.

" 'Charlotte,' he rapidly began, 'you saw me turn the torpedo from the Moon. We'll never strike it. Christopher Spencer—damn him—well, he'll get there, and stay there alone! Do you hear me?' he demanded.

" 'Yes, I hear you! And I know what you've done. Your devilish intent shall be exposed! Why, you're not fit to be here, Felix Claudio, or anywhere!' she replied, raising her voice to a firm high tone.

" 'Listen! Listen to me, Charlotte. I swear to turn the torpedo back, so that we shall strike the Moon as designed, if you will only ask me to be your husband.

Charlotte, don't you see that I love you? Can you not discern that you're killing me by your coldness—by your haughtiness? Oh! I know how unworthy I am to be the husband of such a beautiful and womanly woman as you are. Ever since you reached the age of one hundred years, I have worked and planned, and gladly would I have given many successive lives to place myself in your way, so that you might notice me—love me sufficiently to take me to your heart and make me your husband. Oh, don't you see! Will you not see the terrible strain I am undergoing? Don't say you can't take me. I don't care what you do with me, just take me to your heart and say you love me—only once—and I swear, Charlotte, to be ever loyal. I swear it! I swear it! Please, I implore, do not refuse me! What do you say? What do you say, Charlotte? Answer! Now, answer!' he said as he broke out in great suppressed sobs.

" 'I feel sorry for you,' she quietly said, displaying a sense of pity toward him. 'I can imagine how hard it is to love and not have love returned. But I never courted you. In fact I never loved you—nor could I if I tried. That is the truth. I love another. You know who that other is. I would give my life for him if necessary.'

" 'Then you'll do so now!' he fairly screeched, and in a voice that must have been heard by every one awake at that moment. Then leaping forward he seized Charlotte in his strong arms as easily as a child grasps a doll. Holding her close to him, he rapidly descended the gallery stairs to the floor below, all this, before she could recover from fright or surprise, or realize what had actually happened.

"He had taken several paces forward before she designed his purpose, or realized that he was carrying her in the direction of the great two-foot waste pipe in the center of the room.

"She was so horrified at the thought of being cast down this long pipe into the freezing cold of space, that for a moment she could not utter a cry beyond a low gurgle or rattle made by the throat as she weakly attempted an alarm. Not until he had released her from the pressure of his frenzied grasp and was in the act of laying her upon the floor, did she manage to cry: 'Hel-l-l-p! Hel-l-l——'

" 'Shut up!' he hoarsely whispered, and he quickly jammed a small silken cloth in her open mouth. 'This is your end! I have you now, and I hate that accursed love of yours—Spencer! The sleek hypocrite! I hate him! I. . . .' "

CHAPTER XLIII

REVIVING HOPES

"CHARLOTTE experienced no particular inconvenience or sense of discomfort at being held upside down by Felix Claudio, but on releasing his hold she anticipated being shot through, and, on reaching the outside ether, expected to become a human icicle, as Claudio had predicted. As it was, however, she began to gently slide, and so slowly that she was enabled to secure a firm grip with both hands to bolted projections on the sides. To these she securely hung, her feet alone extending above the floor level.

" 'Get down in there,' cried Claudio, striking the soles of her sandals, first with the flat of his hand, and then, finding it impossible to close the cover, he viciously began kicking her feet, hoping that the nervous pain caused would compel the loosening of her hold. Just as he was about to make another lunge with his foot, Charlotte plainly heard the sound of scuffling, accompanied by a rapid rain of blows, as if two people were fighting. Now there came the sound of a heavy thud as if some one had fallen to the floor. For a moment all was still. 'What could it mean?' she asked herself.

"There was no awaiting an explanation, as without warning she felt some one seize one of her feet. Holding her with a steel-like grip, a voice reassuringly said, 'Don't be afraid, Charlotte. It is I, Doctor Elizabrat. You're safe now.'

" 'Thank God for that,' Charlotte replied with a heavy sigh.

" 'It is fortunate for you,' returned the Doctor, 'that a steady stream of warm air was drawn through the pipe, otherwise you would have surely frozen.' Thus saying, he drew her up easily and closed the cover.

" 'Yes, and it is fortunate, also, that there is a very little more up than down at the present moment, otherwise the rush of blood to my head might have produced unconsciousness,' she replied, as she arose to her feet. Then Charlotte hurriedly explained to the Doctor how Claudio had wantonly attacked her in the gallery.

" 'There he is now, look—just coming to,' pointing to Claudio's prostrate form lying full length upon the floor. 'Men,' commanded the Doctor, to a group now gathered around, 'take Felix Claudio to his room, and there he must remain until we reach our destination. Allow no one to communicate with that inhuman—we have with us a son of the Devil.'

" 'I was about to arouse you all, and was stealing away, when he discovered me,' she addressed the Doctor. 'Something has occurred that I must tell you about.' Thereupon, she related her experience with Claudio in the turret, this, after being aroused by the singular shock which tallied with the Doctor's own experience.

" 'Let us go to the turret,' said the Doctor.

Both hurriedly started for the stairway leading to the gallery. As they reached the turret, both simultaneously gazed in the direction of the Moon.

" 'Oh, Doctor, are we lost, are we lost? Claudio said we were,' she moaned. 'What shall we do?'

" 'We are not lost yet. Keep a brave heart, Charlotte,'

he said kindly. 'If you display the least excitement before these people, we shall have immediate trouble on our hands. Please be calm,' he added.

" 'Oh, I shall try to be, Doctor. Please, please tell me what to do, something, something. I can do it—only tell me what?' she said excitedly.

" 'Now, I'll tell you what to do. Make haste, call up Christopher. Tell him all and that we are several points off our course. Tell him I will take charge and try to correct the course. Tell him we need him. Perhaps he can overtake us. Be sure to tell him that!'

" 'Yes, yes. I will, I will,' said Charlotte, brightening up, and unceremoniously taking the stairs two steps at a time, she hurried to her apartment. She had only gone a few minutes, when she returned, rushing pell-mell up the gallery stairs, excited and out of breath. 'I told him, I informed him, Doctor,' she shouted, in an excited loud voice. 'He's coming! He's coming! My, I'm glad,' and she danced up and down the gallery floor in one careless whirl, bumping into everything nearby, and all but knocking the Doctor over in her mad and happy dance. Suddenly she stopped, and pointing ahead she exclaimed in still more astonishment: 'Look! Look, Doctor! We are now pointing toward the Moon!'

" 'Yes, while you were down stairs I corrected the course by exploding the air from the rear left-hand tubes, until we pointed in the exact direction,' he quietly explained.

" 'But, I neither felt the sensation, nor did I hear anything,' said Charlotte in astonishment.

" 'No, nor did any one else. There is far too much noise aboard, and then, I was more careful in graduating the pressure than Claudio. Whether you had discovered him or not, he is the only one beside myself who is familiar with the automatic machinery controlling the discharge of air, therefore I would have soon known him to be the culprit.'

"'Are we safe now?' asked Charlotte.

"'Until Christopher comes we are. Now, Charlotte,' remarked the Doctor kindly, 'go to bed. Claudio is under restraint, and you may take charge of the turret during the day. How do you like that?' he asked.

"'That will be fine,' she replied as she turned her face wistfully towards Mars. 'I can sleep now, Doctor. Christopher is coming. He's coming soon—I feel it. Oh, I'm so happy!'—and, unconsciously, she kissed the Doctor's hand.

CHAPTER XLIV

THE CHASE

"When Christopher ran to the House across the street he found it crowded. Every member seemed to be present. Even the staid astronomers of three thousand years and over were alert that night, sitting comfortably and listening to reports from observers of the torpedo, from observatories throughout the realm, as well as to the 'phone news messages automatically announced every few minutes. One of the observers had already reported that the torpedo appeared to have changed its direction, but all the others had promptly denied this as being preposterous.

"As Christopher came rushing into their midst, a message was being automatically read by the *readograph*, which closed by saying, 'Doctor Elizabrat and Charlotte Dudley are in the turret. The latter is dancing about as if in great glee.'

" 'I can't believe that,' said Christopher, looking confused, 'I have but this minute been talking with her.' After a moment's hesitation, he shouted: 'Citizens! Citizens, will you gather in the Assembly Room immediately. Send out a 'phone call for all absent members living within the five hundred mile community zone. Tell them to be here within ten minutes. Citizens, we have no time to lose. There is trouble on the torpedo. We must act at once.'

"For awhile all was turmoil and excitement. Every
408

one was wondering what had happened. In their anxiety to learn the trouble, they completely surrounded Christopher, and with great persistence plied him with questions. All to no purpose, however, as he maintained a discreet silence, saying he preferred to deliver the message when all had assembled. It was just thirty minutes past twelve in the morning when the last straggling member arrived. All the members were assembled, eagerly listening to the message delivered by Christopher.

"While Christopher was still addressing them and urging immediate action, a message came in over the *readograph* stating that Doctor Elizabrat had succeeded in correcting the torpedo's direction. It read: 'We will hit the Moon, but I cannot accurately figure where. Send Spencer.' It also went on to say, 'We have no astronomers aboard of sufficient experience to accurately figure our present speed, and to calculate our position and direction. If Spencer commands, we will slacken our speed by suddenly releasing liquefied air from the front tubes. Sufficient, indeed, to form a leverage. This would slacken the speed enough to allow the second torpedo which Spencer will command to overtake us a day or two before being due to reach the Moon. The danger of adopting this method is the enormous quantity of liquefied air required to produce the shock by rapid explosions that would lessen the speed. We are ignorant of the quantities we must employ. Can the speed of the second torpedo be increased sufficiently to overtake us?'

"A reply was immediately dispatched, that the House would take action that night, and assurance given that the Doctor would be advised as to the result of their deliberation.

"The question to decide was now clear. For the second torpedo to overtake the first, it must be shot off with greater force with a view to increasing its speed, or the first one must slow down. Before deciding any matter, Christopher's opinion and suggestions were sought. Very naturally, when new ideas were promulgated they developed a certain percentage of hostility among the members. The newer and more startling the idea, the greater the opposition. In this particular, humanity throughout the universe is the same. The Martians are wont to say: tell me how great is his imagination, and I will gauge the quantity and quality of his charity towards a new idea. But imagination is a born human endowment that no one may hope to acquire by any process of learning in one life. The quality of imagination in the human mind is the only sure proof of our superiority above the animals.

"While the necessity for quick action in forming a definite conclusion was apparent, and urged by the more intelligent of its members, there began a war of words on the part of the orators. An orator is rarely a thinker, he is rather a good advertiser forever over-rated. Not even Mars, with its superior civilization, is free from the orator pest. Every other disease has succumbed to the onward march of science," said Marcomet.

"It was early in the morning when one of those patient mortals, who, always willing to listen to others so long as anything interesting is being said, became worn out by the incessant oratorical batteries. He began a short, crisp attack upon them, and at the end of a hundred-word address succeeded in applying a noise silencer. It was at this moment that the speaker called on Spencer for his opinion upon the subject.

" 'Doctor Elizabrat is right. We must immediately load the tubes with double the quantity of liquefied air, and, when ready, I am ready,' said Christopher.

"More than a score of astronomers immediately jumped to their feet, objecting to so hazardous an undertaking, without first figuring on the effect of so heavy a firing charge.

" 'How long do you think it would take us to figure the matter out?' asked Christopher coolly. As no one replied, he volunteered, 'I will tell you. It would take at least a dozen of you men during one year, to reach a scientific certainty.'

"Still they talked on the hazard of an untried experiment, until Christopher won them over by the simple statement that ten thousand lives were more precious than his. It was taking a chance.

" 'When nature's laws are understood,' he continued, 'all undertakings are scientifically proven in advance, and, except in cases of emergency, chance is almost an unknown word.

" 'The torpedo is constructed to withstand a certain amount of resistance in the firing, but if the charge is doubled you must take the risk of its cargo—I will take my own. If we are blown to atoms, it will be at least a year before you can equip a duplicate torpedo.'

"In all their records, no case was known where one torpedo would attempt to overtake another in space. The proposition to have Spencer try to overtake the first torpedo thrilled the members with a new excitement and created additional interest.

"It was about twelve noon of the same day, when announcement was made that the additional explosives neces-

sary had been safely loaded into the torpedo tubes, but
that it would take several hours extra to clear an additional zone of safety for the people. This delayed Christopher's departure.

" 'I shall be just one day, or about 2,836,561 miles behind it, when the second torpedo is fired,' remarked
Christopher to his friends. 'I cannot tell how soon I may
overtake them, until I am well out in space and can figure
my speed. I have doubled the charge and calculate it
will double the speed of my craft.'

"It was but a few minutes after leave-taking of his
friends, that he arrived on board, and without delay adjusted his safety air-bag. Suddenly he felt himself
hurled back and forth across and around the spacious
room located just under the torpedo's turret. This, with
such rapidity that it seemed as if his air-bag was striking
the floor, ceiling and all sides of the room at one and the
same time. The noise produced by the rapid shocks
nearly drove him mad with pain. Ten thousand black-
smiths striking their anvils with hammers driven at electric speed would have been, in comparison, a soft summer
zephyr striking the sensitive drum of the ear. The din
nearly drove him mad, but soon produced unconsciousness,
and mercifully assuaged his suffering. It was several
hours before he again regained his senses, and then but
partially. Through dulled senses, he slowly began to
realize his position and what had happened, but found he
could not move though repeatedly making the effort.

"As consciousness gradually returned, the pains spread
increasingly all over his body. At last he failed to suppress the agony, and gave vent to his feelings, breaking
forth in long and rhythmic groans so full of suffering that

it resembled the cries of unnumbered human hearts bowed
low in pain and sorrow. It seemed to him a life-time, spent
in being punished by a thousand demons. When at last
the pain began to wear away, hot tears fell as a fitting
climax. Yet, he believed he heard the soft, sweet voice of
Charlotte midst the din and roar and dizzy whirl. He
tried to speak, but found that he did not possess the
strength to form a word. Finally, his eyes opened, but all
was blackness. The air bags were impervious to light.

" 'She is calling me—calling me, and I cannot answer,'
he cried. Then slowly feeling around, he found himself
almost devoid of clothing. His silken garment was in
rags, and his head and body seemed to be bleeding. 'Is
this death? Am I dying?' he thought.

"The tube that supplied air from the bag to his mouth
was disconnected. Feverishly groping inside the bag, he
found the end, but was unable, through weakness, to
place it in his mouth. After much effort he was able to
reach into the folds of his tattered robe where he carried a sharp knife, so that in just such an emergency
he might cut his way out of the silken air bag. To his
horror, he found it was gone. 'Must I be asphyxiated?'
he cried. The horror of the thought rendered him desperate. 'Where has it gone?' he hoarsely whispered. ' 'Twas
there, and now it's gone! What shall I do—hark!' his
breath stopped short. 'It is the voice of Charlotte. Yes,
she! 'Tis she! I'm coming! I'm coming to you! Wait
for me—I'm com——,' and his whisper merged into deep
and labored sounds of breathing. 'God, I must not sleep,'
he again whispered as he tried to arouse himself—unconsciousness fast overcoming him. The effort seemed
to partly turn his body, for as he rolled over, his hand

touched something cold. The slight shock brought him to a full realization of his condition. 'What's that?' he whispered, and as his fingers moved a little upon it, he suddenly started. 'It's the knife! It's the knife! I've found it! Ha, I've got it! You shall not—not—go—now,' he whispered, between fast and labored breaths. He was able to grasp it in his hand, and, raising it high above his head, plunged it into the side of the air-bag. It struck and ripped a hole of eight inches, from which the pent up air burst into the room with a long report. He then collapsed, falling upon his face, but through the small opening the air of the room returned to refresh him.

" 'Christopher, why don't you answer?' came Charlotte's voice from the *readophone*.

" 'I hear you. I'm coming,' he said in a failing voice—accompanied by a groan. But she heard him not."

CHAPTER XLV

"CHRISTOPHER's revival was rapid as the air-bag flew open, but his terrifying experience left him weak and sore. After several futile attempts, he finally extricated himself from the tangled folds of the bag, and with some uncertainty stood on his feet a few moments. With difficulty he made his way to a rubber air-chair and wearily sat down. A few moments of rest revived strength and interest in his surroundings. Drawing a small looking-glass from his tattered robe, he beheld himself. His head and body were black and blue from bruises, and from his mouth, nose and ears, blood trickled, saturating his garments. So dulled had been his senses, that until now he had not realized the *readophone* voice. It had been speaking for several minutes.

" 'Christopher,' came the name again.

" 'Why, that's Charlotte's voice,' he cried, as he staggered to his feet only to fall like a log to the floor. He was much too weak to stand, so along the smooth, hard floor he crawled slowly toward the instrument. Each call of Charlotte's voice appeared to give him added strength, yet urged him to a frenzy of anxiety. 'I'm coming,' he would shout as he slowly and painfully made his way forward. 'I'm coming—I'm here! Here I am, Charlotte. I'm again all right,' he cried with all his might, but his

415

message could never have been heard. It was far too indistinct. He breathlessly listened to hear her reply, but
—all was silent. Worn out, he soon fell into a heavy sleep.

"The *readophone* was again speaking, when he awoke.
'Spencer, Spencer. Are you there?' came the voice which
he immediately recognized as that of Docter Elizabrat.

" 'Yes, Doctor! Doctor, how is Charlotte?' he feverishly asked.

" 'I'm sorry to report that she is very weak. She
fainted over two hours ago and has not revived. We've
put her to bed. I shall inform her, however, as soon as she
awakes, that you are safe, but I feel she will not speak with
you for several hours. You have relieved us all. For an
hour after the explosion, she tried to communicate with
you. I believe, if it were not for her superhuman self-
possession she would have gone mad. I'll tell her you
are alive and well! That will impart supreme happiness.'
Then the voice ceased.

"Christopher sat listening for several minutes, expecting the Doctor to return. He hoped to hear, when Charlotte had learned he was safe—that her restoration to a
normal condition would be immediate and complete.

"As the minutes slipped by and no word came, he busied
himself by trying to repair some of the damage done to his
body and raiment. After taking a bath, dressing his
wounds and donning new garments, he felt that his first
duty was to learn the torpedo's speed and direction. 'Before I sleep,' he said determinedly, 'I must investigate my
surroundings and measure the speed of my steed. I am
anxious to obtain a view of that wonderful land of
"Nowhere." '

"Cautiously setting the turret motors in motion, he

was delighted to find that the delicate machinery was undamaged. Then, examining the lighting switches, electric air-valves, and motors, he was further pleased to find all in working order. Turning on the power which automatically raised the turret and gallery, he prepared to take his first view of space. The machinery responded instantly and when the magnifying glass windows of the turret were about an inch above the torpedo's surface, he became so impatient to look out, that he stopped the machinery and leaped to a window. Then he stood in silence —petrified by the marvelous glory of the scene that met his gaze. 'I see them ahead,' he cried to himself. 'They are pointing exactly for the Moon—so am I.' A smile of intense satisfaction bedecked his face. 'I am satisfied. Sleep first, then I can figure the speed without fearing to sleep over the problem.' He said this aloud, as if talking to a companion.

"He was not certain how long he had slept. But, refreshing himself with a hearty meal, and again redressing his bruises, he raised the turret, full height, and began to figure the speed.

"The scene was magnificent. He stood several minutes, opening and closing his eyes, in order to accustom himself to the transcendent beauty, the whole universe appearing bathed in delicately variegated colors.

"Several times during the hours allotted to mathematical calculation, he found time to inquire of Charlotte's condition, and communicate with friends back on Mars. Charlotte was better, they replied. He had said nothing regarding his own condition to Doctor Elizabrat, fearing it might add to Charlotte's nervous condition.

"He promised the Doctor that when he found the rate

of speed he would immediately communicate the result. 'I will also let you know when to expect me to pull up and take you in tow,' he told the Doctor. He then instructed them to prepare several two-inch flexible steel ropes, ready to securely bind the torpedoes together.

"Realizing that he had no time to waste, he began a series of rapid calculations. He found it was a little past ten in the morning, or about eighteen hours since the starting. Taking this as a basis, he rapidly figured the distance to Mars as 2,592,000 miles. He found that he had been flying at the enormous rate of forty miles per second. While the charge used in firing had been doubled, the speed attained was only a quarter more than that of the first torpedo. Without waiting to study the cause, he ran to the *phonescope* and, calling up Charlotte, told her the good news. Doctor Elizabrat still answered. 'We have been unable to arouse her until a few minutes ago,' he said. 'Now she is awake, but I have advised her to remain at rest. She sends her love. I have assured her of your safety.'

"Christopher then delivered the doctor a long and affectionate message for her. 'Please tell Charlotte that in about three days from fifteen seconds past four o'clock this afternoon, she will be 14,182,827 miles on her journey to the Moon, and at about that hour you may expect to find me drawing up at your side. This, provided I am successful in slackening my speed eight miles per second. I believe I can slacken speed so that I shall be with you at that time.'

"He was enabled to see, through the magnifying observation glass, that the torpedo had reached several million miles ahead. While it now appeared to be somewhat out of its course, the variation would amount to only a few miles. This difference, Christopher knew he could correct, but in order to overtake them, he must change his own course. This, however, he decided as not necessary, until he was within an hour or less in overtaking them. Constant communication between the torpedoes and Mars had been and was now maintained.

"On the fourth day, about 3 P. M., by a rapid calculation he found that he was nearly 144,000 miles behind the first torpedo.

" 'In a little more than an hour I shall be with you,' he shouted to the Doctor through the *transtelautophonescope*.

"He could see Charlotte standing in the rear window of the turret, looking back at him, waving her hand, and dancing up and down in her delight to have found him. She looked pale, as if her mind had undergone some shock. Yet, it was evident that the Doctor had enjoined a strict course of treatment, for Charlotte had not been permitted to talk with him. 'The Doctor is wise,' he mused to himself. 'He desires to have her at her best when she again meets me.'

"Christopher now discovered that the critical time had arrived. He must lessen his speed, and correct the discrepancy in direction, if he expected to overtake and remain side by side with the other torpedo. There must be no accident by collision, nor would it be safe to permit his torpedo to pass beyond the other.

"He began by releasing sufficient air from one of the side-rear tubes, to correct the course. This he accomplished by rapid and successive explosions. From the tubes large volumes of liquefied air belched forth, terminating in heavy, rapid explosions in the outside ether.

This, to some extent, lessened the speed, still he found he was gaining rapidly on the one ahead. He waited to within a minute of the time when he should overtake the other torpedo, when again he released the air in the front tubes—now in larger quantities. He estimated the other torpedo to be about ten miles ahead. The speed of his torpedo had been reduced to about thirty-two and one-half miles a second. By this calculation, he would be up to them in about twenty seconds more. When but five miles away, he again released the air, until the speed was now thirty-two and one-quarter miles per second. In this manner he kept reducing the rate of speed until the other torpedo was within a few hundred feet ahead. By careful manipulation of the air, he was thus enabled to direct his course, so that he came alongside and within a foot of the other torpedo.

"One of the first peculiarities noticeable, as he drew up, was the great mass of refuse that appeared directly under the first torpedo. After close inspection, he found that the accumulation was directly under the refuse chute, and consisted of everything in the way of waste food, dishes, liquids, a dead dog, in fact everything that had been discharged through the refuse traps. All were solidly frozen and immovable. The dog had fallen through one of the torpedo traps, while in the act of barking. Upon striking the outside, he was frozen stiff in less than one-tenth of a second. His body silently brought along with the torpedo, his mouth remained open as if howling, while his feet, bent in the act of pawing the air, he must indeed have been frozen alive. Though tissue paper and other light materials appeared in the mass, they were as immovable as a mountain.

"Great was the rejoicing on board when Christopher drew up in his greater torpedo close to them. After some delay, both torpedoes were lashed together by running the twisted cables through the air pipes. In this process large asbestos tubes six feet in diameter were employed to bridge the space between the torpedoes, the ends connecting through the air pipes at the sides of both. It took many laborious hours to fasten them securely together, connecting their operating machinery, so that both were controlled from one turret.

"All being ready, Christopher walked over the bridge into the other torpedo, and great was the rejoicing when he appeared. With loud welcomes they greeted him upon his magnificent achievement, extending the ovation far into the twilight night.

"Again Christopher and Charlotte were together, destined now never to be parted. Their happiness knew no bounds. It was near the dawn of the everlasting day before they sought their separate apartments.

" 'I have a surprise for you in the morning. It will make you happy,' said Charlotte, as they were about to separate.

" 'What is it? I am very happy now, you know,' he replied.

" 'Oh, pardon me now. You must wait, Christopher— yes, until ten o'clock in the morning.'

"This is all the information she volunteered.

"It was nine-fifty o'clock the next morning when Mrs. Dudley invited Spencer into her apartments. He had hardly entered when he heard the quiet laugh of Doctor Elizabrat and Charlotte, who were both standing over a small paper lying on the table before them.

" 'Christopher,' began the Doctor in a serious tone, 'I have news for you.'

" 'If it's good news, I'm ready to hear it,' replied Christopher.

" 'It is the best of news,' continued Doctor Elizabrat. 'Charlotte's going to marry you to-day—now,' he laughingly announced.

" 'Oh, joy! That's the best I have yet heard. I'm ready—indeed I am,' he exclaimed with unsuppressed delight. 'I see I have the consent of her parents, and they have already signed the certificate, using the same form as at home on Mars. But—and he looked puzzled—where in thunder, or in what place, is this marriage taking place?'

" 'We must know,' replied Doctor Elizabrat, 'in order to fill in this certificate properly, for I, as the Doctor, am held strictly accountable, you know,' he said laughingly.

"For a moment every one present glanced at the document inquiringly. Then Charlotte looking up said, 'Why this is "Nowhere." '

" 'You are right, married "Nowhere" is correct. It's the first marriage, so far as universal history discloses, to be made—"Nowhere." '

"And then the Doctor added, with a twinkle in his eye, 'a happy marriage, celebrated—"Nowhere." ' He then added: 'Each sign in my presence, and I give my consent to your fitness. I declare you both married according to the custom of Mars, and pronounce you man and wife. Let me now embrace you both. Where shall I kiss the bride?'

" 'Nowhere,' interposed Christopher with a look of mock severity.

"Great was the rejoicing when all learned of the marriage.

"The contrivance installed to control both torpedoes from one turret, allowed of Christopher and Charlotte taking up their abode in the second torpedo. So their happy honeymoon passed quickly by, as they rushed on towards the Moon.

"Nearer and nearer they now approached the great disk. When both torpedoes were within three hundred miles from the Moon's surface, by releasing liquefied air from the front ends, the speed was reduced to less than a mile per minute.

"Shortly after entering the attraction of the Moon, the torpedoes' speed began to increase, very slowly at first, but far more rapidly as they commenced to descend. Again great volumes were shot out from the front ends, bottoms and sides. This enabled the torpedoes to so turn that they would descend horizontally through the atmosphere to the Moon's surface. This feat, once accomplished, hundreds of tons of air were again released from the bottom tubes, absolutely controlling the speed. As they passed downward, their speed decreasing, like unto great winged monsters, the torpedoes settled in a valley near the base of Mount Appollonius, close to the great sea of Tranquillitatis on the Moon.

"The expedition had come to a successful end. All were safe. A new nation was born—to begin life in a new world."

CHAPTER XLVI

"THESE new people of the Moon prospered from the outset. Being in communication with many of the nearest planets, including Mars, from which other expeditions were dispatched later, their uplift was rapid. While the Moon's inhabitants sent out successful emigrating expeditions to other planets, none was made to Mars, as the latter's air blanket had become too thin to overcome the weight of any machine against gravitation.

"The Moon's people had determined upon progressiveness. They believed in organization. The home was made sacred. Once over its threshold, none had any right to follow. A certain number of homes, within defined lines, constituted a separate community. The community being sufficient unto itself, yet exchanging its surplus and conveying things from where they were plentiful to where they were scarce. As on Mars, they had no use for money, for each was obliged by custom to do his part in work. They had no written laws, hence no courts, judges, lawyers, nor other non-producers. As no money prevailed, banks were dispensed with. Each owned an aerochair, therefore, there was no use for railroads or steamboats. There being no incentive to extravagance, waste was unknown. The keynote of all teaching was 'Know

424

thyself.' Naturally, the highest ideals obtained and good results followed.

"Since there were neither rich nor poor, there was no trace of class hatred or competition—no straining to mimic at the sacrifice of health, liberty, and happiness. The people ruled themselves and customs constituted their only laws. Publicity constituted the punishment of any slight wrongdoing, therefore, prisons were eliminated. To harm another was to harm one's self. While they knew the imperfections of mankind, they realized how impossible it was to improve by law alone. Justice is no higher than the interpreter of the law.

"The best protection to society resides in good homes and a liberal education. Prevention, or 'begin all reforms at home,' was the watchword of the Moon people. Each parent was responsible to the community for the acts of his offspring. Goodness was the highest attainment, and to reach its ultimate, the people constantly vied with each other.

"Pure air, a solubrious climate, a prolific soil, and the absence of manual labor, rapidly carried the inhabitants to great intelligence and the upbuilding of communities of happy long-lived people. Indeed, disease had been completely mastered. It was a common thing to find people exceeding the age of ten thousand years or more. A person of five thousand years was deemed young.

"New fruits, flowers, trees, and even species of useful and productive animal life, were constantly created. The animal and vegetable had been successfully crossed. The donditto, a species of cow, continued to be the most important meat-animal on the Moon, as it had been on Mars. Almost all the vegetables used were grown upon trees, after the manner of fruit. There were trees that grew substances resembling the meat of chicken, lobster, fish, lamb, and pork.

"The people wore sandals, and on their bodies were draped beautiful and loose silken robes of brilliant and variegated hues. No part of the body was subject to restraint nor were natural lines modified, hence the person waxed strong and perfect. Thus, for many million years, the inhabitants lived and prospered, all save a few growing toward perfection in each succeeding life. Those who strove hardest to master their proclivities, came back improved in each succeeding existence. Well they knew that each, for advancement, must alone depend upon himself. The goodness of father or of mother is no safe guarantee for virtue in the offspring, as the child's personality must begin where it terminates in the previous life.

"While life is eternal, all else disintegrates with change. Even planet bodies must each pass through the ever-continuous reformations from birth to death, and from death to birth; hence, when at last the Moon's atmosphere was discovered to be drying up, through percolation of its surface water, its atmosphere grew correspondingly more rarefied. Its astronomers, anticipating future danger, advised the people thousands of years in advance to prepare and emigrate to Earth, the latter being ready for development.

"From Moon to Earth was a matter of only two hundred and thirty-eight thousand miles. Yet, it required nearly five thousand years of preparation before the initial start. The Moon's inhabitants were then transported safely to Earth in passenger torpedoes. The largest one, however, containing all records, plans, and all the accumulated information of millions of years, the machinery and every important device, as well as large quantities of concentrated foods, was lost. This unto-ward circumstance threw Earth's people back to a con-dition of absolute savagery, and constitutes the saddest tale in human history. No calamity in the universe of worlds makes record of a people landing upon a new planet whose struggle for existence began against such odds. With the loss of every human invention, the race sank to a level that, in appearance and action, they were little above the animals. This was the beginning of Hell," pursued Marcomet, his eyes indicating intense agitation, though his body and his silent thought re-mained unaffected.

"Who was responsible?" I asked eagerly.

"A descendant of Claudio. Indeed, he was a counter-part in all his jealousy and bitterness. Though his name had changed thousands of times, yet the same *Malality* was there."

Marcomet stood in deep silence for some time before resuming his narrative.

"The fate of this precious cargo would never have been discovered had not this man, its intended pilot, been seen as a passenger on the torpedo leaving immediately after the one of which he was supposed to be in charge, had been fired. It reached the Earth, but was totally de-stroyed in its descent through the Earth's atmosphere. The pilot had, through fancied wrongs and jealousies, purposely never boarded the machine. Through his action, the Earth's civilization was set back at least twenty millions of years.

"Thus began the advent of man upon Earth, without food or knowledge. Through the atmosphere was filtered upon its surface the germs of all pestilences, in the form of bugs, birds, reptiles, as well as almost all domesticated and useful animals. Some, becoming wild and uncontrolled, were finally a menace and danger to the inhabitants. Earth's history, therefore, in man's combat with the enemies generated in uncontrolled nature, kept him, for millions of years, but little better than the wild and savage beings about him. Thus he changed from the once highly intelligent to the lower, gorilla-like form of man. Through these varying vicissitudes, he marched again upward and forward, only step by step.

"While the domesticated animal returned to his native and natural condition, man, though scattered over the Earth's surface—a savage to fight for his existence, and forever fighting and opposing his own brother man— nevertheless, everywhere has voluntarily pushed onward, until to-day he stands far above his former condition, revealing his supremacy over many of the elements that surround him, and proving his divine origin. The battle, withal, is not yet won. From now on his mighty strides toward a higher and more perfect human will be rapid.

"Spirit of John Bacon, my story is ended. Transmit it to your people of Earth and,—and remember Yezad."

I then left, accompanied by a *mal*ality companion.

CHAPTER XLVII

THE calm of evening had set in, as that on the morning of our opening this strange story.

The stately old Bacon Homestead, as ever, majestically rears its roof a little back from that old friendly road still winding its course down the long hill into the all but now deserted little country village. Its cultivated fields and well-kept front lawn, together with the well-preserved and freshly painted buildings, offer a singular contrast to the farms of the country around. Most of these have either been long since deserted, or so neglected that the buildings are all dilapidated, and the land given to the reign of weeds.

A few of the barefoot boys and girls of the new generation infrequently pass along the weedy side paths in summertime to sell their berries, on journey errands to the village general store. For the greater part of the year, pedestrians and vehicles are rare. The robin, the meadowlark, the chipmunk and squirrel, in fact, all the wild life familiar to the boys and girls of former generations, are there as in bygone days. But no longer is seen the old and solemn-looking village parson of former time. His frequent self-invited ministerial calls upon the ever-loyal members of his scattered flock have long since ceased. To have him grace their homes with his distinguished but funereal-like presence was deemed both an honor and an inspiration, so that competition among the chosen flock to proudly entertain him had become a settled ambition.

These occasions were celebrated by preparation of bounteous repasts in his honor, at which the younger members of the household were, alas, never invited. On these visits he squared himself with the younger folk for persisting in making faces in the midst of his too long prayers. The punishment he meted out was to admonish their parents with uplifted hands and eyes, that "children should be seen and not heard." This meant that they should invariably keep out of sight while he was present. Of course, the torture of smelling the good things cooking and not being permitted to appease their hunger—until the Parson and invited guests had all but eaten everything up—aroused their bitter resentment and induced an itching desire to get even.

With the Parson had departed many of the honored and respected old families, whose rugged honesty and quaint sayings and methods, long gave tone to the community. Indeed, it had become the sacred duty of the elder folk to patiently listen to the Parson's sermons every Sunday, the ever-recurring and threadbare subject—"Hell, fire, and brimstone." All this had now departed, to the greater glory and increase of happiness to a too long-suffering and simple-minded people. Out of sight and far away have gone the children and grandchildren—lost in the swirling vortex of humanity in the depths of the far-away cities.

But, Sam Willis, the village liar, now old and grey, bless him, still lives on. So do the pleasant memories of many happy hearts and smiling faces he had made. At last, all else have departed—scattered no one knows where. Nancy and Jasper, and all, are but sweet memories to Sam, who only complains to the passing stranger that "it's a queer world" that permits its great men and women to die off without substituting some others "just as good."

New faces now peer through the old frame windows of the Bacon Homestead. In pleasant weather, a young man and woman, accompanied by a little girl, may be seen walking or playing on the great piazza extending along the entire house front, or in the woods and fields adjacent.

Two families still occupy this spacious and historic old landmark. Since the demise of John Bacon, and the early passing of his wife, the families of Paul Bacon and Finley Douglass have occupied the mansion. Here, with marked love and harmony, were the children reared. Robert Douglass—an only child—twenty, strong, sturdy and intelligent; Minna and Brenda Bacon, the former a sweet girl, willowy and agile, while Brenda is still the "little girl."

"We've been studying about fish to-day, about their 'stream-like' bodies. I hate it," said Minna to Robert as they stood out on the front lawn, just at twilight. "Professor says all fish lengths are proportioned about as one is to eight," she continued. "Now, I measured some eels that mother has for supper, and they were two feet long and not over an inch wide. I'm going to tell him in the morning, Cousin Robert, that all fish don't have the 'stream-like' body," and Minna tossed her head in supreme contempt.

"Positive and negative pressure of the currents of water," replied Robert, "exactly equalize one another upon the body surface of a fish. He therefore travels through the water with little energy and no resistance, attaining remarkable speed, and——"

"Why, Cousin Robert," she exclaimed in surprise, "I'll have to ask the Professor to let you tell a fish story, you know so much about them."

"Well, Minna, you must admit that I have studied the habits of birds and fish around on this dear old place since we were all big enough to notice things," he replied, as he tenderly touched her upon the arm.

"Oh, silly. I was only fooling," she replied, laughing, her face turning crimson. "Don't be sensitive!" she added. "I've watched them, too—with you—but somehow I never could see what you do, Cousin Robert."

"Never mind, Minna, it's a pleasure to me to explain—to *you*. I've watched the birds so long, and I've watched you so long, too—Minna," he said, passionately, taking her hand in his, "that I could construct a pair of wings for us both, and soar away through air, until far above the clouds—'way off yonder to that beautiful 'rising Moon'"—pointing upward.

"Please don't do that, Robert," she said, making only a faint effort to extricate her hands from his strong grasp, and then, innocently looking up into his face, she continued: "How do birds soar, Rob—Cousin Robert?"

"Yes, how do they soar, Rob—bert?" exclaimed Brenda, as she arose from the ground where she had been vainly hunting for four-leaved clovers; then turning toward them she quickly continued: "Oh, look! Look at that Moon!"

"We've been looking at the Moon, Brenda," quietly replied Robert.

"I've often noticed large birds moving rapidly through the air, their wings extended and perfectly still," said Minna with a little tremor in her voice—the cool evening air chilling her a little. "And when we all went to Bermuda, did you notice the seagulls following the boat? They kept pace with us, easily, going along at the same speed. Their wings often stood out perfectly still for minutes at a time, yet they were going right up with us. I've wondered and wondered how they could speed along so without moving their wings."

"You're getting chilled, Minna," Robert said, solicitously.

"No, I'm not. Let's stay out a little while."

"All right, have your way."

"Now, all I know is only what I've observed. No one has ever solved the mystery, but I know what I've seen, and that's good enough for me," he blurted out, with no little show of conceit.

"But, do you always see straight, Rob? You said I had the largest hunk of pie last night, and when we measured it yours was the bigger," laughed Minna.

"Now, if you're going to——," began Robert, coloring.

"Oh, go on, Cousin Robert. Don't pay any attention to Minna. She's just plaguing you. I heard her say that she liked——"

"Now you cease that, Brenda Bacon. Don't you dare to say anything regarding private matters," said Minna, moving towards Brenda in a threatening attitude.

" 'Tain't private. Mother knows it, too," said Brenda, dancing up and down in apparent glee for having occasioned her older sister some discomfort. "She likes him, too," she added with a grin.

"I'll send you into the house if you don't behave," and then, seeing Brenda start to sniffle, she realized that her severe tone had hurt her sister's feelings.

"Come here, little one. Forgive me for being unkind," she said. "Now get close to me, and we will listen to Cousin Robert."

"Not much to listen to," he returned, "except that birds must have 'air-like' bodies, the same as fish must possess 'stream-like' bodies. Both are four to five times longer than they are broad. Positive and lesser air currents so equalize the pressure against their entire surface, that when they move in still air they encounter no positive currents against the body, not equalized by the same amount of negative currents.

"In other words, the bird's wing is so perfectly constructed to move in the air, that there is just as much push as pull of air currents against the bird's body."

"Then there is no increase in resistance, as it increases its speed?" inquired Minna in surprise.

"Exactly. The faster a boat is driven through the water, the more resistance, and the greater amount of power required. Not so with birds. The air currents are so distributed against their bodies, that, while some currents tend to retard their progress, others push or forward their movements. The two currents of air, exactly equalizing, all the bird's energy is expended in speed, none for resistance in comparative still air."

"Why, that's fine, Robert. I never thought of that before."

"Wait, Minna," he said, excitedly. "I will tell you how a bird soars. It spreads its wings out straight, to their fullest expansion. Each feather is spread out in a stiff, fan-like shape. The bird would fall to the earth if he was not an expert aviator, and this is where he beats them all. When the bird wishes to soar he spreads these feathers out, and opens them apart, formed like pairs of stairs in succession, so that there is an air space between the wing feathers, just as there must be an air space between the planes of a flying machine."

"Then, why don't they build flying machines like that?" asked Brenda with interest.

"Because—well, they will some day," answered Robert with a little hesitation.

"If Grandad Bacon had only known—what I believe I know—what I seemed to have always known, maybe he would be with us now. Poor Mother, how tenderly she speaks of him. Say, Cousin Minna, he must have been a wonderful man."

"Maybe he did know all you know about machines—you know he had a splendid reputation for flying," said Minna, half reproachfully. "And then, maybe, if he was here, you would not be"—she sorrowfully added.

Neither spoke a word for some time. Finally, Minna said: "How would you build a machine? What would it look like? I'll bet it would be funny looking."

" 'Twould doubtless be a queer looking craft. The planes would not be over eighteen inches wide, and I'd have enough of them so that they'd look like a broad flight of stairs extending upward for sixty feet. The planes would not be directly over each other, no more than the feathers of a soaring bird are over one another. They are spread out stairs-like. The feathers are apart, air space between, and so should the planes be. If they were directly over one another, the air between the feathers would be 'dead air,' and, therefore, would weigh down and impede the progress of the bird. In order to get the benefit of lifting surface, the planes must be apart, but not over one another. A feather is long, narrow, and curves down on both sides. So must the planes. Grandfather's planes were too wide. No matter how long they are, they must not be over eighteen inches wide."

"How do you know that? Did you ever study air currents?"

"No. But I intuitively know that. I know it is so, but I cannot tell you why. No one, to my knowledge, has ever put forth these ideas before."

"Why don't you build a machine?" said Minna, suddenly growing enthusiastic.

"Don't, Minna. The thought sends strange feelings through me. I cannot help thinking about how to make them safe, but it frightens me to think of building one, or mounting into the air with one. It renders me absolutely dizzy to think of it. I shudder when I am even off the ground. I would be a mortal coward in the air."

"I'll never let you fly. I won't let you"—tearfully exclaimed Minna. "There, then. I won't let you fly," she tenderly said.

"You look white, Cousin Robert," remarked Brenda, pityingly.

"Yes, you do. Are you ill, cou—Robert? Let me have your hand. We'll go into the house. What can be the matter with you?" Minna anxiously asked. It was now very evident that she took more than a cousinly interest in him.

"I'm not—er—I'm all right. I just then felt a little

dizzy. I had a feeling as if I were falling. Every time I begin to talk aviation, I get a fainting, falling sensation," said Robert, brightening up a little.

"Mother says your stomach's out of order, Cousin Robert," said Brenda.

"Why, Brenda Bacon, can't you see your Cousin Robert has been taken ill? Why don't you say something nice to him?" said Minna, reproachfully.

"Why don't you?" replied Brenda.

"Yes," he hesitatingly said in a low tone. "Say something nice to me," and he softly pressed her hand in his. She blushed and stood before him, not daring to look him in the face.

"There goes Sam Willis' son Henry. He's studying to become a minister. They say he's lovely," broke in Brenda.

"Does he tell the truth and avoid all the girls?" asked Paul, smiling.

"He's truth itself. He never even looks at a girl," spoke up Minna, earnestly, as if to emphasize Brenda's remark.

"Then, he's not his father's son. But no matter about Rev. Henry Willis, where do I come in, Minna?" said he tenderly.

"Right through the door, of course," she replied, with a little laugh, trying to appear unconcerned.

"Don't fool with me, Minna. You know I'm in earnest. Tell me, quickly—where do I come in—in your—your opinion?" he said, drawing her closer to him.

"Why, Rob—Cousin Robert—I have a *very* good opinion of you," she evasively replied, still trying to act with indifference regarding his caresses.

"No, no. I do not mean *that*. You know what I mean, won't you tell me? Quick, quickly—tell me, please, Minna," he said, passionately.

"Oh, I'm going to tell Mother. You're both spooning —I can see it in your faces. You're both guilty, guilty, guilty. I'm going to tell. I'm going to tell," said Brenda, opening her eyes in astonishment and skipping towards the house.

"Brenda! Brenda! Come back here. Don't be foolish. Mother knows," and Minna called to the retreating figure.

But Brenda did not wait. Into the house she ran, not heeding the calls of her older sister. But Robert and Minna stood there 'twixt the twilight and moonlight, firmly holding each other's hands. For some minutes neither spoke.

Soon a woman appeared at the door, and in a clear, sweet voice called out—"Come, children, dinner is ready."

"How about it, Minna?" asked Robert, turning suddenly again to her.

"I don't know what you mean, Rob," she evasively answered.

"Oh, yes you do, Minna. Quick! Before we go into the house—tell me," he said in a decidedly subdued tone of voice.

"Tell you what? I don't know what you want me to say," she answered, smiling and hanging her head.

"You are contrary, Minna. You do know," he hurriedly and passionately replied. "Am I first, second, third?—Answer me now—please, Minna," he said, pleadingly.

"Why, you're first in everything with me, Bob. Oh, look! The Moon is up! It's full! Doesn't it look red and big? When it gets up high overhead it induces sadness—makes me long for something, I can't tell what," she said, her beautiful face still upturned.

"You can't?" he said almost fiercely. "Is it me? Does it make you long for me?"

"Oh, I never thought of that," she quietly answered, her eyes still watching the full, round disk. After a pause, she slowly added: "No, it makes me long to be 'way up there," and she pointed her finger while speaking. "It gives me a queer sensation; it makes me melancholy to look at the Moon."

"Oh, thunder. Why do you aggravate me? It's not the Moon; it's you that makes me melancholy."

Before she could reply the same familiar voice called again—"Chil-dren! We're waiting for you. Come, hurry!"

"Let me kiss you before we go in, Minna," he said, putting his arms around her waist. As she made no attempt to draw away, he passionately whispered, "Please—Minna—please do."

"Only as a cousin—Rob," she said, her cheeks suffused with blushes, while laying her head upon his shoulder.

"Now, kiss me—please," he commanded, after he had kissed her several times upon the lips.

She put her arms around his neck, and timidly kissed him on the cheek.

"Hurry, Bob, they're waiting for us," she whispered, suddenly releasing herself from his embrace and taking him by the hand and gently pulling him, in silence, towards the house.

As they entered the dining-room together, Finley Douglass, Robert's father, was the first to speak.

"Ha, ha. Your faces are red. What have you two been doing out in that front yard, where everybody in the neighborhood might watch you if they wanted to?"

"Yes," chimed in Paul Bacon, Minna's father. "Brenda says you were hugging one another and——"

"I don't care, I love Robert, so now, you can make all the fun you want to," replied Minna, breaking into tears.

"Now, hush," said Ellen, Robert's mother. "Haven't you two men more sense than to comment upon the divine rights of these two children? Would you have them lose or lessen their loving desire for one another?" Then, addressing Robert: "Pay no attention to anybody in your love affairs, Robert, my son,—and you, dear, sweet Minna. I love you both," and she threw her arms around both and kissed them several times.

"I haven't been doing anything I'm ashamed of," said Robert, bravely, and with some show of feeling.

"No, my son, you have not. Papa's only plaguing you," replied his mother. "You should not talk to your son like that. What they do naturally in sweet love, I reverence! Some people deserve the torment of Tantalus for their itching propensity and hatefulness in interfering with love's true course. Robert and Minna have my entire sanction," she said with decision.

"Well, well! Listen to sister. Did you swallow a dictionary by mistake, Ellen? I love a lover as much as you do. He's the most natural and God-like fellow on earth," replied Paul, positively, bringing his hand down with a bang on the chair arm.

"Robert," said his Uncle Paul, rising from his chair and walking towards him, "there's no hypocrisy in our family. Here's my hand. Love 'em all—but only support one."

"Paul! This is no joking matter," said his wife, Hester, trying hard to look severe.

"No, this is no joke. My congratulations to you both, on your engagement," said Finley quietly.

Robert and Minna, while silently regarding each other, intuitively felt they were engaged—neither desiring to deny it. With feelings of deep appreciation, they expressed thankfulness to all.

The evening meal was merrily progressing, when suddenly little Brenda startled the company with—"I want to be 'stream-like'—like a fish," and then realizing that every one at the table was endeavoring to suppress the amusement her remark created, she immediately added: "Robert knows what I mean." Whereupon that young gentleman was forced by the entreaties of all to explain the theories advanced to Minna. When he ceased speaking all highly complimented him on his keen observation.

"It makes him sick to think of flying," said Brenda.

"Yes, mother. Intense thought of flying in the air makes Robert dizzy," said Minna, solicitously observing Robert.

"I don't feel sick now," said Robert, smiling, as he took a second helping of gooseberry pie.

"How many planes would you construct for an aeroplane?" asked his father.

"Twenty-four," he quickly replied.

"Why just twenty-four?" asked his Uncle Paul, leaning forward with the keenest interest.

"It will carry more, but I will tell you, Uncle Paul, why Minna and I together decided there should be just twenty-four. There is in very old Persian mythology a certain spirit, said to have created twenty-four good spirits, and with a view to keeping them from the power of the Evil One, enclosed them in an egg. Now, there was a certain Ahriman—the spirit representing evil—who pierced the shell. Since then, there is no good without some admixture of evil.

"Each of the twenty-four planes would represent one of our friends—a good spirit. But, since nothing is perfect, doubtless, somewhere, its combined goodness will be pierced by some evil spirit, pierced, but not subdued."

"Yes, that is true. Nothing is absolutely perfect. But where did you obtain that information?" asked his Uncle.

"At the Village Library. I looked it up about a year ago," quickly responded Robert.

"Has it a name?" persisted his Uncle with increasing interest.

"That's the interesting part of it," he quietly replied with a far-away look in his eyes. Then turning quickly, as though reminded of something, in an eager tone he said: "You please tell Uncle about it, Minna."

"No, Robert, you can explain it best; you inform him," she replied, blushing.

"All right, then. Well, one evening about a year ago Minna and I sat together at the window"—pointing— "over there, silently looking out upon the full Moon. As we dreamily gazed upon the great disk, its rays streaming in, Minna suddenly broke the stillness by asking: 'Does its light make you feel melancholy?' 'Yes,' I replied.

Noting the wonderment in my gaze, she asked: 'What do you see in the Moon, Robert?' 'I see a letter.' 'Why not write it down,' she said. Taking a card from my pocket I wrote the letter."

"What was the letter?" interrupted his Aunt Hester.

"Let me first explain," replied Robert, somewhat excitedly.

"Then Minna asked me the same question four times in quick succession. Each time her question was put I gazed intently, and there seemed to appear a different letter distinctly standing out within the circle of the bright disk, until I had written five letters upon the card. When, finally, she asked the sixth time, 'What do you see further, Robert?' I was forced to answer: 'Nothing,' for though I had strained my eyes intently, no other letter was revealed. When Minna and I later examined the card, we discovered the letters had formed a word. In searching for the word, I found it in Persian mythology."

"That's queer," said his mother.

"It's very interesting," corrected Uncle Paul.

On being asked for the word, Robert answered: "I have it on the card in my pocket," and handed it to his uncle.

"Y—E——," began his uncle aloud, and then quickly stopped.

"What is the matter, Paul?" suddenly shouted Finley, starting up, as he saw the man tremble and turn white. His head had fallen forward on the table, while his frame had assumed an unusual rigidity.

"It's Father!" said Paul, finally raising his head a little, and passing the card tremblingly to Finley.

"The word written upon the card is 'Yezad,'" hesitatingly announced Finley, addressing Ellen and Hester in a husky voice.

"Paul is right!" said Ellen. "Father has returned!"

APPENDIX

An unabridged work of the theories of **Dr.** Klouse is in preparation; but, to comply with the urging of friends, the following extracts are now presented:

"Nature always crosses. Great men are born of great mothers. All great women have great fathers.

"Nature chooses the strong. The Amazon will have boys, if her husband be effeminate. When the father is physically stronger, the child will be a girl. When the mother is physically stronger, she will generally give birth to boys. If she be stronger in all ways all the time, then she will have nothing but boys. On the other hand, if she is weaker than her husband at all times, then she will give birth to girls. This theory is of daily observation and may at all times be proved.

"I have shown to my own satisfaction, that the male and female molecules vie with each other, and even continually fight one another for supremacy, from the very inception of life. Every molecule of the human body has some part to play in the construction of the cell. This is true of all Nature.

"With the human body, if certain molecules be destroyed, it means, that part of the body can never more be built up. Every cell of the body is constructed and kept in daily repair by an army of molecules. When the human body begins its formation, the molecules from the father and mother vie with each other, and fight for supremacy. Each set desires to build the body in its different parts, in the way it has been accustomed to do. Hence, a new being may have the ears of the father, and the nose of the mother, or it may have a compromise of both. So with every part of the body.

"Every male and female contributes millions of these molecules from each cell of the human system, held in constant reserve in every body after puberty. When a new body is being created, the molecules of both male and female start to build. Each molecule will build in the way its ancestors have led. The result is, you have the strongest resemblance from the dominant molecules of either sex, and presented by both. You may have the likeness or appearance of either father or mother, or, a composite of both, the stronger forces always dominating —as either body tends.

"The cells are constantly demolished, and as regularly are they repaired and built up, so long as the army of builders live. The nose, ears, eyes, and indeed the whole body may be reconstructed many times, and each time differently. To-day the child may look like its mother, and twenty years from now, it may resemble the father most. Or, it may resemble its grandmother of any distant blood relation. The physique and face are ever changing.

"It appears furthermore that these molecules, as time lapses, die off, just in proportion to their over-energy in any part of the body. If the physique be overworked in any one direction, the little builders die. For every moment the body is used, its cells are being demolished— broken down throughout the body. 'Doesn't he look tired!' or you say, 'She looks tired!' This, simply means, that millions of the surface cells have broken down. Perhaps the person has had but little time for sleep or perfect rest, which means, that the work of repair can best go on while we sleep, or when we enjoy the latter state.

"Could we but examine the body under a powerful microscope, at the close of day when certain work was done, it would reveal the surface of the body in a mass of wrinkles, indicating that millions of cells through use have broken down. Compare the surface of the face before you retire, and its appearance in the morning after a refreshing night of rest. Provided you have had a deep and quiet sleep, void of dreams to disturb slumber, you will be surprised in looking through the microscope, to observe, that nearly all the millions of wrinkles seen the night before have filled out. Then, will you appear to others 'rested.' Perfect sleep is the most essential item in retaining health, keeping the cells built up and affording greater protection against disease.

"As I have indicated, if you walk, talk, sing, read, or write too much, that part overused becomes depleted. It matters little if all other parts of the body be strong and healthy, they will not assist in saving the part affected. Indeed, the part so affected, will, to the contrary, tend to debilitate the whole body.

"If, to wit, the wheels of a wagon be used in disproportion to its body, they will be the first to wear. Whatever part is overworked most, in proportion to its strength, will become useless. Weak legs on a big body are like unto delicate wheels on a cart. Fat men should inherit or build up strong legs. Wrinkles mean, that that part of the body where they occur, has caved in, that the cells controlling the wrinkles are broken down. If the little builders are living, and the opportunity be afforded them by the body absolutely resting in sleep, then, the cells will gradually repair and the wrinkles will disappear. Therefore, the heavier our burden in overwork, overplay, or overindulgence, the greater the task of repair for this vast army of cell builders. The more frequent and persistently they are called upon, the sooner will wrinkles and early decay occur to the individual. Science may foolishly stretch the skin, rub, heat or vibrate the wrinkles, but there is only one cure, if the molecules that care for each cell are still living, and that is absolute rest. Indeed, no science can restore the cells, nor their builders.

"Every movement of the body costs the lives of many workers devoted to sustaining these cells intact. Each molecule selects and carries sustenance from the storehouse of material in the stomach. From the air in the lungs, the oxygen is carried. Their work is to gather, select, manufacture, build, repair, and discard at the same time vast quantities of material, eaten or breathed into the human body. Every human body is, indeed, an inmassed system of intelligent workers, capable of doing more wonderful things, than we, as individuals do, all of which, are essential to our existence and protection.

"If you find yourself growing fat, moderate your eating a week or two, and these tiny workers will remove the surplus they have stored for this very contingency. They will employ it to rebuild the broken cells. Fat people have active armies of molecules ever working. But fat, like wealth, becomes a source of worry and a burden to carry. Too much fat, or carbon, is a disease, and interferes with the delicate machinery of the human system and destroys it."

GLOSSARY

A

AEROLITE: A body falling through the atmosphere to the earth from outer space; a meteorite, properly a meteorite stone.—*Century*.

AEROPHOBIA: In medicine, a morbid dread of a current of air.

AERO-ELECTRIC-CHAIR: Chair propelled by electricity through the air at tremendous speed on Mars. A word designed by the author.

AH'RIMAN or AHRIMA'NNES (4 *syl.*): The angel of darkness and of evil in the Magian system, slain by Mithra. —*Character Sketches*.

AZ'RAEL (3 *syl.*): The angel of death (called Raphael in the *Gospel of Barnabas*).—*Al Koran*. In Jewish angelology, the angel who separates the soul from the body at the moment of death, for which he watches. He appeared on a white horse.

AUTOREADOGRAPH: An instrument used on Mars, similar to the Autoreadophone. Word designed by the author.

ALPHA CENTAURI: According to *The Pith of Astronomy*, by Samuel G. Bayne, this is the nearest sun to our Earth. It is calculated to be twenty-five thousand billions of miles from us, and would take an express train 73,000,000 years to reach it from the earth.

ALPHACENT: The author coined this word by combining *Alpha* with the first four letters of Centauri, an imaginary Planet of which Alpha Centauri is made the great Sun.

ANAXAGORAS: A native of Ionia, b. about 500 B.C. A Greek philosopher.—*Century*.

APENNINES: Mountain of the moon, near the western rim, a little north of its equator and east of the Appolonius volcano.—*Century.*

APEPSIA (Gr.): Defective digestion.—*Dict.*

APPOLONIUS: Volcano near the Western rim of the moon, north of its equator and west of the Appennines mountains.

ARISTILLUS: A volcano of the Moon.—*Enc. Brit.,* 11th, Vol. 18, p. 804.

AS'MADAI (3 *syl.*): The lustful and destroying angel, who robbed Sara of her seven husbands (*Tobit,* iii.8). Milton makes him one of the rebellious angels overthrown by Uriël and Ráphaël. Hume says the word means "the destroyer."—*Paradise Lost,* VI.365 (1665).

AS'MODEUS (4 *syl.*): The demon of vanity and dress, called in the *Talmud* "King of the Devils." As "dress" is one of the bitterest evils of modern life, it is termed "the Asmodeus of domestic peace," a phrase employed to express any "skeleton" in the house of a private family.—*Character Sketches.*

ASTEROIDS or PLANETOIDS: Between the orbits of Mars and Jupiter there is a space of nearly 400,000,000 miles. In 1801 Piazzi discovered the minor planet Ceres. Since then more than 400 have been found. Ceres is the largest with a diameter of 600 miles. Some of the smaller of these asteroids run down to twenty miles in diameter. They all revolve around the Sun.—*Bayne.*

AUTOREADOPHONE: Self-reading-voice. A word coined by the author.

AVERROES: Born at Cordova about 1126, d. Morocco, Dec. 12, 1198. A distinguished Spanish-Arabian philosopher, physician and commentator on Aristotle.—*Century.*

B

BEATRICE: Wisdom that comes of faith.

BEGINNAN: A planet of first magnitude. Coined.

*Bon*ALITY (bôn. F.) : Meaning Good(ality). A compound suffix of Latin origin. The word *Bon*ality was created by the author.

BRUNO (brö′nō), GIORDANO: Born at Nola, Italy, about 1548: died at Rome, February 17, 1600. An Italian philosopher charged as being a heretic and burned at the stake.

C

CAICUS: A region of Mars in lat. 30° N., long. 50°, as shown on Lowell Observatory Map (1905) of Mars.— *Mars and Its Canals*, Lowell.

CAUCASUS MOUNTAINS: Situate about half way between the center and northern extreme of the Moon.—*Enc. Brit.*, 11th ed., vol. 18, p. 804.

CHATOOKEE: An Indian bird, that never drinks at a stream, but catches the rain-drops in falling.—*Account of the Baptist Missionaries,* ii. 309.

CHRYSORRHOAS: Situate long. 70° N. at Mars equator.— *Lowell Observatory, Map* (1905) *of Mars.*

CHICOT: Jester of Henri III and Henri IV. Alexandre Dumas has a novel called *Chicot the Jester* (1553-1591).—*Character Sketches.*

CLEOM′BROTUS or AMBRACIO′TA OF AMBRAC′IA (in Epirus) : Having read Plato's book on the soul's immortality and happiness in another life, he was so ravished with the description that he leaped into the sea that he might die and enjoy Plato's elysium.—*Character Sketches.*

CLITUMNUS: A present canal on Mars shown on *Lowell Observatory Map* (1905) about long. 60° N. of the equator.

CROSSE (Krôs), ANDREW: Born at Broomfield, Somerset, England, June 17th, 1784; died there, July 6, 1855. An English electrician, noted for his experiments in electro-crystallization.—*Enc. Brit.*

D

DEE, JOHN (1527-1608): English mathematician and astrologer. Imprisoned, charged with magic. Instruments destroyed by mobs. He is credited with having written 79 works, most of which have never been printed. His most notable work is *Monas Hieroglyphica* (1564).

DONDITTO: An animal from Dodon, region of Mars, nearly double the size of the cow, that gives from twenty to thirty pounds of meat juice daily. The juice quickly solidifies and may then be cut into tender steaks within thirty minutes. It obviates the necessity of killing animals to secure meat food. Of course, the whole thing is an invention of the author.

DODON: A canal of Mars in long. 50°, in lat. 0°, at the equator, as shown on Lowell Observatory Map (1905) of Mars.—*Mars and Its Canals*, Lowell.

DUALITY: Used in the sense of *Malality*.

E

ELO'A: The first of seraphs. His name with God is "The Chosen One," but the Angels call him Eloa. Eloa and Gabriel were angel friends.—*Character Sketches*.

ELECTRO-AEROCHAIR or ELECTRIC-AEROCHAIR: Chairs propelled by electricity at great speed through the air. A word coined by the author.

F

FRANKENSTEIN (3 *syl.*): A monster, constructed by a student, out of the fragments of bodies collected from dissecting rooms and churchyards, in human form, without a soul. The monster had a great muscular strength and animal passions. It longed for animal love and sympathy, but was shunned by all. It sought with persistency to inflict harm to the young student who had called it into being.—Mrs. Shelley, *Frankenstein* (1817).

FRAIL (MRS.) : A demirep. Scandal says she is a mixture of "pride, folly, affectation, wantonness, inconstancy, covetousness, dissimulation, malice and ignorance, but a celebrated beauty" (act i.). She is entrapped into marriage with Tattle.—W. Congreve, *Love for Love* (1695).

FONS JUVENTAE: Shown on Lowell Observatory Map (1905) of Mars, in long. 60° and lat. 80° N.—Lowell, *Mars and Its Canals.*

FIRMICUS: A volcano in the lower western side of the Moon.—*Ency. Brit.*, 11th ed., v. 18, p. 804.

FRIBBLE: A contemptible molly-coddle, troubled with weak nerves. He "speakes like a lady for all the world, and never swears. . . . He wears nice white gloves, and tells his lady-love that ribbons become her complection, where to stick her patches, who is the best milliner, where they sell the best tea, what is the best wash for the face, and the best paste for the hands. He is always playing with his lady's fan, and showing his teeth." He says when he is married: "All the domestic business will be taken from my wife's hands. I shall make the tea, comb the dogs, and dress the children myself."—D. Garrick, *Miss in Her Teens,* ii. (1753).—*Character Sketches.*

G

GA'BRIEL (2 or 3 *syl.*): According to Milton is called "chief of the angelic guards" (*Paradise Lost,* iv, 549); but in bk. vi, 44, etc., Michael is said to be "of celestial armies prince," and Gabriel "in military prowess next."

GALILE'O (Galilei): Born at Pisa, but lived chiefly in Florence. In 1633 he published his work on the Copernican system, showing that "the earth moved and the sun stood still." For this he was denounced by the Inquisition of Rome, and accused of contradicting the Bible (1564-1642).—*Character Sketches.*

GANGES, RIVER: Now a canal of Mars, extending lat. N. 20° to 15° S. in long. 50° to 70°, as shown Map of Mars (1905), by Lowell Observatory.—*Mars and Its Canals.*

H

HERCULES: In Greek and Roman mythology, a mighty hero, worshipped as the god of physical strength, courage and related qualities.

I

ITEM, A MONEY BROKER: He was a thorough villain, who could "bully, cajole, curse, fawn, flatter, and filch." Mr. Item always advised his clients not to sign away their money, but at the same time stated to them the imperative necessity of so doing. "I would advise you strongly not to put your hand to that paper, though Heaven knows how else you can satisfy these duns and escape imprisonments."—Holcroft, *The Deserted Daughter.—Character Sketches.*

J

JUDAS ISCARIOT: Klopstock says that Judas had a heart formed for every virtue, and was in youth unpolluted by crime, insomuch that the Man-of-Sorrows thought him worthy of being one of the twelve. He, however, was jealous of John, because the Messiah loved him more than He loved the rest of the apostles; and this hatred towards the beloved disciple made him hate the lover of "the beloved." Judas also feared that John would have a higher post than himself in the Kingdom, and perhaps be made treasurer. The poet tells us that Judas betrayed Jesus under the expectation that it would drive Him to establish His Kingdom at once, and rouse Him into action.—*Character Sketches.*

K

KARTAPHILOS: The wandering Jew, who struck Jesus, also

was doorkeeper for Pontius Pilate.—*Character Sketches*.

L

LIMPKIN (TONY): The rough, good-natured booby son of Mrs. Hardcastle, by her first husband. Tony dearly loved a practical joke, and was fond of low society, spending much of his time at the tavern, where he could air his conceit and self-importance. He is described as ''an awkward booby, reared and spoiled at his mother's apron-strings''; and ''if burning the footman's shoes, frightening the maids, and worrying the kittens, be humorous, then Tony was indeed a humorous fellow. By his blundering he first gets everybody into difficulties and then by fresh blunders brings everything right again.—Oliver Goldsmith, *She Stoops to Conquer* (1773).

LUCUS LUNAS: Perhaps a large lake bed, in long. 70° S., lat. 20° as shown on Lowell Observatory Map (1905) of Mars.—*Mars and Its Canals*, Lowell.

LUCIFER: Is described by Dantê as a huge giant, with three faces: one red, indicative of anger; one yellow, indicative of envy; and one black, indicative of melancholy. Between his shoulders, the poet says, there shot forth two enormous wings, without plumage, ''in texture like a bat's.'' With these, ''he flapped i' the air,'' and ''Cocy'tus to its depth was frozen.'' ''At six eyes he wept,'' and at every mouth he champed a sinner.—Dante, *Hell*, XXXIV (1301).

LINNE (The Heir of): A great spendthrift, who sold his estates to John-o-the-Scales, his steward, reserving for himself only a ''poor and lonesome lodge in a lonely glen.'' Here he found a rope, with a running noose, and put it around his neck, with the intention of hanging himself. The weight of his body broke the rope, and he fell to the ground. He now found two chests of gold and one of silver, with this inscription: ''Once more, my son, I set thee clear. Amend thy life or a

rope must end it.'' The heir of Linne now went to
the steward for the loan of forty pence, which was
denied him. One of the guests said, ''Why, John,
you ought to lend it, for you had the estates cheap
enough.'' ''Cheap! say you. Why, he shall have
them back for a hundred marks less than the money
I gave for them.'' ''Done!'' said the heir of Linne;
and counted out the money. Thus he recovered his
estates, and made the kind guest his forester.—Percy,
Reliques, II, ii. 5.

LOURDIS: An idiotic scholar of Sorbonne.—*Character
Sketches*.

LYRE: Low and to the right of Cygnus, and a little outside of the Milky Way, in the constellation Lyræ, the
Harp, marked by the beautiful and very bright bluish
star, Vega. It has no other star of greater magnitude
than the third.—*Newcomb*.

M

*Mal*ALITY (mal. F., <L. malum, evil, malus, bad) (-ality):
A compound suffix of Latin origin. The word *mal*ality
was created by the author.

MARCOMET: A word formed by the author from the first
three letters of Mars, and the word Comet.—*Mar comet*.

MICHAEL: Milton makes Michael the leader of the heavenly host in the war in heaven. The word means
''God's power.'' Gabriel was next in command to the
archangel Michael. ''Go, Michael, of celestial armies
prince.''—*Paradise Lost*, VI.44 (1665).—*Character
Sketches*.

MES-CARICUS: A section of Mars shown on Lowell Observatory Map (1905).—*Mars and Its Canals*.

MESSEIS FONS: In lat. 10° N., long. 80°, on Mars.—*Lowell
Observatory Map* (1905).

METEORITE: The universe swims with meteoric stones.
They revolve around the sun and are governed by the
same laws as all other bodies. They have their region
of travel around the sun. Prof. Peirce states that the

heat which the earth receives directly from the meteors is the same in amount which it receives from the sun by radiation, and that the sun receives five-sixths of its heat from meteors that fall on it. When they come near enough to the earth they are attracted by it and rush into our atmosphere with such velocity as to produce a degree of heat sufficient to vaporize them and turn them into meteoric dust. During this process of burning they appear to us as shooting stars. Many may be seen on clear nights.—*Ext. Bayne.*

MILLIE, BESSIE: Of Pomo'na, in the Orkney Islands, helped to eke out her living (even so late as 1814) by selling favorable winds to mariners, for the small sum of sixpence per vessel.—*Character Sketches.*

N

NICHT WAHR: A German expression meaning: Not true.

NOSMNBDSGRSUTT: The land of flying men and women.—*Character Sketches.*

NOUKHAIL: The angel of day and night. The day and night are trusted to my care. I hold the day in my right hand and the night in my left; and I maintain the just equilibrium between them, for if either were to overbalance the other, the universe would either be consumed by the heat of the sun, or would perish with the cold of darkness.—Comte de Caylus, *Oriental Tales* ("History of Abdal Motallab," 1743).

O

OFFERUS: Later changed to St. Christopher (see *St. Christopher*).

P

PATCHE (1 *syl.*): Cardinal Wolsey's jester. When the cardinal felt his favor giving way, he sent Patche as a gift to the King and Henry VIII considered the gift a most acceptable one.—*Character Sketches.*

PERSONALITY: Used in the sense of *Bon*ality.

PHONESCOPE: An abbreviation of Transtelephonescope.

PILATE, PONTIUS: The Roman governor of Judæa under whom Jesus Christ suffered crucifixion. He came in A.D. 26. He ruled 10 years, quarrelled almost continuously with the Jews, and in A.D. 36 was recalled.— *Enc. Brit.*

PLATO, originally Aristocles (Gr.): So surnamed from his broad shoulders. Born at Ægina, 429 or 427 B.C.; died at Athens, 347. A famous Greek philosopher.

PSYCHOLOGRAPH: Mind writing, recording and communicating. A word designed by the author.

R

READOGRAPH: An instrument, when attached to permanent records reads aloud or in like manner records the voice. A word coined by the author.

READOPHONE: An instrument similar to the Readograph.

RELÆSTHESA: Ability to sense distant objects.

S

SECCHI: A volcano in the extreme west center of the Moon, as shown on copy of photo taken by Lick Observatory, October 27, 1890.—*Enc. Brit.*, vol. 18, p. 804.

SERENITATIS: *Maria* or *Sea* of the Moon.—*Enc. Brit.*, 11th ed., v. 18, p. 804.

SIDERITE METEORITES: Meteorites which are composed chiefly of iron, or pyrrhotite, schreibersite, graphite, etc.

SKINFAXI ("shining mane"): The horse which draws the chariot of day.—*Scandinavian Mythology.*

SPECTROSCOPE: An instrument which makes known to us the composition of celestial bodies. With a system of prisms it divides the light from them into lines on a band or ribbon. The order and position of these lines denote the chemical composition of the body under examination, so that we can determine exactly all the

GLOSSARY 459

substances that compose it and their percentages. It is, in fact, the autograph of the substance, written with lines in colors. The astronomers by its aid can as easily tell what the Sun or Sirius are composed of as a chemist can analyze the composition of gun-powder.—*Bayne.*

SPECTRUM: The continuous band of light showing the successive prismatic colors observed when the radiation from such a source as the sun is viewed after having passed through a prism.—*Cent.*

STAGNUM PEGASEUM: In lat. 30° N., long. 55° of Mars, as shown on Lowell Observatory Map (1905). Lowell, *Mars and Its Canals* (1906).

ST. CHRISTOPHER: Real name Offĕrus, a native of Lycia, very tall, and fearful to look at. He was so proud of his strength that he resolved to serve only the mightiest, and went in search of a worthy master. He first entered the service of the emperor; but one day, seeing his master cross himself for fear of the devil, he quitted his service for that of the Satan. This new master he found was thrown into alarm at the sight of a cross; so he quitted him also, and he went in search of the Saviour. One day, near a ferry, a little child accosted him, and begged the giant to carry him across the water. Christopher put the child on his back, but found every step he took the child grew heavier and heavier, till the burden was more than he could bear. As he sank beneath his load, the child told the giant he was Christ, and Christopher resolved to serve Christ and Him alone. He died three days afterwards and was canonized. The Greek and Latin churches look on him as the protecting saint against floods, fire and earthquake.—James deVoragine, *Golden Legends* 100 (13th Cent.).—*Character Sketches.*

T

TRANSFUSION: The chapter relating to this subject was written by the author about January, 1912. The volume was completed in the present form September 30th, 1915, but owing to various reasons was not issued 'til November, 1922. On October 11, 1922, there appeared in the New York Evening *Sun* the following item, which speaks for itself:

"Paris, Oct. 11.—A revolution in medical practice is foreseen if the profession adopts the system of transfusing animal blood into human beings just perfected by Dr. Crouchet of Bordeaux. He states that it is no longer necessary to depend on human blood transfusion even in the gravest cases.

"Dr. Crouchet, who commenced his experiments with transfusion between animals, says that in sixteen cases he has succeeded beyond his fondest hopes in injecting animal blood mixed with a citrate solution. He used both horses and sheep for his initial experiments.

"In only a few cases did a light fever develop, but this quickly passed, the patient showing immediate signs of amelioration. Some even insisted on a second transfusion."

TRANQUILLITATIS, *Maria* or *Sea*: A sea bed near the center of the Moon, as shown on a copy of photo, taken by *Lick Observatory*, October 27, 1890, and published in *11th edition of Enc. Brit.*, vol. 18, p. 804.

TRANSTELEPHONESCOPE: Send-far-voice-and-view. An instrument of great power in sending and receiving messages with a near view of the person or object, across millions of miles of space. A word invention of the author.

TRANSTELESCOPE: An instrument used on Mars for viewing scenes on far-away planets.

U

URIEL (3 *syl.*) or ISRAFIL: The angel, who is to sound the resurrection trumpet. Longfellow calls him "the minister of Mars."—*Character Sketches*.

Uzziel (Uz'zeel): The next in command to Gabriel. The word means "God's strength"—Milton, *Paradise Lost*, v. 782 (1665).

V

Vega: "Astronomers have agreed on 19 stars of first magnitude," 13 of which are in the Northern hemisphere. "Vega-of the Lyre" is advancing toward the Earth at the rate of 44 miles a second. "The constellation of Lyre is noted because of Vega, the most beautiful and one of the largest stars of the sky. It may be recognized by the formation of a small equilateral triangle with two minor stars. By latest decisions of astronomers the solar system is flying towards this point. Vega can always be seen on a clear night, but is more brilliant when overhead in Winter."—*The Pith of Astronomy*, by Samuel G. Bayne.

Vaporum: *Maria* or *sea*, about the center of the Moon. Now probably dry.—Lick Observatory Map (1890), *Enc. Brit.*

Veron'ica: The maiden who handed her handkerchief to Jesus on His way to Calvary. The "Man of Sorrows" wiped His face with it, returned it to the maiden, and it everafter had a perfect likeness of the Saviour photographed on it. The handkerchief and the maiden were both called Veronica (*i.e., vera iconica,* "the true likeness").

One of these handkerchiefs is preserved in St. Peter's of Rome, and another in Milan Cathedral.—*Character Sketches.*

W

Weissnichtwo (*vic-nect-vo*): No-where. The word is German for "I know not where," and was used by Carlyle (*Sartor Resartus*, 1833).

Wetzweiler (Tid), or *Le Glorieux*: The court jester of Charles, "The Bold," duke of Burgundy.—Sir W. Scott, *Quentin Durward* (time, Edward IV.).

WHANG: An avaricious Chinese miller.—Goldsmith, *A Citizen of the World* (1759).

WILD (JONATHAN): A cool, calculating, heartless villain, with the voice of a Stentor. He was born at Wolverhampton, in Staffordshire, and was the son of a carpenter. He was executed. (1682-1725.)

Y

YEZAD or YEZDAM: Called by the Greeks Orama'zês (4 *syl.*), the principle of good in Persian mythology, opposed to Ahriman or Arimannis, the principle of evil. Yezad created twenty-four good spirits, and, to keep them from the power of the evil one, enclosed them in an egg; but Ahriman pierced the shell, and hence there is no good without some admixture of evil.

Oroma'zês (4 *syl.*), the principle of good in Persian mythology. Same as Yezad (q.v.).

Zoroaster, Persian philosopher (800 B.C.), teaches that the Universe is a constant scene of conflict between the good and the bad. Each of these principles possesses creative powers but the good is eternal and will finally triumph over the bad. He believed in an infinite deity called Time without bounds, Worship, Fire and Sun.—*Character Sketches of Romance, Fiction and the Drama.* Revised edition of the Reader's Handbook by Rev. E. Cobham Brewer, LL.D. Edited by Marion Harland, 1892.

Z

ZEPH'ON: A cherub who detected Satan squatting in the garden, and brought him before Gabriel, the archangel. The word means "searcher of secrets." Milton makes him "the guardian angel of paradise."—*Character Sketches.*

ZOPHIEL (Zo-*fel*): "Of cherubein the swiftest wing." The word means "God's spy." Zophiel brings word to the heavenly host that the rebel crew are preparing a second and fiercer attack.—*Character Sketches.*

Zanga: The revengeful Moor.—Edward Young, *The Revenge* (1721).

Zad'kiel (3 *syl.*): Angel of planet Jupiter.—*Jewish Mythology.*

Zenodochium: The name given by the Greeks to a building erected for the reception of strangers.—*Enc. Brit.*

Zim'ri: One of the six Wise Men of the East led by the guiding star of Jesus. Zimri taught the people, but they treated him with contempt; yet, when dying, he prevailed on one of them, and then expired.—Klopstock, *The Messiah,* v. (1771).